THE CURSE

"I pray you'll tell me my fortune, Mistress Bell," he mocked. "What do you espy in your crystal?"

She regarded him out of reddened eyes. In a low voice she said, "I see a long, long road, Richard Veringer. As you have broken your oath and destroyed my home and more— more than you know—so will your home be destroyed and so will those you love be loathed and feared as they go forth upon the byways of this world and have no resting place until they find some plot of ground which will receive them. But the searching will be arduous and the way fearful. That will be the fate of the Veringer household—and that is my curse upon you, Richard Veringer. I am not finished with you!"

Florence Stevenson is a well-known playwright, and the author of over 30 books in print. She is also the winner of the Theater Americana Award for Best Play of 1951.

HOUSEHOLD

FLORENCE STEVENSON

LEISURE BOOKS NEW YORK CITY

A LEISURE BOOK

March 1989

Published by

Dorchester Publishing Co., Inc.
276 Fifth Avenue
New York, NY 10001

Printed in the United States of America

Part One

One

Tattered, tarred and weathered swung the late Jack o' Diamonds, as he had called himself when with pistol in hand and a swift horse under him, he hid in culverts, lurked behind trees or, dismounted, lay low on the ground, his leathern garments artfully blending into the high, autumn-tinged grasses that bordered the King's Highway.

Richard Veringer, riding towards the Hold, passed the gallow's tree with a cursory glance at its fruit. Had he not received his mother's letter, he would never have been able to identify the Jack. The highwayman looked uncommonly bony. The crows had made short shrift of his flesh, and his skull, gleaming white between shreds of dried and shriveled skin, would soon tumble to the ground. Before it did, Richard intended to have the men from the Hold give it a decent burial, Fulke being underground and unable to countermand the order.

A smile played about Richard's shapely mouth. Slaying the Jack had been one of his late brother's last deeds of "derring-do." It had won him the gratitude of the county and, according to his mother, he had been called "hero" and "savior" for ridding the community of such a rascal. People's memories were damned short, Richard reflected. That fact, coupled with a wish to respect the Veringers for what they had been over the centuries rather than the figure his late brother had cut, glorified the dispatching of old Jack and scotched the rumors that he and Fulke were hand-in-glove. Richard wondered what had caused his falling out with Fulke. Probably he had kept more than his share of the loot. It little mattered. Richard firmed his lips in order to banish the pleased expression that came and went like the sun on a cloudy day. It had been more rather than less in evidence ever since the messenger had come to the Kirk bearing the news that Fulke had been shot by the irate father of his latest conquest. He wondered how many brats Fulke had sired in the course of his three-year majority. Veringer features had been familiar in village cradles ever since Fulke's fourteenth birthday.

Richard could not decry his taste in wenches for it had kept him unwed, and if there were bastards aplenty who could call him father, none could lay claim to the earldom. He, Richard Veringer, could now don that mantle with its yellowed ermine and the velvet that needed patching. He was now the sixth in his family to inherit the earldom of More—to which could also be added the older and earlier title of Baron. He touched the flank of his horse with a light flick of his whip. Fulke would have dug both spurs into the animal's hide and galloped toward the grey battlements and towers outlined against the horizon. With the Hold looming large in front of him, he drew himself up, an instinctive bracing against the pressures which would presently be directed towards him. His answers, which were already framed and would remain the same, were embodied in the person of his mother.

He could imagine her now, austere in the black she had worn at his father's death and never removed in the last three years. Mourning had become habitual, and she would use her grief as a weapon, a sword to bring him to his knees, agreeing to her wish that he would stay and manage the property.

Richard snorted. As if they did not have a steward capable enough to fulfill that obligation. He had always been expected to be the obedient son, but he had not been obedient four years ago when sent to study for the ministry. His father had exacted his acquiescence with a whip, laid across his bare shoulders until the blood ran. He had hated his father for that and hated Fulke for his laughter.

"Ye'll die a martyr to your lack o' faith, brother mine," Fulke had said to the angry youth he had been, smarting from the flogging and the inexorable command he must obey. The first son had the title, the second was destined for the church and the third for the army. But there had been only Fulke and himself squeezed out of his mother's spare loins, else he might have exchanged professions with the sibling that never was. He was certainly not suited to instill his flock with the fear of the God in whom he was not at all sure he believed. He could contain his smile no longer. The disciplines were at an end. Fulke was as his boon companion, the grinning Jack o'Diamonds on his gallows tree, and he was the Sixth Earl of More.

Lady Veringer was thin as a stick and pale as a wraith, a wrathful wraith, Richard thought unlovingly as he listened with diminishing patience to the diatribe she was finally concluding.

". . . tenants and those who depend on you," she finished with a baleful glance.

"There's the steward. I'll give him my instructions," Richard said, pleased with a succinct answer that put his mother in her proper place, not that she gave any indication of accepting it.

She glared at him out of eyes that looked cavernous in her wasted countenance. Meeting that reproving and, at the same time, accusing stare, he was uncomfortably reminded of the Jack's empty eyesockets. She said in a voice to which she had added a quaver, a touch of artistry she had omitted from her earlier efforts, "I little thought that you would evade your responsibilities in this manner, Richard. You are the Earl of More and you must live up to all that it means. Your poor brother . . ."

"Lived down to it," Richard muttered.

"I fear I did not hear you."

"No matter," he retorted impatiently. "I shall be leaving

for London at sunrise.''

"It does not cause you any distress to know that you are breaking your mother's heart?'' she demanded with a bitter twist of her pale lips.

"I do not anticipate that that particular rupture will occur,'' he said, shrugging. "You've borne two deaths admirably. Surely a mere departure could not exert such pressure.''

Astonishingly, she was able to squeeze out a pair of tears, one in each eye. Clasping her narrow hands over her meager bosom, she moaned, "You leave me with no words.''

"It's just as well.'' Richard produced a second shrug. "There is much I must do before my departure. I pray you will have left my brother's wardrobe intact. My own suits are all in greys and blacks, excellent for traveling, but I've no wish to look like a country parson at London gatherings. And it will be several days before I will have found a tailor to my liking.''

He was confronted by a virago. "I'll not allow you to touch as much as a . . . a button of your sainted brother's garments!'' she shrilled.

"Sainted?'' he echoed and burst into laughter. "Oh, Mother, I thought you had no sense of humor, but I see I was mistaken.''

"You are a villain, a rogue, a . . . a whited sepulcher of deepest dye!''

"Better and better . . .'' Richard was thoroughly enjoying himself. The old tigress had had her teeth drawn, but four years had sapped her strength. From being a thunderstorm she had dwindled to a drizzle. He continued, "I cannot agree that I have left you without words. Your vocabulary is, if anything, much improved since I was last here.'' Richard turned on his heel, thought better of it and came back to her. "I think it is my brother's death that has loosened your tongue. Or perhaps it was that of my father. Between 'em you had little chance for self-expression.'' He turned away from the stiff figure of his mother and then bethought himself of something else that must irk her even more. "I intend to give old Jack a decent burial in consecrated ground,'' he informed her gravely.

"Consecrated ground!" cried Lady More. "Not on your life! Let the rascal hang there until he rots!"

"That's just it," Richard replied. "The process is underway. Damned unsightly, I call it."

"He serves as a warning to all malefactors!" Lady More's eyes flashed.

"Do you think so?" Richard regarded her in some surprise. "It's my belief that all malefactors faced with the Jack are of the opinion they'll outsmart him, outrun him, outlie him. If anything his ending encourages rather than discourages thievery, serving as a challenge, as it must."

"You make a mockery of your cloth!" snapped his mother.

"Quite," Richard replied. His eyes, a blue-grey, became for a moment, entirely grey and cold. "And have done since I was forced to don it."

"You are no son of mine!"

"I wish that were true, but the benefits accruing to the title provide some compensation." Richard sketched a bow and started up the chill and shadowy stone steps that led to the upper floors.

Lady More looked after him and raised a bony fist, shaking it. "I curse you," she cried. "I curse you, Richard. One day your sins'll find you out!"

"I pray you'll not be so medieval, Mother." Richard laughed and continued on up the stairs.

There was a loud reverberating crash in the hall which he might have taken as an expression of heavenly pique had he not suspected that Lady More, in the very ecstasy of passion, had knocked over one of the two suits of armor that stood on either side of the door.

The upper floors of Veringer's Hold were as dingy, as cold and as ill-lighted as the Great Hall. Lady More, as her garb implied, was of a saving nature, and she, too, had a strong Scottish strain in her ancestry. Consequently, there was a short supply of candles, and these were not wax but tallow dipped in the castle kitchens. One of them was guttering in a holder on a deal table just outside the first in the series of vast, chilly sitting rooms and bedchambers. Richard picked up the candle. It had been a long time since he had crossed that particular threshold and, he remembered, his last visit had been in the company of his late brother. They had come to admire Fulke's likeness, painted by a man from London at what Richard suspected was a reduced rate, considering the results. Fulke, he recalled, had been uncommonly pleased with them, but no one had ever accused him of being a connoisseur of portraiture.

The gallery was even colder than the hall, for one of the windows was open and a breeze troubled the flame of Richard's candle. Fortunately, he discovered a candelabrum containing three candles, two nearly melted down to the holders but one with about three inches yet unburnt. Richard lighted all three and set his own down on a long table pushed against the far wall. He shut the window and stared at the painted visages with more satisfaction than he had felt since first riding over the drawbridge which had groaned with what had seemed to him mechanical reluctance when lowered over the moat.

"My happily buried ancestors," he muttered, paraphrasing Shakespeare and casting an eye toward the Second Earl of More, a staunch Catholic until 1536 and the Dissolution of the monasteries, a Protestant until 1554 and the ascension of Mary I, and in 1558 a Protestant again and thereafter, having been favorably impressed by the preachings of John Knox. The second Earl had been a second son like himself but the first of the heirs to bear the name Fulke; until then they had all been Richard. Coincidentally, the second Earl had dark red hair and a yellowish-green eye, the same coloring as his late descendent.

The third Earl, also a Fulke, resembled his father in appearance though not in deeds. If he were less changeable in his religion, his politics were definitely questionable. Richard strolled to his portrait; he looked sober enough in black with puritanical white collars and cuffs. No one could tell by looking at his solemnly righteous expression that some dry rot had attacked the roots of the family tree. A staunch Puritan with all the benefits accruing to a Royalist turned follower of Oliver Cromwell, he had cast a jaundiced eye on the Protector's son and heir (a Richard) and sent considerable money to Charles II with the result that alone out of the countryside the Veringer family retained property and title. The resulting gossip had been a bitter blow to his wife, the stern-faced lady who hung by his side. Richard made a face at her since she looked a great deal like his mother. He strolled away from her and back several generations to Lady Janet, who had been the bride of Richard, the third Baron of More. She had a mane of fiery hair and flashing green eyes. The third Baron had seen her during a foray across the border to attack her sheep-purloining family's castle and had made off with her immediately. He had locked her in the west tower and had had his face well-scratched, his neck bitten, his shins bruised and his toes mashed before the lady gave in, marrying him only when her belly was rising to accomodate the fourth Baron. She faced subsequent generations with a twinkle in her eyes and a smile on her lips. Richard smiled back and then frowned as he glimpsed the latest addition to the collection.

Moving toward it, he stared or rather glared at his brother's countenance. The man who had done the painting had little in common with Van Dyke, one of the few artists with whom Richard was familiar, but he had captured Fulke's scowling expression and arrogant posture. His brush had also duplicated the red-gold of his brother's hair. Fulke, in common with himself, had scorned the practice of wearing a wig. It was odd, Richard thought, that the two of them were so dissimilar in type. His hair was as black as his brother's matched that of Lady Janet, while Fulke's eyes were a yellowish green under tufted eyebrows. His own brows were sleek and one was higher than the other, giving him a quizzical expression, even when he was not being quizzical. When he was in a questioning mood, the eyebrow went even higher.

"Devilish" had been the comment of more than one parishoner of his kirk when seeing the eyebrow in action. Devilish, too, was the smile that often played about his lips, they had said. Richard smiled again, thinking that the church elders were as glad to see him go as he had been to leave. They had accepted him only because of his lineage. A poor parish at the edge of the Scottish border was unwilling to turn away the son of a belted earl. He frowned and dismissed parish, church and congregation from his mind. He continued to stare at his brother's portrait, not really seeing it now but seeing instead the living Fulke, captured in his mind's eye, strolling about and casting aspersions on such females as graced the walls.

He had begun with the incumbent Lady Veringer, painted as was the custom shortly after her wedding to his Lordship, the fourth Earl and, as usual, looking as if she had just swallowed a sour pickle. Her gown, white satin trimmed with blue and pink flowers and lavishly embroidered, would have been very becoming to some pink and white miss. On his mother, gaunt even in her youth, it was most unflattering, especially at the bust, quite flat where it should have swelled. The artist had added a quirk to her lip, obviously in an effort to convey the notion of a smile, but he had not succeeded in erasing the frown with which she must have regarded him.

"Probably estimating the cost of the colors" had been Fulke's comment. "Lord, what a horror our Mama was. 'Twasn't for the fortune she brought, the old man'd not have had her in his bed, I'll be bound. Damme me, if I'd ever wed such a prune-faced wench." He had cocked a derisive eye at Richard. "It's Christina Dysart I'll be having when the time's right."

That statement had infuriated Richard. The three of them had known each other since they were children—Christina being the only daughter of Sir Gerald Dysart, who lived several miles down the road from the Hold. Christina, however, had seemed to favor Richard above Fulke who was always intimidating her with the rough games he liked to play. Richard had adored Christina, too. However, when she had come of age—18 to his 17—and had been given the ball that took place just before he was sent off to study for the ministry, she had saved most of her dances for Fulke.

She had told the wounded swain he had been at the time, "I hear you're off to be a minister, Dickie. 'Tis a noble calling to be sure, but I'm not cut out for that sort of cloth myself." She had flung back her golden head and laughed. He had hated her.

He smiled. To his certain knowledge, Christina was not wed yet. She would be 23 and perhaps would be expecting him to come and pay his respects to his late brother's fiancée.

He doubted that she'd have been receiving much in the way of respect from Fulke. They had been betrothed for something less than a year. Perhaps, just for curiosity's sake, he'd pay his old love a brief visit before going off to London.

He glanced at his brother's portrait and seemed to see a corroborating gleam in those tigerish eyes—though that, he hoped, was only the glow from the tallest of the three candles. Without looking at the rest of his ancestors, Richard strode out of the gallery and went downstairs. In a few more minutes, he was waiting for his horse to be saddled and a few minutes after that he was galloping in the direction of Dysart Manor.

Years ago the Manor had pleased him considerably more than the Hold. It had been erected at the end of this century, and though like the castle it had been constructed of stone, it was all of a piece—not sprawling all over its land like the Hold, which had suffered both Tudor and Cromwellian additions as well as the wear and tear it had sustained in the 500 years of its existence. A pleasant stretch of grounds led up to the Manor, and Richard could remember when he and Christina had raced their horses up its winding length, the last race taking place when she was 17 and he 16. He had won and lifted her down from her horse, claiming the prize of a kiss. She gave it to him readily enough, flinging her arms around his neck and whispering, "Well run, Sir Knight."

She had loved the Hold, he also remembered, loved it as a child because its high slit windows figured in their game of "Damsel in Distress." He had always been her knight in those days with Fulke scorning to join in their silly "child's play." He preferred jousting and tumbling with the rough lads of the village. Richard frowned. Banishing these encroaching memories, he spurred his horse up the curving road, thinking that even given the fact that it was close on November the place had a desolate look he never recalled having seen before, almost as if the grounds themselves had gone into mourning over Fulke's death.

The servant who obsequiously ushered him into the hall was gone a long time before returning with the information that Sir Gerald and his lady would be delighted to receive him in the small drawing room. Joining them, it seemed to him that her ladyship looked very peaked in the black she wore for the late bridegroom, and also she seemed to be both discomfited and pleased to see him. She was at pains to tell him that Christina, currently resting in her room, would be down very soon. She added that though the girl was naturally grieved over the death of Fulke, she had recovered her spirits to some extent although as was only natural she had her good and bad days. She stopped talking midsentence and went off to fetch her daughter, something she might have delegated to a servant but which she obviously preferred to do.

Sir Gerald, who had mumbled a greeting of sorts, glowered at Richard and then made a palpable effort to produce a smile. He had been, Richard noted, looking extremely gloomy and downcast, a condition which could have been attributed to his gouty leg. Now, with an effortful smile, he cleared his throat twice before saying, "Remember how close you and m'daughter used to be. That's true, ain't it?"

"We were, sir," Richard agreed. "Before I commenced studying for the ministry."

" 'Twasn't long ago, though. Not more than three years," growled Sir Gerald.

"Four, sir."

"Four! You'll never tell me that!" the baronet exclaimed accusingly.

"I was eighteen, sir, and am turned twenty-two."

"*Twenty*-two . . . twenty-*two*," his host muttered. "My gal's twenty. Time does fly, don't it?"

Richard nodded, reflecting that for Sir Gerald, time must fly backwards since Christina was nearing her twenty-fourth birthday.

"Been a bit cast down my girl has . . . sewing the trousseau, you see."

"A sad loss." Richard decided that he really wasn't lying in making this admission. Certainly Fulke's death must have been a sad loss to his fiancée.

"Indeed, yes. Cut off in his prime, damned rascal . . ." Sir Gerald fastened his eyes on Richard. "I'm talking about old Hodges that did for him. Hanged, sir, I'll see him hanged as high as the Jack o' Diamonds. Though that'll be your prerogative, I'm thinking."

"If he can be brought to justice, Sir Gerald."

"Has been," the baronet rasped. "Down with the rats in Oldfield's Keep, didn't you hear?"

Richard hadn't heard, and now he made a mental note to secure the man's release before setting off for London. He was about to say something soothing and noncommittal to Sir Gerald when Christina made her entrance, moving very slowly, her mother fluttering behind her like a nervous moth.

Christina was not wearing black. Her gown was a pale blue brocade, almost the color of her eyes. Her golden curls were elaborately dressed, or at least that was his first impression. A second hinted at a hasty gathering and pinning with some three or four locks straying to one shoulder when only two should have been there. She was wearing quite a bit of rouge over the leaden-white paint, much favored by ladies determined to ape the London styles.

Richard, who had been inwardly amused at his reception, felt a quick pity for the girl he once had believed he loved. In those years, Christina had been beautiful and slim. Despite her makeup and despite the fact that the gown, its wide skirts fanning out to the imminent danger of any small table or chair in her immediate path, was designed to emphasize a slender waist, Christina was neither beautiful nor slender. Her face was puffy, and it would have been better had she worn mourning, for the black would have minimized the thickness of her middle. His suspicions were not without foundation. He wondered how soon she would be dropping the brat concealed by her skirts and mentally damned his brother.

Remembering his manners, he bowed low. "Christina," he murmured, kissing the back of her plump and trembling hand. "How well you look." Unfortunately, his eyebrow had quirked up and he hoped that Christina, who had once known him so well, would have forgotten that telltale mannerism.

Fortunately, Christina, sinking into a deep curtsy, did not appear to have noticed, but it soon became obvious, through a series of grimaces, that she needed help in rising. Her mother hastily provided it, murmuring, "Poor Christina is quite weak with grief."

"You have my deepest sympathies, Christina," Richard said.

She raised her eyes and Richard, seeing that they were blazing, realized that the eyebrow had not gone unnoticed. "I thank you, Richard. You were . . . most kind to come and see me."

"We have thought of you so much. I know Christina has missed you sorely," Lady Dysart gushed. "You were all so close when you were young . . . and Christina hard put to choose between you, were you not, my love? And poor dear Fulke . . . such a tragedy."

"Indeed," Richard agreed solemnly.

"Have you come home to stay?" Christina asked.

Had he heard the barest hint of hope in her tone? He was not sure. To his surprise, it gave him considerably less pleasure than he had anticipated to reply, "No, as it happens, I'll be leaving for London on the morrow."

"Really, so soon!" Lady Dysart exclaimed, distress written on her face.

"I must go." Richard felt it incumbent upon him to add, "There are matters concerning the estate that need my immediate attention."

"Have you no man of business?" Sir Gerald asked.

Richard, regarding him, found fury in his stare. "I am thinking of changing solicitors," he replied.

"And how long do you intend to remain in London?" Christina spoke a trifle breathlessly. She was smiling now, her eyes masked by her lengthy and artfully-darkened lashes. "I hope it will not be a lengthy visit, now that we have you home at last." She attempted but did not quite achieve a coquettish smile.

Pity warred with ire at the deception Christina was willing to practice upon him for her effort to legitimize his brother's bastard. "I do not know," he said. "I'd think I would be there upwards of six months to a year."

"Six months to a year!" Sir Gerald roared. "Now what in hell would ye be doing in London for so great a time?"

"My dear . . ." his wife protested.

"Mama . . ." Christina suddenly moaned, her hands pressing down against her wide skirts.

"My love." Lady Dysart was at her side, her eyes wide with concern. "What is it?"

"I . . . I told you . . . it was better, I mean . . . I . . . ohhh . . ." Christina groaned loudly. "The physician," she gasped. "The physician . . . you'll need to f-fetch him . . . I was . . . not wrong. The pains—"

"Oh, gracious, sit down, love. Something she ate," Lady Dysart moaned in Richard's direction.

"My horse is just outside," Richard said. "He's a swift goer. I'll ride for the physician."

"No, please." Lady Dysart flung out a protesting hand. "Gerald?"

"Oh, let him go," commanded the baronet, an eye on his gouty leg. "Do you imagine the young scapegrace hasn't cottoned to the situation ere now? He's another like his thrice-damned brother, may he be burning in hell!"

"That I'm not," Richard countered as he turned toward the hall. "And I promise you, that whether he's my nephew or she's my niece, the babe'll be provided for."

"A pox on ye," Sir Gerald yelled. "D'you think I'd not maintain my daughter's bastard? I curse ye and the lot of ye."

"Curses," Richard said, moving swiftly into the hall. "Curses, as I told my mother earlier this evening, are extremely medieval. This is 1758, my dear Sir Gerald!"

Since he did not have a handy suit of armor to fell, Sir Gerald had evidently concentrated on the nearest china ornament. Richard heard the crash but could not tell what it might have been, because by the time it landed he was just closing the door behind him.

Having seen the physician ride off on his mission of mercy, Richard was put in mind of the other or, rather, the most recent brat his brother had sired. He rode at once in the direction of Oldfield's Keep, intending to do as he had promised himself he would and demand the release of old Hodges.

The Keep had once been a castle, but time and the warlike natures of several generations of Oldfields had damaged it to the point that Squire Oldfield had built a new manor house. The round stone Keep, all that was left of the original building, had been let out as a prison. It was a damp, unhealthy bastion with several floors, all occupied by male-factors of various stamp. Some were political prisoners, some were poachers, some vagrants and some, like old Hodges, were there because they had taken what was euphemistically termed the "law" into their own hands, righting wrongs no one else was willing to face.

Richard was positive that even his prudish mother believed Emmy Hodges had suffered but little at the hands and the other less visible extremity of Fulke. She would maintain that Mr. Hodges had acted with an overweening pride. That the Emmys of this world were put there to serve the young master was a fact with which no one of his class would argue. Unlike Christina, these females were treated like rutting animals and sent to workhouses or prisons when they were in trouble. Their parents usually had a brood of them and one wouldn't be missed.

Mr. Mercer, the gaoler at the Keep, reflected this attitude. He could not imagine his Lordship should take any interest in old Hodges, a cantankerous prisoner if there ever was one! He was astounded when Richard asked if the man might be set free.

"Oh, no, no, no, my Lord. His Lordship, the Justice of the Peace, would 'ave my 'ead. 'E's got to come up before Asizzes. 'E 'as'n like as not they'll 'ang 'im an' good riddance. Can't go about shootin' the gentry. Sets a bad example to the young."

'Well, perhaps I could see him and make life a bit easier for him," Richard persisted. "What he has left of it."

To say that Mr. Mercer was surprised was a considerable understatement. However, he was also pleased. His Lordship's mention of making life easier for the old goat could mean only one thing. He wanted to give him money, and that sort of largesse would eventually find its way into *his* pocket. Mr. Mercer had a stock of comforts to lighten the sufferings of those who could afford it. Plugs of tobacco, beer, watered down to be sure but still tasty, and sundry other items were among his stock. "I'll see wot I can do, if you'll take a seat, my Lord." Indicating a battered wooden bench, the gaoler hurried off.

His fortnight in the Keep had not improved old Hodges'

looks, and certainly it had wrought on his temper. He came stomping into the room, clad in malodorous garments, his face covered by a dirty grizzled beard, his eyes hot with an anger hardly assuaged by his surroundings. His hands were chained, as were his feet. He glared at Richard out of those small, reddened eyes and growled, "Wot're ye doin' 'ere? Come to look at the animals in the menagerie?"

"On the contrary, my good man," Richard began.

"I'm not yer good man," snarled the prisoner.

" 'Ere that's no way to talk to 'is Lordship," the gaoler protested, evidently envisioning Richard's money fading away.

"Never mind," Richard said. "I am sure Mr. Hodges has been sorely tried. I have come to offer my sympathies, since I can do little else. I'd hoped to free you, sir."

"Free me!" Mr. Hodges howled. "Free 'im wot killed yer own blood brother? Yer another just like 'im, not a scrap o' conscience between ye. An' my poor Emmy saddled wi' one o' yer good-fer-nothin' brats. Free me, indeed. T'was my pleasure to do wot I done'n I be willin' to pay the price." He raised both hands and shook his chains. "I'd kill ye, too, if I 'ad my way 'n rid the world o' all the Veringers, all o' 'em, d'ye 'ear?" He spat on the floor. "My curse on ye, Richard Veringer, may ye rot in 'ell wi' yer brother afore yer much older!"

"I'd best take 'im below, your Lordship," said the discomfited and disappointed gaoler.

"I expect you must," Richard agreed.

"Aye, take me away from 'im. 'E's got a prettier face but 'e's just like his damned brother. Curse 'im, I say. Curse 'im."

Richard waited until Mr. Mercer returned. Producing a half-crown, he handed it to the astonished man. "See that he has a few creature comforts," he said gently.

"Oh, I will, I will, never you fear, sir," the gaoler promised as Richard strode out of the Keep.

He was whistling as he rode toward the Hold. "Three times is the charm, if one believed in that sort of thing," he muttered to himself. "Ah, superstition! That is the real curse . . . keeping the common mind in thrall. It's fortunate that I'm among the enlightened, holding with neither curse nor oath, God nor the devil!''

At that moment, a cloud passed over the moon, briefly darkening the landscape. As it sailed away, Richard added with a quirk of his eyebrow, "Nor do I believe in so-called portents. The natural cannot be joined with the supernatural—since there is no supernatural!''

Lady Veringer, lying in her curtained fourposter, heard her second son come whistling up the stairs. She muttered several words that Fulke and his father had been known to employ when in a temper. She was glad that she had had the opportunity to lock up all of her late son's clothing. Richard would need to appear at London gatherings looking like a country parson—or not at all.

TWO

"And here I was of the opinion that you were man of the cloth, Lord Veringer," Sir Frances Dashwood said as the condemned man, purple-faced from the tightening noose, jerked about on the gallows.

"Not I." Richard was glad to shift his gaze from spectacle to speaker. Though a visit to a Tyburn hanging was one of the great sights of London, he had not found it much to his liking. His new acquaintance, Sir Francis Dashwood appeared to be enjoying it greatly. He had also compared the hanging to several others witnessed over the past few weeks. "Quite the best of the lot," he was now assuring Richard. "This rogue's lasted at least five minutes longer than any of the others. "I'll make money on it. Lost last week . . . great hulking fellow, strong as an ox, but heavy. If I'd thought about it, I'd've known the weight would pull him down. It's the small ones that usually take the longest. Remember that, if you lay any bets on 'em, Lord, look at him dancing. Ah, that's it. Dead and fifteen guineas for me!"

Richard was reminded of the Jack o'Diamonds which put him in mind of his mother, which put him in mind of what Sir Francis had said about his presumed calling. He frowned.

The remark was based on the clothes he had been forced to wear until his new suits could be finished. He glanced down at himself and smiled.

Nothing could be less clerical than his blue coat, flared at the back and matched by tight-fitting breeches of the same material. His vest was heavily embroidered with red and blue threads in a swirling pattern, and over the fall of lace at his throat was a black ribbon called a solitaire. He had clubbed his hair at the nape of his neck and tied it with a silk ribbon. He could guess what they would have said at the kirk had they caught their minister in such garb.

"But," Sir Francis said suddenly, "you *were* a man of the cloth."

"I was," Richard admitted reluctantly.

"And left it? Why?"

Richard found that Sir Francis' eyes a mild grey, were alight with curiosity. He wondered briefly whether he were of a religious persuasion and preparing to harangue him on his duties, but doubted that such a one would be laying bets as to the longevity of an expiring criminal. He decided to be frank. "I left it because I came into the title on the un-expected demise of my elder brother. Quite truthfully, I had been most reluctant to take holy orders, having little vocation for the ministry."

"But you took 'em," persisted the baronet.

"I did." Richard smiled wryly.

"And how long were you in the ministry?"

"Upwards to two years—ordained."

"Ah, but that is excellent," Sir Francis rubbed his small, rather plump hands together and also smiled, more broadly than Richard's effort. He bowed. "I trust we'll meet a third time."

Nodding cheerfully, he strolled away, disappearing amidst the multitudes and leaving Richard puzzled. He had remembered where he had seen Sir Francis before. It was a fortnight ago, just after his arrival in London and a new friend had taken him to Whites. He had been feeling un-comfortable and out of place in his rusty black clergyman's attire. He had exchanged a few words with Sir Francis and probably had excused his garments, as he was in the habit of doing to everyone he met. He wondered about the baronet now. Judging from his friendly attitude, it would seem he might have asked his direction and suggested another meeting, but he had not. Still, and Richard did not know why he was so sure of it, he was positive that Sir Francis intended them to meet again. Shrugging, he threaded his way through the crowds and strolled toward his lodgings, keeping as near to the street as carriages, wagons, sedan chairs, hawkers, herb and fruit sellers, beggars, street musicians, running footmen and horseback riders would allow. He had no wish to find himself drenched with the contents from a slop jar, a not unlikely prospect during any walk in London.

By the time he was in his parlor, Richard had forgotten about Dashwood in contemplating what he would wear to the theater that evening. He had three hours in which to make this momentous decision, the play not commencing until six. However, he had reasons for wanting to look his very best—rather, *a* reason.

Her name was Catlin O'Neill. She was appearing in *The Lover's Stratagem*, a play he had seen on Tuesday evening, Wednesday evening and would see again tonight, Thursday evening, when it would close, having had, in the eyes of some spectators, far too long a run for the indifferent farce it was. Richard, however, could have seen it every night in the week, even though he must needs suffer through the ludicrous work that preceded it—something about a Dane named Hamlet, whose indecision almost proved his undoing, had it not been for his best friend Laertes, brother of Ophelia to whom Hamlet was engaged. It was Laertes who warned Hamlet that his uncle was preparing to poison him. Consequently Hamlet turned the tables on Claudius, spearing him, and marrying Ophelia, who had supposedly drowned, but actually had swum to safety, collapsing on the river bank and being nursed back to health by a friendly fisherman.

It was a great mystery to Richard why the audience preferred this work to *The Lover's Stratagem*. He usually slept soundly through it and, indeed, had slept that first night waking up just in time for the face of Catlin. Ah, Catlin, Catlin! It was a name that warmed his heart and heated his blood. He had gone backstage to the Green Room to meet her, only to be informed that she had left the theater directly after the curtain fell. This information was provided by the Ophelia, who, judging by her winks and smiles and flutters with her fan would not have been adverse to his company. However, Richard, who judged her old enough to have been a young aunt or an elder sister, if not his mother, ignored the lady's blandishments and persisted in his desire to meet the charming Miss O'Neill.

"You'll not be having much luck with her," snapped the affronted Ophelia. "She be an Irisher and they're all crazy! This one brings her nurse to the theater along with the old lout who purports to drive her here in her own coach. To my notion, he's keeping her though he don't look like he has two groats to rub together. And I warn you, he's a tough one."

Last night, Richard had managed to get to the Green Room in time to see the beautiful Catlin who, unlike Ophelia, was even lovelier without her makeup. Unfortunately, she was met by a grave, elderly Irish woman in a shawl, obviously the nurse, who elbowed her way through the crowds to join the girl. Seizing her arm, she hustled her past a group of young men, which Richard found himself eyeing just as sternly as the nurse. Their remarks, directed at Catlin, were probably intended as compliments but they bordered on the obscene. If he had not been so intent on following Mistress O'Neill, he would have made them pay for those ill-advised witticisms. He came out of the stage door just in time to see an immense man join the woman and her charge. This new arrival had bright red hair, bright blue eyes and a pugnacious expression on a wide, freckled, snub-nosed face. There were rolling muscles on his arms that not even a frayed green coat could conceal. With the help of the nurse, he whisked the young actress into a waiting coach and they were off.

Tonight, Richard vowed, would be a different matter. He had learned his lesson. He would linger outside until it was time for Mistress O'Neill to emerge. Meanwhile he would bribe the pugnacious coachman. A pound should do it. Judging from his threadbare appearance, the huge Irishman would pocket it gladly. And after he had Catlin in his grasp . . . Richard frowned.

He had not really decided what he would do once he was face to face with the ravishingly beautiful girl and eventually side by side with her in the coach he would hire for the occasion. He could, of course, kiss her passionately but while such an action was delightful to contemplate, he was not precisely sure how it would be received. She might yield immediately. That would be wonderful, but also disappointing. Much to his surprise, he found he did not crave an easy conquest. He wanted a show of reluctance on her part, even fright. Then he would soothe her, assuring her that he meant no harm. Once she trusted him, he would take her to supper and afterwards . . .

He was angry at the heat he felt on his cheeks and forehead! A man of 22 was blushing at visions which should have been realities four years earlier, save that there had been Christina four years earlier, and he himself had been the perfect knight, Chaucer-style. Later, though there had been rawboned lassies wandering about the kirk, he had still been too much in love with faithless Christina to attempt anything so bold as a kiss. As for the lassies, they giggled when he passed but seemed too awed by his occupation to give him so much as a come-hither look, not that he wanted one. Eventually, he had lost his uncomfortable virginity at an inn with a mob-capped maid-servant, who also giggled but was eager and surprisingly accomplished. That relationship had sufficed until she married. There had been no one since Meg; her name, he recalled, had been Meg MacDonald. It was difficult to affix a face to the name since their meetings had always taken place in the dark.

Richard stopped thinking about Meg. It seemed almost obscene to couple his faceless paramour with the beauteous Catlin, even in his thoughts. He set about deciding what he would wear to the theater. As yet, he had only two choices—back or white. He wished he had hired a valet. Most of them were knowledgeable about clothes, but he had been too eager to see the various sights of London to cool his heels in an employment office. Besides, the thrifty habits he had learned while an underpaid minister in an out-of-the-way kirk still remained with him. He was able-bodied, and consequently he could bathe, shave and dress himself! And, at this juncture, he was better off without a servant. Servants gossiped, and it would not help Catlin's reputation to have her name bandied about. If she partook of a midnight supper with him, he must needs serve it himself.

He decided on the white suit.

Two hours later, standing in front of a long glass, he surveyed himself with pardonable pride. There was a fall of fine lace at his throat, a diamond glittering amidst its folds. His vest, a cream-colored brocade, was patterned with large, stylized chrysanthemums. A silk braid edged his buckram stiffened vest. His coat, also brocade and pure white, stitched with silver, was similarly stiffened. Though not really comfortable, it was certainly fashionable. His breeches matched his coat. His stockings with the dark embroidered clocks were silk, white, of course, as were his shoes. He did not wear high heels. Though these were the very epitome of fashion, they were uncomfortable, and he did not need the extra height, being two inches over six feet. However, as a concession to the occasion, he wore red heels and buckles studded with seeming diamonds.

He hoped his garb would impress Catlin and her coachman. He flushed. He had been well on his way to forgetting that he was a rich and titled Lord rather than an impecunious Honorable, of which there were many floating about the city without so much as a shilling in their pockets. After tonight, he would see about hiring a valet. More than that, he would also purchase a house. If he were to have as beautiful a mistress as Catlin O'Neill, he could scarcely lodge her in a hired set of rooms. He would have to give her her own coach and four. He would pay her bills at the mantua maker and he would buy her jewelry—rubies, diamonds, sapphires, emeralds and pearls. He loosed a long sigh as he envisioned her lying on a white chaise longue with silken sheets . . . no, those belonged on the bed he would also buy along with the rest of the furnishings for his house. The bed would be a wide oval, resting on swan's wings. He had seen something similar imported from France. It would have a canopy hung with brocade curtains. It would also be heaped with pillows and upon these Catlin would lie, looking like a Titian painting he had once seen in the house of a friend. However, judging from what could be seen of her shape in the gown she wore for the play, her waist was thin, suggesting slim hips, a nymph rather than a goddess. And nymphs would not have so plump a form or so full a belly unless . . . he flushed a second time. If she were to bear him children, he would see that his bastards wanted for nothing and . . .

A small crystalline chime interrupted his ruminations.

He started. The clock on his mantel was striking the half-hour. It was time to summon the coach he had hired, the coach which this evening would bring the beautiful, the exquisite Catlin O'Neill to his door. He took his cloak, also white brocade, from a hook in the hall and flung it about him. He picked up his stick, something he certainly didn't need but which was another fashionable necessity. He was ready for the theater, for Catlin O'Neill, for love!

The alley which stretched behind the Little Theater in the Hay was narrow, ill-lighted and crammed with tottering old buildings which, to Richard's mind, must have been there before the Great Fire that leveled most of London 90 odd years ago. They looked as if they were within minutes of falling in on each other, but in spite of their undoubted antiquity, numerous people appeared to dwell in them, befouling the street with their reeking slops and with their no less odoriferous selves. They seemed to fall into two categories—pale, haggard young women with inexpertly painted faces or thin, ragged, drunken men. Both sexes patronized one or another of the small gin shops that vied with the old-clothes merchants for the trade of the quarter. They walked or lurched past Richard, seemingly unaware of him, but a sixth sense informed him that they were like so many jackals, circling nearer and nearer, hoping to knock him down, grab his purse and, before he was aware of it, strip him as clean as vultures at carrion. It was not a pretty notion. It was not a pretty street. It looked even more forbidding at this present moment because of the continuous drizzle which seemed to be getting heavier. Mentally, he chafed at the idea of Catlin being subjected to such sights each night. However, now was not the time to dwell on that. He had just clambered out of his waiting coach at a signal from the huge Irishman.

Richard was really elated. Matters had gone very smoothly. At first, the coachman had been as pugnacious as his appearance indicated, but only at first. Confronted with two golden guineas rather than the pound Richard had originally meant to offer, the scoundrel's eyes had widened, and he had become shades less belligerent. He had listened to Richard's plea and later to his plan with a flattering interest. Subsequently, the rascal proved most agreeable—to the point of offering a few helpful suggestions of his own.

"There'll be a regular crowd at the stage door, and since it be rainin', I'll guide her to yer coach and she none the wiser. Ye'd best be standin' out in the street so she won't set up a holler when she sees you inside." He jerked his thumb at Richard's coach.

"What about the old woman?" Richard demanded, wishing he could strike this reprobate down.

"Oh, you give me another half crown 'n I'll settle up with her."

The leer in the Hibernian's eyes was a bit of a disappointment. Richard had the definite impression that the beautiful Catlin must have been "kidnapped" more than once. However, upon due consideration, the fact that her favors were for sale made him feel much less guilty. The seduction of a virgin had given him qualms, but no one could seduce a whore and, as another new acquaintance had opined, "all actresses are whores, my dear fellow."

She did not look like a whore, but she was an actress and consequently pretense was one of her tools.

It was beginning to rain harder. Richard wished he had not worn his white silk. He wished, too, that he had brought his heavier cloak, but still he was sure that the white could not fail to make a good impression upon Mistress O'Neill; not only was it becoming, it was costly. She would be assured he could pay well for her favors and . . . another whistle reached him. She had come out of the theater and soon the coachman would guide her to him.

His heart was pounding somewhere near his throat or even at the roof of his mouth, which was absurd for a sophisticated man of the world. He put a stop to his inner qualms, and his eyes widened. She was only a few feet away from him, leaning on the arm of the coachman. He strode in her direction, and in that instant, the coachman turned, his pugnacious contenance one huge snarl. His fist shot out and connected with Richard's jaw.

Lightning flashed through Richard's brain. It was followed by pain; he staggered, trying vainly to keep his balance, and then fell. He had a last look at her before lapsing into unconsciousness. His last thought was that she had seemed shocked and pitying.

Richard worked his jaw back and forth. He did not believe it broken, but it did ache abominably. His back also hurt, and equally painful was the assault to his dignity and the damage to his garments as he lay in the filth of that rain-spattered street.

A group of spectators were standing around him, laughing immoderately and making grabs at various portions of his person. The feel of air on his neck told him that his lace cravat with the accompanying diamond had been ripped away. The fact that he could move both sets of toes assured him that stockings and shoes were also gone. He was mournfully pleased that the diamonds in the buckles were paste. He did not know what else was missing. He had just regained con-sciousness, and there was no telling how long he had been lying there. Fury shook him as he thought of Catlin's perfidious coachman, who had cheated and betrayed him! He groaned deep in his throat as a vision of Catlin flashed into his mind; she had looked so incredulously beautiful, even more beautiful than the previous night. She had definitely smiled at him, and he thought he heard her cry out when her coachman had so basely floored him.

"Dear, dear, dear . . . shocking I say."

Richard twitched and stared upwards in a surprise quickly succeeded by shock. Bending over him was Sir Francis Dash-wood. "You," he croaked.

"My dear young man," the baronet murmured, a look of pity in his grey eyes. "But come, let me help you up. You cannot continue to lie here in all this muck."

Though slight of build, Sir Francis proved to be sur-prisingly strong. He actually lifted Richard to his feet and, keeping a sustaining arm around him, said, "I'll take you to my coach."

"No need." Richard took an experimental step and winced as he felt the wet cobblestones hard beneath his feet. His head was also going around in circles. Though he had sustained a hefty clout, he could walk, albeit painfully. He said, "My coach is nearby."

"And its driver did not come to your aid?" queried the baronet, raising thin eyebrows.

"No, by heaven, he did not!" Richard muttered, realizing that the man could not have stirred from his perch nor the footman neither, and they had both been well paid! However, the pair of them had not been very large. Perhaps they had been afraid of the huge Irishman. But afterwards . . . surely they could have helped him up. Why hadn't they? He suppressed a groan. His head was aching, and it was hard to concentrate.

"Where's your coach?" Sir Francis demanded. "You should certainly give the man a dressing down."

"I shall . . ." Richard began and paused. His coach had been across the lane, but it was no longer there. "It's gone!" he exclaimed.

"Dear me. Well, you must take advantage of my offer, must you not? Here, let me assist you." Sir Francis drew him toward a huge coach standing close by.

"I thank you," Richard mumbled.

Half-dazed as he had been, he never remembered exactly how he came to Sir Francis's comfortable town house. He was even more confused when he awakened in a large chamber paneled in dark wood and filled with morning sunshine. He stared about him in a consternation relieved only by a few flashes of memory. Someone had given him a shot of brandy. He vaguely remembered a bell ringing. A man in livery . . . grey livery? Yes, he thought it was grey. The servant told him he had been instructed to put him in the east chamber.

"I will be able to go home, if your coachman will drive me."

"No, no, no." Sir Francis had entered and suggested the binding of his wounds, telling him he would be better off not going home.

Recalling that he had no valet, he had finally agreed. Afterwards he had been grateful for soothing emollients rubbed on his head and back. Someone had undressed him and put him to bed. Oddly enough the pain he sustained the previous night had largely disappeared, that is the bodily pain. As his mind grew clearer, anger warred with anguish as he imagined how he must have looked to Catlin, once her coachman had laid him low on those filthy streets.

His unwelcome recollections were interrupted by a soft tap

on the door.

"Come in," Richard called.

A small slight, dark man in grey livery entered. Bowing, he said in French-accented speech, "I trust Monsieur has slept well?"

"Very well," Richard replied, aware now of a soreness in his jaw. He frowned as the sensation set off a score of mingled questions and regrets. These were accompanied by vivid images of Catlin as she came toward the coach with the old woman behind her. She had stared at him, her beautiful blue eyes wide with interest and subsequently pity. Yes, he was sure he had read both emotions in those cerulean depths. How the devil was he to see her again? He could make inquiries at the theater, but even were he to receive her direction, how might he pass the barrier of coachman and nurse? Both were definitely of the dragon persuasion.

The small man cleared his throat. "If Monsieur is feeling more himself, Sir Francis would welcome his company at breakfast."

Breakfast! Richard suddenly remembered he had not eaten since four o'clock yesterday afternoon. There had been a midnight supper in his lodgings but that must be sadly spoiled by now, and he was ravenously hungry. "Tell Sir Francis," he said gratefully, "that I would be delighted."

"But, of course," Sir Francis said after hearing the whole of Richard's account over an excellent repast of chicken, roast beef, rashers of bason, scrambled eggs, several side dishes of excellently cooked vegetables, a meat pasty, a bottle of port and a pot of hot chocolate, "You must bring her to Medmenham Abbey."

"Medmenham Abbey?" Richard frowned. "A Papist retreat?"

Sir Francis laughed softly. "Papist? Bless you, my dear young sir, do I appear to you as one of Roman stripe?"

"No," Richard answered hesitantly. He was hard put to understand his exact feelings regarding his host. Sir Francis was certainly pleasant and charming, yet something about the man disturbed him. He was not sure what it could be and probably he was mistaken. After all, who else would have taken a chance acquaintance into his home, cared for his hurts, given him a bed, a fine meal and sent his servant to that same stranger's lodgings for a change of garments? There was but one answer to that. No one else in the whole of London acted out of such disinterested kindness. He said apologetically " 'Twas the word abbey that confused me, Sir Francis."

"But it must not. Oh dear me, no, it must not and will not when you see it," replied the baronet with one of his soft laughs. "The description is purely facetious. In some aspects, however, it differs little from that crumbling and ignoble institution which its adherents call 'the holy Catholic church.' We have our brothers and our sisters, monks and nuns, if you prefer. Also we have our masses and similar solemn ceremonies—with a few distinctive alterations."

"And what would they be?" Richard asked. "I am not sure I understand you."

"You cannot understand me until you have been there," Sir Francis said reasonably. "However, if you wish to be alone with the beautiful Miss O'Neill, there could not be a better spot than Medmenham. And I can arrange matters for you."

"At an abbey?" Richard still felt puzzled both by the offer and the location.

"Not *an* abbey, my dear fellow. Medmenham Abbey! Our grounds are extensive and full of delightful little nooks and crannies that absolutely beckon lovers. You need only promise me one favor."

Richard regarded him narrowly. His host was still smiling, but his eyes had darkened and hardened, turning a steely grey in which no smile lingered. There had been a strange intonation to his voice as well, an inflection which seemed almost threatening. For some reason he was reminded of Marlowe's Dr. Faustus being asked to forfeit his soul, an odd conceit for himself who did not believe in souls.

He said, "What must I promise?"

"We are a secret society. If I reveal any of our secrets to you, it means I trust you. In turn, I expect you to be worthy of that trust. If anyone should learn that you had been my guest at my estate in West Wycombe, I would prefer you did not mention the abbey."

Richard's own gaze was hard as he answered coldly, "That is one favor you need not have asked of me, Sir Francis. I am, I am sure, an honorable man."

The baronet smiled genially. "I know that. I did not intend to impugn your honor in any way, my dear . . . may I call you Richard?"

Richard nodded a trifle curtly. He was still annoyed by the implications of Sir Francis' request.

"As I was saying, I did not intend to cast any slur upon your honor, but as the Abbot of Medmenham it is my duty to ask each prospective monk the same question. It is so ordained in our charter."

"Monk?" Richard frowned.

"Because of our reverence for each other and our lack of reverence for the aforementioned Roman establishment, we choose to call ourselves the Monks of Medmenham. I am surprised that no word of our doings has reached you."

"You have just told me that they are secret," Richard said confusedly.

"Secret to some, not secret to others. But a man of the cloth such as yourself . . ."

"I am no longer of the cloth."

"Just so," Sir Francis said meaningfully.

His meaning escaped Richard. He was too disciplined to probe further on that particular subject. "How does this concern Miss O'Neill?" he inquired.

"I presume that the lady being of Irish extraction is a Papist?"

"I do not know. I've had no opportunity to converse with her," Richard admitted regretfully.

"Nor would you be speaking of such a matter were an opportunity presented," murmured the baronet.

Richard felt one of his embarrassing flushes warm his cheeks. "I do not expect we would," he mumbled.

"Well, whether you would nor not—and whether she is or is not a Papist—the lady, from what I was able to see in the theater and outside, would make an admirable and adorable addition to our . . . ceremonies. There are many actresses among the young nuns who join us."

"Nuns?" Richard questioned.

"I believe I mentioned that we welcome both monks and nuns," Sir Francis reminded him.

"I see . . ." Richard found that he was breathing harder. "But I do not believe she would consent to be a nun. Nor do

I think she'd consent to come.''

"Consent is not always a requirement." Sir Francis favored him with another of his ready smiles.

Richard stiffened. "You would . . . would . . ."

"I would do exactly what you had in mind to do last night, my dear young friend, save that I should succeed in all matters save one."

"One?"

"Her possible . . . virtue would remain intact . . . at least until your arrival at the abbey."

Richard said huffily, "You suggest that I . . . I . . ."

"I suggest, my dear young man, that you did not have your coach waiting for the young lady because you wished to escort her home. I cannot help but think you had other matters in mind and that, I imagine, was exactly the opinion of Big Tim O'Donovan, which is the name of her coachman, an old family servant, who, I might add, would gladly lay down his life if such were needed for his young mistress. He would, however, be far quicker to lay down the lives of those who would unlawfully solicit her favors. He is extremely honorable as servants go and cannot be bribed," the baronet sighed. "However, there are others ways of dealing with that particular barrier."

"I would not want him hurt," Richard began and paused. "I mean if . . . but it is preposterous. I could not take her out of London. I would be charged with . . ."

"Nothing, Richard. The young ladies who join in our revels at Medmenham enjoy themselves hugely. Not one has ever complained of her treatment. I presume you'd not allow that lovely young creature to return home empty-handed?"

"I did not propose to treat her as my whore!" Richard retorted hotly.

"Of course you did not," Sir Francis said soothingly. "Only as your mistress, I am sure. Your first mistress, unless I am deeply mistaken."

Richard breathed hard. He longed to contradict Sir Francis, but his brief visits to Meg could hardly glorify her with the title of mistress. Besides, he hadn't kept her. Half the time, he was out of pocket from hiring the room, and she had loaned him small sums of money. He had always paid them back.

He sighed and said, "Yes, she would have been my first."

"Come, we must not speak as if all hope were dead, my dear Richard. It is perhaps dormant, resting, even dozing, but not yet to be buried in a mausoleum. If you'll leave the particulars to me, I can promise you that by this time—shall we say, the day after tomorrow—you'll not be sitting at my table in your dressing gown but you might be wearing that same apparel at another table with a much prettier face in view."

Richard glared at Sir Francis. "I do not think . . ." he began angrily.

"I pray you'll not be hasty." Sir Francis raised his hand. "I have it on the very best authority that the lovely O'Neill returns to Dublin tomorrow or, at least, starts her journey toward that city. Once there, she'll not be coming back to London, and Ireland, I might add, is full of gallants who are not fond of the English, as well as a coachman who does not hanker for the sight of you."

"She is going to Ireland!" Richard cried despairingly.

"Tomorrow morning at dawn, unless she is prevented from taking this most disastrous step."

"Oh, God." Richard buried his face in his hands.

"You do not believe in God, so I doubt he can be counted upon to intervene. However, there are earthly powers which might prove equally effective."

Richard regarded him confusedly. "I expect you must be referring to your own once more?"

"Naturally."

"But why would you do this for me?"

"Because I knew from the first that you were a man after my own heart, a minister who dared to forsake the church. That took considerable bravery. It also suggested that, in common with myself, you are done with the shibboleths of religion. Nor can I believe you are bound by custom or snared in the meshes of what passes for morality in this kingdom. You are open-minded and a freethinker. In other words, you should belong to our fraternity, my dear Richard, and it is my hope that by the time a few days have passed, you'll be of my—or rather *our* persuasion."

"I do not know quite what to say . . ." Richard began.

"You need say nothing until you've been introduced to

our brethern, and until you have held the beauteous Catlin in your arms.''

Richard gave him a long troubled look. "She is the apple of your tree in paradise?"

"The apple?" Sir Francis questioned and then laughed. "Ah, you mean, am I trying to bribe you? Nothing of the sort. I want only your happiness, and I cannot think you'll be happy if the beauty does as she intends and sails off to Ireland tomorrow morning."

"Oh, God," Richard muttered again.

"Rather say, 'Oh, Francis.' I am not nearly so amorphous, and I do have connections in many, many places."

Richard fixed tormented eyes on his host. "It sounds . . ."

"How does it sound?"

"As if . . ."

"I hope you're not going to disappoint me," the baronet murmured.

"It doesn't seem quite honorable," Richard commented gruffly.

"All's fair in love and war," Sir Francis replied. "But I should protest, for you are impugning my honor now. I might add that my man, when he fetched your clothes, told me of an elegant supper spread for two—food for rats or, possibly, mice? I think not."

"No," Richard said wretchedly. "I had hoped . . ."

"And need not hope any longer, if you agree. If you do not, she'll be lost to you forever."

Her face, as he had seen it the previous night, had been incredibly beautiful, her eyes, compassionate yet alarmed, her mouth so soft, so perfect. Would she always remember him as lying in the dirt at her feet, and would he always remember her as a fleeting image as insubstantial as a dream?

He said slowly, "I think I must agree."

"Good man," Sir Francis said heartily. "I knew I could not be mistaken in you. We'll leave for Medmenham tomorrow night!"

"And she?" Richard asked eagerly. "Will she accompany us?"

"She'll go by another route but will arrive as quickly, never fear." The baronet wiped his hand with a fine linen napkin and thrust it out. "You have my handclasp and my word on it."

Richard found Sir Francis' grip surprisingly hard for so plump and white a hand. "I thank you, sir," he said.

"And I thank you," the baronet returned. "I am sure you cannot fail to appreciate what we have to offer you."

"I am already in your debt," Richard replied.

"Yes, you are, aren't you? But I beg you'll not give it another thought."

It was a strange answer and vaguely disquieting—but again, Richard was not sure why—and in a few seconds, he had forgotten all about it, dwelling on his Catlin's charms.

Three

In after years, a regretful Richard, dwelling on the brief period he spent at Medmenham Abbey, was wont to groan over his folly in agreeing so readily with the practiced persuasions of his host. Instead of returning to his lodgings where presumably he might have devoted some time to second thoughts, he allowed Sir Francis to send for his luggage, as earlier he had procured his suit. Moreover he had also, though not without protest, donned the rusty black garments he had worn at the kirk.

"I cannot think why you want me to wear them?" he had said. "I am no longer a minister."

"I know, dear lad, but you'll be riding and 'twould be a shame to spoil your new clothes. Save for a brief stop at an inn, we'll be in the saddle for most of the day."

At another time, Sir Francis' sartorial suggestions may have been suspect, but Richard, his mind and heart occupied with Catlin, was beyond logical thought. He had become obsessed with the idea of her. The fact that she was leaving for Ireland filled him with actual terror, edged round with horror. He agreed with Sir Francis that once she set her little foot upon the green sward of that misty island, he would never see her again. Catlin . . . Catlin . . . her image troubled his dreams and dwelt in his mind's eye to the point that he was even oblivious to the pleasant countryside through which they rode to West Wycombe in Buckinghamshire, some 31 miles from London.

In fact, Richard was so concentrated on Catlin's charm, beauty and in speculating on what would happen once he held his promised prize in his arms, he was never sure what road they followed or how long it took to arrive at their destination. His concentration on his probable mistress remained all but unbroken until Sir Francis said in terms of pride that bordered upon the rapturous, "We are here, dear lad. Look you, Medmenham Abbey!"

Raising his eyes, Richard turned in the wrong direction which was toward the banks of the Thames. Since they arrived in the late afternoon, the river reflected a sky dyed scarlet by the descending sun. And there, apparently in those pellucid depths, rose the dark mass of ruined tower, gables and chimneys of Medmenham. Gazing at it, Richard was uncomfortably reminded of the flames which, at the irate demands of the elders in his kirk, he reluctantly described as providing eternal torment for sinners who merited it; these same flames were seemingly engulfing the abbey. Despite his disbelief in all matters pertaining to religion, the image sent an atavistic shiver coursing through his veins.

The sensation passed swiftly as he looked at the structure itself and remembered that behind its facade was Catlin O'Neill. At Sir Francis' bidding, he dismounted and remanded his tired mount to the care of the grooms who came hurrying toward him.

"We'll use the eastern entrance," Sir Francis said.

Following his host, Richard noted, not without inner amusement, that while the abbey bore a great resemblance to one of those religious houses partially leveled during the Dissolution, the architecture was modern and, unless he were deeply mistaken, no more than ten years old. Probably, Medmenham Abbey had sprung from the same medieval fancies that brought Horace Walpole's gothic mansion at Strawberry Hill into being.

Reaching a large recessed doorway, Richard noted that there was an inscription carved over it, the words being in antique French and reading, "Fay ce que voudras."

"Fay ce que voudras," he repeated out loud. It was hardly a religious sentiment. "Do what you will?" he questioned.

"Ah, c'est vrai," corroborated Sir Francis with a smile. "Here, my dear boy, one may do as one wishes. I quote from Rabelais, of course. 'Tis a command I hope you will obey. Most of our members do."

"Do you have many members?" Richard inquired.

"We have twelve who are charter members of the abbey. On occasion, we also have honorary members. These may or may not want to join our ranks. While they are here they enjoy the same privileges as our twelve brethern, provided they adhere to our code."

"And that is?"

"Later," Sir Francis promised. "I am sure that you must be saddle-weary and will want to refresh yourself."

It seemed to him that his new friend was being unnecessarily provocative. Upon another occasion, Richard might have demanded a further explanation, but Catlin still dominated his thinking and it was her name that leaped to his tongue. "What of Catlin?" he asked. "Is she here yet?"

"She has been here for some three hours. I am sure she'll be of a mind to welcome you."

"Three hours!" Richard exclaimed. "How is that possible?"

"She left in good time."

Pleasure at this information warred with conscience. Since they had ridden out of London shortly after dawn, Catlin must have been on her way earlier, perhaps pulled from her bed. And what had happened to her servants? He found himself reluctant to speculate on that. Once more desire drowned his scruples. "When shall I see her?" he asked eagerly.

"A few preliminaries must be observed, and then we'll take you to her."

"Preliminaries?" Richard repeated. He did not like the way his host was looking at him. The grey eyes glinted with humor, and he had the uneasy feeling that Sir Francis was enjoying a joke at his expense.

"Sure you'll be wanting to cleanse yourself of the dirt acquired on the road. There's a bath awaiting you in one of our guest chambers. Afterwards everything will be explained, I hope to your satisfaction.''

Impatience was a lump in his throat and a glitter in his eye, but a strong infusion of common sense told Richard that protests would avail him nothing. Coupled with that conclusion was a growing unease for which he had no cogent reason. Part of it might be attributed to the fact that the dimming light in the hall was further diffused by stained-glass windows, which threw a pattern of red and green on Sir Francis' visage, distorting his features and making him look, indeed, as if he were wearing a devil's mask.

''Dear boy,'' Sir Francis continued, ''before taking your bath, let me give you a glass of wine.''

Richard did not want wine. Everything Sir Francis proposed seemed designed to lengthen the time that stretched between the present and his meeting with Catlin. Yet, since it would have been ill-mannered to refuse such ready hospitality, he said reluctantly, ''A drink would certainly be welcome.''

''We must go to the south drawing room. 'Tis on the next floor. Come.''

Following his host up a circular staircase, Richard saw that there were paintings on the walls. Though these, too, were cast into shadow by the diminishing light, several bathed in the red glow from a higher window brought an actual blush to his cheek. It was an unusual abbey that could boast the picture of a nymph lying beneath a Hercules whose might was not limited merely to his muscles. There was an equally graphic rendering of Cupid with Psyche. The mental images to which these paintings gave rise caused Richard to regret the postponement of his meeting with Catlin even more. In the interests of self-protection, he averted his eyes from the walls, staring straight at Sir Francis' plumpish back. Over his host's shoulder, he saw an alabaster statue which, on closer examination, proved to be a beautifully sculpted but subtly distorted depiction of the Holy Trinity. Examining it closer as he passed, Richard's lip curled. He found this juxtaposition of the spiritual and the profane depressingly adolescent.

The room into which Sir Francis ushered Richard was in sharp contrast to the shadowy hall; candles flamed in wall sconces, in candelabra and in the great crystal chandelier that centered on a painted ceiling. Glancing upwards, Richard saw what first appeared to be a clasical scene typical of those decorating many a contemporary mansion. However, a second and longer look showed him that the godlike Grecian youths were engaged in a Bacchanalian orgy complete with supplicating maidens whose pleas were very obviously going unheeded. The work was detailed enough to bring forth a most embarrassing reaction. Looking away quickly, Richard encountered his host's eyes and found them full of glee. Had he noticed? Of course he had, Richard thought with some annoyance, and now he realized that some of the furnishings depicted in the painting were duplicated in the room. Among them were couches covered with green damask. These were very long and very wide, designed, Richard guessed, for similar dalliance.

Indicating a nearby divan, Sir Francis said genially, "Sit down, dear boy." He strolled to a long side board on which were several crystal decanters of wine along with delicate crystal goblets.

Richard, meanwhile, found his couch almost indecently soft, filled, he guessed, with the finest swan's-down. Everywhere he looked he saw evidence of sybaritic luxury; tables, bearing baskets of beautiful fruit, were inlaid with semi-precious stones. Huge malachite pillars flanked a fireplace in which a roaring fire had been built. There were Roman marbles upon the mantel, and in one corner of the room stood a statue of a well-endowed Apollo carrying a lyre. The other corner was occupied by a companion piece—a young, naked and voluptuous nymph with a roguish smile on her face and a finger against her lips, as if requesting silence. The other hand was upheld in a beckoning gesture.

"Charming, is she not?" Sir Francis remarked. "I call her Phyrne." He proffered Richard a goblet filled with dark red wine. "I hope you'll find this to your taste. 'Tis well aged and comes from one of Italy's finest vineyards."

"I am sure I will," Richard murmured, strenuously trying to appear as casual as his host. He feared that he had not quite succeeded in hiding his surprise at finding such voluptuous surroundings beneath an abbey roof. As he accepted the glass, Sir Francis held up another goblet of wine.

"A toast, my dear Reverend Veringer!" he said lightly.

"I am not a reverend," Richard replied coldly. "As I have

explained, all that is behind me now.''

"I remember, dear boy," Sir Francis nodded, "but I cannot help wondering . . . does one ever doff the principles learned in childhood and early youth? If I were to direct this toast toward the health of say . . . Satan, what would your response be?"

Richard regarded him with more than a little disappointment. He had misjudged his host. All of Sir Francis' aftermentioned reasons for bringing him to Medmenham could be discounted. Despite this man's avowal of an enlightened atheism that marched with his own, Sir Francis was proving to be an impious fraud. He must be engaged in some manner of devil worship! And undoubtedly the abbey was the headquarters of a Satanic circle. The studied irreverence he had marked in the Trinity pointed to that. There had been similar groups among the undergraduates at the seminary, an adolescent response to a repressive rule. Generally, these did not survive graduation, but some young men, he knew, did continue their adherence to these societies. He knew of several "hell-fire" clubs and thought them both puerile and pathetic. He had deemed Sir Francis too intelligent to concern himself with such arrant nonsense. How could any reasoning individual lend credence to the notion of a personified evil? It was almost as ridiculous as believing that a supreme being guided the destinies of mankind. However, much as he would have enjoyed debating with his host and battering down his beliefs with opinions he had held ever since he had been old enough to reason, he did not want to involve himself in anything that must keep him from Catlin. If paying lip service to a "painted devil" would please the man, he had no objections. Catlin was all that mattered.

He said, "I would be delighted to toast Satan or Beelzebub or Lucifer or the whole hierarchy of demons, if you prefer."

"Ah." Sir Francis had seemed tense but now he visibly relaxed. "As I think I told you before, my dear young sir, you are a man after my own heart. To Satan, then!" He clicked glasses with Richard and drank deeply.

"To Satan." Richard drained his glass.

"And I bid you welcome to Medmenham," Sir Francis said approvingly. "I am pleased we understand each other. I presume you'll want to take your bath now?"

"Immediately!" Richard responded enthusiastically.

The bathtub was set in the middle of a large chamber furnished with a huge fourposter bed and a tall mahogany armoire. Richard had been brought to the room by a light-voiced, soft-footed lad with the beautiful sexless face of an Italian choirboy. He had been clad in the grey livery common to all of Sir Francis' servants. Helping Richard undress, he had assisted him into the bath. However, an offer to scrub his back had been curtly rejected.

Lying in waters that were pleasantly warm, Richard wondered if pedastry were the order of the day at the abbey, but dismissed that notion as he recalled the paintings. That Sir Francis was both hedonist and Satanist he was willing to believe, but he must be exonerated of what men called the French vice. Certainly he was a strange man and a disappointment, yet at least a question troubling him ever since the previous evening had been resolved. He had wondered why Sir Francis was so eager to forward the course of true love and, for a stranger. Undoubtedly, the baronet imagined he had left the church because he had lost his faith in God. Probably he would have been extremely disappointed to learn that the erstwhile Reverend Veringer had no faith to lose and that he had loathed every moment spent in seminary and pulpit! Yet, as he was quick to assure himself, that was just as well. If Sir Francis had not imagined him to be an apostate ripe for devilish mischief, he never would have invited him to Med-menham and Catlin would now be in Ireland. He grimaced. They were taking a damned long time bringing them together, and to think about her as much as he did was intensely frustrating, especially for one who had not held a woman in his arms since Meg deserted him.

"*Abstinence, dear Richard, maketh the heart grow fonder.*"

Richard started, causing some of the water to spill over the tub's edge. The whisper in his ears was in his brother's voice. Fulke had said those words to him when he had deprived him of Christina, and why was he now thinking of his damned sibling—hopefully damned, he amended, wishing he could believe in such heavenly reprisals.

Banishing Fulke from his mind, he clambered out of the

bath. There was a rough towel lying on a chair. Wrapping it around him, he rubbed himself dry. His heart was beginning to pound heavily. It was time—it had to be time for him to join Catlin. He strode to the armoire, expecting to find his second-best suit of clothes, but on peering inside, he found only a long brown cassock which ordinarily would have been made of sackcloth and tied with a rope. This garment was fashioned from heavy silk and belted with a twisted silken cord. On the floor beneath it was a pair of leather sandals. He eyed the costume angrily. He was not going to dress up like some damned mountebank! He strode back to the bed where the boy had laid his black suit only to find it gone.

Additional anger shot through him. He pulled open the door to his room, hastily slamming it as he heard a spurt of girlish giggling in the corridor and remembered belatedly that he could not be the only guest at the abbey. His choice was clear. Either he donned that damned robe or he remained here. Was he to greet Catlin in this Papist attire? The idea was deeply repugnant, but since he had no choice he finally put it on, feeling like a damned fool. As that thought crossed his mind, he smiled unwillingly. Those who did obeisance to the so-called foul fiend could also be called damned—and fools, they undoubtedly were. "I'm in good company," he muttered, as he slipped his feet into the sandals and knotted the cord tightly around his waist. He was about to open the door when he heard a light knock. A thrill of anticipation went through him. Catlin, at last?

It was not Catlin who waited outside in the hall. It was the boy who had brought him to the chamber. "If your Lordship will be so good as to follow me," he murmured.

Once more Richard was going down the hall, descending the stairs to another floor and then down the stairs he had mounted upon arrival. Only this time, the same stillness did not prevail. Though no one save his guide was in evidence, he heard muted conversations and, he thought, light feminine laughter. He stared around the entrance hall, seeing several doors. Where did they lead? More specifically, where was he being led?

The boy opened one of the doors and beckoned Richard to follow him. They were in a dimly-lighted corridor; on either side of them were paneled walls similar to those on the upper floors but unadorned by paintings. At the end of the corridor, Richard saw another portal. Reaching it, his guide knocked loudly three times.

Three for the holy trinity, Richard thought amusedly as the door swung slowly open. Though the boy went inside, Richard remained on the threshold staring into a small room, lighted by two candles placed on a long flat table covered by a scarlet cloth and flanked by three chairs. Richard's eyes shifted to the cloth on which was emblazoned a golden cross. There was, he thought, something strange about that cross, and another look revealed that it was upside down.

Richard immediately recognized another symbol of Sir Francis' so-called Satanism. A book he had found in the seiminary library had contained a description of Satanic practices. The text had been spiced with such adjectives as "horrid," "abominable" and "evil." Richard could not see anything abominable or evil about the reversed cross nor, he told himself, would any other enlightened person.

"Enter, my Lord," someone ordered in deep sepulchral tones.

Richard looked about him but saw no one. Then, a panel behind the table slid slowly open, and three men in cowled robes similar to his own appeared and took the three chairs. Richard concealed a threatening grin as he noted their cowls were up, leaving their features in darkness. The effect was eerie but not as frightening as they evidently hoped. He faced them boldly, saying ironically, "Good evening, good sirs."

They did not move or speak. Three monkish monoliths, he thought amusedly. Finally, after a long pause, the man on the left said, "Richard Veringer, Lord More, are you present?"

"As you see," Richard acknowledged.

"Do you know why you are here?" inquired the man on the right.

Richard's patience was swiftly leaving him, "No. At least, I do not know why I have been summoned to this room."

"You have been summoned here, Richard Veringer, because we want your word that you'll reveal nothing of what has or will take place during your stay." It was the man in the center who had spoken, and Richard recognized Sir Francis Dashwood's tones.

"You have that," he replied brusquely. "And indeed you need not have asked."

"On the contrary, it is important to ask, important, too, that you swear on the head of our Prince Satan, guardian of the Monks of Medmenham, that you will abide by our rules. Will you swear?"

"If I must," Richard said.

"You must," the man on the right said solemnly.

"And if you forget your obligations to us," the man on the left spoke in a deep monotone, "you'll pay the price and suffer the consequences. Do you understand?"

Richard nodded. The thought of Catlin was in his mind again, or rather it had never left his mind. He had an impulse to tell them all to go to hell, but, under the present circumstances, such an order must prove singularly ineffective.

He said, "I understand."

"And will swear."

"Very well," said the man on the left, "repeat after me. 'I, Richard Veringer, do solemnly swear to keep faith with those who sit in high places and whose hearts and souls are in thrall to the Prince of Darkness, whom I now recognize as my liege Lord.' "

Richard, repeating the requested oath, wondered what more he must suffer before seeing her. He was really going through hell! He bit down a threatening laugh as he realized that in the eyes of the trio on the dais, he was doing just that!

"Is it enough, Brother?" asked the man in the middle.

"It is enough, Brother," the other two repeated in unison.

"Very well, Richard Veringer, Earl of More, you are admitted to our circle and may partake of all the joys therein—for as long as you remain under our roof."

"I am indeed honored," Richard said with a touch of sarcasm he could not quite conceal.

"You are, and more than you imagine." Sir Francis threw back his cowl and clapped his hands. "Ahriman, will you escort my Lord More to the Corridor of Delights?"

The boy who had led Richard into the room moved to his side. "If your Lordship will follow me . . ." he said softly.

A few minutes later, they returned to the hall, and the servant led him into another passageway. Once more Richard heard that sibilant merriment, muted giggles and beguiling feminine tones merging with the deeper voices of men—men and women together, but where? When his guide held up a candle, Richard saw doors on either side of him. Little grills were set into them, not unlike those in a prison, Richard thought with shock, but it was from them that the voices issued and, he noted, each of the rooms, or rather cells, was lighted. Again he followed the boy called Ahriman down the corridor to a door nearly at its end. Stopping in front of it, he motioned Richard to go inside.

As he entered, he heard a gasp of fright. In the dimness of this darkened chamber, Richard saw a figure huddled on a large bed. The only other furniture in the cell was a night stand on which stood a tall candelabrum. Extending his taper, the boy lit its seven candles and left the room. To Richard's amazement and subsequent anger, he heard a frightened female voice.

"Oh, help me . . . help me . . ."

He whirled. Thanks to the illumination provided by the candles, he finally beheld the beautiful but tear-stained face of Catlin O'Neill. Compunction stirred. She must have been badly frightened, kept here in semidarkness and not knowing why she had been spirited away to this strange place. How, he wondered, could he soothe her fears and put her at her ease. Words sprang to his lips and died as on glancing down, he found that, in common with himself, she as in religious garb—a nun's habit, complete with coif and veil though neither headdress nor gown hid her charms. Both were fashioned from a gossamer fabric and, again in common with himself, beneath that transparent material she was naked. He flushed, as inadvertently his eyes strayed to her small but perfectly shaped breasts with their rosy nipples inviting his kisses.

"Do . . . do not look at me," she whispered and shrank away, pressing her body against a mound of silken pillows. He wondered why she had not reached for the coverlet and saw, then, that her hands and feet were tightly bound.

"Good God," he exclaimed angrily. "Let me remove those ropes."

"Do not t-touch me, F-Father . . ." she began and paused. "B-But you're no priest nor monk, neither, to be in such a place. Oh, where am I and why was I forced to don this unholy garb? Please, sir, if you have any pity, help me. Get me away from here.''

Her pain and distress were, he decided, real enough. The poor little wench was unused to such unorthodox methods of seduction. He never would have agreed to such proceedings, himself, he thought crossly, beginning to loathe these psuedo-monkish trappings. They could only give rise to horror in a person who had any religious leanings, which she obviously did. Sir Francis was more of a fool than he had believed and he, Richard Veringer, was an even greater fool to have countenanced her kidnapping! If he had realized what it entailed, he most certainly would have refused to lend himself to such a scheme!

''Please, you must let me free you,'' he said gently, soothingly. ''Those ropes must be hurting you.''

''They are that.'' She sounded a shade less frenzied. ''My fingers are numb. Could you . . . would you help me to get away?'' Her beautiful eyes were bloodshot and tears stood in them again.

His annoyance increased. The girl was so frightened, it would be a Herculean task to calm her down. He said soothingly, ''Certainly, if that is what you wish, my dear.''

''What I wish?'' she repeated incredulously. ''Why would I not wish it?''

''Softly, softly,'' he murmured, wishing she were not wearing that damned headdress. He would have liked to stroke her hair, but perhaps it was better not to make an overture yet. ''Let me undo those knots,'' he said.

They were more difficult to untie than he had believed; it took some little time before he could loosen them. As he struggled with the cord, his anger against Sir Francis mounted even higher. Why had he been so hard on the poor girl? Finally, the knots yielded, and he pulled the cords away. ''There,'' he said triumphantly.

''Oh, I do thank you,'' she whispered.

He caught her hands, holding them gently. ''Let me rub your wrists and bring the circulation back.''

''No.'' She tried to pull away.

''Come, you needn't be afraid of me,'' he murmured. ''I'd not harm you, believe me.'' Taking her right hand, he pressed a kiss against the palm only to have her utter an outraged squeak and pull it back, slapping him smartly across the face with her other hand. Evidently, forgetting that her feet were still bound, she started up from the bed only to fall heavily upon the floor.

Richard knelt by her side. "Catlin . . ."

"Keep away from me!" she cried. "How dare you touch me in such a way? Oh, may the Blessed Mother protect me, for sure I've fallen amongst thieves and ravishers."

He had been on the verge of anger at the untoward response of this little whore. However, on hearing her wild words, his mood changed to one of amusement. She was a clever bit o'muslin, staging a tragedy for him, by way of punishing him and at the same time doing her best to increase her worth in his eyes. While he did admire her acting ability, he was weary of waiting for her promised favors.

"Come, my dear," he said impatiently. "I am sorry for the way you were brought here, but your servant cheated me, as you well know, and 'twas only right I should retaliate. Still, I bear you no ill will for my tumble in the muck and should have pursued you in the proper way had I not been informed that you were off to Ireland in the morning. I promise you that now we're together, I'll be kind to you and, as for ravishing you, I should like to know how one may steal what has already been lost?"

"Lost?" she cried furiously. "You are speaking about my . . . my . . ."

"Maidenhead, my darling. And may I compliment you upon your dramatics. I vow they're worthy of a Clive or a Prichard."

"Dramatics?" She regarded him with a mixture of anger and fright. "I am not acting. I am a virgin, and but for you, I'd have been in Ireland with my brother, who is . . . is *the* O'Neill—Mahon O'Neill, Lord of Munster, descended from the Kings of Ireland!"

"Better and better," Richard approved, smiting his hands together in teasing applause. "And are not all the Irish descended from such dubious royalty?"

"You may laugh, curse you!" she cried. "But 'tis the truth. I am Lady Catlin O'Neill and . . ."

"And what is such an exalted personage doing upon our humble English boards?" Richard demanded between chuckles which were, if the truth be told, becoming rather forced. Judging from his recollections of her in *The Lover's Stratagem*, she had been lovely, charming and beautiful to look upon, but he could have sworn she had not the ability to simulate such sincerity as she was now displaying.

Tears were rolling down her cheeks. Her whole body was wracked by sobs which certainly seemed genuine as she moaned, "My brother lost heavily at . . . at the tables and I . . . I thought I might earn the money to stake him again. And I . . . I did and he won back the whole of what we'd lost and more. And today I'd have been on my way back to our castle instead of being here in this horrid place amongst these devils, who make a mockery of all that's pure and holy. You think I do not know you for what you are, but I do, and oh, may Christ and all his saints have mercy on me!"

Disappointment and chagrin warred with a deep sense of shame. Richard knew she had to be telling the truth. Much as he wanted her, he could never take her under these conditions. He had to save some of the shreds of his honor. Striding to the door of the cell, he called loudly, "Let us out. I beg you'll let us out!"

Laughter greeted his cry—laughter from the other cells—but there were also footsteps in the hall, swift footsteps that brought the young servant to stare wide-eyed through the grill.

"What do you wish, my Lord?"

"I wish to be taken to Sir Francis," Richard told him curtly.

Still in his monk's robes, Sir Francis joined Richard in a small octagonal chamber furnished with an octagonal table flanked by eight chairs. Pushed against one wall was a long graceful sofa, carved with gryphons and unicorns and covered with his favorite green damask to match green walls, ornamented with genuine Persian miniatures. Through tall French windows, Richard could see a portion of the garden. A wind had risen and the swaying shadows of the tree branches were moon-projected upon the floor.

"Well," Sir Francis said, eying Richard with some surprise, "you seem to be in a sad taking, my friend. Did my servant inform me correctly? Is your Catlin actually a virgin?"

"Indeed, she is, damn it," Richard muttered resentfully. "I know truth when I hear it. She's a virgin and a lady."

"Both conditions are subject to change," Sir Francis murmured.

"Not through me," Richard snapped.

"A man of honor, I see."

"I wish that were true," Richard said heavily, "but I fear you'll not get her to agree. I acted impulsively, foolishly. I thought . . . but no matter. I pray you'll send her home."

"If that is you wish . . ."

"It is what she wishes," Richard stressed.

"Very well. I'll have her removed from the . . . Corridor of Delights. As a virgin, I am sure she's of no mind to be stimulated by what she hears." Moving to a silken tassel hanging on the wall near the door, Sir Francis pulled it twice. In a few seconds, the boy returned. "Bring me Miss O'Neill," Sir Francis ordered.

In a short time, Catlin came in. Evidently, she had been weeping bitterly, and though she was now making an effort to subdue her sobs, she was not successful. Her face was suffused with blushes, and she clutched her transparent robe about her with hands and arms employed to hide as much as possible.

"Obviously, a virgin," Sir Francis commented. He gave her a reassuring smile. "My dear child, a great effort has been made and I, a party to it. My sincere apologies. I pray you'll sit down." He waved at the sofa. "You see there are pillows. I beg you'll make use of 'em until I send for your garments."

She nodded miserably, and sitting down, she clutched the proffered protections tight against her, looking at neither man and keeping her shamed gaze seemingly upon a bouquet of golden flowers embroidered on a green satin pillow.

Moving swiftly to a decanter standing on a side table, Sir Francis poured wine into three goblets, handing one to Catlin, who shook her head, evidently still unable to speak for the sobs that wracked her slender body.

"Come," Sir Francis said softly. " 'Twill calm your nerves, and you need not fear it. I, too, am drinking from that same bottle, and I hope Richard will join us. Poor lady, as you can see he's much cast down for sure. As I think you must agree, virgins are at a premium upon our English stages.'' Sir Francis held out the third goblet. ''Richard?''

Richard accepted the drink. ''I thank you,'' he responded dully, wishing he could throw that same wine in his host's smiling face, but that would serve neither himself nor poor Catlin O'Neill, whom he belatedly recognized as one he would be proud to have as his wife. Unfortunately, in lending himself to this scheme, he had lost her forever!

''To Ireland and its green hills! You must drink to that, my poor child,'' Sir Francis addressed Catlin. '' 'Twill make you feel more the thing.'' Taking a sip from his own glass, he added, ''I, at least, will drink to Eire. And will not you, Richard?''

''I will.'' Richard sipped his wine, thinking it tasted more pungent than before and finding it more to his liking. Catlin, he noticed, had stooped weeping and was watching them narrowly. She was still suspicious, not that he blamed her, he thought resignedly.

''You'll not drink to Ireland?'' Sir Francis visited a gentle smile upon Catlin. ''And to your safe journey back to its shores?''

''I . . . I will drink to that,'' she said on a note of relief. ''You will take me home?''

''You'll leave by dawning. My own yacht will bear you back to Ireland. You have my word on it.''

Catlin visibly relaxed. She took a sip of the wine. '' 'Tis delicious,'' she admitted almost reluctantly and took another.

''From Italy's finest vineyard,'' Sir Francis repeated, moving toward the door. ''I'll see why they've not brought your gown, my dear. Also I must make plans for your departure.''

Catlin sipped her wine. ''I wish I might go now.''

''Alas, 'tis not possible . . . the roads at night. I'd not send my worst enemy out upon 'em. Never fear. You'll be waked in good time.'' With a bow, he left, closing the door softly behind him.

An uncomfortable silence fell. Richard could not bring himself to look at the girl he had wronged so grievously. And she, he knew, must be hating him. He drained his glass and summoning his courage looked at Catlin, finding to his surprise that she was clutching an empty goblet. She stared back at him, and it seemed to Richard that there was much less animosity in her attitude. He said tentatively, "I hope you are feeling better?"

"I am that," she murmured with a slight smile, eyeing him. Could it be appreciatively? Richard wondered with some amazement and decided he must be three-parts drunk if he thought that.

"Should . . . should you care for another glass of wine?" he asked hesitantly.

"I think I should." She nodded. " 'Twas mighty calming."

Richard rose immediately. For a moment, the room spun about him, which annoyed him. Generally he had a hard head, but he had not supped since early afternoon, he remembered. He walked carefully across the room and brought the decanter to a table near the sofa. Setting it down, he poured a full goblet for Catlin and one for himself.

"I hope that's not too much," he said, sitting down gingerly at the far end of the sofa and half expecting her to either order him away or jump to her feet. She did neither. She merely took the glass and tilted it to her lips, not sipping it this time but drinking deeply, something Richard, himself, was quite unable to keep from doing. They finished at the same time, setting down their goblets in unison, their laughter also mingling.

Catlin put out her little tongue and ran it slowly around her lips. "That was delicious." She stretched out so that the tips of her bare toes were touching Richard's thigh. Her pillow had dropped to the floor, but she did not seem to notice it.

"Delicious," Richard agreed. His heart was beating faster, and he was as sure of that as his desire for her was mounting. "More wine?" he asked.

"Is there more?" She glanced at the decanter.

"Enough," he assured her huskily. Again he tipped the decanter, filling her glass a trifle fuller than his own and praying she would not notice it. She did not, but he noticed that she did not drink the wine as quickly as she had before. She sipped it slowly, eyeing him over the rim of the glass and smiling at him with so heady a mixture of innocence and sensuality that he could not refrain from caressing her delicate little foot. It was beautifully shaped. Almost without volition his hand was moving slowly up her ankle. He expected that at any moment she would pull away, but she did not. Looking up, he met her eyes again and caught his breath as he read excitement in them, an excitement that matched his own. Her mouth was slightly parted, and he could see her breasts rising and falling. She was breathing quickly, almost as if she had been suddenly robbed of breath, and she was gazing him as if she expected . . . wanted . . . as if, indeed, her desire matched his own! Then, incredibly, amazingly, she reached out her hand and lightly caressed his hair.

"Catlin," he whispered and knew somewhere in the depths of his numbing brain that they had been given a stimulant—an aphrodisiac, perhaps. He must warn her, apologize, explain . . . but these scruples dissolved even as they formed, flitting out of his mind, leaving only desire behind.

Outside, a wind was blowing and tree shadows danced on her face. He must brush them off. He shifted his position. He was lying against her now, his lips on her throat, and beneath his hands he felt her hardening nipples. He tore at her gossamer garment and it yielded easily; soon that flimsy barrier lay in shreds. Her body was very white where the shadows did not darken it, the tree shadows flicking against her belly and her thighs and against the soft golden fleece that bloomed between them. He had stopped trying to brush the shadows away. He would kiss them away, instead. And that was when the men came, the men in the dark robes, wrenching the two of them apart and bearing Catlin away, her sudden screaming echoing in his ears.

Four

"Catlin . . . Catlin . . ." Richard cried in fear and agony, then found Sir Francis at his side, soft-voiced and reassuring.

"You'll see her soon again, lad."

He spoke as if he were addressing a boy of 12 rather than a man of 22, Richard thought resentfully. But why did he, himself, feel so dull and dizzy, and what had happened to Catlin? He caught Sir Francis' sleeve. "Where is she?" he demanded furiously. "Why did they take her away from me, and who was it? Tell me so that I can carve his guts out!"

"Lord, you are a firebrand, dear Richard, but you must release me. There are matters to which I must attend—immediately." Sir Francis made an effort to pull himself out of Richard's frenzied grasp.

"I'll release you," Richard said between his teeth, "when I know where you've taken Catlin. She must be allowed to go home. She's no wanton. She's a virgin!"

"I quite understand." Sir Francis still spoke gently. "And you, dear boy, were bent on relieving her of that particular asset, were you not? Well, I promise you, your thirst will not go unslaked, but meanwhile you must be patient."

"Damn you!" Richard tightened his grasp on Sir Francis'

sleeve. "I do not . . ." Whatever else he would have said died in his throat as he felt himself grabbed from behind, his arms pinioned by a huge man in a monk's habit. Cursing and struggling he tried to free himself but to no avail. The hands that clutched him were iron to his wood.

Moving back, Sir Francis shot Richard a commiserating look. "Sorry, dear boy, but you'll see her again and very soon." He glanced at Richard's silent captor. "I suggest you bring him with us."

Though Richard struggled fiercely, he was no match for the man who held him. He was forced to follow Sir Francis, for his captor fell into step behind him and there were others in back of them, a procession. Down the stairs they went, and as they reached the ground floor, they were joined by dancers in motley, leaping in front of them through the open door and out into the windy darkness, where in the shadows a violin screeched, a fife squealed and someone beat a drum. Someone also was singing incomprehensible words in a loud ugly voice, yet there was an odd rhythm behind this deliberate cacophony. Richard could actually feel the strange strident music coursing through his veins. His ears were ringing, and oddly he found himself moving in time to it. He cast a glance over his shoulder and found that the whole procession was infected by that shrilling, pounding noise.

The wind had risen. The sawing tree branches were silhouetted against a huge round moon and shards of clouds skittered across its white face. Some of his dizziness had left him, and Richard realized that the drug from the wine was wearing off. Concurrent with that realization, his captor's arms fell away but he was borne onwards by the surging crowd behind him—the roistering monks and the giggling nuns.

"To the caverns . . . the caverns," someone yelled.

"The caverns . . . the caverns," other voices echoed shrilly, eagerly.

Richard was being pushed down. He tried to fight against the pressure but fell on his knees, feeling sharp jagged rocks through the silk of his cassock. He was being urged to crawl over this sharpness through a narrow opening that he could barely see in the darkness. He tried to rise but stumbled and fell against a boulder. He was yanked to his feet and saw

moonlight through a hole in a rocky wall. Just as he realized
he was in some sort of a cavern, he was urged forward again
by those behind him. He stumbled and fell down again,
swallowing a groan as he scraped hands and knees together on
crusty protuberances rising from the floor, little stalagmites
gleaming orange under the light from torches stuck in
brackets along the craggy walls, throwing a lurid glow on the
faces of the assembly as well.

"Catlin . . . Catlin . . . Catlin . . ." Richard roared and
thought he heard a faint reply coming from a cavity in the
wall, a few feet away. Staggering to his feet, he took a
tentative step in that direction only to be pulled back by a
small, strong hand on his arm.

"Richard Veringer, stay here with me," a low, insistent
feminine voice urged.

He turned and looked down, finding one of the so-called
nuns beside him. She was short and dark and her eyes seemed
filled with fire, but that, of course, was only the reflection
from the torches. Her body was slender and shapely but failed
to stir his senses. He thought of Catlin's small, round breasts,
those beautiful fruits from the trees of Paradise! Where had
they taken her? Was she lost to him? He groaned deep in his
throat, needing the relief, the release of his passions so
summarily denied him. His head was spinning again, and he
coughed as perfumed smoke entered his nostrils. Incense!
They were burning incense in the cavern. He had heard that
the stuff was used in Papist ceremonies. And now he saw little
prie-dieus, prayer benches, lined up across the cavern. Was
he in some manner of church? Sir Francis had said he was a
nonbeliever, but if one recognized the existence of Satan,
conversely one also believed in God. He moved forward again
and almost bumped into a statue of the Virgin. Staring
angrily at it, he noted something wrong with its profile and
coming around the front saw that the face beneath the
traditional blue veil was that of a hog with a tremendous
snout and small red eyes! Laughter bust out of him. Even in
the midst of his worry over Catlin, he had to appreciate the
impudence of that unknown artist.

The small nun stepped to his side, whispering that a
ceremony was about to begin and that he must come back to
the others.

"What others?" he whispered, wondering at her evident nervousness.

"Come!" She grasped his hand, pulling him toward the back of the cavern. "You must not be conspicuous," she warned. "You'll anger them and they are already angry."

"Who are they, and why are they angry?" he asked.

"They are always angry on these nights—angry and dangerous. They're frightened, you see."

"Of what?"

"You'll understand presently."

A bell rang.

All the company sought out the prie-dieus and knelt. Richard had no such intention, but the girl at his side yanked at his hand and upset his precarious balance. As he fell, she pushed a bench in front of him, saying at the same time, "Don't be a damned fool."

He clutched it. "Are they not all damned fools here?" he whispered, appreciating his own jest and beginning to laugh.

"Hush," she hissed. "Look there." She thrust out her hand and pointed.

Obeying, Richard saw a man in monk's robes mounting a small flight of rough-hewn steps toward a bowl-shaped platform, carved with strange signs. A pulpit, Richard decided and then swallowed a cry as the man faced the congregation, if so it could be termed. He was wearing a mask—a goat's head, incredibly ugly and, Richard guessed, frightening to a goodly number of the people present. The goat was a symbol of Satan. He wondered why that particular animal had been chosen. He had never been particularly fond of goats. He did not like their odd eyes nor did he appreciate their penchant for eating everything in sight. As a child, he had lost a favorite hat to the voracious appetite of a black and white billy goat.

"My children, hear me." The voice issuing from the mask was hollow and echoing. It recited Latin prayers, but how odd they sounded—not like the Latin Richard had learned in school to the accompaniment of a ruler over his knuckles each time he missed a declension.

Around him, the crowd of "monks" and "nuns" were muttering those prayers, were intoning other responses, were rising and kneeling. In the glimmer of torchlight, he saw an altar. Rising behind it was another reversed cross on which was stretched the tortured image of a man in a loin cloth, his tongue lolling out of his mouth and two horns buried in his hair. His legs ended in hoofs. Richard smiled derisively—more mockery of Papist symbols. Sir Francis had to be a believer, else he could not have taken such pleasure in degrading his faith!

A scream rang out, which was choked off quickly, but not before Richard recognized Catlin's voice. He rose and was pulled down once more by the surprisingly powerful grasp of the small girl by his side.

" 'Tis too late. You can do nothing as yet," she said obscurely.

"Do nothing? Catlin needs me, I tell you," he yelled, forgetting that she could not know who Catlin was.

"You cannot go now. You'd be torn to pieces. Wait. She is safe enough."

Unwillingly, Richard knelt down again. He had to believe her. He also agreed that there would be danger if he were to interrupt the ceremony. He could not quell a cavernful of fanatics!

The tinkling of a small bell was in his ears, and a strange chant arose from the congregations. Though the words had a familiar ring, he could not make out what they were saying. It sounded like gibberish.

"Name thy be hallowed, heaven in art who father our . . ." they sang.

"Our father who . . ." Richard automatically reversed the phrase and realized why the words had sounded so strange. The prayers as well as the crosses were reversed. More sacrilege, he thought contemptuously, finding the reverse more confusing than perverse. It was all child's play!

"Come to Communion," boomed the figure in the goat mask. "The host is ready. The red host is ready and the altar prepared! Come to thine altar, my dear children, and eat of the flesh and drink of the blood of our Lord Sathanas, long may he reign on earth as he does in Hell and heaven, Amen."

Richard recognized Sir Francis' tones—Sir Francis with a goat's head clapped on his shoulders! Sir Francis, who knew where they had taken Catlin, now stood behind the altar, awaiting the faithful who worshipped Satan!

He was being urged to his feet by his companion. She wanted him to join the line of men and women surging toward the altar, he guessed. He did not resist her this time. Once he reached Sir Francis, he would shake him like the dog he was and force him to reveal what he had done with Catlin.

"Be calm," murmured the voice he now knew. The girl was behind him and obviously concerned about him. He wondered why.

They moved with the line. They were passing the altar to partake of the wafer, that which was called the "red host." He knelt and knew that for appearance sake he must take the biscuit in his mouth and drink from a silver communion cup shaped like a goat's hoof. As he swallowed the wafer, he would have sipped from the cup but it was tilted and the liquid poured down his throat. He swallowed convulsively once, twice, thrice before it was taken away. It had a strange pungent taste, but it was not unpleasant. In spite of his concern for Catlin, he wished he might have had more of it.

Someone pushed him to his knees crying, "Kneel in the Presence!"

Falling forward, Richard reached out to save himself, grasping the altar and feeling flesh! He stared down, seeing now that the silver dish containing the scarlet wafers was not resting on a linen or a cotton table cover. It lay on a nude body, a woman's beautiful naked body. Her breasts were like apples, tipped with hard little red nipples. Her face, however, was as pale as death, her blue eyes open and filled with horror.

"Catlin!" Richard reached for her, only to be thrust aside and held, straining against a powerful grip, while the rest of the congregation passed by and the man in the goat mask gave them the blood-red wafers, lifting each from the dish reposing on Catlin's belly.

A gong boomed out, and the cavern was filled with a brighter light. Almost magically, the prie-dieus were gone, pushed away by some of the monks. People were talking all at once—talking, screaming, laughing, singing, embracing. In another second, they were writhing together on the floor, the monks tearing at the transparent robes of the nuns and wrenching them off, while the women kissed and embraced them.

Richard was feeling very strange, as if, in fact, he were outside his body, looking on. At the same time, hands were reaching for him and pulling him down. He struggled to free himself from their determined grasping, yet there was an excitement rising in him. He wanted to be part of that wildness, wanted to throw himself down and feel those knowing caresses, but he could not because of Catlin. Catlin—who was she? He was no longer sure. Someone had caught his sleeve. He looked down and saw the small girl, who had guided him through the ceremony. She pushed her thumb against his palm, stroking it and sending shivers through him.

"Take me," she begged. "Take Erlina Bell."

He stared at her. Her face seemed to be melting before his eyes—her body, too. He reached out to touch her, and she held his hand between her naked breasts. Her flesh was firm and warm. He wanted her. No, . . . he had to find Catlin. He staggered away from her, looking toward the place where the table had been and saw her still lying there. She was no longer alone! The man in the goat's mask was poised over her, stroking her with hands curved like talons!

Richard rushed toward them, stepping over and on hands and arms, unmindful of outraged screams. He fell and rose again and finally reached her. He thrust the man in the goat's mask aside, and when the latter with an outraged scream tried to tangle with him, he lifted him bodily and threw him down. He lay where he had fallen, and Richard pulled Catlin into his arms, holding her against him, uttering soothing little sounds, as if comforting a frightened child.

"Catlin . . . Catlin." His mouth was against her ear. He smoothed her tangled hair back from her beautiful face and looking down saw that she was bound hand and foot. He carried her to a corner of the cavern and worked at the bindings. Finally she was free, and with a moan she flung her arms around his neck, burying her face against his chest.

He held her gently, patting her back, still uttering soothing little sounds, but it was difficult to touch her without wanting her. In spite of his good intentions, his desire for her was increasing. He needed her. Her back was so smooth beneath his fingers as he ran his hand the length of it.

He wanted her, and amazingly she seemed impelled by the same desires. She slipped her hands beneath his robe, fondling him, caressing him until he could no longer disobey the promptings of his own body. She was beneath him. He thrust himself against her softness and her hardness until the thin barrier of her maidenhead was pierced and her sharp cry of pain was in his ears, then silenced as he possessed her and she, ignited by his passion, climaxed with a moan of pure pleasure.

Moments later, lying beside him, she turned and put her mouth against his ear. "I wanted *you*," she whispered. "He'll not have me now."

"He?" Richard demanded furiously.

She trembled. "He said I was damned and being damned was ripe to bear his child, but 'tis your seed I'll have growing in my womb. I'll birth no goat-headed demons."

He had to tell her she was talking foolishly. Unfortunately it was difficult for him to think clearly, yet even in his current state of confusion, he was annoyed that this lovely girl should give ear to such folderol! Beauty without intelligence was a combination he did not admire, but he must remember she was a Papist, one that had been used as . . . as what? His head was getting heavy again, and looking at Catlin, he found her blurry and indistinct. It must be the drug. A man jumped between them, and he heard Catlin cry out. He lunged at the intruder, who eluded him and ran away. Richard stared after him and then turning looked toward Catlin, but the space where she had lain was empty.

Richard got to his feet, staring woozily about him, "Catlin . . . Catlinnnnn," he called, but his voice was drowned in the howls and laughter and screams about him. He stared out across the smoky cavern, across the sea of writhing, copulating bodies, and wrinkled his nose. A strong odor of sweat rose from the group, and looking at them, he was aware of various imperfections—huge flaccid bellies, hairy backs, posteriors ornamented with boils, pendulous breasts, scrawny limbs. True, there were some amidst the assembly that were well-endowed but . . . his thoughts abruptly ceased as hands grabbed him, pulled him down, caressed and stroked him. Mouths pressed against his mouth, seeking tongues thrust his lips apart, knees parted his legs. Caught in that orgiastic maelstrom, he dizzily tried to evade those that lay upon him, crawled over him, sidled against him, but it was useless to contend against them. He must needs respond to their urging, mindlessly, mechanically, until at length, he lay naked and exhausted in the arms of he knew not whom. His eyes were filled with strange patterns of light that formed and reformed, lights and shapes together, with sounds, music. Yes, there was music and chanting . . . somewhere . . . somewhere.

A name forced itself into his half-numbed brain and he whispered, ''Catlin . . .'' and wondered upon whom he was calling.

''Take me! Take Erlina Bell.''

Richard forced his heavy eyelids open and found that the dark girl was beside him again. ''You . . .'' he mumbled.

''Take Erlina Bell,'' she commanded.

Rolling over on his belly, he stared down at her, seeing that her body was hard-fleshed and thin. He did not want her. He was too weary, too spent, yet she was caressing him now. There was fire in her touch. It burned through him, arousing him, driving his weariness away. Her caresses were blotting out all that remained of any coherent thought, leaving only desire. He had to possess her. He had no choice. As he mounted her, she screamed shrilly like a female cat under a tom. A second later, he screamed, too, as her sharp teeth sank into his shoulder. The pain infuriated yet excited him. Snarling, he bit down on her back. The taste of her blood was on his tongue. Her nails dug into his back.

''You . . . you . . . you . . . where are you?'' came a sobbing scream.

''Don't listen to her,'' Erlina Bell cried, clutching him the harder.

Richard had heard, had listened. He found the strength to wrest himself from that spasmodic grip. Clambering to his feet, he stared about him and saw her and knew her, too. ''Catlin,'' he mouthed. ''Catlin, Catlin . . .''

She was standing a short distance away, and he cleared the distance between them in a single heap, clasping her tightly in his arms. He moved back hastily, feeling the stickiness of blood against his hands—her blood. Staring down at her back, he saw that she had been flogged. There were stripes across her hips and buttocks and scratches on her breasts, her belly and her thighs. "Who has hurt you?" he asked hoarsely.

"The goat . . . to punish me," she moaned. "He said you'd robbed him and I must be chastized. You as well. He said were both damned to . . . to eternal flames." She began to cry.

Richard held her tightly again, wishing he might throttle the man who had flogged her, and yet at the same time, in a tiny corner of his brain, he wished she had the wit not to swallow those ridiculous threats whole. Then his passion for her blotted out that minor quibble. Stroking her hair, he said softly, "He lied. Neither of us will be punished. This is all a great travesty, my own love, a mockery of something that means nothing." He fell silent as a wind suddenly howled through the cavern extinguishing the torches.

Stygian darkness like a smothering blanket fell upon them all, and the shrieks of laughter turned into wails of terror as it grew colder and colder and colder.

"Come." A familiar voice was in Richard's ear and a small hand fastened on his arm. "Come with me."

Hardly knowing what he was doing, he lifted Catlin in his arms and let Erlina Bell lead him away. They were guided toward a rocky crevasse. As they moved inside, at the girl's whispered directions, the sharp points of the stones cut his feet and lacerated the flesh of his thighs, but he made no sound; nor did Catlin, quivering against him.

"He'll try to take her," Erlina Bell muttered, "but if you promise to help me, I will help you. And I can get you away from here, Richard Veringer."

"How do you know my name?" he demanded.

"Suffice to say that I know it," she replied. "And I will get you away from here if you swear by the Great Mother, by the Horned God and by Ahriman, that you will do as I ask."

"Ahriman . . ." He wondered where he had heard the name. Ahriman was what Sir Francis had called his servant. Why was she naming him in such an oath?

"Why . . . Ahriman, the boy that served Sir Francis?" he whispered.

"He's not what you think, *my* Ahriman," she emphasized with an ominous note in her voice.

His mind was clearing now, but what she was saying still sounded like so much gibberish to him. Gibberish or not, he found himself oddly reluctant to accede to her demand. Still Catlin, alternately moaning with pain and babbling now about a cat named Grimalkin and a witch called Molly and some sort of curse, must be his first concern.

"How could I help you?" he demanded.

"There is a small cottage on your land. It is stone and far from the castle or Hold, as you call it. In the forest it is. Do you know it?"

"Know it . . . a cottage?" he repeated, trying to concentrate. He did know it, but it was still hard to fix his mind on anything. He must have been drugged. Yes, he had been drugged, heavily. That was why he had particiapted in the orgy. He did not want to think about that, could not dwell on what had happened, had to concentrate on what she was saying about the cottage. and this woman, who was she? How did she know him? To his certain knowledge, he had never seen her before. No matter, he must concentrate and think about the cottage in the forest . . . the cottage, the cottage. "Yes," he cried triumphantly, "I do know of it. It belonged to some manner of hermit, a hundred years ago. How did you happen to hear of it?"

"Suffice to say that I did hear of it and want it. I want it to be mine for as long as I need it. Will you swear that I may call it mine?"

"You may have it," he said. "I need not swear, though. You have my word. And now when I think of it, there's none will venture near the place. They say it's accursed, which, of course, is fool's talk. 'Tis yours."

"You must promise that it is mine by the Great Mother, the Horned God and by Ahriman," she said stubbornly.

"As you choose." He was weary and confused. There was something about this dark girl that filled him with repugnance, especially when he recollected the savagery of their mating. They had come together like a pair of wild beasts. He would not think of that. He must consider Catlin, poor little wench, thrust into terror through no fault of her own. "I swear by the Great Mother," he said. "Is that right?"

"Yes. Continue!"

"Ahriman . . . and the horned owl?"

"God!" she snapped.

"I beg your pardon. God, then. That the cottage is your's as long as . . . as . . ."

"I might need it."

"You might need it. Are you satisfied, Erlina Bell?"

"I am satisfied," she answered. "And you must remember that you've sworn an oath, Richard Veringer. An oath is much more binding than a mere promise."

"Not my promise!" he said frowning.

"No matter. I am satisfied," she repeated.

It was, Richard decided, a mere coincidence that a cloud sailed over the moon as they crawled from their hiding place into the windy night. The cloud made it impossible for anyone to see their naked bodies, and they were able to follow Erlina to a small cave, just wide enough to contain the three of them. Crouching down, Richard stiffened, as he heard Catlin's name called and recognized Sir Francis' voice. The man continued calling, his tone coaxing then furious, screaming her name until he was hoarse, until at last he could manage no more than a croak.

Hours later Erlina led them back into the great cavern, now emptied of all who had worshipped, feasted and copulated there. Lighting one of the torches, she indicated a passageway buried deep in the rocks and which, she insisted, was unknown even to Sir Francis.

"And how do you know of it?" Richard asked curiously.

"I am Romany born," she explained. "Our tribes are possessed of much lore that is hidden."

It was an answer that sufficed for many of his questions, including her mention of the hut on his grounds. He could now acquit her of any arcane abilities and was angry that he should even have entertained so ridiculous a notion!

Erlina found them some discarded monks' robes and guided them to an inn, where she was known. The host, who seemed in awe of her, provided changes of garments merely on the promise of future repayment.

A month later, it was Erlina Bell who was sole witness of the weddng of Catlin O'Neill and Richard Veringer, conducted in the rose gardens of the castle. The ceremony was secret because the bridegroom's mother had died before his return and the nuptials should have been postponed. They could not be postponed for the regulation year of mourning since the bride was already suffering the pangs of morning sickness.

Erlina left hastily before the minister pronounced his blessing, passing out of the gardens and losing herself among the trees that bordered them.

Richard, embracing the beautiful Lady Catlin Veringer, did not take a second look for his erstwhile helper; he was wholly concentrated on his bride, who had turned deathly pale. Uttering a low cry, she fell to her knees, her hands over her ears.

"What is it, my love?" he demanded concernedly. Catlin had been prey to some strange moods ever since that terrible night.

"You cannot hear?" she demanded in a trembling voice.

"No. What do you hear?"

"Molly . . . 'tis Molly," she whispered, clutching his hand. "Molly, the witch, and her cat Grimalkin. Do you not hear her screamin' and himself howlin' out their torment?"

"I can't say that I do." Richard stifled a sigh as he added, "And who, my love, would Molly be?"

"Ach, many years ago she was burned at the stake as a witch on evidence given by Macklin O'Neill, my great, great, great, great-grandfather, whom she'd helped until he grew feared o' her. An' as she was writhin' in the flames, her cat came an' leaped up at my grandfather, who threw him, yowlin'n spittin', into the fire with her, an' when there's a doom for the O'Neills they come back to warn an' to gloat. They're here. They're here an' 'tis because I've been wicked."

It occurred to Richard that he had never heard her speak with so thick a brogue, and moreover did Irish aristocrats sound like the women who sold lavender on Dublin's streets? Fortunately he remembered that it was mainly the great families of Ireland who boasted banshees. He said gently, "You haven't been wicked, my dearest."

"I have," she moaned. " 'Twas my body was used as an altar for those unholy doings."

He was glad that her 'g's had returned. He said, "I pray

you'll not be troubling yourself about that. There's no more truth to that ceremony than there is to the supposition that the moon's made of green cheese.'' Taking her in his arms, he felt a strong surge of desire. "You are my goddess, my angel—and my altar, too, where I will worship.''

"Ach, you shouldn't be saying that," she chided. " 'Tis a sacrilege!"

"Then let me be damned for it!" Richard responded lightly, thinking of Erlina Bell now. He owed her a debt of gratitude for insisting that the ceremony be held at twilight. In the month that had elapsed between the nights of Sir Francis' Satanic revels, Catlin, while remaining at the Hold, had turned virtuous and refused him so much as a peck on her cheek. All that was changed now. With his ring legally on her finger, not to mention his child in her belly, there was no reason why they shouldn't enjoy themselves to the full.

Lifting his beautiful bride in his arms, Richard carried her carefully back to the castle. Once in the huge bed where generations of Veringers had fulfilled their marital obligations, Catlin, evidently reassured by heavenly sanction, responded in a way that vanquished the burgeoning regrets that had been plaguing Richard of late.

Part Two

One

Catlin was dreaming.

As she moved restlessly on the wide mattress, beneath her the wood, sawed and fashioned into a bedframe, 180 years ago, creaked and groaned. Richard, aroused from a deep sleep, knew from his wife's mutterings that the cat-encumbered banshee was riding through her dreams.

In the interests of self-protection, he edged carefully away from his wife's flailing arms and quivering body both of which could inflict severe physical pain upon his spare form. He added a grimace to his second sigh, needing a woman and wishing that it might have been Catlin. A vision of what she had been when he first saw her and through the earlier part of their 19-year marriage, rose to tantalize him. Once she had managed to put the terrors of Medmenham out of her mind, or rather to the back of her mind, as he found out later, she had proved to be a gracious hostess and an ornament to the Hold. In those years, the neighboring gentry had flocked to the castle. Catlin, and on occasion, her brother Mahon, entertained and charmed them. She had been depressed when her first child had been born dead, talking a great deal of nonsense about Molly, the banshee, and her cat Gremalkin come to warn her. However, she recovered from the blow, particularly when she became pregnant almost immediately afterwards. Then she had started talking about that damned banshee again and a miscarriage had followed. She had cheered up mightily at the birth of Richard Anthony, a dark-haired, blue-eyed bouncing baby, who, Richard smiled, was the image of himself. Now 16-year-old Richard, called Tony, was already displaying a strong sense of responsibility as became his heir.

Catlin had been full of hope for the child she conceived only two months after she bore Tony, but she lost it during her third month, muttering about Molly again. It was after that miscarriage that she began to put on a little weight, he remembered. She gained more after her next baby was born dead, and she fell into a depression which seemingly could be appeased only by food. She was, however, only pleasingly plump at Kathleen's birth. Their first daughter had been a scrawny, three-pound infant, but he had another smile for the tawny-haired, golden eyed beauty she was at only 14. Catlin cheered up mightily, and while she did not lose the weight she had gained after Kathleen's birth, she was still beautiful and happy with her two adorable children. He would have been pleased, he recalled, if she had had no more lyings-in. Unfortunately it seemed that he had only to make love to her once for her to conceive. Before the births of Colin, twelve, and Juliet, ten, one child had been born dead and the other survived only until his first birthday. But why could not Catlin, like himself, have been satisfied with the four lovely children who had lived? Colin and Juliet were the equal of their older brother and sister—the boy dark and handsome, the girl fair, blonde and the image of her mother with her huge blue eyes and sylph-like slimness. He shuddered, praying that Juliet would never balloon out like the near-monstrosity that lay beside him.

As slender and willowy as Catlin had been when they first met, she had become a caricature of that ethereal beauty. Her lovely eyes and straight little nose were minimized by her enormous cheeks. At least four chins augmented her own, and from the size of her belly it was hard to believe that she was not expecting triplets!

It was not only the loss of her looks that depressed him. It was the superstition that seemed to rule her life at present. As often as he had told her that it was ridiculous to imagine that these children were born under a dark star and destined for misery, Catlin refused to believe otherwise. She had told him that that damned figment of her imagination, the banshee, had said as much. Moreover the creature had, she insisted, come to wail on their castle battlements to the neglect of her Irish haunts.

Thinking on it, it seemed incredible to him that he could have married a woman who saw portents in stones, brooks, trees, animals, birds and, as for the moon, sun and stars, not a day passed that one or another was not giving her cause for alarm.

Of recent years, she had spent hours on her knees in the old partially ruined chapel, which had been a storeroom until she refurbished it with her damned Papist crosses, statues and paintings. If he had not waxed so adamant, she would have installed a resident priest as well! Even so, she was always after him to bring one in—and always for the same reason. Ever since the death of her last child, she had believed herself doomed and damned by her participation in the revels at Medmenham.

" 'Twas an altar for evil, I was," she had cried as they had put the little coffin containing the remnants of Mahon, their late son and last infant into the family crypt in the churchyard. "It's damned I am and my children, too."

He had done his best to convince her that what she had observed had been naught but a cleverly designed mask along with winds which had probably been churned up by some sort of gigantic bellows. He spoke to deaf ears. Catlin's one answer was to point out the loss of six children, tragedies she blamed on the terrible moments when she inadvertently had participated in that Satanic Mass. There was no convincing her that she had been victim rather than perpetrator, for then she would remind him of her subsequent actions when she had behaved as shamelessly as any Covent Garden drab.

"You were drugged," was always his response.

"I was possessed and could not have been possessed were not there evil in my own soul," she had answered on more than one occasion. As she interpreted it, the evil had been in her wanting and welcoming his caresses, she, a virgin and a good Catholic girl. There were times in these last years when he wondered how their life would have been had he not fallen in with Sir Francis' plans and instead had followed her to Ireland. Would he have wanted her as much once he got to know her? He was not being fair, and he knew it. Until her banshee-augmented depression had settled on her, she had been delightful.

"Lud, man, what's happened to my sister of late?" Richard winced. That was the voice of Catlin's brother Mahon on his last visit, shortly after the death of his namesake. "She had such a sense of fun, and now she's as grave as a nun." Mahon had eyed Richard suspiciously. Though the Irish were known to be poetical, Mahon had not been speaking in rhymes; he had been shocked and depressed by the appearance and mental attitude of his sister. He had not visited them again, and Catlin rarely mentioned him. She was not given to saying very much on subjects other than sin, sorrow and fate. Richard winced. Of late, she had been constantly adjuring him to remember his immortal soul, something that appeared to trouble her greatly. Much as such references annoyed him, he did not argue with her on matters spiritual or ecclesiastical. Her voice had grown in proportion to her size, and she could shriek like her apochryphal banshee when aroused.

Operating on the theory that "soft answers turneth away wrath," his conversations with his wife were, more often than not, a series of nods. He used an emphatic nod for agreement, a hesitant nod for disagreement and a medium nod for almost everything else. It was amazing and gratifying how well that worked. He was quite sure that Catlin, who of late talked enough for them both, was quite unaware of his silences. It did not make for a particularly felicitous relationship, but he had ceased to expect felicity. Most men he knew never sought for it in the confines of marriage. They had mistresses to warm their beds and wives to bear their brats.

He did not have a mistress. If the truth were to be told, his desire for sexual adventures had been largely quelled on the night of the orgy, aspects of which could still bring a flush to his cheeks, amazing in a man who had just recently celebrated his forty-first birthday and was consequently in the "the yellow leaf of his life." That melancholy reflection brought forth a groan, one he regretted immediately, for with a gargantuan wheeze, Catlin, who was evidently also awake, heaved herself closer to him and placed a heavy hand on his stomach.

"Richard . . ." she moaned.

He produced a yawn almost as prodigious as her wheeze, hoping it would quell her enthusiasm for chatter in the night. "Yes, my love," he burbled through a second yawn.

Neither proved effective for she said fearfully, "Do you hear the cat?"

"No, my love," he said soothingly.

"I do. I hear Molly also."

"You've been having another one of your bad dreams."

A pillow, dislodged by Catlin's vigorous shaking of her head, slammed against Richard's face. " 'Tis no dream. There's evil all around us. I feel it," she intoned. Edging closer to him, she added, "Hold me, Richard, my dearest, for I am sore afraid."

It was no small task to perform but Richard, thinking it was high time they had separate rooms, dutifully made the effort, while his wife sobbed noisily in the semicircle of his straining arms.

On a higher floor in another wing of the Hold, Juliet Veringer awakened from a deep sleep, her ears alerted to the keening of the banshee and the howl of her cat. Surely, she thought resentfully, Grimalkin must have been the most ill-dispositioned animal in the world. However, with her quick faculty for understanding both sides of any given question, Juliet could imagine the poor creature wouldn't enjoy being rooted out of whatever airy kennel it occupied merely to notify the O'Neills or those related to them of impending doom.

She frowned, wondering why she, only half an O'Neill and alone out of all the Veringer siblings, could see the cat in all its grey-striped glory, with the halo of fire around its head and its huge eyes green as the grass that grows on Ireland's sward. She did not remember where she had heard the latter description, but guessed it had been confided to her by Molly in one of her quieter moments when she wasn't wailing out one of her forecasts of doom.

Juliet had seen Molly, too. Thin as a bone she was, with the pale freckled skin common to the redhead she swore she had been in her younger years. Now her hair was white as the snowdrops that bloom near the lakes of Kilarney. That, Juliet recalled, was another of Molly's descriptions, told to her when she was a wee thing and the banshee had come to pass the time of day with her before she set up a howl on the castle ramparts. Molly also had green eyes, and she could make them shine like a beacon in the night but hadn't a notion of where she'd learned the trick of that. And why, Juliet wondered, were they disturbing her sleep tonight? Probably they were also disturbing her mother and Colin, as well. Though they couldn't see them, Colin, Tony and Kathleen could hear them. It had been a long time since the pair had set up such a chorus, and now there were no more babies to die. Juliet swallowed a large lump in her throat. There were still the four of *them* and their darling parents, as well.

She slid out of bed and pulling open the heavy oaken door of her bedroom, she dashed down the dark cold hall toward Colin's chamber. It was only after she was inside and the door banged behind her that, in the act of leaping on his bed, she feared he might not care for this late invasion.

He didn't.

"You jumped on my arm," he stated sleepily and crossly.

"But I didn't wake you," she commented knowledgeably. "You heard them, too. Didn't you?"

"I have been asleep," he replied pointedly.

"You heard, you heard, you heard!" Juliet chanted.

Out of natural curiosity, her brother capitulated. "Did you see them?"

"Of course, I didn't. They're outside. Poor Molly. It's cold tonight."

"She wouldn't be feeling the cold. She's dead," Colin reminded her.

Juliet shivered. "It must be dreadful to be dead. I hope it never happens to me."

"If it does, you'll just have to make the best of it like Molly."

"Oh, you!" Juliet punched him. "You'd miss me, wouldn't you?"

"I don't expect I should." He shrugged. "At least, I'd sleep the night through."

"You weren't sleeping tonight. You were listening to Molly and Grimalkin." A sudden thought struck her, and she shivered again.

"You're cold. You'd best get under the covers."

"I'm not cold," Juliet told him, but she also accepted his invitation, snuggling up against him. "I was shivering . . . out of fright."

"You?" he scoffed. "You're never frightened."

"I was, too," she said indignantly. "The last time Molly screamed like that—and the time before that—was because of the babies dying. You . . . you don't think one of us'll die?"

"Hush," Colin soothed. "It could not be for that. They were all little."

"Little people aren't the only ones who die," Juliet sobbed. "Molly was old and she died . . . burnt to ashes."

"No one's going to die, silly," he said with conviction. "She's here for some other reason."

"I wonder what," Juliet murmured sleepily.

"*You* could ask her," Colin said enviously.

"I'd never ask her," Juliet said yawning.

"Why not?"

"I do not want to know."

"You are a silly," Colin sighed.

Juliet didn't answer. She had fallen asleep. Colin, looking at her moonlit face, smiled with a tenderness his favorite sister was never likely to see, and despite the keening of Molly, who was certainly going on longer than usual tonight, he followed Juliet's lead and went peacefully to sleep.

Kathleen Veringer, woken out of a sound sleep, glared in the direction of her window. Usually she awakened the minute the first rays of sunlight hit the panes, but it wasn't the sun that had roused her. It was Molly's blasted howling! It seemed particularly loud tonight—an eldritch screech, she thought—and she was pleased, having just added "eldritch" to her vocabulary.

"Eldritch, eldritch, eldritch," Kathleen muttered, almost tasting the new word. She loved to read but loved to ride just as much, and thinking of Jenny, the mare given to her on the occasion of her fourteenth birthday, a fortnight since, she could be up and riding into the forest. Wasn't Molly loud tonight! She wondered what more was going to happen to this "accursed" family, her mother's words. Thinking of her mother, Kathleen made a face. She would have to rise before dawn if she were going to ride that morning.

Every time Molly howled, her mother made them all go into that horrid cold chapel and pray! Papa didn't hold with that, she knew, but for some reason he never argued with Mama on this matter. He only looked long-suffering and rolled his eyes around. It was a pity Mama did not spend less time in the chapel and more riding, but would there be a horse in the stable could bear her? She seemed to be getting fatter and fatter with every passing day. She wasn't even pretty any more—and she had been beautiful. There was that portrait in the gallery, painted just after she married Papa. She had also been slim and smiling. She seldom smiled any more and was always so cross—and if Kathleen went riding on a Molly morning, she would be very cross indeed.

"I will go," Kathleen whispered mutinously. "And she'll not stop me."

Tony Veringer frowned as he stood at the window of his room, looking out on the moonlit towers of the Hold. Molly's wailing filled him with frustration. If there were only some way to communicate with her and find out what dire event was soon to take place. Only Juliet could do that, but he would not dream of waking Juliet. He did not want his sister communing with such dark powers. She must have nothing to mar her sunny childhood, such a little treasure she was with her corn-gold hair and those deep blue eyes, both inherited from Mama.

Thinking of his mother, Tony frowned. Of recent years, she had become so unhappy, so haunted. By what? The deaths of his siblings? The indifference of his father? Tony's frown deepened. He loved his father devotedly but he wished that he would be kinder to his mother. He spoke to her so brusquely, and Tony wondered if only he were aware of how often his father avoided looking directly at her immense body. He did not think that even his mother knew about that. She was too wrapped up in some private misery. She practically never laughed as she had when he was little. Oh, she had been beautiful then. It was a pity the younger children had never seen her as he remembered her.

What was preying on her mind?

The hours she spent in chapel were increasing. Sometimes she went in of a morning and did not emerge until mid-afternoon. If only she would speak to him. Once he dared to question her about the terrors he read in her eyes. He would not do so again, for she had fallen wailing to her knees and actually beat her breasts while she gasped out that she was accursed for her great sins. Her shrieking had held the same keening sound he was hearing now from the banshee. They had left him no wiser, only with the feeling that inadvertently he had grievously hurt his mother, whom he adored. He adored his whole family. He wanted them to be happy, but how could they be happy with Molly screaming and the cat with her? He had heard that when the cat cried, too, the doom would be particularly dire. His father scoffed at that, but his father also refused to believe in the presence of Molly or her cat. He blamed his wife for instilling the children with her Irish superstitions.

Tony went back to bed, but knew he would not sleep and did not. The dawn was a thin red line across the Eastern horizon when Molly ceased her howling. Tony, tossing restlessly in his bed, heard the sound of hooves on the path leading to the forest and was surprised. It was early for anyone to be abroad. Perhaps, he thought half-humorously, it was a pooka, come galloping out of Ireland especially to bear Molly and her cat back to the O'Neill's castle where they rightfully belonged. More likely, it was his sister Kathleen on Jenny, bent on escaping a long prayer session in the chapel. He wished he might take his own horse and join her but that would grieve his mother, and this morning she must already be sorely afflicted and would need him at her side in chapel.

Jenny, her eyes wild and burrs in her mane and tail, galloped into the stable without Kathleen, sending all the grooms into a frenzy. Lady Kathleen was a prime favorite with the stable crowd—the grooms, the boys and even with Dobbin, named after a horse and half-witted. Seeing Jenny coming back riderless had made Dobbin drop the two buckets he was carrying to water the horses, sink down in the wet hay and the horse manure and begin to blubber, both fists shoved into his eyes, his whole misshapen body shaking with grief. The grooms were bringing out horses so they could ride and find her or the body, when Kathleen, her elegant new habit mud-stained and with brambles in her hair, came limping in.

Dobbin saw her first and ran screaming to seize the torn hem of her habit and rub it across his face and to jump up and down, making the sounds that passed for speech and which only his mother understood.

David, the head groom, came to her side. "Are you hurt, lass?" he asked. "Lady Kathleen?"

"I'm not hurt, David," she told him, her lip quivering. "But I . . . I must find my mother. I have seen . . . and I . . . I vow 'tis her fault, my fall . . . The way she looked at me . . . and those others . . . they were . . . I don't understand but . . ." Tears began to roll down her cheeks. "I must find my father!"

"You've found him, and what's amiss and where's Jenny?" Richard demanded, just having entered the stable.

"Jenny!" Kathleen cried, not answering her father immediately. She looked at David in horror. "Did she not come home?"

"She came home and is in her stall," he said comfortingly. "She took no hurt, milady."

"Jenny, Jenny, Jenny." Kathleen ran to her darling mare's stall and found her there with her head in a sack of oats and the burrs already combed out of her mane and tail. "Jenny," she sobbed, kissing the horse's foam-streaked side.

"Kathleen!" Richard caught his daughter's hand, pulling her out of the stall and looking anxiously down into her sherry-colored eyes, which were not the same color as those of his brother Fulke, he always assured himself, even now in the midst of his concern for her. "You've had a tumble, my dear?"

"It . . . it . . . it was she who *made* me fall," Kathleen stammered.

"Jenny?"

"No, the small woman . . . all of them . . . they pointed

at me and said things." Kathleen lowered her voice. "When I first came upon them, they were all on the ground and they were singing and moving together in an odd way . . . and they weren't wearing any clothes. It was like horses when they mate, only they were people. Then . . . then they saw me and they all shrieked at me . . . and the small woman pointed and Jenny . . ."

Richard paled, remembering and not wanting to remember. "Where were they?" he rasped.

"In a . . . a clearing. There was a fire burning and the small woman came and pointed at Jenny, and she shied and threw me down." Ever since she had passed her fourteenth birthday, Kathleen had considered herself entirely grown-up but now, as she gasped out the tale of her encounter in the woods, she clung to Richard like a frightened child and wailed because a strange, small, naked woman had glared at her out of wild, wide eyes which seemed to be full of fire and had said incomprehensible words and pointed at her horse. Jenny, who never shied, had done so emitting a high whinny that sounded almost like a human scream, tossing Kathleen from her back and fleeing while all the naked people continued to yell and point at Kathleen. She had run from them further into the woods, stumbling and falling often and twisting her foot, but still she had run, feeling as if they were pursuing her; she still felt as if they must come dashing after her into the stableyard to pluck her from her father's embrace.

Through kissing, petting and murmuring words of comfort, Richard finally succeeded in calming Kathleen. When she could speak coherently, he asked, "Did this small woman . . . I mean, was there a cottage anywhere near there? A stone cottage?"

"Yes," she corroborated excitedly. "I saw it through the trees. I never knew there was a cottage in the woods. Oh, Papa, who is she? She was horrid like a . . . a witch . . . and those others . . . what were they doing?"

Richard, his head packed with visions which had intermittently filled him with horror over the past 19 years, made a great effort to sound unconcerned, calm and even a little amused. "I would not know, my dear, unless I were to see these wonders for myself. As for witches, you know that's all fancy.''

Kathleen did not argue. She only said, "She was so horrid. She looked at me as if she hated me." She shivered and repeated something she had heard from her nurse when she was just a wee thing. "She looked as if she were ill-wishing me.''

"Nonsense," Richard replied bracingly. 'I can see you're monstrously upset, my child, and sure you've had a fright and a tumble, but I beg you'll not brood on it. That woman cannot harm you.''

"Do you know her then, Papa?" Kathleen gazed at him in wonder.

"I've some knowledge of her." Richard strove for a neutral tone. It would not do for his daughter to witness his anger, more than anger—fury, if what he guessed to be taking place was indeed happening.

"Come," he urged, "I'll take you to your room." As if she were still a baby, Richard lifted Kathleen and bore her inside. That she did not protest or proclaim her nearing adulthood was a measure of how deeply she had been frightened. Richard, remanding her to the care of Mistress MacGowan, the nurse who had cared for all his children, also noted that for once Kathleen seemed to welcome her cluckings as the old woman began to tend her.

The spectacle poor Kathleen had witnessed brought to mind bits and pieces of local gossip Richard had heard over the years and dismissed. Two girls from the village had gone to evening service one night and mysteriously disappeared on their way home through the woods.

They were found naked and distraught in a meadow not far from the castle. One died from exposure; the other lived on in a near-mindless stage, unable to account for anything that had happened to her or her friend. Later it was found she was pregnant. She died in childbirth, the babe with her. Gypsies had been seen in the neighborhood, and, as usual, the blame fell upon their bold-eyed men. They were not so kindly treated the next season, but a gypsy girl disappeared, too. She had been discovered dead and also nude. It was generally believed that she had been the victim of some village rowdies bent on reprisals. And yet another girl, turned out of her house for being pregnant, had spoken wildly of being ravished by the devil in the woods.

"Girls . . . always young girls," Richard muttered to himself. Was there any connection? He ground his teeth. In his present mood he was glad Catlin had sought the solace of her chapel. With an unusual rush of sympathy for his wife, he decided to keep the tale from her. Going back to Kathleen, he exacted her promise that she would confide nothing of what she had seen to her brothers, sister or mother. It proved easier than he had anticipated to convice Kathleen that she should keep her own counsel. His daughter did not want to think about it, and telling her family would have meant that they might never have stopped mulling over the subject.

After leaving Kathleen, Richard strode back to the stables. He planned to enlist some of his grooms and keepers to lead a raid on Erlina Bell's cottage—Erlina Bell, who until this moment he had forgotten, or had he merely relegated her to the back of his mind? Unwillingly, he remembered that night. Odd, the several ways it had been brought back to him in the last few hours. There were Catlin's dreams and Kathleen's terrors, and he himself had been thinking about it, lying wakeful beside the mountain of flesh Catlin had become.

How would Erlina look?

Thin, he thought. Scrawny, perhaps. Thin women often become bony when they reached middle age. It must have been an unpalatable sight for Kathleen, seeing a bag of bones naked in the woods. Inadvertently, he recalled the Jack o'Diamonds, bare bones buried in consecrated ground in defiance of his mother's wishes and eliciting a string of curses from her, superstitious old bitch! And Catlin, equally superstitious! He had been unfortunate in his choice of women, he thought bitterly, but why was he dwelling on the past? Because the past was present in the person of Erlina Bell, doing God knows what in the woods!

Who would have thought that when she asked him for the cottage and made him swear she could keep it until . . . he halted midstride. He had promised her the cottage, and now he was of a mind to thrust her out—on the evidence of a frightened child. He needed more proof than that. He needed to see what might be taking place there for himself. He would enlist the services of only one man, David, whom he could trust. David knew the woods well. His father had been a keeper, shot by a poacher, and his son brought as a mere lad into the Hold because he was good with horses.

They would need to leave before sunup, perhaps long before. The moon was full, and they would not ride but would walk. He continued on his way to the stables, his anger now mixed with a certain avid curiosity which, had he been challenged on it, he most certainly would have denied.

Much to Richard's surprise, David was reluctant to venture anywhere near the stone house. He knew about it, had seen it as a lad, had even been inside and had also been glad to abide by Richard's stipulation that that part of the woods was out of bounds. David had been sure that Richard must agree the place was haunted.

"All dusty 'twere 'n dark wi' weird drawin's on the walls, faces'n the like. To look at 'em made you feel all peculiar. An' bein' there, you 'eard things." David did not elaborate but the shudder that shook his husky frame emphasized his fears better than any description he could have provided. David did not shudder easily, Richard knew. His head groom had been one of the lads who helped pluck the fruit of the gallow's tree and lay old Jack in the ground.

"We'll not need to enter the cottage," Richard assured him. "It's not for that I'm going."

"I've heard . . ."

"I am sure I've heard whatever's reached your ears, man, and I tell you, there's no such thing as ghosts."

David looked patently unconvinced, but typically he agreed to go.

The trees grew high near the stone house. In the bright moonlight, they were dark against it, their long branches lying over its half-shattered roof like spindly but protecting arms. Crouched in the high grass to the side of the cottage, Richard and David watched. They had been there nearly an hour, and though there were dim, flickering lights in the windows, none of them were blue, as David had insisted they would be. In fact, nothing to excite their curiosity had occurred until this moment when two figures in dark-hooded cloaks carried torches out to a clearing just behind their hiding place. It was wide and, in David's eyes, ominously circular. "Brownies'n bogles'n witches, they do dance in such," he muttered to Richard.

Somebody must have been doing something in that circle, Richard reasoned, for the grasses were broken and flattened. He did not attribute that condition to David's cited causes, for he had just seen a flat stone within the circle. It was about six feet long and two feet wide. The word that sped to his mind was "altar." In the darkness back of his eyes, he saw the table altar of the cavern and its fair burden—the lithe and beautiful body of Catlin O'Neill. The flame of desire flared and flickered out, doused by present reality. Richard glared at the stone, wondering if what he was beginning to suspect could possibly be true.

Beside him, David emitted a long, low whistle. Glancing up, Richard saw a thin man with a fiddle tucked beneath his chin, his body gleaming naked and white under the torch-light and the moon. The music he had begun to play was strangely beguiling. Others poured forth from the cottage. Mentally counting them, Richard found that there were twelve: six men and six women. Leading them was the thirteenth, the small woman. She did not appear to be much more than a girl. Her hair, dark and wavy, flowed over her bare shoulders. Her body was slender and incredibly graceful as she went through the patterns of a whirling, leaping, incredibly sensuous dance, bringing her followers close together in a sort of weaving motion.

David was watching. Richard guessed that the groom must be on fire with a lust he was experiencing himself. The wild music, the naked dancers, the suggestive movements were almost unbearably provocative.

"Take me . . . take me," her pleas echoed in his head, as he stared at Erlina Bell, so little changed, so slim, so firm. He had taken her, unable to resist that plea because of the drug. Had she whispered her invitation at this moment, he would need no drugs to comply. Fortunately his anger was as great or possibly even greater than his desire. There was no need to fan the flames of that. She, who had asked for a haven, had brought the madness of Mednenham to his own woods!

"I cannot watch," David groaned. "I want . . . I want . . ." His lean body was tense, his eyes ablaze. He started to crawl forward.

"David!" Richard held him down, gritting his teeth as a long woeful shriek reached them. Under his hand, he felt David relax.

" 'Tis a girl," the groom muttered.

"Very likely." Richard drew and expelled a long breath as the cry was repeated. A second later she was thrust into view; she was no more than 16. Her hair was long and fair, her naked body a little plump but shapely. She struggled desperately.

"I know her," David hissed. "She is Meg MacAlpin, the blacksmith's oldest lass. I must help."

"You must stay where you are," Richard cautioned. "They'd tear you to pieces, man."

"I'm a match for . . ." David tried to free himself from Richard's grasp.

"One's no match for thirteen," Richard whispered. His own anger increased as he watched the girl sobbing and struggling. Erlina stepped forward. She held a cup, and fixing her eyes on Meg, she muttered something. The girl suddenly turned passive, staring blankly at her. A moment later, she took the cup and drained it. A silly smile appeared on her face. She started to giggle and continued giggling as two of the men lifted her onto the stone altar.

"God's guts," David muttered. "What be that?"

Richard's attention was diverted to a figure that had just dropped its dark cape to reveal the scarlet vestments of a priest beneath the head of a goat!

" 'Tis Satan!" David moaned.

" 'Tis a mask," Richard contradicted through gritted teeth. "And I beg you, be silent."

His warning was not needed. David was silent and rigid with horror as the whole obscene ceremony of the caverns was duplicated, complete with the orgiastic aftermath. Richard found himself acutely depressed. These puerile ceremonies had partially ruined his marriage. Poor Catlin believed the loss of so many babies was her punishment for having participated, however unwillingly, in a similar ritual. Over the years her conviction that she was damned for all eternity had grown. He had been unable to make her believe that she was the victim of a pack of sex-crazed lunatics. He wished that he could bring her here and show her this revolting spectacle, but it was too late. Let her know that such things were actually taking place on t grounds of the Hold and she might very well lose her fragile grip on sanity! He had a long sigh for the Catlin he had known at the beginning of their married life. If anyone ought to be damned for all eternity, he thought bitterly, it should be Sir Francis!

It was not until after sunrise that they could make their way back to the stables. "Take a couple hours sleep," Richard advised his pale and shaken groom. "Then gather men you trust and join me here at nine." He added tersely, "And I charge you, bring axes, crowbars and sledge hammers."

Erlina Bell looked better by dusk than by daylight was the thought that entered Richard's mind as he faced her. The rough homespun gown she wore hid the luscious curves of her body, and her hair, piled untidily on the top of her head, resembled a rat's nest. She stared at him and at the six grim men who stood a few paces behind him. Her dark eyes were wide, and surprise was the only readable emotion reflected in their obsidian depths. Time, Richard realized, had been less kind to her than he had imagined. There were deep lines on either side of her mouth. More seamed her forehead. There were flecks of grey in her hair. Yet, surprisingly enough, she still exuded a certain sensuous appeal, which he wished he had not noticed.

Tilting her head to one side, she said, "It's been a long set of years since we've met, my Lord. Have you missed me and come to pass the time of day with me? If that's the way the matter stands, I must needs bid you welcome."

There was audacity and a challenge in her speech. Richard, with the events of the night large in his mind, longed to put her over his knee. Unfortunately such a gesture might not have resulted in the punishment she richly deserved. He said coldly, "I think you must know why I have come."

Her eyes narrowed. "We made a bargain, you and I. My need has not grown less with the years. This house, I recall, was given me until I chose to leave. I do not so choose."

"The choice is no longer yours, Mistress," Richard stated. "I said you might . . ."

"You swore," she interrupted.

"I swore you might remain here, but I did not give you

leave to abuse your tenancy. Meg MacAlpin was found naked, ravished and raving in the fields this morning. They fear for her sanity.''

''If Meg MacAlpin's the blacksmith's child, her sanity is a precarious thing at best. But why should you come to me with these tales?''

''Who better?'' Richard snapped. ''I saw the whole of your . . . ceremony last night.''

''You . . . watched?'' she whispered accusingly.

Richard knew basilisks did not exist, but if they had, their fabled stare might have been very similar to the one he was currently receiving from his soon-to-be-late tenant. He said calmly, ''I watched, and so I think it'll not surprise you when I tell you, I want you out of this place and quickly.''

Her hands curled into fists. ''Need I remind you . . .'' she began.

''You need remind me of nothing.'' He flung the words back at her. ''I renounce that oath and warn you that if you're not off this land within the hour, I'll have you thrown off. My men are aching to do it.''

''I warn you not to insist upon this desecration,'' she cried. ''Else my curse shall follow you . . .''

''Desecration? One desecrates a church or a temple or a shrine, but not such a place as this. As for your curses,'' Richard's smile combined insolence with mockery, ''curse away, my dear Erlina. I'll add them to my collection. Now go and be quick about it. My men are as anxious as myself to see the last of you!''

The fire faded from her eyes. She sagged against her door which was, Richard noted, battered and hanging by one hinge. The whole house was, as he remembered, a crumbling wreck, barely livable. Erlina Bell's look, he also noted, was actually conciliating, and he guessed he had really frightened her. Fool, he thought contemptuously. She and Dashwood were both fools, substituting one so-called eminence for another in their futile quest for earthly power.

''Please . . .'' Erlina Bell whispered. ''I will go, but I have no place as yet. I pray you let me remain until I find another.''

''You may remain as long as it takes you to gather such belongings as you can carry, Mistress. I give you an hour, then my men will escort you to my gates. No doubt, you'll find some other fool to take you in.''

Her assumed humility dropped with amazing swiftness. Her eyes actually flamed. "I warn you, Richard Veringer," she cried hoarsely. "I warn you that . . .''

His patience fled. "Too many warnings, Mistress, and too little action. I think we must needs supply that." He gestured to the men behind him. "Have at the house, and I charge you, do not leave one stone of it standing."

She shrieked then, a long wail, as they rushed forward, thrusting her aside, their hammers and crowbars poised. "No, damn you, damn you, double-damn you a hundred times. My elixir . . . my glass, my elixir . . . my potions!" she howled.

"Poisons, you mean. Noxious poisons, drugs to dull the senses, let them shatter and sink into the earth!" Richard exclaimed.

She screamed again and ran in amongst the men only to be thrown violently back by David. She fell in a heap and struggled to her feet. The sound of their tools was loud against the crumbling stones. She ran forward a second time, striving to grasp a tall beaker which even as she touched it was knocked from her hand, shattering into a thousand pieces as it hit the stones. A scarlet liquid soaked into the earth, and she howled in agony. Then she reached down and retrieved something else, clutching it protectively against her bosom and dashing out. The sun's gleam was caught in the object, and Richard, blinking against its brightness, saw that it was a witching ball. "I pray you'll tell me my fortune, Mistress Bell," he mocked. "What do you espy in your crystal?"

She regarded him out of reddened eyes. In a low voice she said, "I see a long, long road, Richard Veringer. As you have broken your oath and dstroyed my home and more—more than you know—so will your home be destroyed and so will those you love be loathed and feared as they go forth upon the byways of this world and have no resting place until they find some plot of ground which will receive them. But the searching will be arduous and the way fearful. That will be the fate of the Veringer household—and that is my curse upon you, Richard Veringer. I am not finished with you!"

Behind him, the ancient walls of the cottage crashed down

upon each other, leaving only a heap of stones. Richard stared at Erlina Bell with grim amusement. "I might tell you, Mistress, that I do not believe in curses or omens, gods or devils or any of the fantasies concocted by charlatans such as yourself to confound mens' minds."

She stared at the heap of stones, blinking against the dust that arose from them. "Do you not believe, my Lord? One wonders what you'll be saying in seven years?"

"I do not anticipate a change in opinions I have held for the whole of my lifetime," he retorted coldly. Reaching into an inner pocket, he brought out some coins and handed them to her. "Let these keep you until you find another roof."

She took the coins and, spitting on them, flung them at his feet. "There are those who'll give me shelter, right enough. I tax you, sir, remember me when seven years have come and gone!"

He laughed into her furious face. "I doubt I'll be able to remember you in seven days, Mistress Bell." He turned to David. "Escort this woman across the bridge that spans the moat." With a wave of his hand, he mounted his horse and rode home in high good humor.

TWO

Colin was lost and had no notion how he had become lost save that while riding toward the Hold, he had been thinking about Kathleen or, rather, Juliet. Her birthday present lay in his knapsack, the prettiest little ivory fan he could find. It was not too small because the spokes must be wide enough to accomodate the names of the men who would wish to dance with her at her forthcoming ball. He supposed he should have waited to present the gift. His sister would not be 18 until mid-November, but at her earnest request, the ball would be given within the week.

He agreed with her. November in Northumberland was no time for a birthday ball, not with the roads piled high with snow and the drawbridge icy over the frozen moat.

His thoughts shifted to Kathleen, who had met Sir John Driscoll, the man she later married at her birthday ball, given three years ago when she turned 18. He wondered if Juliet would find the man she would eventually marry on this occasion. He doubted it. According to her letters, she had been in and out of love no less than four times in six months! Kathleen's temperament was entirely different. Colin suspected she did not approve of Juliet's flighty ways. She would never admit to such a thing, though. Family loyalty was strong in them all. He smiled fondly. Kathleen would soon be brought to bed of her first child, and due to the fact that Sir John had been sent to Madras three months earlier, his sister would be having her baby at the Hold. He was glad of that and suspected that Kathleen was, too. She had not wanted to leave the castle—none of them did. His smile vanished. He would have to leave it eventually since Tony stood to inherit. He frowned, sighed, and since it did no good to ponder upon the inevitable, he fixed his mind on his present dilemma. How he could have lost his way—and so close to home?

The forest path onto which Miranda, his mare, had unaccountably wandered while his attention had been diverted was narrow. The trees were so dense they blotted out the waning light. He would have difficulty finding the road again and though he could be no more than a league from the Hold, he would probably have to hole up in another tavern for the night. There would be only a small sliver of a moon to light the sky and, in his last letter, his father warned that there had been a veritable plague of highwaymen upon the roads of late.

Colin frowned, cursing his absent-mindedness. He had been looking forward to spending this night beneath the castle roof. In addition to the pleasure of seeing his family again, he was weary of putting up at indifferent hostelries and like as not sharing a bed with some flea-ridden stranger. He was also sick of the food, either overcooked or raw. There seemed to be no happy medium. As for the wine, it was all corked, or so it had appeared to him.

Miranda suddenly neighed and reared, nearly unseating Colin. Startled, he reined her in and looked about to see what might have frightened the animal. Not surprisingly, he could see nothing. It was even darker now, and he must concentrate on trying to find a way out of woods that seemed to be growing more impenetrable with every step his mare took. Wheeling her around, Colin started back the way he had come. Surely the path must branch off and they would find themselves on the highway.

He was considerably relieved when at last they emerged upon a broader road. Still it was one he did not immediately recognize. Fortunately there was a light flickering in a window less than half a mile distant. Seeing a painted signboard swinging in the evening breeze, Colin realized he had found his inn. He patted Miranda's flank gently and a short time later entered The Green Dragon, an inn which looked very old, a fact substantiated by the host.

Identifying himself as Mr. Horatio Chubb, he welcomed Colin with a large smile, exposing teeth almost as green as the faded dragon on the sign. He was a small, stout man with a tic in one eye which made it appear as if he were always winking. As he led Colin into the common room, he said, "This 'ere place were built afore an 'Anover set 'isself on the throne. It were 'ere afore the Stuart kings, too. It were built when Whitby Abbey were filled wi' monks." Having delivered himself of this gratuitous information the host indicated a table adjacent to a small fire burning in a great hearth.

Colin, sitting down in an old wooden chair, found himself the sole occupant of a musty chamber with a low, beamed ceiling and smoke-begrimed walls. The air was heavy with the odors of mold, greasy food and stale beer, none of which was likely to pique his appetite. Nor was he much taken with the antiquarian-minded innkeeper. Aside from the tic, which he could not help, he was grimy and unshaven, and his apron carried stains on top of stains. Rubbing his hands on this limp garment, Mr. Chubb regarded Colin almost affectionately.

"Not many come 'ere today'n those that did left afore sunset. Ye'll 'ave a chamber to yerself tonight."

"That is gratifying," Colin lied. He cast a glance toward the grease-befogged window and concealed a sigh. The small panes were dark. Any hope of inquiring the path to the main highway was flouted. If he left the inn, he would be in danger of becoming lost all over again. Yet he could not like Chubb, and furthermore he did not trust him. The man put him in mind of all the traveler's tales he had heard—most of them centering around dark, lonely, deserted inns and unprepossessing landlords with an eye to robbery or murder or both. That host and inn met at least two of these qualifications was undeniable. Colin was not ready to acquit him of the third and fourth. Fortunately, there was a pistol in his greatcoat pocket, and though he was passing weary, if there was not a stout chair or a nightstand to place against the door, he was prepared to remain wakeful through the night.

"Would ye be 'avin' wine or ale, sor?" inquired the host.

"Ale will do, thanks," Colin said.

"I'll be fetchin' it, sor. We be short o' 'elp'n . . ." Mr. Chubb paused at a loud knock on the outer door. His small eyes sparkled. "Maybe ye brought me luck," he said. "There be another."

He had not added victim but Colin was ready to supply the missing definition as the host hurried off to answer the door. Hearing his unctuous, "Good evenin', sor," Colin envisioned him bowing and rubbing his hands, the actions he had used when he ushered him into the room. He had difficulty smothering a laugh as Mr. Chubb, bowing even more deeply, brought in a tall, slender young man. Leading him to an adjacent table, he rubbed his hands while saying, "Sit 'ere, sor. I'm just after 'elpin' this 'ere guest'n wot'll you 'ave to drink. Ale or wine?"

"Wine, my good man, if there's any fit for my palate," the newcomer drawled wearily.

"Wine it is, sor." Mr. Chubb hurried off.

The young man loosed a long sigh and fixing a lackluster eye on Colin, he said wearily, "Are we the only victims then?"

Colin started, then laughed. "I vow you must have peered into my mind. 'Twas the same thought that occurred to me."

"Alas, I wish I were so perspicacious." The stranger smiled. "Think how such an ability would serve one at the gaming tables."

Colin regarded him interestedly, noting that he was very well dressed. His greatcoat was of fine cloth and stylish. Only two capes graced his shoulders rather than the several attached to Colin's older coat. The newcomer's boots were polished to a high shine, and his hair, dark and wavy, was tied with a black ribbon. Though he must have just dismounted, not a lock of it was out of place. He had set a round hat on the table before him rather than the cocked version Colin still wore. In fact, his style and his neatness were enviable, and having seen several equally fashionable young men frequenting the gambling clubs in London, Colin wondered if he might not be a professional gamester.

"Are you a gamester, sir?" he asked.

"I have been, but luck's not favored me of late."

"I'm sorry," Colin said politely.

"I do not repine." The other shrugged. "Luck has a way of turning. Down one day, up the next. And you, do you gamble?"

Colin shook his head. "No, I am at Oxford."

"Oh, indeed. But that should not keep you from the tables if you've a hankering for them."

"I haven't." Colin shrugged. "Unlike you, I've never been particularly lucky at either cards or dice, and so I don't play."

"You're not one to take chances. I can understand that and I admire it, too. I wish it might have been so with me. Though," he lowered his voice, " 'twas quite a chance to take coming to this unsavory hostel."

Colin leaned forward. "Do you know anything about it?" he whispered.

"Does one have to know anything? One needs only to employ eyes and nose."

"True." Colin grimaced. "But I'd no choice. I was lost and my father told me that the roads are reputed to be dangerous, else I should have pressed on. I had every intention of reaching the Hold tonight, save that I took a wrong turning, having made the error of thinking while riding."

"That is an error . . . particularly when it brought you here. Do you live far from this place?"

"I do not think it can be too far." Colin paused as Chubb came back bearing a tray on which was a foaming mug of ale and a glass of wine."

" 'Ere ye be, gentlemen, the best o' my cellar." Setting down the glasses, he grinned and quitted the room.

"Well," Colin said, regarding the other man ruefully, "your health, sir."

"And your's." The stranger lifted his drink and taking a sip suddenly hurled the glass across the room. "Faugh, damme me if I've ever tasted such!" He wiped a hand across his mouth.

Colin set down his mug. "Was it so bad?"

"Vile, like all else in this miserable inn. If I had any place to go, I'd not stay here another minute."

"I fear we've no choice," Colin told him ruefully. " 'Tis very dark out."

"I see as well by dark as by daylight," his companion snapped. "You say that you do not live far from here?"

"Not far, but the road . . . I think it's through the forest."

"I have a nose for direction. If I could bring you to your home, might I have accomodation for the night?"

"If you could, you'd be more than welcome," Colin said. "But I doubt . . ."

"Do not doubt." The stranger rose. "Be assured that if you give me your location, I'll find it." Lowering his voice to a half-whisper, he added, "I'd not drink any more of that ale. 'Tis my opinion both wine and ale are drugged."

"Do you think so?" Colin demanded, surprised and alarmed at having his own fears corroborated.

"I do, else why are we the only travelers to be honored with mine host's dubious hospitality?"

"That did occur to me," Colin admitted. "But are you sure you could find the way?"

"As I have told you, my night vision's quite remarkable and has served me well in the past."

"If you really believe . . ."

"I do," was the positive reply. "My name, by the way, is Simeon Weir. And you are . . . ?"

"Colin Veringer."

"Veringer's Hold!" Weir exclaimed. "But I know it. And we are less than thirty minutes away!"

"You know it! Here's good fortune," Colin exclaimed, rising. "Would you be acquainted with my brother Tony, perhaps?"

Weir shook his head. "I am familiar with this part of the country but I have no close acquaintances here. My home's outside of Edinburgh."

"That's quite a distance yet."

"Yes, I've many leagues to ride." Weir spoke wearily. "And there'll be small rejoicing when I arrive. My father recently died and my stepmother resents me. She'd rather my young half-brother came into the baronetcy and, in consequence, she'll be hard put to receive me. I wish I might postpone the visit but I stand to inherit the property so I must be on my way.''

"Need you be there at any given time?" Colin asked, pitying him.

"Any time between now and eternity." Sir Simeon Weir's lips twisted mockingly. "Closer to the latter, I'm thinking."

"Why, will you not remain with us for a day or two . . . longer if you choose?"

Weir shook his head. "I cannot think I'd be welcome for more than this night."

"Nonsense, man, you may stay as long as you choose. Perhaps you might come to my sister's birthday ball."

"You have a sister?"

"Two." Colin smiled. "Juliet's having the birthday and Kathleen's expecting a birth."

"And relatives and guests to come. I wish them both happiness, but I cannot think you'll have room enough for me." Weir spoke a trifle wistfully.

"Come . . . the Hold's large enough for a regiment and has quartered many in times gone by, when we British were at loggerheads with you Scots."

"Ah, yes," Weir said with a tinge of mockery. "The King over the water and the 'Forty-five. Such a pother. So much good red blood soaking into the ground."

Colin regarded him with some little shock. "You're the first Scot I've met who does not . . ."

"Either bemoan or proudly prate of Culloden?" Weir questioned contemptuously. "You've met Highlanders, I fancy. We of the Lowlands are less romantic. We do not sell our souls for a callow charmer with a long tongue, a worthy descendent of the whoring Queen of Scots, who lost her head long before the English clipped it."

"Lord man, hold your fire," Colin said, laughing. "All that's ancient history."

"Ancient?" Weir stiffened, then relaxed. "But of course, and memories are far too long in Scotland. Meanwhile we're putting off our departure. Let us pay our charming host and have done."

Despite Sir Simeon's assurances, Colin, riding after him

through the dense forest, had been full of qualms. Once they had left the inn, he was more than a little inclined to doubt his companion's vaunted night vision. Much to his surprise, they had not strayed from the path often, and when they had, that could be blamed on Miranda. She had been acting skittish ever since they left the inn, and Colin suspected her of wanting to devote her attention to oats, water and sleep. However it was also possible that she was being made nervous by an overabundance of annoying and unexpectedly brave bats.

For the last quarter of an hour or more, they had been swooping out of trees and skimming over the heads of the horses, which Colin found very odd and a trifle unnerving. The bats at the Hold preferred the heights. Colin wished heartily that these would have been of a similar persuasion. Though he could hardly see their dark shapes, he heard their shrill twittering. It sounded unexpectedly eerie in the darkness. He wondered if it disturbed his guide as much as himself. Even as the thought crossed his mind, Weir suddenly cried out and waved his arms as if warding them off. There was a rush of wings, a loud squealing of many bat voices and then stillness. To Colin's amazement, they all dispersed and, at the same time, Miranda, uttering a high whinny, reared. It took all his strength to bring her down without unseating himself.

"Lord, man! Are you hurt?" Weir called back.

"No," Colin answered breathlessly. "Miranda's steadier now. The bats must have frightened her."

"I'm not surprised, poor creature. They certainly alarmed me."

"I thought 'twas the other way around."

"What would you be meaning by that?" There was a cold edge to his companion's voice.

"They almost seemed to fly away at your command."

Weir laughed now. "Then you'll need to be afraid of me."

"Afraid?"

"I'd be frightened of anyone who could scatter bats by willing it. Also I'd be grateful for his presence. I hate the pesky things myself."

"I don't suppose I hate any animal," Colin mused.

"You're a good-natured young man," Weir commented.

"And you're a good-natured old man." Colin's merry laughter rang out. "I doubt that you could give me many years."

"I'm twenty-two."

"My twentieth birthday's but a month away."

"And you are the eldest son?" Weir had reined in his horse waiting until Colin came up beside him.

"No. Tony's the eldest. Rather he is named Richard, but is called by the second of his names to distinguish him from my father."

"And your sister? I presume this must be her eighteenth year, else she'd not have been given a ball."

"Juliet will be eighteen come November." Colin explained the reasons for the ball. "Probably," he added with a small pang, "she'll be wedded and off by November. Half the county's in love with her, and she's in love with them. My sister Kathleen also married at eighteen as did my mother."

"You seem very fond of this Juliet," Weir commented.

"She's my favorite sister," Colin admitted. "We're the closest in age, you see, and she's such a merry little thing, a real tease. I shall miss her when she's away from the Hold. We all will, I expect."

"Very likely." Weir nodded. "I've not had a sister, but I did have a favorite brother, older than myself."

"He's dead?"

"Long ago," Weir corroborated.

"A childhood disease?"

"Aye, one that was like to have felled the lot of us, but I recovered. He did not."

"You have my sympathies." Colin put out his hand to touch Weir's shoulder, but at the same time the latter's horse snorted and moved away.

"Aldeberan's anxious for stable comforts," Weir said. "We'd best be on our way."

"Yes, we should," Colin agreed, falling in behind him once more.

In another few minutes, they took a turn, and amazingly the shrubbery and trees thinned out and Colin looked once more upon the highway. "By all that's holy, man!" he exclaimed. "You've brought us through the dark forest. However did you manage it?"

"I've told you—'tis my night vision."

"I wish I possessed that gift."

With a spurt of low laughter, Weir said, " 'Tis not quite the blessing you'd imagine. My eyes by day are not nearly so dependable. In fact it has been my habit to rest a good part of each day, rising when the sun is sinking and the light less painful to me. My friends have dubbed me a modern Arisitippus for my slothful habits, as they term them. I let them think that I, too, live for pleasure."

"Why do you not tell them the truth?" Colin inquired sympathetically.

"I am not a seeker after pity. Let them spend that elsewhere, that's what I say," Weir said loftily. "I've told you only that you may understand and perhaps explain my infirmity to your family, though I fear they may find it very strange and not to their liking."

"And I promise you, they will not," Colin assured him. He stared down the road. To his surprise, he saw the massive outlines of the Hold. Once more he was amazed. "Good Lord, man, we're close to home. I never dreamed we'd arrive so quickly! Come!" He rode up to join Sir Simeon once more.

The latter said tentatively, "You're sure of my welcome?"

"Never more. You have my word on it. Come," Colin repeated, urging Miranda toward the drawbridge.

An hour later, Colin, preparing for bed, was joined by Juliet. "You're here!" she shrieked and flung herself into his arms.

"I am that." He hugged her and, pushing her away, smiled down at her. "But I'd not wanted you to greet me at such an hour. You should have been long asleep."

"How might I sleep and you not under our roof when you were expected long before?" Juliet inquired.

"I was delayed upon the road."

"But not waylaid. With the way Molly was carrying on, I thought you might be, and poor Mama feared the same thing. And Papa talked of highwaymen, and I . . ."

"I do not hear Molly now," he interrupted. "Has she been

at it again?''

"When has she not, these past seven years?''

"And still refuses to tell you why?''

"She's grown very grumpy. She'll not speak to me at all any more. To my mind, she misses Ireland.''

"I wish she'd go back there.'' Colin tilted his head. "I think I do hear her, but faintly.''

"She's weary, I expect.'' Juliet frowned. "I, too, wish she'd return. Poor Mama's quite beside herself.''

"Lord, that would be difficult.'' Colin commented with a grin he hastily smoothed away.

"What do you . . . oh!'' Juliet shook her head and her finger as well. "I beg you'll not be so cruel. 'Tis an unceasing pain to her that she's gained so much flesh. 'Tis difficult for her to walk. She spends most of her days in her chamber.''

"She's grown even greater?''

Juliet nodded and looked at him unhappily. "She says she'll not even come down for my ball and Papa's sleeping in another bedchamber.''

"So I learned when I spoke to William about accomodations for Sir Simeon Weir, who came with me.''

"Sir Simeon Weir? Who might he be? You've brought home a friend for me? From Oxford? Oh, you never said you'd do that.'' Juliet's blue eyes shone. "What's he like? Tell me!''

"He's not a friend, minx, and I didn't bring him for you. I'm not saying he mightn't be a friend, but at present he's but an acquaintance, a most helpful one at that.'' Colin explained his encounter with Weir.

Juliet listened attentively. "He does sound fascinating. I've never met anyone who could see at night as well as we can by day!''

"No more have I. I wasn't inclined to believe him, at first, but it's true. There wasn't even a good moon, and he rode as if he knew every inch of the path!''

"Marvelous!'' Juliet smiled brightly. "I am glad he insisted you leave that horrid inn. I had feelings about you tonight, and I expect that's why.''

"Feelings?''

"I thought you might be in some sort of trouble.''

"Oh, yes, I expect father's been talking quite a bit about

all the highwaymen in the district.''

"More than that." Juliet regarded him oddly.

"What more?"

"I don't know." She frowned. "But you're here, and all my fears are assuaged. Oh, Colin, I have missed you so dreadfully!"

"And I have missed you." He looked at her lovingly. "Now get to bed. I'd like to ride with you in the morning, and if we do not stop talking, we'll both remain abed all day like Sir Simeon Weir."

"Does he sleep all day?" she demanded.

"He says that the sunlight's hard on his eyes."

"Oh, poor man. I do love the sun."

"And so do I. And if I am to see it, you must leave me now."

"No," Juliet said pouting. "I want to remain here with you."

Colin shook his head. "You may not."

"Why not?" she demanded crossly.

"You know very well why not," he returned. "We're not children any more."

"Nor lovers, neither," she responded audaciously. "I could not love you in that way."

"Nor I you." He grinned.

"Then let me stay." She shivered. "I am still afraid."

"Why?" Colin's grin vanished. Generally she put small stress upon such feelings, especially now that she had grown older.

"I do not know." Juliet's expression was puzzled. "Please let me stay. I'll lie very far from you, and I'll leave early before the maids come to bring hot water."

He was never proof against her pleading. "Very well, minx." He kissed her on the forehead. She, in turn, flung her arms around him and kissed him on the cheek. Afterwards she bounced into the huge fourposter, lying as near to the edge as possible until he joined her. Then she rolled over to tickle him.

"Enough." He pushed her away and laughed.

They both laughed and, as they had when they were children, fell peacefully asleep—at a proper distance from each other.

* * *

Fulke's laughter was in Richard's ears as he awakened out of a rare dream of his brother. He felt as he had in childhood when Fulke, for no reason at all, pointed at him and guffawed, as if he were some figure of fun. It was the same sort of sniggering merriment which had roused him. He turned toward Catlin, then remembered that she was no longer beside him. The reasons for that caused him to wince. In the last seven years, she seemed to have put on at least seven more stone. On the rare occasions when she dressed, it took two maids to put her into her gowns and three to bathe her. The doctor had suggested she eat less but, seemingly, she could not. She had a craving for sweets, and the cook, nothing loath, sent jellies, pastries and comfits to her.

"If I'd known . . ." Richard muttered. Against his will, he thought of Dashwood and Medmenham. He could see Catlin in his mind's eye. Had she ever been so lovely and so slim? It seemed impossible, but it was not—and then, of course, his thoughts strayed to Erlina Bell. He didn't need her curses. Through his own folly, he was cursed with a wife who looked like some carnival oddity!

If he could have brought himself to believe in a supreme being, he would pray that none of his children grow to resemble their mother and thought immediately of Juliet. It would be terrible if that slim, delightful little creature were to become so gross. She was such a lovely child—though child no longer. The day after tomorrow she would have her birthday ball. Seventeen and seven months she was and, of course, he must lose her soon. He had no doubt that Juliet, like Kathleen, would marry early; perhaps, again in common with Kathleen, she would meet her future husband on the night of the ball.

Strange to think of his hard-riding little girl ready to drop her first child. Would she prove as fecund as her mother? He did not dwell on that. His thoughts turned to Tony, in love with Lady Felicity Campbell—so pretty a girl, but delicate, or so she appeared. Looks could be deceiving, and no one knew that better than himself. And Colin was home! Parkins, his valet, had brought him that news, knowing him to be concerned. And who was Sir Simeon Weir? It did not matter; he would meet him on the morrow. He glanced toward the window. It was still dark, and Parkins had mentioned something about Sir Simeon guiding Colin home in what was practically the dark o' the moon. Odd, but at least the boy'd sleep under his own roof tonight; all his four were together again. They were such handsome children. Once more Richard thought of his dream and heard his brother's mocking laughter in his ears. It was a pity Fulke could not have known of his four fine *legitimate* children. He almost wished that there were ghosts. Surely if his brother floated through the halls, it would irk him mightily, especially when he remembered that he had been slaughtered for the wanton sowing of his own seed—and no legitimate heir to succeed him. Smiling, Richard went back to sleep.

"Molly and the cat, too." Catlin, lying awake, thought she had never heard them so loud. She reached out a trembling hand and encountered only a pillow. Once she would have wept, but having discovered long ago that tears were useless, she merely closed her eyes and thought of *The Lover's Stratagem* and the young man in the audience, who had looked at her so ardently. How would her life have been had she not fallen in love with him that very minute? It had been wicked of him to have her kidnapped, to be sure, and her own wickedness lay in yielding to him. True, she had been drugged, but she had wanted him and wanted him still. Catlin reached for the tray that was on the nightstand. There was a small selection of cakes and bonbons upon it, which meant crumbs in the bed in the morning, but Richard was not there to complain. Tears threatened. She reached for a cake and stuffed the whole of it into her mouth. Swallowing it, she had another . . . and another . . .

Kathleen, new to the delight of feeling the kicking of her child in its efforts to escape its nest, smiled and patted her belly, wishing she could hold her baby in her arms. She never would have guessed that the joys of motherhood could replace the excitement of galloping across the fields. It had been close on seven months since she had ridden. A giggle escaped her. Indoor sports had more than compensated for the lack, and once John returned from Madras and her babe was born, she'd put the child out with a wet nurse and save her bosom for he who was lover as well as husband. Her mother would have chided her for such wanton thoughts, she knew, but she'd never been minded toward confidences in that lump that lay alone in the master bedroom. She had only pity for her poor father and wondered why he did not take a mistress! The banshee's wailing reached her, but faintly. Kathleen wondered what it might be and was prayerfully pleased that Molly was not keening for Colin, who was home again.

Tony, heavily asleep in his room, dreamed blissfully of Felicity.

Juliet met Sir Simeon in the rose garden at twilight and decided immediately that he was uncommonly handsome but that she did not like him. She was surprised at her feelings, especially since she had the strongest reasons in the world to like him. He had brought her brother home safely from an inn about which Tony had made inquiries, learning that it had a malodorous reputation. Also, it had been at Sir Simeon's insistence that they had left that inn. Consequently Juliet had every reason to like him and possibly even to love him. She had often envisioned the man she thought she could love, and though she was sure she had been deeply enamoured of at least four young men, none had had the coal black hair, the flashing dark eyes and the handsome features she preferred.

Sir Simeon had coal black hair, and if his rather somber eyes did not flash, they were a deep brown which was almost as satisfactory as black. His features were definitely handsome, and he was also charming. Thus, she found it very odd in herself that she had conceived so immediate a dislike for him. Searching for a reason, she fell back on one that was patently ridiculous.

He had startled her, appearing so unexpectedly behind her on the graveled path. She had been clipping roses to bring to her mother's room, that lady being in even lower spirits than usual. With the intention of going back to the house, Juliet had turned and found him there. She had not even heard the crunch of gravel beneath his feet, even though she heard it all well enough afterwards and the explanation for not having heard it had been eminently reasonable. He had been walking on the grass rather than the gravel.

Sir Simeon's own reaction to her had proved far different. His graceful speech, full of such words as nymphs descending from Olympus, should have thrilled not embarrassed her. Here was a man of the world come from London, still a magic name to Juliet, who had yet to visit it and who envied Kathleen greatly for not only visiting it but living there. Sir Simeon, bowing over her stiff little hand, complimented her on her beauty, but here a second set of quibbles arose. Though he was quite right about her beauty, her mirror telling her no different, his hand was very cold and his lips similarly chill. That suggested thin blood, a condition one could only pity, but his touch had made her shiver. She had been intensely pleased when Sukey, one of the maids, came to tell her that she was wanted inside.

Juliet's opinion of Sir Simeon, detailed later that evening to Colin, surprised and annoyed him, a fact he did not hesitate to reveal. "I would think," he began coldly, "that when a man has saved my life, you'd be kinder in both your thoughts and your actions. You deliberately avoided him in the music room tonight!"

They were in Colin's bedchamber again, and Juliet took an anguished turn around the room, coming to stand opposite her brother.

"I have tried to be kind to him," she stressed, "but I do not care for him." She regarded Colin unhappily. "I pray he'll not ask me to dance tomorrow night."

"I am sure that he will," Colin said pointedly. "He praised your beauty to me. And if he does wish to inscribe his name on your fan, I beg you'll not refuse."

"Oh, dear," Juliet sighed. "Have I no choice in the matter?"

"It would be the only courteous way to behave," Colin affirmed. "Which reminds me . . ." Reaching into his pocket, he produced the fan. "This comes from London, my dear."

She gazed on it delightedly. "Oh, Colin. The sweet thing!" She flung her arms around him. "I do love you so much. I will even dance with Sir Simeon, but you must ask me, too."

"I will, dearest child, but I fear that even were I near you, you'll be surrounded by lads who'll not give a mere brother a chance."

"I expect that's true," she agreed seriously. "So you must be the first to inscribe your name here and now."

Colin laughed, and taking the fan to his desk where there resposed an inkhorn and quill, he wrote his name on the first of the spokes, "You've a great deal of confidence in yourself," he commented as he returned it to her.

"Papa has said that I am the most beautiful girl on either side of the border." She smiled up at him. "And I say that I have the most handsome brother in the whole world."

"Your brother thanks you . . . and believes you are a bit short-sighted."

"I am not in the least short-sighted!" she exclaimed.

"Very well . . . but I charge you, be nice to Sir Simeon."

"Oh, all right," she said, pouting. "But I am doing it only for you."

On the night of her birthday ball, Juliet, sitting at her dressing table and having her curls piled up on top of a wonderfully intricate metal structure tricked out with horse hair, soon to be powdered and topped by a spun-glass coach and four, watched with less interest than usual. The excitement she had been experiencing all that month and for months before that had abated. She felt both tired and out of sorts mainly because of a dream she had had the previous night, one she blamed on Sir Simeon Weir. She was well aware that she was being unfair. It was not his fault that she had dreamed of him, nor her's neither, she thought bitterly. Still, if he had not been at the Hold, she would not have spoiled her night by dreaming about him.

"It seemed so real . . ." she muttered.

"I beg your pardon, mademoiselle." Monsieur Vigot, the hairdresser, a little hoptoad of a man, blinked at her in surprise.

"Nothing, Viggie. I was thinking out loud." Juliet flushed and flushed again remembering that ridiculous dream. In her dream, she had awakened suddenly to find Sir Simeon Weir seated on the edge of her bed, smiling down at her.

"Why are you here?" she had questioned, adding rudely,

"Go away." In her dream, she had not been surprised that he should be there, only annoyed.

She was still annoyed and her annoyance increased as she remembered his reply. "I am here because I love you."

Now why had she dreamed that?

Kathleen had once told her that she willed herself to dream of John making love to her. Juliet had willed no such thing. She could not imagine anything more horrid than having Sir Simeon make love to her. Still, in the dream she had suffered his kiss. It had been horrid. He had not kissed her lips, rather his mouth had fastened near her throat, remaining there for at least . . . she did not know how long. Then, whispering that he loved her and would return, he had gone. She had awakened immediately and had felt very odd—dizzy and weak. She had been unable to remain awake, and in the morning, the condition still persisted. However she was feeling better now.

"Helas," 'tis the season for the mosquito, but perhaps a little powder . . ." the hairdresser murmured.

"I beg your pardon, Viggie?" Juliet apologized. "I was not attending. What were you saying about powder?"

"See, there is a little mark on the whiteness. A mosquito must have bitten you . . . and twice." He placed a long finger on her throat.

"Perhaps it is not . . ." Juliet put her hand to her mouth to stifle a sudden giggle. Meeting the hairdresser's curious gaze in the mirror, she gave him no explanation. It would have been dreadful had she said, "Sir Simeon may have bitten me." She would be making a joke, and Monsieur Vigot, to whom gossip was as precious as gold, might have taken her seriously and have bruited her tale through the household. Colin would never have forgiven her! "Perhaps it is not a mosquito but some other insect." She leaned forward and found to her amazement that there were two little marks on her neck. Something had bitten her in the night, though she doubted it could have been Sir Simeon Weir. She looked anxiously at her hairdresser. "Do you think my necklace will hide these?"

"Ah, your necklace . . . I was forgetting that. Of course, mon enfant, diamonds hide much!"

At last she was dressed. Looking into the glass, Juliet hardly recognized herself. Her gown, with its immense panniers of white and gold satin over a pleated underskirt in white satin, again patterned with golden lilies and edged with gold scallops along the hem, the whole held up by an immense hoop, was magnificent. Her close-fitting bodice was laced tightly in the back, cut low and square in the front, accentuating the slight fullness of her bosom. Her sleeves were edged in fine lace. Diamond earrings matched the diamonds that clasped her throat, and there were also diamonds set in the heels of her little white satin shoes.

"C'est magnifique!" exclaimed Monsieur Vigot, and Maria, her maid, gasped, "Lor, I'm struck dumb, milady."

Juliet wanted to nod but thought better of it. Despite all the pins in her headdress, it still felt as if it might topple and send the coach and four skimming to the floor. She would also need to take care how she walked, for despite the fact that she had been practicing for this night all of her life, or so it seemed, the hoop needed managing. She smothered a giggle. It was well the entrances were wide. And Colin, who was waiting in her sitting room to escort her to their mother's bedchamber, would also guide her down the stairs.

"But you are beautiful, too!" Juliet greeted her brother, who was looking at her dumbfounded. He was, she thought, in his white satin coat, his gold embroidered waistcoat, his white satin breeches and his white stockings with their embroidered clocks. He wore his own hair but heavily powdered and tied in the back with a black ribbon. Diamonds sparkled in the lace at his throat. A flurry of compliments flew between them and then he offered his arm.

"Come, let's get to Mother."

Catlin, propped up on a mound of lace-edged pillows and wearing a pale, rose-colored negligee, looked at her two children through a haze of tears. Colin, clad in white, much resembled Richard as he had been on that night, over a quarter of a century ago, before Tim, her protective coachman, had sent him sprawling in the street. Juliet? Juliet as usual, was looking very beautiful but . . . Catlin frowned. It seemed to her that the girl was paler than usual. It was on the tip of her tongue to comment on it, but now was not a time for criticism.

She said, "I wish I might be present, my own darlings, but

be assured that all my thoughts will be with you. I pray you'll have a lovely time.''

''Oh, Mama.'' Juliet stepped forward impulsively, wanting to kiss her.

''No.'' Catlin raised a protesting hand. ''Best not bend or stoop too much with such a head.''

Juliet moved back. ''It is rather silly, isn't it? I am sure Colin thinks so.''

''I never said that,'' he retorted indignantly. ''And 'tis my honest opinion you are not the most beautiful girl in three counties but in all of England and Scotland, too.''

''Indeed, she is.'' Richard, attired in royal purple, stepped into the room and moving to Catlin dropped a kiss on her cheek. ''I wish you'd be with us, my dear,'' he said and swallowed an unexpected lump in his throat as he met Catlin's eyes, adoring and unreproachful. They were, he thought, still as blue as the lakes of Kilarney. Bottling up a sigh, he escorted his radiant children from the room.

Once she set foot on the dance floor, Juliet's unaccountable malaise vanished. Besieged by partners, she disappointed all of them by opening the ball with Colin and then proceeded to be gracious and generous as well. She was extremely glad that Sir Simeon did not become one of the number eagerly soliciting her for minuets, gavottes and country dances. However she did meet him during one of the figures of a dance and, much to her secret embarrassment, just managed not to grimace. She did have to agree with Colin that he was a good-looking man. Powdered hair became him, and his eyes were really quite beautiful, deep and dark, twin wells into which one could fall. She banished that surprising thought. Even if she had dreamed of him, she could never become attracted to him!

As she had opened the ball with Colin, Juliet closed it with Tony, who was looking remarkably handsome in a plum-colored suit stitched with silver.

''Well, infant,'' he said as the music ended and the weary musicians set about packing their fiddles, flutes and harp, ''have you fallen in love?''

Juliet smiled up at him. ''There are so many,'' she complained. ''I thought I loved Christian Rivermead, but the stream's run dry.''

"Ugh," commented her brother, pretending to shudder at her witticism.

Juliet flushed. "Colin would have laughed," she accused.

"I am sure of that." Tony regarded her gravely. "You are mighty close with Colin," he observed.

She glared at him. "Not so close as that, Tony. I *want* to fall in love."

"And what do you think of Sir Simeon Weir? He has been casting sheep's eyes in your direction all this night."

"I wish he were a thousand leagues from here," Juliet said positively. "Imagine a man who sleeps the whole of the day away. I could not exist without the sun!"

"He is a strange sort," her brother agreed. "I am not at all sure I like him."

"I am sure I don't like him," she stated. She gazed across the ballroom at those guests who still remained. "He's not here now. I expect the sunrise has sent him off to bed."

"It should send us all to bed. You're looking very weary yourself, infant."

"Oh, Tony," she scolded, "you should not call me 'infant' when I am seventeen and seven months."

"A great age," he teased.

"I do not see Felicity," Juliet observed.

"She left early." He frowned. "She wasn't feeling quite the thing."

"A pity. She did look so beautiful in that blue gown."

"Yes," Tony agreed. "A picture."

"And one you'd like to add to the gallery upstairs," she accused.

Tony flushed. "It is my hope," he admitted.

"And her's as well," Juliet commented. "If anyone's affianced this night, 'twill be you. La, Tony, I think I am quite envious of you."

"There'll be other balls, infant."

"Oh, I do hope so!" Juliet exclaimed. "I do love to dance!" She whirled around the polished floor, looking at her image reflected to infinity in its four facing mirrors, and was caught by Colin, who whirled her around again, while Tony stood watching and frowning slightly. He was glad that Colin must soon return to Oxford. They were almost too close, the pair of them. Then he forgot them, as looking into the mirror he seemed to see himself and Felicity. She had looked beautiful tonight, and though it had been entirely wrong to voice his sentiments and intentions before speaking to her father, he had offered and she had glowingly accepted. He would wait on Sir Robert Campbell tomorrow.

Near six in the evening two days after the ball, Kathleen went into labor, and the Hold was in an uproar—mainly because Catlin had told of Molly, rushing howling down the castle corridors with the spirit cat shrieking behind her.

Upbraided by a harried and anxious Richard, Catlin merely sobbed and wailed, "You must believe! Why will you not believe I hear them? And the children do, also."

Richard, dispatching messengers for the doctor and also for a midwife, was glad Catlin's formidable bulk prevented her from leaving her bed. He had had enough of hysterics from the maids who, without one shred of evidence, believed implicitly in Catlin's damned banshee and had crazy anecdotes of their own to prove the improbable. His main concern was that these tales of the creature's overwrought behavior must not reach the ears of his suffering daughter.

Unfortunately, despite all his determined efforts to keep Kathleen from finding out about Molly's so-called peregrinations, on entering her chamber he learned that she knew all about them, as did Tony and presumably Colin and Juliet, who had not yet come to their sister's room.

"Superstition," Richard proclaimed, looking into his daughter's agonized face. " 'Tis naught but superstition."

Below in the great hall, Colin was bidding farewell to Sir Simeon Weir, who cloaked and booted, was just inside the door. "I thank you for your hospitality," he said gratefully.

"We were pleased to have you," Colin replied politely, hoping that his thoughts were not mirrored in his eyes. Though he was reluctant to admit it, the fact that Juliet had conceived such a dislike for the man had influenced him adversely. However he did not agree that Sir Simeon had an unhealthy pallor, something he had ascribed to the fact that his guest ate very little, merely picking at his food. Tonight, he was looking very well. There was color in his cheeks, and his eyes were certainly brighter. The rest had obviously done him a world of good.

"I was quite taken with your little sister Juliet," Sir Simeon was saying, "but I fear she did not feel the same for me."

"Oh, well," Colin temporized, "Juliet does not know her own mind and . . ." He paused, cocking his head. He was hearing Molly now, wild and piercing. He thought immediately of poor Kathleen and wished Sir Simeon would hurry with his farewells.

"I must go," Sir Simeon said. "And I thank you again. I am in your debt indeed, and I hope that some day I will be able to repay your hospitality."

"I wish you a safe journey," Colin said, following him outside and watching him mount his horse and ride off into the gathering shadows. Coming back into the hall, he had a mind to seek out Juliet, whom he hadn't seen since they had gone riding early that morning. She had dreamed of Sir Simeon again, she told him gloomily. "He quite ruins my nights," she had concluded.

She had looked tired, Colin recalled. He should tell her that, if out of common courtesy, he had not actually speeded the parting guest, he had at least seen him off. However, Molly's howling was loud and agonized. He hurried back to Kathleen's chambers.

Juliet had been feeling tired ever since the ball and, in fact, had found it very difficult to rise this morning. It had been a real chore to go riding with Colin, but she had not wanted to forego that pleasure. However, upon coming back, she had fallen into her bed without removing her garments, even though they smelled most unpleasantly of horse. She had been so weary that when Sukey came to tell her that Kathleen was in labor, her first thought had been one of actual annoyance. Even though Kathleen would never know, she felt very guilty about that, and certainly she must soon go to her sister's apartments. She, too, had heard the keening of the banshee and the yowling of the cat. That spelled danger, she was sure of it—but it was so difficult to bestir herself. She longed to rest. She dared not rest for she would fall asleep, and Kathleen would never forgive her. She rose and was about to ring for her maid when there was a soft tap at her door.

"Come," she called, expecting Colin, but it was Sir Simeon Weir who stood framed in the aperture and, even as her surprise was turning to anger, he stepped inside, closing the door behind him. Indignation boiled up in her bosom, "What are you doing in my room?" she demanded.

"I have come to say farewell," he said, coming toward her.

"Oh," she said with considerable pleasure. "You are finally going?"

"Within the hour," he asserted. "I would you were coming with me."

"Whatever for?" she inquired rudely.

"I find you very beautiful."

"Oh," she said, "everyone does."

He smiled. "You are passing vain, little Juliet."

"If you've come to chastize me, 'tis hardly your place," she flared.

"I would not presume to do that. I love you."

"I do not love you," she retorted. "And perhaps when you are gone, I will cease to dream about you!" That had been a sad error, she realized immediately, wondering what had made her blurt out the fact that he haunted her dreams. It would only increase his vile self-importance.

"You've not dreamed of me," he said.

"I have so," she contradicted and wondered why she had been so insistent. She should have agreed that she hadn't dreamed of him; thus she had missed another opportunity. Of a sudden, she knew why and wondered why it had not occurred to her before, but it *had* occurred to her, she recalled. She really was not thinking clearly at all—or had not been—but was now. He had no right in her rooms. She would tell him that before he was much older. And how old was he? She had the curious impression that he was much, much older than she had originally imagined.

"You've not dreamed of me," he insisted.

She glared at him. "How can you be so certain?" she demanded. "I have, but I'll not argue about it. I want you . . ."

"And I want you, my little love." He moved toward her swiftly and clasped her in his arms.

Juliet tried to pull away. "I did not say I *wanted* you, like *wanting*," she emphasized. "You did not give me a chance to finish what I meant to tell you.''

''I know that.'' He brought his lips down on her throat. She struggled fiercely at first, then ceased to struggle. ''I thought it was a dream,'' she said plaintively, when at last he released her.

''It was no dream.''

''Molly,'' she whispered. ''She must be at my door. How loudly she is shrieking.''

''Never mind her.'' He ran his hand gently through her hair.

''Can *you* hear her?''

''And that cat.'' He nodded.

''That's very strange. Are we related?''

''We are, my love,'' he smiled. ''By love.''

Anger rose in her and died. She could not quite remember why she was angry. Yes, she did remember. ''I don't love you,'' she said positively.

''You will,'' he murmured. ''You'll love me as you've never loved anyone in this life.'' Lifting her in his arms, he put her down on her bed and stretched out beside her.

She was surprised to find him at her side, but she was too tired to protest. She suddenly wondered where Colin was, and something like a pain throbbed in the vicinity of her heart—then was gone. Sir Simeon put his arms around her, and she forgot Colin as his lips were once more fastened on her throat. ''That feels . . .'' she murmured.

He lifted his head, and she saw that his mouth was very red. ''How does it feel, my love?'' he asked.

''Nice,'' she said, surprising herself. She raised her hand to touch his lips and found that her finger tips had turned scarlet. She regarded them incuriously, regarding him with an equal lack of curiosity as he lifted her hand and kissed the blood from each finger.

She lifted her head slightly, ''Molly . . .'' she whispered. ''It's very odd.''

''What's odd, my darling?''

''Molly's crying in a different way.''

''How is it different?''

''I don't remember.'' His lips were on her throat again, and she was feeling very sleepy.

* * *

Much to everyone's surprise, Kathleen, to the accompaniment of Molly's increasing howls, brought forth a fine baby boy. In spite of her long labor, the delivery was easy. The doctor and the midwife congratulated each other on it.

Richard, who had insisted on remaining throughout the ordeal, came into the sitting room adjacent to Kathleen's bedroom to tell his anxious sons the happy news. "Where's your sister?" he asked, looking around for Juliet.

Colin had been listening to Molly's wails now blending with those of her cat. It had seemed to him that there was a difference about them, a pain that was usually lacking in her perfunctory performances. He knew that Tony had heard them, too. He had a feeling that his brother had also noted the difference, for he had stared anxiously at him from time to time. Suddenly it seemed very strange that Juliet had not joined them, for surely she, too, would have been aware of Molly's inexplicable sorrow. As a child, she had seen and spoken with the banshee, he recalled.

Juliet had been tired after their ride this morning; he had seen that but had not marked it, remembering that she had danced unceasingly until dawn on the night of her ball. That, however, was two nights ago. A fear he did not comprehend caused him to rise and stride to the door in practically a single step. "I'll fetch her," he said through stiff lips.

"I'll come with you." Tony's tone suggested that he, too, was anxious.

"I'll bring the good news to your mother." Richard fixed a frowning gaze on them. "Your sister Juliet had better have a good reason for not attending Kathleen."

Colin and Tony hurried to Juliet's rooms. Pushing the door open, they strode to her bedroom where Colin came to a sudden stop, causing his brother, who was on his heels, to crash against him. Tony's muttered apologies were silenced as Colin said softly, "She's asleep. I'd best wake her though."

"Yes," Tony agreed. "She'll want to know."

Coming to the side of the bed, Colin bent over Juliet. "Minx," he said, "wake up. You are now the aunt of a bouncing baby boy."

She did not stir—but it was a full minute before he realized that she wasn't breathing.

Three

When she woke, it was dark, so dark that she could hardly believe she was in her own room, yet she could not have left it. She had fallen asleep on the bed, and she had dreamed—dreamed what? She had dreamed that Sir Simeon had come to bid her goodbye—and in her own bedroom. She giggled, and the sound of her laughter startled her. It sounded hollow and echoing as if, indeed, she were not in her chamber but in another place. That confused her. She must still be dreaming. She blinked and blinked again, staring into the blackness and seeing nothing. She put out her hand and gasped. Instead of the bed, she felt hardness against her hand. She moved and felt a similar hardness against her whole body as if, indeed, she were closed into something like a chest. She raised her hand and again encountered hardness only inches above her. She pushed against the hardness, but it did not budge. A scream formed in her throat and ecscaped only as a long sigh. And then, she did cry out for a voice was in her ears.

"Gently, my love . . . gently, gently, do not struggle and do not be afraid. I am here to help you."

She knew that voice, or thought she did. No, she was not

sure. "Where am I?" she asked. "Why is it so dark? And . . ." She suddenly remembered her sister. "Kathleen . . . has Katie had her baby?"

"That need not concern you, my love," the voice said. "Now I am going to lift the cover. You'll not need to lift it when you become accustomed to your situation."

"My situation," she repeated confusedly. "What . . . where am I? Am I not in the Hold? Where am I?" She was becoming panicked again.

"Explanations must wait, my love."

She did recognize that voice. It belonged to Sir Simeon Weir. In her mind flew fragments of images. Sir Simeon at her door—no, nearer, beside her on the bed! The bed! And she had fallen asleep but not with him beside her. She never, never could have done that! But he had been on the bed. He must have drugged her and kidnapped her.

Low laughter filled her ears. "That was not the way of it, my love. I did not need to drug or kidnap you."

"But where am I? Where have you taken me?" she cried, and only then realized that he had answered her thoughts—but how was that possible? It did not matter! It did matter! She was dreaming, had to be dreaming!

"No, 'tis no dream. Though that is often the belief in the beginning. But enough. I am not here to torture but to advise." Something flew back, and Juliet blinked against the brightness of refracted moonlight shining through an arched window.

Hands clasped her hands and drew her up. "Now, step over the side," came the instruction.

Juliet raised her foot and stood there for a moment. "Step over what?" she demanded. Looking down she saw a long narrow box that seemed to be constructed from stone. "Where have you taken me?" she cried.

"I have taken you nowhere, my dearest. 'Twas your family brought you here, three days since."

"My family!" she exclaimed and stepped out of the box. Looking in the direction of the voice, she saw Sir Simeon Weir, standing in a pool of moonlight. She said furiously, "You're lying. Why am I with you? I don't want to be with you. Oh, I must be dreaming!"

"Look around you and tell me what you find," he

ordered.

"I won't. Why have you brought me here?"

"This is your dwelling place as long as you wish it to be. I pray that will not be long."

"I do not understand you," she whispered, aware now that understanding was hovering at the periphery of her mind and that she did not want to let it seep into her brain.

"Look about you," Sir Simeon repeated.

She did not want to obey him either, but in some strange way, he was forcing her to it. She turned her head slowly and saw them, the great oblong stone boxes lying on thick stone shelves and knew what she might have already known, had she been willing to admit it to herself.

"The crypt," she whispered. "They brought me here to the crypt? My family? Colin? You're lying. Only the dead lie here."

"And the undead," he added.

"The *un*dead? What . . . are they?"

"You've never heard of the undead?" he asked incredulously.

She shook her head.

"I mislike the term . . . but they are also called vampires."

"Vampires," she repeated. Her mother had told them folk tales, until forbidden to do so by her father. She, Kathleen, Tony and Colin had been alternately entranced and terrified by those same tales. There were vampires in Ireland, horrid creatures with flaming red eyes, who lived by sucking blood from their victims. They were evil.

"They are evil," Juliet said.

"They are not evil, unless it is evil to wish to survive."

"They survive on the blood of . . ." she paused, staring at him. Into her mind came a vision of his lips dyed scarlet.

"They survive on the blood of those they love."

"No." She spread her fingers wide, envisioning the redness on their tips. "You are . . ."

"I am," he admitted. "And you, also."

She wanted to scream, to faint, but could do neither of these things, could only listen as he said, "Now that you have opened yourself to knowledge, let it flow into you."

"No, no, no." Juliet ran to the door of the crypt, tugging

at its handle, trying to open it. It did not yield, but there was a narrow crack from top to bottom, and unknowingly knowing, she passed through it and was out in the churchyard. Looking back and seeing the door still closed save for the crack which was no wider than the length of her fingernail, she sank down on a tombstone staring up at the half moon, which gave off a radiance that was proving almost as blinding as the sun.

She could see so well! She could see the churchyard and every separate leaf that clung to the branches of the hemlock trees. Looking down, she found a spider in the center of its web. She could hear its minute movements as it digested the moth it had just caught. Now that she was listening, there were so many strange sounds, but she knew them! She could identify the twitter of the bats and the sleepy murmur of the hedgehog as it lay in its burrow under her feet. She could hear the rougher grumble of a badger and the velvety flutter which were the wings of an owl flying overhead. Useless, useless, useless to cling to the notion that she was dreaming!

"Useless," he agreed.

He was standing beside her but she had not heard him come, she who had heard so much.

"You must learn to deal with sounds, the new sounds. You must choose what you will and what you will not hear. But you will always be able to hear *them*, no matter how lightly they tread. You will always know what they are thinking. Only when you sleep, will you not know . . . and then will you be vulnerable to them."

"Them?" she asked and knew the answer, but did not want to know it.

"Mortals," he said brutally, because he knew she knew.

She wrung her hands, "Why . . . why did you do this to me?"

"Because I love you. It is not given us to love often. I knew I should love you when first your brother mentioned your name. I could see you, even as he spoke. You'll be able to do the same with your lovers."

"I do not want lovers," she cried. "I want to be married and to have children and live in the sun!"

"Marriage is not for us, and the sun would be your true death," he said reasonably and coldly.

"I know," she said reluctantly. More was coming to her, flowing into her mind, even as he said it must. But not everything, not yet. "Why did Colin bring you to our home?"

"It was so ordained."

"Ordained? How could that be?"

"Because you were cradled in evil, my dear child, cradled and cursed—the lot of you. Why do you suppose that hag of a banshee and her cat have the run of the Hold?"

"Because . . ." Juliet hesitated and then pressed her hands against her ears, but could not stop the knowledge from pouring into them, the fearful knowledge which flooded through her so that she knew what he knew. She knew everything. It battered against her brain.

She huddled down on the tombstone, putting her hands against her tearless eyes. "I want my family . . . I want to be with them, live with them . . . I want Colin!"

"Whom you loved too much," he accused.

" 'Tis not true!" she cried. "He was my friend." She finally looked up at him and saw his disbelieving smile. "I do not care what you think. It is true. Oh, he will miss me."

"They will all miss you and then they'll forget you, as I have been forgotten. I have not seen my family for a hundred years."

"I cannot imagine they'd feel the poorer for that," she said with a flash of her former spirit.

He glared at her. "You'll do well not to alienate me," he growled. "I can teach you much."

"Your knowledge is already mine," she retorted. "I do not want it. I will not be as you, frequenting the Green Dragon, awaiting the hapless traveler who strays off his path."

"Those who come there . . ."

"Have not strayed but are guided," she finished, with a shudder. "Is there so much evil in the world?"

"Is there not?" He moved to her. "You've absorbed much and quickly, my dearest. I knew 'twould be so, but still you need me."

"I neither need nor want you. I will not be as you. Tomorrow when the sun rises, I will be waiting."

His laughter was ugly. "So be it, little Juliet. Yet it may be that you will change your mind."

"Never," she moaned. "I love the sun."

"And do you not love the moon?" He pointed.

She would not look at it. "The moon is cold and . . . and dead, forever and ever, wandering through space and lost, lost as I am lost."

"Without the moon, the seas would not roll. Without the moon . . . but 'tis early to convince you, my love."

"I am not your love!" she cried.

"You are my love, while your blood warms my veins."

"My blood!" She glared into his handsome, evil face. "Oh, you are cruel. I am . . . I *was* only seventeen. Could you not have let me live a little longer?"

"I have given you eternal life," he said softly. "The stones of your castle will crumble. Those you loved will be dust in their tombs, but you will not die, not if you are careful."

"I will, I will . . ." she sobbed. "I will die at dawning."

"Your misery will pass," he said calmly. "Mine did."

"You . . ." She stared at him and speaking out of her new knowledge said, "You rejoiced in this life from the very first. You wanted it, sought it and were rewarded accordingly."

His dark eyes glowed red. "I cannot deny it. And you will learn to rejoice in it yourself. You will come to me and beg me to help you. Tomorrow night, I will stand outside the crypt and you will drink with me."

"I shan't! Go away, go away," she moaned. "I will stay here and await the sunrise!"

His laughter echoed in her ears and then he was gone.

She sat on the tomb, clutching her knees and staring up at the star-filled sky and at the moon. It was a beautiful night. The stars seemed so close. They were round, too. Billions of little moons clustering around the half-dark planet. She found suddenly that she loved the moon. She had never realized that in its way it was as wonderful as the sun.

She lifted her head. She heard footsteps. She turned, and though the churchyard was hedged, she could see through the greenery, see the man quite clearly, a drunk lurching home after a night at some tavern, his blood blending with his drink. She moved her tongue and felt them to see if they were there. They were—her sharp little fangs, sharp and retractable. They could not always be seen, she knew.

Meanwhile, he was walking—walking away from her? He must not walk away. She leaped to her feet. A hunger she had never known before, a hunger that consumed her, was activating her. He could not get away, must not, must not. She streaked across the grass, easily evading the tombstones. The hedge presented no barrier; as she had managed the crack in the door, so she managed the hedge and emerged a few paces behind him. She stepped to his side.

He stared at her blearily, blinked and grinned. "Good evenin', little lady. Where you goin' this hour of the night?"

"Walking," she said.

"Walking, is it? Yer a pretty piece. Walk a bit o' the way wi' me."

"I will." She could hardly speak for the desire mounting in her. But how could she approach him? How might she sip the wine that was sweeter and headier than anything she had ever drunk? He would have to stand still. How could she force him to stand still? She wrung her little hands while he went on walking and grinning at her. Then, of a sudden, he grabbed her, holding her tightly and pushing her down on the grass. His loose mouth was upon her mouth, and she knew what to do.

Yet even as the first swallow warmed her body, she shuddered and fled, sobbing, sobbing, back to the crypt, slipping inside, rushing to her coffin and flinging herself down on the hard padding. "Oh, what have I done?" she moaned.

"Nothing well," observed a hateful voice beside her. "But you'll learn. Where there's a will, there's a way."

Two nights after his mother's funeral, Colin tossed and groaned in his sleep, finally blinking himself awake. Another vivid dream of Juliet had troubled him. He did not want to dream of her; it had been a year since her inexplicable death, and his grief should have been assuaged by now. He doubted that it ever would be. Each time he returned to the Hold, he could see her in his mind's eye, running down the stairs to greet him, her beautiful eyes beaming with love for him.

Tonight she would have wanted to be with him, sleeping on the far side of the bed because she would need comforting in her grief. Still, one could not really grieve deeply for their poor mother, who had finally, gratefully breathed her last in her husband's arms. His father, however, had seemed extremely stricken, considering how much he had avoided her in the latter years. He had wept as much over his late wife as he had over Juliet, but Molly had been surprisingly silent as well as Grimalkin, too. However, now Colin could hear them both. He shuddered wondering what more could come to afflict them?

Unwillingly, he recalled the grief in Molly's tones on the night Kathleen's son Mark was born. The household had feared for mother and child, but it was Juliet who died, so strangely, looking so pale and drained—and the doctor talking of anemia and dubbing it an odd but not entirely unusual occurrence. He had mentioned it again when attending his mother in her final moments. There had been other similar cases in the community, though none so severe as that which had killed Juliet. Only one had died in the last year, a young woman named Ruth Ellersbee, who sang in the church choir. She had succumbed some six months after Juliet's passing.

Colin groaned and stared into the darkness. "Juliet," he whispered. "My dearest, dearest Juliet . . ."

"Oh, Colin," she said yearningly as she stepped to the foot of the bed. "I didn't mean for you to see me. I shouldn't have come. He said I shouldn't, but I have missed you so dreadfully."

Colin closed his eyes and opened them again, seeing her still standing at the foot of the bed, bathed in moonlight. She was looking at him with that same pleading expression he had been wont to see on her face when she begged him to let her remain with him through the night.

"I'm dreaming," he said uncertainly.

"I said the same thing once, my dearest, but you're not and I . . ." She sighed. "I wasn't either."

"Are you afraid of me? If you're afraid, I'll go at once. I expect I'd be afraid of you if . . . No, I wouldn't. I could never be afraid of you, Colin. And as for me, I won't harm you. I promise you that. I really haven't harmed anyone, not so they'd die of it. I take very small sips. He laughs at me for it, but life is so beautiful. I don't want to deprive anyone of it or of the sun, though I have found I can make do quite well with moonlight.''

He listened without comprehension, hearing only her voice yet seeing her—*Juliet*! ''It is you,'' he whispered. ''Oh, my dearest, darling, I thought you were dead.''

''Well, Colin, my dear,'' she said reluctantly, ''I am, after a fashion.''

''You . . . you seem mighty solid for a ghost.''

''A ghost? Well, I am not precisely a ghost. Mama's not either. I thought she might remain at the Hold, but she's gone. I'm glad of that. She was so unhappy. And I am sure she'd not have enjoyed the company in the churchyard. Take the Crusader . . . but I do not want to talk about him, though it is odd to see him looking so very respectable, his effigy, I mean, lying on top of his tomb with his wife at his side. She looks even more respectable. I don't like her at all, though I expect we ought to be more in sympathy. But she does speak the most peculiar English. It is very difficult to understand her, and you'd not believe her French. And . . .''

''Juliet,'' he interrupted impatiently, ''you are babbling.''

''Oh,'' she said, ''how lovely to have you scold me.''

''I don't mean to scold you,'' he said in stricken tones. ''Oh, Juliet, what happened to you?''

''I expect you need an explanation.'' She sounded equally stricken. ''I wish you could guess. I really hate to say it, even though he tells me I ought to be used to it by now. Oh, I do hate him, and he'd be furious if he knew I'd come here.''

''He? Who is *he*?''

''Sir Simeon Weir,'' she said ruefully.

''Sir Simeon Weir! What had he to do with you?''

Slowly, reluctantly, she told him.

He listened quietly and without comment, managing to quell the rage that boiled inside of him. Yet, when she finished, she gazed at him wide-eyed, saying, ''No, you mustn't, dearest. You'd be powerless against him.''

He made no attempt to deny her unspoken accusation. ''*He* is powerless after sunrise,'' he said through gritted teeth, ''and then he must seek his grave. Does he lie in Scotland?''

''No,'' she said. ''He needs only a stone, a stone as small as a pebble to put into his coffin.''

"A stone? A pebble?"

"Something from the plot of earth where he first lay, and with it he may rest in any graveyard, any crypt, any coffin. But I do not know where he has chosen to lie."

"You're not telling me the truth," he accused.

"Nor will I!"

"You'd protect him!"

"Colin," she said, shooting him a stricken look, "I am protecting *you*! He'd know if I told you and would seek you out. And before you had a chance . . . Oh, if I had not been so weak to come here, weak to cower away from the sun, which would destroy me. But I am not weak enough to reveal his hiding place. He'd only have to look at me to guess what I'd done. Just as I only have to look at you to know your intent."

"I beg you," he began. "Juliet . . ."

"And I beg you," she interrupted. "Oh, 'twas wrong for me to come, but I do love you so much—too much, I fear. I would not believe it when he told me that it was so. Perhaps it is more of the evil, for we are accursed, Colin, all of us, and that will make us weak and make you vulnerable in the face of those who'll not rest until we are sent forth from here—from the Hold."

He listened unsurprised. It seemed to him that he had always known all she was telling him, and it was knowledge that held no terrors for him, he who loved her as she loved him.

"Why would he know?" Colin demanded.

"We are bonded," she explained. "By blood. While one drop of my blood remains in his veins, he will know. Just as I know about him and the green . . ."

"The green?" Colin questioned.

"Nothing. Oh, I must go. I've said too much and I must go." She moved toward the window. "It is late and I must go."

"Not yet, my dearest, not yet," he protested.

"I must." She looked at him out of anguished eyes. "It grows late and I . . . I am thirsty. If I were to remain I might . . . It is a terrible thirst, Colin, a terrible, terrible thirst. I feel it come over me and when it does, I am not myself. I am its possession, its slave, and I cannot fight it. I must drink.''

''You will stay,'' he said strongly. ''And that knowledge you share with him will also be mine.'' He arose swiftly and enfolded her in his arms. ''You have said we are accursed. I'll share that curse, my Juliet, and as we are touched by evil, you'll not be able to resist.''

''Oh, Colin, nooooo,'' she wailed, struggling against him.

Though she was cold, cold with a cold that seemed to make the blood freeze in his veins, he held her until she ceased to struggle, until her mouth fastened on his neck and her sharp little fangs sank into his flesh. Moments later, she sprang away from him, thrusting the back of her hand against her crimson lips. ''Oh, why, why?'' she cried accusingly, rushing toward the window and throwing herself from it, her wail mingling with the banshee's howl.

Behind her, Colin pressed a finger against the small wounds on his neck and smiled triumphantly. His theory had proved correct. A bonding *had* taken place, and her muttered words about the ''green'' were suddenly very clear.

The following night, Colin went late to The Green Dragon. Any fear that he might have trouble finding it again was assuaged. He seemed to know the way and did not question that knowledge. It was near dawn when he arrived, and rather than going inside, he lingered near the window. Peering in, he saw Sir Simeon, deep in conversation with a young man, who appeared to be three-quarters drunk. With him was a girl who, judging from the look of her, was no more than 18 or 19. She appeared to be very nervous, and it was upon her that Sir Simeon's dark gaze was fastened. She watched him with the frozen look of a rabbit mesmerized by a stoat. In another second, the drunken man had toppled to the floor.

Sir Simeon, rising, sat down beside the girl and casually kissed her. She tried to push him away but her movements were feeble at best. Soon she had stopped struggling. With a silly smile, she gave herself to the predator. Seeing Sir Simeon's lips shift from mouth to neck, Colin shuddered and clutched the pointed stake. His newly acquired knowledge alerted him to the fact that while he feasted, Sir Simeon was impervious to anything save his all consuming thirst. He felt sorry for the victim, but there was no help for her. In common with Juliet and himself, the path had been chosen for her long ago. Laws had been broken, the eternal laws his father had derided.

He ceased thinking. The sky was growing lighter, and Sir Simeon was raising his head. The girl had fallen forward, so that the upper part of her body lay on the table. A thin trickle of blood seeped from a ragged wound in her neck. Sir Simeon hurried outside, vanishing amidst the trees. A second later, the scruffy little host came hurrying into the room. As usual, he was wiping his hands on his filthy apron. Colin watched with a fascinated horror as he used that same apron to wipe the blood from the girl's neck. Lifting her in his arms, he carried her out of the room. A second later, he was back to arouse her drunken companion. Smiling and bowing, he led him into the hall, and as he did not emerge, Colin guessed that he was being shown to such accomodations as the inn might boast. Going to the front door, he tried the handle and found that it was unlocked. He strolled inside and stood there awaiting the moment when Mr. Chubb would return.

She had awakened with a singular feeling of freedom, but in the next moment had been frightened. She had not returned to the crypt until near dawn the previous night and so had avoided any reprisals Sir Simeon might have taken against her. The following night, he had been summmoned to The Green Dragon, that horrid way station for the unwary sinner and those, who like Colin, were not unwary but unaware.

Slipping from her coffin, Juliet hurried into the churchyard. Sir Simeon must have gone already. Unencumbered by his presence she moved lightly among the tombs, nodding briefly to Ruth Ellersbee, who had just emerged, and to Lady Margaret, who was surging forth from the chapel, leaning on the Crusader's arm, queening it over all of them, as usual. It seemed to her that Lady Margaret and her husband were angry. However she did not care to question them. She wanted to be away in the woods, to remember and savor those moments she had spent with Colin, something she must never, never, never do again. Sir Simeon had warned her that it was unwise to visit those one loved, not only because of the dangers of discovery and vengeance, but because of the anguish of parting. She knew that anguish now and knew guilt besides, for her veins had been warmed by her brother's blood. Moaning and shivering, she wandered past the immense old trees, wondering when Sir Simeon would seek her out, wondering what he would do when he found her.

It was late when she returned; the moon was almost down and the sky paling. She hurried into the crypt, wondering now where he was, Sir Simeon, who had chosen to lie near her in the empty sarcophagus which one day would be occupied by her brother.

"Juliet."

She stiffened and saw Colin standing just inside the door. Terror possessed her. "Why are you here?" she whispered.

"I have been waiting for you. I have a gift for you," he said in a low voice. Moving to Sir Simeon's appropriated coffin, he stooped and with some difficulty managed to push back the lid. "Look," he commanded.

Obeying, Juliet saw mouldering bones amidst the dark suit he had worn and saw, too, the stake protruding from his shattered rib cage.

"How?" she whispered.

"No matter," Colin murmured. "It is done."

She threw her arms around him. "How long have you been waiting?"

"Since just past sunset."

"Oh, you should not have waited. 'Tis dangerous!"

"I know." He smiled. "I met the Crusader's lady. I vow, even longevity's no excuse for such overweening self-importance. I found Ruth much more to my liking. She, at least, was gentle."

"Colin . . ." For the first time, she became aware of his pallor. "They did not . . ."

"They did," he nodded. " 'Twas not unpleasant."

"Oh, Colin." She threw her arms around him. "You must go!"

He shook his head. " 'Tis too late, my own. But on the morrow we'll both go. I've written to Tony and told him all that has occurred. I told him that I might not return and have given him my instructions."

"Oh, why . . . why?" she cried.

"I do not care to live without you, my Juliet. And you should not be forced into this existence. Tony will come in the morning and he'll find me. I've left him mallets and a pair of stakes."

"Oh!" she trembled.

"Are you afraid?"

"I will . . . welcome the true death, if I may share it with you, but I do not want you to perish, my love, my love."

"Shhhh, be of good cheer, minx." He bent to kiss her, and sagging in her arms, he died.

"Good God," Richard strode into the library to find Tony standing by the hearth, feeding a paper into the flames. "Why will you light a fire in June?"

It was a moment before his son could reply. "There were some letters I . . . wanted to destroy," he said huskily.

"Love letters?" A brief smile flickered in Richard's somber eyes.

"And the like." Tony thought he had never heard Molly wail so loudly or the cat screech so incessantly, but since it was impossible to guess whether or not they wanted him to abide by the instructions in his brother's letter, he chose to believe that they approved his decision.

Part Three

One

Lucy Veringer sat in the library pouring over a large framed square of canvas spread out on the desktop in front of her. Called a family tree, it really did look like a tree. Her great-uncle Colin had taken up painting shortly after his transition, as her grandfather preferred to term it, and he had done branches, curling ones with green leaves and, if you looked close enough, little faces peeping between them.

Lucy wished he would paint more pictures. The portrait he had done of her Uncle Mark, as a young man, pleased her, though as her great-aunt Juliet said, Uncle Mark pleased no one. She looked up his dates on the tree. He had died in 1828 in his forty-seventh year, four years before she herself was born. It had all been a great scandal, and the bullet that felled him was in the desk drawer. Impulsively, Lucy opened the drawer and fiddling among sealing wax, quills and other paraphernalia finally found it. She held the bullet up to the candle flame. Though flattened and discolored, it still gleamed silver. The shepherd who had fashioned it wanted it back, but it had not been returned to him.

"Lucky, he wasn't hanged."

Lucy started and looked around, but of course she couldn't

see him. One didn't see the Old Lord (so called to distinguish him from his son, the present Earl of More); he made himself known in other ways mainly because, as he had so often told her, he was not going to stalk about the ramparts like the ghost of Hamlet's father. He was still angry about finding himself in a similar condition.

In his lifetime, despite all evidence to the contrary, he had convinced himself that there were no such things as ghosts, banshees, witches, werewolves, vampires or, for that matter, devils, angels and the Creator, Himself. The circumstances in the household caused him to change his mind but realization had come after death, and there he was, caught like a fly in amber, which was his simile. However there was no one to say that he must materialize and nothing to hinder him from keeping an eye, as it were, on his descendents. Consequently, one never knew when he was about or if he had eavesdropped on one's innermost thoughts, until he deliberately made himself known to the two humans, who could communicate with him—herself and her great-grandfather.

Lucy said placatingly, "You know why the shepherd had to kill Uncle Mark."

"*You shouldn't know*," came the explosive retort. "*Disgusting to burden a child with such information.*"

A door opened and slammed.

"Lucy." Mark Driscoll, Jr., a handsome boy of 13 strode to the desk. He was looking himself again, his red-gold hair smoothed back and his golden eyes full of humor, a sharp contrast to the other night when they almost hadn't got him chained in the cellar in time.

"Oh, I thought you were grandfather!" she exclaimed.

"Why should you think that?"

"Great-grandfather, I mean."

"Is he here?"

"Oh yes, and in one of his rages. I expect that's because of the tree."

"The tree?" He gave her a puzzled stare.

"This tree." She indicated the painting.

He came nearer to the desk and stared down at it. "Oh, that. Why does it fascinate you?"

"I think it's interesting."

"It doesn't interest *me*," he said loftily, sitting down in a chair near the desk. "Anyhow, it's all finished, at least as far as we're concerned. This branch is deadwood—or it will be when Great-Uncle Tony dies."

Lucy looked distressed. "I wish you wouldn't talk of him dying. Anyway, why couldn't you inherit the title?"

"For the same reason you can't . . . I mean couldn't, if you were a man."

"I'm not a werewolf!" Lucy exclaimed and then flushed. "I . . . I am sorry, Mark. I didn't mean . . ."

He looked at her fondly, "That's all right," he soothed. "Just as long as you don't mention it when there are strangers about."

"I never would!" she cried.

"Anyhow, my being a werewolf has nothing to do with it. I couldn't inherit because my father didn't marry my mother, either."

"*Common prostitute! Doxy! Trull!*" growled the Old Lord.

"Great-grandfather!" Lucy protested.

"What's he saying?" Mark asked.

"Nothing you should hear."

"You do queen it over us, you little witch!" he teased.

"I am not a witch!" she cried indignantly.

"You can talk to Great-grandfather and also to Molly and her cat. You'd think I could, too. I do hear them but I've never seen them."

"Grandfather says that lycanthropy is a disease."

"*Accursed . . . accursed . . .*" groaned the Old Lord.

"Yes," Lucy said seriously, "I expect it is part of the curse, just like Great-aunt Kathleen and Uncle John being murdered in Madras when your father was but a babe in arms."

"And being bitten by that strange woman he met on the moors." Mark nodded. "I'm glad she wasn't my mother. I'd be a double-werewolf, then." He wriggled his fingers and hunched his shoulders. "It's bad enough the way it is."

"Oh, dear, are you uncomfortable? I thought it wasn't so painful last time."

He flushed. "It's a bit better, but changing still causes a severe muscular strain."

"I do wish I could see it happen," Lucy said, her blue eyes

bright with interest. "I almost did the other night."

"You wouldn't want to see it," he said with a slight shudder. "And you are lucky they got me below in time. Was I growling?"

"A bit."

"I . . ."

"Lucy, what are you doing in here?" A tall spare woman with a hard angular face and narrow eyes stalked into the room. Her dark grey gown blended in with her greyish skin and iron grey hair and was almost the exact hue of her eyes. "I told you," she continued harshly, "that you were to remain in the kitchen."

Lucy flushed and slipped off the chair but said with a certain defiance, "Grandfather wanted . . ."

"You'll not refer to that man as your grandfather!" the woman snapped.

"But he *is* her grandfather, Mrs. Crowell!" Mark exclaimed indignantly.

Mrs. Crowell rounded on him. "We do not know for sure who fathered my misbegotten daughter's nameless brat."

"You do know!" Mark flared. "Everyone says that Lucy's the image of Lady Felicity."

"Humph, anyone can have blonde hair and blue eyes. Could've been any one of the young sprigs who chased her. I always knew she'd come to a bad end. Didn't I tell her time and again . . . but enough. You get back to the servants' room where you belong. It's time you was in training, miss. And don't look at me with that better-than-thou-expression. You'll be lucky if you ever get to be first parlormaid much less a housekeeper like myself. And you're to start as a kitchen maid. I have it all arranged with my niece who works as cook in Newcastle."

"Grandfather said . . ." Lucy whispered.

"Don't you 'grandfather' me." Mrs. Crowell crossed to the child and struck her across the face, a stinging slap that brought tears to the huge blue eyes, even though Lucy never uttered a word. "You're a whore's leavings and a blot on my good name. You should've died with Mary. And . . ." She suddenly screamed as a large book was hurled through the air striking her on the chest and felling her. She was up immediately, her expression wrathful. Pulling Lucy from the chair, she shook her roughly. "You little devil, throwing that book at me!"

"Stop it," Mark caught her arm. "She didn't. You know she didn't."

"Don't you come between me and what is mine," yelled the housekeeper. "This is the last straw. Today she goes forth from this house and into service. We'll see how her airs 'n graces will serve her there."

"I beg your pardon, Mrs. Crowell," a cold voice said from the doorway. "Lucy will remain at the Hold and you will cease to torment her."

For all that she was facing her employer, the housekeeper's anger gave no sign of abating. "She is my daughter's child, my Lord. I'll deal with her as I see fit."

"She is my son's daughter," he returned coolly. "Mary Crowell died before he could give her his name."

Mrs. Crowell sniffed. "He could've given her his name any time during the nine months her belly was blowing up like a hot-air balloon! But he was in London with his other doxies, not that I blame him. Mary was a light woman. She went against the teachings of God and was punished for her sins, and no good will come to this brat, either. She was born of sin and . . ."

"You'll leave this house today." Tony's blue eyes were stern and his lined face grim. "I kept you here because I felt I owed it to you. I wanted to atone for my son's behavior. However, I have long wanted to rid the Hold of your presence. You are unkind to the maids and delinquent in your duties. I should not have tolerated that, and I will not tolerate your cruelty to this innocent."

"Innocent! Give her another ten years and you'll see her whoring in the stable loft like her mother before her."

"Lucy." Tony turned to the child. "I do not want you to believe ill of your poor mother. She was a sweet, gentle girl and my son was a heartless rapscallion, who eventually died of his dissipations." He turned back to the housekeeper. "Yet he would have married your daughter had she survived. I'd have seen to that—or else I'd have married her myself. I will arrange for my steward to pay you, and you will go as soon as you are packed. I do not think it can take you longer than two hours."

"I will not go without Lucy, who is my daughter's child," the housekeeper retorted. "You have no hold over her, my Lord."

"Nor have you, Mrs. Crowell." Tony said. "This child is the image of my late wife, and as for being nameless, I will adopt her and then she'll have the name my son could not provide."

"Could not, would not," snarled Mrs. Crowell. "I'll not consent to this adoption. I know my rights and . . ." She suddenly screamed loudly as the inkwell flew from the desk and sprayed her with its contents.

"Oh, Great-grandfather, that was wonderful!" Mark clapped his hands loudly.

"Yes, it was," Tony agreed. He turned to the house-keeper. "I suggest that you leave before my father inflicts greater harm upon you. He's quite capable of throwing you out of the window, and I do not know what he'd do if you were to punish this poor baby any more than you have already."

Mrs. Crowell, her hair, face and gown splattered with black ink, stared at them, her mouth opening and closing. Then, with a harsh scream, she ran out of the room.

"Here now, Lucy, don't cry," Mark suddenly said.

Turning, Tony saw tears running down the child's sensitive little face. "Come, Lucy, the worst is over and she'll soon be gone."

"She'll make me go with her," sobbed the child. "She will!"

"She will not, for we will keep you here with us until the carriage I am about to order has taken her across the bridge that spans the moat. And then we shall lock the gates behind her and give the keepers orders not to let her near the Hold." Tony patted Lucy's head and looking down saw a dark red mark on her wrist. "Here, what's this? You've hurt yourself."

"It's nothing." Lucy put her hand in her lap quickly.

"Let me see this nothing." Tony retrieved her hand and examined it closely. "It's a burn. How did you get such a burn?"

"She . . . I was careless," Lucy murmured. "With the ironing."

"What ironing?"

Lucy kept her eyes on the tree painting. "The . . . ironing," she said as if that were all the explanation they needed.

"I say, she never made you do part of the ironing, did she?" Mark demanded angrily.

"Some of it," she said diffidently, not wanting to think of the huge cold laundry room and the hours she spent there, laboriously ironing aprons and caps with the maids sneaking in to help her when her grandmother wasn't looking. The discovery that Annie was helping her had resulted in the girl being sacked and in the burn that marked her wrist. There were other burns, and she was glad her sleeves covered them as well as the black and blue spots from her grandmother's pinches. She did not crave pity. She might be nameless, but Veringer blood ran in her veins and the Veringers were brave!

"Oh, Lucy," Tony said, stroking her wrist, "you do not need to be loyal to that termagant." His faded eyes flashed. "She's been hurting you all along, has she not? And you've said nothing."

"She never would." Mark actually growled. "I wish she'd have come to the cellar, that woman."

Tony shook his head. He had a serious look for Mark. "You do not wish anything of the sort, my boy."

"No, I do not, sir." The boy flushed. "But she shouldn't go unpunished. I wish *they* were here—except that her blood would taste very sour, I'm sure."

"Juliet says that it all tastes the same," Lucy reminded him.

"I shouldn't be surprised if it did." Tony moved toward the door. "I'll go and speed the parting . . . guest." He went out, closing the door softly behind him, only to have it fly open again and shut with a tremendous crash.

"They're alike in that, my uncle and great-grandfather," Mark observed to Lucy. "I shouldn't have mentioned Colin and Juliet."

"No more should I." Lucy looked at him regretfully. "It does upset them both so much."

"But never you," Mark said amazedly. "You are a marvel, Lucy. And just think, you can stay at the Hold with us—forever and ever!"

"Do you suppose I can?" she asked dubiously, her thoughts taking her back to the drab rooms she shared with her grandmother, to the eternal exhortations on the subject of her inherited sin, to the threats of service or worse, yet, apprenticeship in a factory. The times when she was able to escape to the library and cheer herself up by dwelling on the glorious past of her ancestors were few and far between. She knew her grandfather was fond of her but he was much preoccupied with the affairs of the estate. She also knew that he spent long hours in the chapel praying for the souls of his mother, his father and above all for that of poor Lady Felicity, dead in childbed with Felix, who had been her father. Lucy, herself, had occasionally gone to the chapel to pray for her grandfather, Mark, Colin and Juliet—though Molly had told her prayers were of little help to this family.

"It's the curse, d'you see?" The banshee had loosed a gusty sigh. "And it's doubly cursed I am. Ach, I miss the auld sod, but there's no goin' back until it's at an end, and Himself knows when that will be."

"Will the curse really end?" Lucy had asked, feeling sorry for the banshee. She did look so wrung out and the cat's whiskers were drooping.

"Aye, it'll end." Molly nodded. "When they find a place to receive them. That nasty piece o'goods Erlina Bell'll do her best to see they do not. A murrain on her, I say, no proper witch she wi' her indecent goin's on. Scandalous, I call it. I never did more'n make a few cows run dry'n raise a storm or two . . . an' for that I was toasted to a fare-thee-well'n Grimalkin wi' me."

"A place to receive them? What about the Hold?"

Molly had shaken her head until her white locks had fluttered about her thin old face. " 'Twill not be here. 'Tis not given to me to know where, but 'tis out on the road the lot o' us will be. Mark my words'n be off with you. I should not be speaking to you as 'tis but there's so few can see me an' 'tis lonely bein' here wi' poor little Juliet away so much . . ." Molly had faded then and the cat with her.

Sitting in her chamber, braiding her hair, Lucy was thinking about her long-ago conversation with Mark. She looked out of her window at the span of the drawbridge and envisioned Mr. Matthais Veringer riding across it, unless he came by carriage. His visit, ostensibly to pay his respects to the elderly or rather ancient Earl of More, Tony having just celebrated his eighty-ninth birthday, was actually to view the estate he would soon inherit. Her gorge rose. It wasn't fair. Mark ought to inherit or Colin. They both loved the place so much but Mark was illegitimate and a werewolf while Colin was a vampire and, for all intents and purposes, dead. There was only one slim hope that the family could remain in the Hold, and it rested on her shoulders. If Mr. Veringer were to take a liking to her or, in fact, love her . . . Lucy frowned. She had doubts about Mr. Matthais Veringer. Four years ago, on her sixteenth birthday, she had discovered that she had the gift of prescience. No one had expected Juliet and Colin would be there to help her celebrate that event, but she knew they would come and knew when. She had been right. She was dolefully sure that she was right about Matthais Veringer, and wistfully wishful that she was wrong. Matthais Veringer, a coming event, was casting his shadow before him, and she didn't like the looks of it.

She finished braiding her hair. Staring into the mirror, she did think he might approve her. Lucy wasn't vain but she couldn't help knowing that she was beautiful. As so often happens with girls, she took after her father's side of the family and, as Tony had averred, she was the image of her grandmother. She had Felicity Campbell's wide blue eyes and her pale golden hair. The slight tilt of those same eyes might be attributed to Juliet. Her nose was straight and beautifully shaped. Her mouth was full but not too full, and the lips were a lovely pink. Her high cheekbones were about all she had inherited from poor Mary Crowell. She was very slim with a waist that Mark could span with his two hands quite easily.

Poor Mark. She was quite aware that he loved her, and she loved him but only as a brother. That, of course, was fortunate. Actually, he should never marry. The population of werewolves ought not to be increased. She sighed. Mark's plight always brought tears to her eyes. He was so gentle and kind in his normal state, but tonight the moon would be full and already he was in the cellar. If he howled too loudly, they would have to concoct some story about a rabid dog. It was fortunate that the cadet branch of the Veringers dwelt in Oxford. There had been little communication between the two families, but of late there had been correspondence and an engraving of Colin's painting of the family tree had been forwarded to Matthais. Lucy grimaced. Though her grandfather assured her it was necessary to provide the heir apparent with this information, she regretted the necessity. It meant that she and Tony must needs entertain him alone. They might, with the excuse of special diets, have been able to get about the fact that Colin and Juliet could not join them at dinner but unfortunately, their portraits hung in the gallery and naturally Matthais Veringer would expect to be shown through it. Colin had painted his sister's picture which was a marvelous likeness while his own portrait, done when he was 19, was a faithful but not particularly inspired rendering. Of course Colin could have grown a moustache for the occasion, but she could understand his reasons for refusing. It was difficult to get the caked blood out of the small hairs.

Lucy rose and cast another glance into the mirror. Her grandfather had insisted that she have a new gown for the occasion. It was a blue shot silk over an immense crinoline. It was extremely difficult to manage, but it did give shape to her voluminous skirts. Juliet had marveled over its panniers, saying they reminded her of the gown she had worn on her birthday ball in June of 1786. Immediately upon uttering these words she had frowned and exchanged a speaking look with her brother, who had turned briefly morose. Later, Lucy remembered that Juliet had suffered her transition in July of that same year. It was really amazing! Though the ball had taken place 66 years previously, Juliet still looked 17 while Colin could never be taken for much past 22!

It was a pity they could not entertain Matthais Veringer. In the past half-century they had traveled over most of Europe and had had some very amusing experiences or, at least, they seemed amusing in the telling. Of course, some of the anecdotes, concerning the near loss of their coffins during a rough channel crossing and the time those same boxes had fallen off the cart bearing them to Prague and they had waked at night without a notion where they were, could hardly be shared with their guest. Nor could they relate

Colin's encounter with a scrawny little Corsican Corporal who spoke a villanious French and took umbrage at what he termed Colin's outrageous flirting with a slim Creole wench from Martinique, obviously no better than she should be. That visit to France had certainly been eventful, for Juliet, clapped into prison as an aristocrat, had shared a cell with a Marquis. Upon refreshing herself with a few small sips of his blood, he had amazingly begged her to drink more. He had proved to be a writer and subsequently had named one of the books after her. While these tales could not be aired, there were others equally fascinating. She had said as much to Juliet.

"You will be fascinating, too, my love," Juliet had comforted her.

As usual, Juliet was being kind. No one knew better than Lucy how terrified she was when forced to meet anyone outside of the household. She was painfully aware that everyone in the village and on the neighboring estates knew of her heritage. Her grandmother, leaving in the highest dudgeon, had not been silent on the subject of her daughter's betrayal at the hands of Lord Felix Veringer. She had added injury to insult with dark tales of the Old Lord and, of course, everyone was aware of the fate that had befallen Sir Mark Driscoll, avoiding his son on the rare occasions he was seen in the village. No tradesmen would come to the Hold and few servants remained there. Only Tony's doddering old butler and his equally ancient cook were still in residence, and that was because both were approaching 80 and could not hope for another position. There were also two brave maids, who stayed because of the high wages, but they talked, too.

Each time Lucy came into town for supplies, she caught looks and saw people making signs to ward off the evil eye. Long ago she had given up going to church because of the looks and whispers that followed her when she entered the Veringer pew. However, tonight she must try to abrogate her shyness while making a determined effort to charm Matthais Veringer. She did not look forward to the task.

They had taken all the extension leaves out of the dining room table and still it was long, far too long for the three people who bowed their heads while one of them, Matthais

Veringer, at his own request, said a lengthy and sonorous grace. Each word that issued from his lips was, in effect, a reproof because his distant cousin Lord More had not suggested a prayer but had left him to rectify the omission. Finally, Matthais ended what was more sermon than grace. Though he sat in the middle of the vast expanse of white linen, shining silver and sparkling crystal, Lucy, who had disliked him on sight, thought he gave the impression of presiding at it, while she at one end and her grandfather at the other were put in the position of being guests. As much as was humanly possible, Matthais Veringer avoided looking or speaking to her. His eyes, large and grey, had beamed their disapproval when she was introduced to him. He had not kissed her hand. He had merely touched it quickly as if he considered himself actually sullied by contact with one so far beneath him in station. Though he resided in Oxford Mr. Veringer had, Lucy guessed, an ear to local rumors. She wondered who his informant had been and did not put it past her grandmother to have written to him. That notion was quickly scotched when she recalled that Mrs. Crowell had difficulty signing her own name. It hardly mattered. Though Mr. Veringer might be uncomfortable and even affronted by her presence at table, she was delighted by his slights. In consequence of them, she was not compelled to speak to him and thus had plenty of time to observe him.

He was not ill-looking. He had the Veringer height and might have been more attractive were it not for the stamp his detestable air of self-consequence had imprinted upon his features. There was a touch of red to his heavily pomaded chestnut locks, and his grey eyes were well-shaped as was his nose. She did not like his mouth which she found too full. He was in danger of adding an extra chin to the one he already possessed. There was also a slight bulge below his waistline. His hands were too soft and white to please her, and there was a foppishness to his dress that made her glad Colin and Mark were not present. Both of them prized simplicity and might have made subtle jests about the immense amount of jewelry he wore. In addition to the signet ring that nearly reached the joint of the index finger on his right hand, there was a large diamond sparkling on his left. His garments, following the latest style, were black for evening. His shirt front was elaborately frilled, and he wore a yellow satin waistcoat embroidered with butterflies.

He ate what was put before him and did not refuse seconds. Eating, she decided, was evidently an activity that pleased him. He deigned to compliment Tony on his cuisine and seemed surprised that Mrs. McCulloch, the cook, was not of French extraction.

"We have always employed a Frenchman in our kitchens," he remarked.

"Have you?"

Lucy, glancing at her grandfather, was hard put not to giggle. He was obviously fighting a strong desire to put down this young man.

For the first time since they had come to the table, Mr. Veringer turned his gaze on Lucy. "I presume, Miss Veringer, that you handle the hiring of the servants?"

She felt a rush of pure anger. His inference was plain. He was trying to put her in her place, which he clearly believed was not, at the master's table. She said softly, "And why should you presume that, Cousin Matthais?"

She was pleased to note an angry frown in his eyes at what he must consider a familiarity unsuited to her position. "I had the impression that you were the . . . er, chatelaine of this establishment."

"My grand-daughter does not serve in that capacity," Tony said coldly. "It is I who have the hiring of the staff, most of whom have been here since before you were born, I am sure."

"Indeed, sir, that speaks well for your treatment of them. We, too, have the reputation of maintaining a contented staff." His eyes rested on Lucy again. "Of course, we do not pamper them." He laughed shortly. "And we do insist upon decorum. Last year one of our maids found herself in the . . . family way, and she was dismissed on the spot."

"And then what happened to her?" Lucy inquired coolly.

The grey eyes fastened on her face. "She was sent to the workhouse, Miss Veringer. As for her unfortunate child, I expect it will be placed in an orphanage where it will learn a trade, something suitable for its station in life."

"I see." Lucy wondered if her grandfather detected the far from subtle insult inherent in the introduction of that pointed anecdote. A swift glance at him assured her that he had missed nothing of the exchange. His blue eyes were absolutely glacial as they lingered on Matthais Veringer's face.

"I have always heard that conditions in the workhouses leave much to be desired," Tony said with deceptive mildness.

"I have never heard that," his guest replied. "I do not believe in coddling the underclasses, sir."

"I see," Tony commented.

"However, I have always found that morning and evening prayers do a great deal to keep servants in line."

"It is my belief that worship is a private thing and best left to the individual," Tony said coldly.

Matthais opened his eyes widely. "Surely you cannot be serious, sir. The girls of that class have no moral fiber. Look at the appalling number of illegitimate births! If not exposed to proper instruction and, I might add, discipline, these young women invariably go astray. It remains for their masters to offer such instruction so that they know that the Lord is watching them at all times. Thus they are guarded from unfortunate lapses."

"I presume you are speaking specifically, sir, rather than figuratively. Those unfortunate lapses that you mention are, from my understanding, often the result of being young, pretty, defenseless and in households where the gentlemen are less concerned with their moral fiber than you appear to be," Lucy said tartly and was immediately regretful. She had no wish to remind her grandfather of what was by now ancient history.

Matthais Veringer flushed. "I hardly believe that this is a fit topic of conversation for a female." He might have said more but old Angus tottered in with the next course which, fortunately, proved succulent enough to take his mind from Lucy's unmaidenly frankness.

Dinner finally ending, Tony suggested that Lucy repair to the music room. "We'll have our port and join you there, presently, my love." He smiled at her fondly, adding, "Lucy performs well upon the pianoforte."

"If you please, sir," Matthais said, leaning forward, "I know it's late but since my time here is limited by my obligations in the city, I should like to see some of the house. If Miss Veringer would be so kind as to show it to me."

"Of course, sir, I would be delighted," Lucy murmured, her gaze falling in a middle space, avoiding both her grandfather and their guest. Now that she had become aware of his condescension, she could even be amused by the lengths to which he was determined to go in order to put her in her proper place which, again, was obviously not in the music room. She could almost see into the workings of his small conventional mind. He was wrestling with the giant problem of how to treat one who, in his estimation, was no better than an upper servant, despite her Veringer connection. He obviously thought Tony a senile old man who, in lieu of any legitimate descendant, had elevated her to a position she had no right to occupy. That, she knew, was also the contention of the families dwelling in the immediate area.

"If you choose," Tony said. "My granddaughter is a fine musician but also an excellent guide." Again his arctic glance belied his smile.

Lucy had not expected that the castle would find favor in Mr. Veringer's eyes. He had already been disposed to criticize before they started on a tour that had taken him through the hall and into the library, the music room and the second drawing room. However, she had not anticipated his utter dismay.

"But everything is so old and antiquated!" he almost bleated as they came forth from the main drawing room. "I doubt if you have so much as a water closet."

"On the contrary." Lucy managed to swallow a sharp retort, "We have quite a few. They are installed in all the bedrooms and have been there for the last fifty years!"

"Ah!" His sigh of relief was explosive. "My Milicent will appreciate that, at least."

"Your . . . Milicent, sir?"

"My fiancée, the daughter of Lord Overbrook. She is Lady Milicent Overbrook. I am a most fortunate man. Had we not become affianced in April, the queen would have claimed her for the Royal Household."

"Indeed. I felicitate you upon your happiness, sir."

"I thank you, Miss Veringer." He moved forward and stumbled. "Great heavens, these halls are dark! It would seem to me that your grandfather would have had gas laid on.''

"He much prefers candlelight, Cousin Matthais." Lucy pressed her lips together to keep from laughing as she actually felt the disapproval welling up within him at this second reference to their relationship.

"Well, I expect that change is difficult for him to accept, Miss Veringer. A man as old as that, approaching ninety, his faculties must be quite impaired."

"If you are suggesting senility, Cousin Matthais, I must hasten to correct that impression. My grandfather has a lively mind and a quite marvelous acumen."

"It does credit to you that you are so eager to defend him, Miss Veringer."

Lucy's little hand tightened on the candle holder she was carrying. The man really was insufferable! Common courtesy demanded that she bridle her tongue and must also keep her from throwing the candle at him. However, at that moment, she longed to give him several pieces of her mind. She contented herself by saying with deceptive mildness, "Should you like to visit the Long Gallery, sir?"

"Yes, I should like that." His tone brightened. "I expect I will find a likeness of my great-great-great grandfather Elias Veringer?"

"There is a portrait, I believe."

"There must be," he said firmly.

In spite of two candelabra, the portrait gallery was sunk in shadow. Lucy, leading him from one end to the other, was forced to carry an extra candle to light Mr. Veringer's way. From his comments, he appeared more impressed with the older generations than with the brood that had sprung from the loins of Richard and Catlin. "Lord Veringer's mother was, I seem to recall, of Irish extraction?" he asked.

"Yes." Lucy hearing the disdain in his tone, added wickedly, "My great-grandmother was Irish born and bred."

"And . . . on your mother's side?" There was an underlying sarcasm to his tone that did not escape Lucy. She doubted that it was meant to do so.

She responded calmly and clearly. "As far as I can determine, sir, they were pure English, though I never knew my mother and my late grandmother did not inform me as to her heritage.''

"I expect she had little time to sit and talk," he replied pointedly.

"That is true." Lucy smiled up at him. "Being house-keeper of so large an establishment as the Hold is a gigantic task, and my grandmother prided herself upon her efficiency."

"I am sure she had every right to do that," he allowed magnaminously. He came to a stop in front of Juliet's portrait painted, had he but known it, by her brother as a present for what would have been her twenty-first birthday. Colin's own portrait hung next to that of his sister. Matthais looked closely from one to the other. "A handsome pair," he remarked. He cleared his throat. "One hears such odd tales in the village."

"Oh?" Lucy, well-aware of what he must have heard, looked at him interrogatively. "What sort of tales?"

"Quite wild," he amplified. "I am sure you must be acquainted with them yourself."

"I cannot be sure of that until I know what you've heard."

"The most arrant nonsense, of course. I'd not thought that old superstitions were so prevalent in this enlightened age."

"Old superstitions, sir?"

"You are not aware of them?" he probed.

"I have learned never to heed village gossip, sir."

"Er . . . very wise, I am sure. And who would this be?" He pointed to the portrait of Felix Veringer as a young man, before dissipation had marked his handsome features.

"That is my father, sir," Lucy said softly.

"Oh, yes, your father . . ." He cleared his throat. "Miss Veringer, I have a question for you which I hope you'll not take amiss, but I feel I must have an answer since your grand-father's decidedly frail. I observed him rather closely at dinner, and it seems to me that his days upon this earth are numbered. I should like to know what you intend to do, once the title and estate are conferred upon me. You have another cousin, too, whom I believe is in much the same circum-stances as yourself. Have either of you given any thought of your future?"

Lucy, caught unawares, experienced a sinking feeling. "We have not, I fear, contemplated our grandfather's death. He is very dear to us, you know."

"That is certainly understandable and your feeling for him does you credit, but we must be practical in more ways than one. I wish that I might offer you both a home here, but Milicent . . ." Though he left the sentence unfinished, his implication was all too clear. He would not subject his highborn bride to the contamination of two baseborn relations.

"You needn't concern yourself about our Cousin Mark or our dearest Lucy. We'll see that they are both comfortable and want for nothing, dear Cousin Matthais," remarked a silvery voice from the shadows.

"Yes, indeed, we will provide for them," concurred a deeper voice.

Lucy, moving back, cast a startled glance into the gloom. "Juliet," she mouthed and, in that same moment, she appeared with Colin a few paces behind her.

Juliet looked particularly fetching in a gown fashioned for her by Charles Worth on her last visit to Paris. Of white peau de soie, it was draped over a huge crinoline. Small lilies of the valley were embroidered on the skirt, and if her décolleté seemed daring for the girl of 17 she still appeared to be, she looked so lovely that one forgot about the proprieties. Colin was fashionably dressed in grey, his shirt pleated rather than frilled, his suit beautifully cut. He presented a marked contrast to his foppish relative. He and his sister looked as if they had just come from a gala evening at the theater, and thanks to their retractable fangs, their smiles revealed nothing more than a general good cheer. However Matthais Veringer, staring at them and then at the shadowy mirror that hung over the fireplace and which reflected everything in the room except that attractive pair, did not respond to their bonhomie.

As they came closer, he tottered away, "Stay b-b-back," he squealed. "In the name of . . . of . . ." There was a loud thump as he toppled to the floor in a dead faint.

Oblivious of her fallen cousin, Juliet surged forward, "You know we'd not let you want for anything, my dearest Lucy," she cried.

"Quite true," Colin agreed with an affectionate smile.

Lucy felt laughter threatening but coupled with it was anxiety. "I do appreciate your concern," she said, "but truthfully, I think it would have been better if you'd not made so precipitate an entrance.''

"Probably you are right." Juliet nodded. "But we couldn't help it, overhearing him. Of all the unctuous, toadying little . . . and *he*'s to be Earl of More! Oh, Colin!'' Juliet clasped her brother's arm. "If only you hadn't been so dreadfully impulsive.''

"It's too late to repine, my love," he murmured. "And I dare say that *he* is part of the curse.''

"A large part.'' Juliet twinkled. "I'd say he weighed at least twenty stone, but I do think we ought to get him to his chamber. He cannot remain here all the night.''

"An admirable suggestion, my dear.'' Colin lifted Matthais and slung him over his shoulder.

"How easily you did that!'' Lucy marveled.

"It's one of the benefits of transition," Juliet explained. "We're both much stronger than we were before.''

"I remember you telling me that," Lucy said, "but I did not realize how strong until this moment.''

Juliet glided to the window. "I do wish you could just throw him out, Colin," she said wistfully.

"Oh, no!'' Lucy exclaimed.

"No, certainly not," Colin reproved. "You mustn't be so bloodthirsty, Juliet.'' His eyes widened as he broke into ironical laughter.

Juliet also laughed. "I could never thirst after that blood," she said frankly. "It must be dreadfully thin and full of impurities. Which chamber have you alotted to him, Lucy?''

"The East wing at the end of the hall.''

"I'll put him to bed," Colin said obligingly.

"I'd best sit by him," Juliet murmured. "He'll need an explanation.''

"You'd better leave that to me," Lucy said firmly. "You'd send him off into another fit.''

"I know," Juliet replied.

It was unfortunate that Matthais, coming out of a long swoon, should hear the protracted howl that arose from the depths of the castle. It was a melancholy sound, particularly horrifying because it combined the wolfish with the human cry and, to the uninitiated, it brought with it a primeval terror especially when, as on this occasion, it was accompanied by low, ferocious snarls.

Listening to poor Mark, Lucy felt only pity for him, trapped in his lupine shape and locked in the cellar. At the same time, she wondered what had set him off. It was seldom that he sounded so loud or, she suddenly realized, so near. Had he managed to break his bonds or had someone freed him? Even as that queasy conjecture crossed her mind, she heard a snuffling at the door while beside her, a voice filled with terror gasped, "In the name of Jesus, what is that?"

Unfortunately, Matthais' ill-advised exhortation brought another louder howl. Coupled with it was a determined scratching on the door.

"There . . . there's a dog out there," Matthais quavered. "A f-ferocious d-dog . . . from the sound of it."

"Not a dog, Cousin Matthais." Juliet suddenly appeared at his bedside. "Just our Cousin Mark. He has spells. However, my father will subdue him." She paused and directed an impish look toward Lucy. "Gracious, I do believe he's fainted again."

Matthais Veringer left the Hold at the same time that the sun cast its first rays through the window. To Lucy, standing beside an embarrassed Tony in the great hall, he seemed entirely different from the smug, self-satified young man who had arrived yesterday. He appeared to have aged at least ten years and despite her distress over the events of the previous evening, Lucy could only be interested in the fact that something she had believed to be entirely apochryphal had proved accurate. A narrow white streak like the stripe in a skunk's back ran down the center of Matthais' Veringer's glossy locks. He was also pale and haggard. The description so beloved of contemporary novelists, "trembling in every limb," could be applied to him. Indeed, as he reached the door, he was obliged to steady himself against it.

From his tone of voice, however, it was obvious that his anger equaled his terror. "I'll not thank you for your hospitality, my Lord," he said, his eyes avoiding Lucy. Evidently he was all too aware of the spectacle he had made of himself. "I will tell you, however, that . . . that when this moldering pile becomes my property, I shall have it razed to the ground and a proper dwelling built. As for some of its inmates . . .'' He shrieked as the door suddenly swung back, throwing him to the floor. A chill wind went through the hall causing the chandelier to swing back and forth, and then the door slammed.

Matthais clambered to his feet. Clutching the doorknob with trembling hands, he wrenched the door open and dashed out, his loud screams resounding in their ears. Caught between regret and laughter, Lucy turned to Tony only to find that he had quietly slipped to the floor in a faint.

"Grandfather!" She bent over him, a hand to his heart. It was still beating, but in that same moment, a great howl rang through the hall. Mingled with it was the screeching of a cat. Molly and her pet were outdoing themselves this time.

"I just swept out another huge load o' 'em, Miss Lucy," Betsy, one of the maids, said. She looked at her with wide eyes. "Must've been fifty o' the pesky things, toes turned up'n dead as doornails, they was, with nobody settin' out traps or poison, not that I know of."

Standing just beyond the door to her grandfather's chamber, Lucy said, "It does seem strange." She hoped that she had injected enough surprise into her response.

"Very strange, Miss Lucy." Betsy shivered. "Must've been 'bout a hundred mice in two days. Somethin's doin' for 'em," she said darkly. Bobbing a curtsy, she went in to relieve Lucy at Tony's bedside.

Hurrying down the stairs, Lucy winced as she heard Molly on the battlements and Grimalkin chasing up and down the hall in full screech. This was one of the times when she really regretted her psychic sensitivity. She had never known Molly to utter such loud, sustained wails and, of course, it was Grimalkin's howling that accounted for the heart failure that had felled so many of the castle's rodent population. It was proving to be a truly vicious circle, for their deaths served to accentuate that fiery feline's frustration at seeing so many savory mouthfuls going to waste—with the result that he howled the louder and slew more.

She had no doubt as to the reasons behind the banshee's increased efforts. Tony was dying, and added to that tragedy was the plight of the remaining household. She was quite sure that the news of his impending demise had spread through the village and equally sure that Matthais was coiled like a serpent, awaiting the moment when he could slither back to the Hold and strike at its inmates. She doubted that any of them would be allowed to remain an instant after the burial of her grandfather. And where on earth could they go? They needed an estate comparable to the Hold and preferably with its own burial ground. Unfortunately, there was no money to purchase such a property. Due to the strain her father had put on the Hold, all the land that could be legally sold had gone. The rest was entailed. It was a problem that, as yet, had no solution.

She came outside. It was a lovely night. The sky was encrusted with stars and the waning moon was reflected in the still waters of the moat. The great old trees were illumined by that chill radiance, and her ears were filled with the sounds of the night. Dolefully she wondered how many more nights she would be able to stand here; not many, she was sure of that. The Old Lord, who often accompanied her on these strolls, was in his son's room. She had felt his grief. Mark was still recovering from the strain of the last two days.

Had it only been two days since Matthais Veringer had gone screaming forth from the Hold? Picturing his ignominious departure in her mind's eye, she wished that Juliet and Colin had not seen fit to take up their figurative cudgels in her behalf, wishing even more that one of those cudgels had not been poor Mark, dragged out of the cellar in his lupine shape. Futile as they had seemed at the time, she found herself dwelling more and more on Matthais' threats. She had a distinct feeling that he was planning something, and she trusted her feelings.

"Lucy . . ." Juliet called.

Lucy started. Turning, she saw her great-aunt gracefully gliding across the grass. She was clad in a long dark cloak and was smiling happily. Juliet was usually smiling, Lucy mused. In the years since her transition, she seemed to grow more and more light-hearted, she and Colin, too. Sometimes Lucy was depressed by their gaiety. There was, she thought, something soulless in it.

Judging from her grandfather's recollections, they had been very different in the old days. He had told her about Colin's pathetic letter and last request as well as his own inability to honor it.

"I had every intention of obeying but once I saw them lying in their coffins, both looking so beautiful and so *alive*, as if, indeed they had only just gone to sleep, I could not pound the stakes into their hearts," he had told her with that old agony coloring his tone. He had added firmly and not regretfully, "In any form, they are still my kin—and I love them."

Yet, in not complying, he had condemned them to the dark realms of the undead. There had been a bitter confrontation between Colin and his brother, after Colin had awakened in his tomb. However that anger had been long forgotten. Lucy was quite sure that he enjoyed his unnatural existence, and though neither had ever discussed it with her, she was equally sure that Colin and Juliet were no longer repelled by the means that must be employed were they to sustain themselves. Still, to give credit where credit was certainly due, they did not seek their prey in the immediate vicinity—only occasionally. They were away for months and even years. Through the help of various individuals hypnotically pressed into their service as well as through their own heightened ingenuity and the shape-shifting that came naturally to vampires, they had gotten their traveling arrangements down to a fine art.

"Lucy." Juliet stepped purposefully to her side. She appeared to be both pleased and excited. "I have had a revelation!"

"A revelation?" Lucy echoed.

"Yes!" Juliet's moon-illumined eyes gleamed. "I think we must all go to Boston. I am sure Colin will agree, once he returns."

"Boston?" Lucy stared at her in some consternation. "I didn't know we had connections in Lincolnshire!"

"Not Boston here. I am speaking about Boston in Massachusetts, which is in America. Judging from what Bob Smith told Jane Warren, while they were making love in the cemetery tonight, it's just the place for us!"

"Boston? America? Why?" Lucy stared at Juliet, wondering if she were hearing right.

"Of course, you are, silly." Juliet answered that unspoken thought. "It's just the place for all of us. Now listen and don't interrupt. I haven't been out yet, and I must go very soon.''

"Out" being a euphemism for activities neither Juliet nor Colin ever described in detail, Lucy said quickly, "Tell me.''

As Juliet launched into one of the lively accounts that had kept her entertained all her life, Lucy marveled at the vivid word pictures she painted. Words came as easily to her lips as colors to her brother's brush. She would have been a marvelous actress.

Lucy could almost see her, waking in the crypt and hearing Bob Smith's young, eager voice. "I'm sorry I must meet you 'ere, love, but given your family . . .''

"I'm not afraid of ghosts, Bob," Jane said staunchly. "Better than my sisters, who'd be rushin' to Pa, tellin' on me. They just live to do that." She paused, adding, "They do say this place is haunted.''

He laughed merrily. "So's the whole o' Boston for that matter 'n you'll find a lot o' the people that live there mucking about in graveyards just to practice.''

"Practice what?''

"Conjurin' up the dead. Mediums, you know.''

"No, I don't know. What's a medium?''

"They communicate with the dear departed. That's what they call 'em—the spirits, I mean. They have circles 'n they make lots of money. Seems everybody in Boston's out to talk to their dead grandfather—college professors, newspaper-men. 'Tisn't a day don't pass that there's not somethin' in the newspapers about it.''

"Wot's a circle," Jane had wanted to know.

"That's what they call the group—sittin' an' 'oldin' 'ands in a circle while the medium supposedly picks up on their energy 'n brings 'em messages from them wot 'as passed over. They don't never say 'died' no more. They've gone 'n passed over, see.''

"I don't see an' I don't want to see," Jane said firmly. "Wouldn't get me tryin' to talk to anyone wot's dead.''

"Me neither.''

The conversation had shifted to topics more felicitous to both parties, but Juliet had heard enough. "Lucy," she said eagerly now, "you could do it—communicate, I mean.''

"I couldn't," Lucy contradicted. "I mean I . . ."

"Of course, you could," Juliet said bracingly. "And father would help, I know it."

"Help?" Lucy asked dubiously.

"He must have a wide acquaintance among the dear departed." Juliet giggled, then sobered. "I hope I have given you something to consider, Lucy. After all we must go somewhere . . . and meanwhile, I will leave you."

The thought of going to Boston had seemed totally mad at first but the more Lucy pondered Juliet's suggestion, the more it appealed to her. A city where the supernatural was not only tolerated but actually esteemed offered limitless possibilities, especially for the five remaining members of the family. They only needed a house ancient enough to please the Old Lord and big enough to suit the special needs of her other relatives. A subsequent conversation with Juliet had elicited the information that she and Colin would be perfectly satisfied with a large cellar, one that could be divided between them and Mark. Of course, they would also need additional chambers on a higher floor, to accomodate Colin's painting equipment and Juliet's mammoth wardrobe.

Though she knew little about America, the idea of Boston, first settled in the seventeenth century, appealed to Lucy. It remained for her to seek out Bob Smith, the butcher's son, whom she knew. As a boy, he had been briefly employed as a groom at the Hold. Lucy had gone riding with him on several occasions, but she had not seen him in three years.

Three days after her conversation with Juliet and on her way to the butcher's shop, Lucy was fortunate enough to meet Bob coming out. She experienced a shock on seeing him. Time had certainly wrought changes in the rather shy lad of 19 she remembered. At 22, he was self-confident to the point of brashness. He was also very nattily dressed, but seeing her he flushed as easily as he had when saddling her horse for her.

"Well, Miss Lucy," he said, his admiring gaze on her face, "I'd 'ardley 'ave known ye. 'Aven't you grown up, though!"

"Not high enough," she said wryly. Her height, which was only two inches above five feet, was a sore point with her.

" 'Igh enough for anyone wi' eyes in 'is 'ead," he

responded and flushed. "Beggin' yer pardon, Miss Lucy."

"Please," she said, "I am complimented. But you've been in America, have you not?"

"Yes, Miss Lucy, I 'ave. Boston. It's a fine place, I tell you."

"And will you return?"

"Yes, ma'am, we'll be goin' back." A proud smile lifted the corners of his mouth. "Me 'n Jane Gordon, we're goin' to get married an' leave on the Eastern Queen come month's end."

After she had congratulated him, Lucy said, "You will be settling in Boston?"

"Yes, ma'am. It's a great little city. I've got me a job there, workin' in the livery stables. I'm doin' well. One o' these days—but I shouldn't be talkin' 'bout that—but, well, America's a place where a man don't need to stay in a rut. 'E can move a'ead without folks puttin' 'im in 'is place."

"So I've heard. Though I expect you'd get ahead anywhere, Bob."

"It's good o' you to say so, Miss Lucy. But America, it's different. It's for me."

"I suppose everything's new in Boston. Houses and . . ."

"Oh, no, ma'am," he interrupted. "There's old and there's new, plenty o' both when it comes to 'ouses."

"And the people, are they congenial?"

"They are that, ma'am."

"I understand that there's some interest in the . . . spiritualist movement?"

Bob's eyes, which were big and round, grew bigger and rounder. "D'you mean to say you've 'eard about that all the way over 'ere?"

Lucy blushed. "I've heard something of the sort."

"Well, you're right, ma'am. 'Tisn't only Boston. It's all over the bloomin' country but it's Boston where I live and they're set on it there. Professors, doctors, scientists even."

By the time Lucy returned to the Hold, she was just as excited as Juliet had been. Judging from what Bob had told her, Boston did seem like the ideal place for them. It lay across the seas in America. Erlina Bell had predicted a long, hard way before they reached their final resting place . . . and did not Boston fill those requirements? The fact that they would be traveling upon the ocean rather than the roads of the world did not weigh with her; it was distance that mattered. And the distance between Northumberland and Liverpool was also considerable. Furthermore, no one would know about them in America, no one except Bob Smith and his bride and they were friends.

Her enthusiasm was a trifle dimmed by the time she presented the idea to Mark and the Old Lord. It was a radical change, and she expected an argument, but amazingly Mark agreed that it was a good idea, and after a few door slammings and window rattlings, so did the Old Lord. His situation had not robbed him of a sense of adventure. As he confided to Lucy, the idea of visiting the colonies had always appealed to him, and not even her reminder that the colonies had been a country for the last 75 years dimmed his anticipation.

Lucy, resuming her vigil by Tony's bed on the evening after the vote had been taken, looked regretfully at her grandfather. It would be better not to tell him of their plans. He loved the Hold.

"Lucy . . ."

She tensed, looking at him anxiously. He had been sleeping, she thought, but now his eyes were open and fixed on her. "Lucy, my child . . ." He spoke with difficulty.

"Grandfather, dearest." She moved nearer the bed, bending over him. "What may I fetch for you?"

"Nothing . . . but my father's not with us now and I . . . wish to . . . to tell you. Do not persist in your . . . scheme. Leave the household. Go far away and make your own life. You should not be accursed, you who have done nothing but good. 'Twas wrong of me to let you remain. I should have sent you to . . . another place . . . another country."

"I could never have left you, Grandfather." She took his hand, holding it tightly, her distress increasing because his flesh was so cold even though the room was passing warm.

"Child, you must. I . . . I fear for you and I . . . beg you to leave while you may." He eased his hand from her grasp and pointed a shaking finger. "See . . . the bedpost."

"The bedpost," she repeated, thinking he must be wandering in his mind. "What of the bedpost,

Grandfather?''

''The one on the left . . . the knob unscrews. Open it now and take what you find inside.''

''But . . .''

''Do as I say,'' he said in a stronger voice. ''Use both hands.''

Since it was better to humor him, Lucy rose and put both her little hands around the left knob. To her amazement, it moved under her fingers. Beneath it was a hollow space filled with old gold coins. There seemed to be quite a few of them. She looked at her grandfather in amazement.

''I collected them as a lad . . . there are angels and sovereigns. They are worth quite a lot by now. I want you to take them for yourself, my Lucy, and go far, far away. Do not let them use you. It's not fair.''

''Use me, Grandfather? I don't understand.''

''You are too sensitive . . . and it will be dangerous, more dangerous than you know, this plan . . .''

''Plan?'' she repeated, wondering angrily who had told him what they had in mind.

''None told me . . .'' he whispered. ''It was given me to know . . . a warning from Molly, who loves you, Lucy.''

His wits were wandering, she decided. Tony had never been able to interpret the words of the banshee. Only she and Juliet could.

''Please,'' he whispered. ''You must promise. There's very little time.''

''Grandfather . . .'' Tears started to Lucy's eyes as she fell on her knees beside the bed.

''The gold,'' he urged. ''Let me see you take the gold and put it in your pocket. Take it, now.''

To humor him, she obeyed.

''Put the knob back in place . . . else he will know.''

''He?''

''Matthais . . .'' Tony whispered. ''He waits, and you must promise . . .'' He broke off, staring past her. ''Ah, my love, my Felicity, is it you then?''

''*Tony, my dearest, dearest, come.*''

Lucy felt rather than heard the words, but on glancing over her shoulder, she saw the girl, slender like herself, and knew that she resembled her grandmother even more closely than the portrait revealed.

She shifted her gaze to her grandfather and saw that his eyes were as ardent as those of the young man he had been so many years ago. He held out his arms, and with her heightened vision, Lucy rejoiced at their passionate embrace.

A second later, Tony lay very still but his lips were yet curved in that tender and welcoming smile.

The Seventh Earl of More had been interred in the crypt for a day and the half of another one when Bob Smith came riding toward the Hold, choosing the same way, had he but known it, that Richard Veringer had come close to a century ago. Passing the battered remains of an ancient gibbet, Bob's horse reared and snorted, snuffling as his rider soothed and gentled him. Crossing the sagging drawbridge, he urged his stallion into a gallop and a few minutes later dismounted and tied the animal to a nearby post.

Running up to the front door, he raised the rusty old knocker and let it fall again and again, slamming it against the plate as hard as he could, until the butler, muttering to himself, pulled open the assaulted portal. He started back with a cry which mingled anger and alarm as Bob rushed into the hall.

"Here, you," the butler proclaimed, drawing himself up to his full height which unfortunately did not exceed that of Mr. Smith's five and sixty inches. "Ye can't come in here as if you was Lord'n Master!"

"I've got to see Miss Lucy," Bob cried.

"Miss Lucy's not receiving."

"I tell you, I've got to see her!" Bob yelled.

"And I tell you, you'll go around to the back door . . ."

"What is it, Angus?" Lucy asked from the first landing.

The ancient butler gazed up at her apologetically. "This person . . ." he began loftily.

"Miss Lucy." Bob Smith hurried toward the steps as she came down them, looking pale and drained in her black gown. On the landing above her, Mark stood watching, his golden eyes somber.

Bob said, "They be acomin' up 'ere, Miss Lucy an' uh . . . Mr. Mark." His glance slid between the two of them. "That Mr. Veringer, 'im wot says 'e's now the earl an' owner

o' the castle. 'E's got 'em, them wot 'angs around the tavern
an' a few o' the lads wot's always spoilin' for a bit o' mischief.
'E's got 'em all riled up. 'E says 'e's goin' to burn the castle
an' them as lies in the graveyard, miss, as well. 'E says e's
goin' to put stakes through their 'earts. 'E's got the carpenter
sawin' up wood for 'em now . . . an' the blacksmith's 'eatin'
up 'is forge to make a silver bullet, same as wot done for your
pa, Mr. Mark, only this time it'll be for you.''

"But . . . but that's madness!" Lucy burst out.

"An' so me'n Jane told 'em, Miss Lucy, but they be all
riled up on account of Mr. Veringer 'n wot 'e's sayin'. Cor,
but 'e be a poor lookin' sort, all bent over'n shakin' in every
limb like 'e 'as the palsy—only 'e says as 'ow 'e were done in
by them wot lives in the castle.''

"It was his own cowardice that did for him," Mark said
contemptuously. "God, I wish they'd let me at him that
night.''

"Shhhh." Lucy shot a warning glance at him. "You know
you don't mean that." She turned back to Bob. "When will
they be here?" she demanded.

"Just after the sun goes down. They'll be goin' to the crypt
first wi' their stakes. They're makin' three o' 'em. One for
the old Lord wot just died.''

"Damn them!" Mark exploded. "Tony's no . . .''

"Will you help us, Bob?" Lucy demanded briskly.

"I will that, miss. Wouldn't be 'ere if I didn't mean to
'elp ye.''

"You'd help us even if there were things we had
to . . . remove from the crypt?''

"I'll help you, too, Miss Lucy," quavered the old butler.
"I'm not afraid o' Lord and Lady Veringer, an' cook'll lend a
hand, too.''

"Me, too," Bob said staunchly.

Lucy regarded them through eyes brightened by her tears.
"You know," she said.

"Of course they know, Lucy," Mark said. "And since that
information's shared by most the village, we'd best get to
work.''

They stood on a distant tree-covered hill but one that
commanded an excellent view of the castle, watching the

small torch lit procession cross the bridge that spanned the moat. Lucy leaned against Mark, who had slipped an arm around her waist. Juliet and Colin were also side by side and, above them, a tree shook violently, even though there was very little wind. A short distance away from them, Bob Smith and Jane Warren sat, arms clasping their knees. Stacked beside them were a pile of canvases taken from the portrait gallery. Those and whatever garments could be piled into three large stout trunks were all that had been removed from the castle. Also with them were two coffins from the crypt and a bag of stones dug from the graveyard.

The small procession went into the castle, and in what seemed a very few minutes, the windows of the great edifice gleamed as red as if they were mirroring the rays of the dying sun.

Above the watchers on the hill a high wind seemed to hurl itself toward the Hold, its shriek even louder than that of Molly and her cat. To Lucy, it sounded like a dirge, but to the Old Lord, who had once been called Richard Veringer, its strident cadences issued from the throat of Erlina Bell.

TWO

The complications attendant on traveling to Liverpool and boarding the steamship Eastern Queen were augmented by the fact that Bob Smith and his Jane could not leave on the same ship after all. Due to the illness of Jane's mother, they had to postpone their wedding to a later date. Consequently most of the arrangements for train and ship were handled by Mark and Lucy. Fortunately, this kept them from grieving too deeply over the demise of Tony and the razing of their ancestral castle.

Since it was not possible to take all the portraits, Lucy left a number of them in storage against the day when they might return, or so she told herself. Though they had booked a one-way passage, it was necessary to think of returning, otherwise the idea of leaving the Hold and England, too, would be overwhelming. Such thoughts had to be given short shrift as they prepared to embark.

The disposal of the two coffins presented a real problem. The man who booked the passage was definitely reluctant to take them aboard.

"I don't know what the passengers'd say, Miss Veringer, if they was to know there was two bodies goin' wi' 'em." He shook his head. "There's enough o' 'em as is queasy to begin with."

Fortunately, he was not proof against Lucy's sorrowful contenance and the sparkle of tears in her gentian blue eyes, as she feelingly spoke of her dearest aunt and uncle's final wish to be buried in the New World they had left only to be felled in England by a virulent attack of the grippe.

Much to the relief of herself and especially Mark, the steamer would sail with the new moon, docking in Boston a scant ten days later, well in advance of the full moon. Still, when she finally stood with Mark on deck watching the shores of England recede, she was much less easy in her mind than she had hoped. Much as she did not want to anticipate trouble, she was thinking of her pending debut as a medium, and she was definitely nervous.

"*No need to be.*"

Lucy tensed and then smiled. Implicit in her great-grandfather's reasoning was his promise that he would aid her. He had spoken vaguely about sources, but he had suggested that his acquaintance with the departed was wide, at least in England. He saw no reason why that should not hold true in America as well. Though comforted, she still wished that Tony might have added his own reassurances.

"*Gone.*"

She nodded sympathetically, knowing that the Old Lord mourned his son and had wistfully hoped he might remain earthbound, too. But Tony suffered enough in life, Lucy thought suddenly, remembering the look of happiness on his face when the wraith which had been Felicity Veringer entered his room. She had looked so young, no more than a girl. She had been young when she died bearing Felix. It was sad to die without ever knowing your child, sad to die leaving behind you another loved one and sad, too, for the bereaved husband. Tony had never wanted to marry again or even contemplated such a step, she knew. Felicity had been the love of his life—but Felix, the son he had also loved deeply, had been the bane of his existence.

"You made up for everything, Lucy," he had often said. And he had made up to her for the lack of father and mother, too. The only real sorrow she had ever known was his passing. She almost, wished . . . no, she did not want him to return!

He was freed from the curse at last and gone with Felicity, who had not escaped it either. And what of herself? Save for Tony's passing, she had been very happy, at least since the departure of her grandmother. But what of the future?

She stared at the receding shore still glowing brightly in the summer sunshine, the days lasting long at this time of year. The port was not a particularly lovely sight, but if she had been looking at the Hold . . . She bit her lip. To think of that, as she had last seen it, a twisted mass of burnt wood and fallen stones with not a single tower remaining, was appalling. She brushed a hand across her eyes.

"Homesick already, miss?"

Lucy, looked up, saw that Mark was no longer beside her. In his place was a tall fair young man with dark blue eyes and a sweep of dark wavy hair. He had a long face, clean shaven, which she liked. His cheekbones were high and a jutting nose had a bump in the middle, as if it might have been broken. She also liked his mouth which was neither thin nor full but suggested strength as did his square, cleft chin. If his features were not classic, they were still handsome. Strangely enough, Lucy felt as if she had known him for a long time, as if she was meeting an old friend.

She smiled up at him, saying, "I'm not really homesick, sir. I . . ." She paused in consternation. She had been about to tell him that she really never had a home, which was ridiculous since she had been born in the Hold and had lived there all her life—but by the bounty of others, she realized. Though her grandfather might have disputed that strongly as well as her great-grandfather, had he been there, which fortunately he was not, she had been an unexpected visitor. She had been dropped from the loins of betrayed Mary Crowell as Matthais Veringer had been only too eager to point out.

The man at her side said, "But you are British, are you not?"

"Indeed, yes," she assented, and hearing a certain something in his tone, she added, "But you're not."

"No, ma'am, I'm American, born and bred. Boston's my home port. Are you bound for Boston?"

"Most assuredly, sir."

"I like the way you said that, as if you had more than a

mere visit in mind.''

"Yes, it will be more than a visit, sir.''

"Lucy!'' Mark had stepped to her side again. He put a possessive hand on her arm, his golden gaze cool as he looked quizzically at the stranger, whom she realized all at once *was* a stranger. She had not felt that way when they were talking. She had actually regarded him as a friend. Meeting Mark's disapproving stare, she said, ''This gentleman's from Boston, Cousin Mark.''

Mark looked startled, as well he might since she had never before addressed him in so formal a manner. "Oh? And whom might I have the pleasure of addressing?'' he demanded, his tone as chill as his glance.

"Swithin Blake,'' the American replied in tones quite as cold as those of Mark. ''And you, sir?''

"Marcus Driscoll.''

"And you?'' Mr. Blake's blue eyes rested appreciatively upon Lucy's face.

"I am Lucy Veringer,'' she said quickly.

"I am delighted to make your acquaintance, Miss Veringer.'' Mr. Blake smiled and bowed. ''And yours, too, Mr. Driscoll,'' he said in less enthusiastic tones.

"Your servant, sir.'' Mark inclined his head, adding peremptorily, ''Lucy, you are needed below.''

"Am I?'' Distress filled her. Had something gone amiss wit the coffins? Had they opened when they were put into the hold? A glance at Mark's face told her nothing. ''Oh, I must go,'' she said nervously.

"I do hope we will meet again, Miss Veringer.'' Swithin Blake's eyes were eager.

"I hope so, too.'' She spoke without thinking and felt Mark's hand tighten on her arm. ''I meant . . .'' She blushed.

"I am in hopes that you meant exactly what you said, Miss Veringer,'' Mr. Blake replied and bowed.

In the confines of her cabin, Lucy listened to a stern lecture on the inadvisability of coversing with strangers, particularly of the masculine persuasion. She had never seen Mark's golden eyes so angry. There was almost a snarl in his voice as he described and denounced her lack of decorum in addressing someone to whom she had never been properly introduced.

She listened abashedly, her eyes downcast, well-aware that she deserved her scolding, yet resenting it, too. However, by the time he had stalked out of the cabin, she had come to her senses. She never should have spoken so readily to Mr. Swithin Blake. She had quite forgotten her situation and her responsibilities. It behooved her to remember that she was not like other young women. She was a member of a household that contained among its immediate members, a werewolf, two vampires, a ghost, a banshee and a phantom cat. Much as she adored them all, she was quite sure that a stranger, even a handsome young man with the most beautiful dark blue eyes, who had looked at her in a way that had loosed flocks of butterflies in her chest and other areas, would not welcome so unusual a set of in-laws. She blushed rosily, wondering why she should think of marriage in connection with someone she had just met and whom unfortunately she must make every effort to avoid during the days it took the Eastern Queen to steam across the Atlantic.

Hard on that decision, she heard a most melancholy wail and accompanying it an affronted screech. Obviously, Molly and Grimalkin were in agreement with her, she thought dolefully, but on listening more closely, she was puzzled. Molly sounded very strange, as did Grimalkin. Rather than issuing warnings, they both seemed to be complaining. In another moment, she was sure she knew why. Not only had they never been so far from the "auld sod" but they were on shipboard and the motion of the boat was not agreeing with them.

"Oh, dear, it is so boring," Juliet muttered to Colin as they stood at the railing looking up at a midnight sky etched with stars seen through a gossamer veiling of mist.

"Boring," he repeated automatically. In his mind, he was garnering the imagery of the night for the canvas he was contemplating.

"Do you not find it so?" she asked. "Visiting them in their cabins while they sleep and never having so much as a proper conversation?"

He fixed a stern eye on his sister. "You are developing into an incorrigible flirt," he chided. "I thought we'd agreed . . ."

"I agree with our agreement," she assured him, "but I cannot help it if I prefer the preliminaries." She tossed her head. "And most of them snore. They also have bad breath. I never notice that when they're awake."

"*I* never look a gift horse in the mouth," Colin said pointedly. He smiled and his fangs gleamed white in the uncertain moonlight.

"Oh, dear, are you going?" Juliet inquired disappointedly.

"I fear I must, my darling."

"I shouldn't have talked about it, then you wouldn't have become thirsty." She spoke to the empty air. Her brother had gone.

Juliet pouted and stared down at the waves. They were touched with phosphoresence and very beautiful, but though she might have admired the sight at another time, talking about *it* had also made her thirsty. She touched her jutting fangs with the tip of her tongue and wondered if the Captain had retired yet. He was a big man, and the veins in his neck were large and inviting. She would not take much from him though. It would not do to have the man at the helm incapacitated.

"Might I ask who you are?" inquired a stern voice to her left.

Juliet turned quickly and saw a tall young officer frowning at her. Mindful of her teeth, she gave him a small closed smile. "Good evening, sir," she said lightly.

His eyes widened as she knew they would once he glimpsed her moonlight-tinted face. Though she had not seen her own features since her transition, Colin had often sketched them for her, and she was well-aware of their effect upon men. He, she noted, was extremely good-looking. His hair was a dark auburn and his eyes an entrancing green. Even his uniform was most becoming. He had, she recalled, asked her a question. "It's a lovely night, isn't it?" she inquired softly.

"That is no answer!" His stern, searching glance did not waver.

"My name is Juliet," she murmured.

"Juliet what?" he snapped.

She gazed at him delightedly. He was going to prove difficult. In spite of the fact that she and Colin had agreed, in fact sworn, not to arouse suspicions by any overt advances, it was quite impossible for her to resist a challenge. And he, the darling boy, was making such a determined effort to resist her.

"Why do you want to know my name?" she asked, her wide eyes on his face.

"I've not seen you on board," he responded accusingly.

"Have you seen everyone on board?"

"Everyone in First Class. Where have you been?"

"Ill in my cabin. This is my first night out."

"I'm not sure I believe you."

"Do you think I'm a stowaway? You're wrong. My passage is bought and paid for."

"Is it?"

Juliet's excitement increased. He still sounded doubtful. He was going to provide rare sport, and he was lovely—so tall, so handsome and, best of all, awake! "Should you like to come with me to my cabin and see my tickets?" she asked softly.

He blushed and replied gruffly. "There's no need to do that. I expect I was mistaken."

"I'd be glad to show them to you," Juliet persisted. Lucy had purchased a sitting room, one reserved for the convenience of herself and her brother. It adjoined Lucy's cabin, but she always went to bed early. Juliet did not think Colin would be using it. Once he arrived at a decision, he stuck to it. She usually did, too, but occasionally she gave herself a little leeway. Her eyes shone as she saw that the officer was beginning to breathe deeply. "Come." She dared to put her little hand on his arm. "I do want to set your mind at ease."

"Well," he capitulated. "I think it would be best."

He was a rather clumsy lover, Juliet decided as she bit deep into his neck. She sipped slowly and thoughtfully, taking just enough and no more. It was so much nicer to be loved, especially by a young man, far better to be excited and exhilarated than merely sustained. He was such a nice boy, too. As for his lovemaking, she was sure that with a little instruction on her part, that would improve. Only she had better keep this encounter to herself. Colin would be extremely annoyed. She did not think she had aroused her officer's suspicions. She was sure of it when at length he awakened. He was extremely embarrassed and apologetic to the point of tears for having fallen asleep in her arms. His fingers shook so much as he put on his garments that she had to fasten all his buttons. However, at the last he said, as she had known he would, "When can I see you again?"

"Tomorrow?" she murmured.

"Unfortunately," he said regretfully, "I have night detail."

"Do you consider that . . . unfortunate?" she drawled.

"Juliet!" he exclaimed ecstatically as he embraced her.

"William," she responded with a touch of that same ecstasy, thinking that he would last at least the eight remaining days of the voyage—that is, if she husbanded those resources, and she would certainly make every effort to do so.

"But I want to take William with us!" Juliet said sulkily. Colin glared at her. "That is out of the question!"

If it had been possible for Juliet to weep, she would have made play with her long tear-tipped lashes but that effort was denied her. "He will be one of us soon," she stated.

"Not if the ship's doctor gives him a transfusion, which he will do," Mark said coldly. "I have alerted him to his condition."

"Mark!" Juliet glared at him. "What gave you the right to interfere?"

"Juliet," Colin said, "our life's complicated enough, and furthermore if your paramour were to die aboard this ship, they would drop him into the sea. I hesitate to contemplate the exigencies attendant upon an undead life at forty fathoms."

"Oh, dear, how ghastly!" Juliet brushed a hand across her dry eyes.

"Cheer up," her brother said briskly. "You'll find someone else. You always do."

"You have no heart," Juliet retorted. Then, looking at him, she added quickly, "Oh, I didn't mean it, you know I didn't." She stretched out both hands to him.

He took them, holding them gently. "I know you didn't, my dear. And I know how difficult it can be . . . all this."

"So difficult." She nodded, moving closer to him. "And I expect you're right. William would be a complication. I suppose I shouldn't have encouraged him, but it's so tedious the other way."

"Extremely tedious," Colin agreed dryly. "But come, my sweet, it grows early and I suggest we go along to rest."

"Yes, I am tired." She yawned. "Good night, Lucy."

"Good night, darling. Good night, Colin, love," Lucy said warmly. "It will be better in Boston, you'll see."

After they had gone, Lucy gave Mark a grateful look. "How did you find out?" she asked.

"One night when I couldn't sleep, I saw them."

"I'm ever so pleased you told the doctor," she said. "But how did you explain his condition?"

"I said he appeared to be anemic."

"Oh, that was clever!" she said approvingly. "If Juliet had persisted, it would have been a most unfortunate entanglement, not only for her but for all of us."

"Speaking of unfortunate entanglements, I must compliment you on the adroit way you've avoided Mr. Blake," Mark praised.

Lucy said resignedly, "What else could I do?" Looking up at him, she added quickly with what she hoped was a realistic yawn, "I really am tired, dear Mark. I simply must retire for what little remains of this night. Tomorrow will be such a complicated day."

"Very well, Lucy," he agreed reluctantly. "I expect you do need your sleep." He kissed her lightly on the cheek, and a second later the cabin door closed softly behind him.

Lucy directed a regretful look at the door. Mark's feelings for her were becoming more and more obvious. Fortunately, he was also aware that it was futile to hope that anything could ever come to fruition between them. He had condemned himself to perpetual bachelorhood, and she, herself, dared not think of an alternate alliance.

She had avoided Swithin Blake by having all her meals sent to her cabin, thus preventing a chance meeting in the dining salon. In taking the air, she seldom strayed far from her door.

Once she had seen him at a distance, but he had been walking with an attractive young woman, who had been visiting languishing glances on his handsome profile. Watching them, Lucy had experienced a sensation closely allied with pain. Yet conversely, she had been pleased that he was enjoying himself—or rather she had told herself that she ought to be pleased, which was practically the same thing, though a smidgin less noble.

She was glad that they were docking on the morrow. Undoubtedly, she would never see him again. Then, it would be easy to forget him. After all, she had only spoken to him once, and no one could fall in love so quickly—or if they could, they shouldn't. Only poets and romantic novelists believed in love at first sight. Lucy, feeling moisture in her eyes, angrily brushed it away.

"I *shall* forget him," she vowed. She meant what she said but much to her chagrin, she found upon waking the following morning that she had no control whatever over her dreams.

She saw him once more, when they were disembarking. She had been confused and daunted by the sight of the bustling port of Boston and by the knowledge that they were an ocean away from England. For the first time she also feared that she would never be able to return to her country again. No use to tell herself that it was far too early to be homesick. How could she be otherwise, faced with this unknown land and hearing such a cacophony of voices, all of which seemed louder than any she had ever heard before? Then, just ahead of her, she saw the tall, slender figure of a young man and did not even need a glimpse of his face to tell her that he was Swithin Blake.

His name sprang to her tongue, but of course she dared not utter it with Mark's hand so firmly on her arm. She could only wish that he might turn around and see her which, of course, he would not do. In common with all other returning travelers, he would be scanning the upturned faces of the crowds below for whoever had come to meet hm. He would not be walking friendless into Boston. And nor was she, she recalled. Mark was by her side, the Old Lord was hovering somewhere about, probably doing a bit of a sightseeing, while Molly and the cat, quite recovered from their ordeals on shipboard, were softly keening. In a short while, she and Mark would have reclaimed their luggage and the coffins, and by the time they arrived at their hotel, the family would be reunited!

Lucy sighed for no reason and stepping forward suddenly caught her toe in a plank and stumbled. Despite Mark's sustaining arm, she was catapulated against Swithin Blake's back.

He turned instantly and steadied her, while she blushed and murmured apologies rendered half-inarticulate by her confusion. She became even more confused on meeting his eyes which, for an instant, reflected a happy surprise. However that faded, almost immediately to be replaced by a chill that also coated his tones as he said, "Miss Veringer, is it not?"

"Yes, Mr. Blake, it is," she acknowledged softly. And then, before she could call them back, the words slipped out. "So good to see you again."

The chill vanished. "My pleasure, ma'am," he replied. "Welcome to Boston—both of you."

He looked as if he might have said more but at that moment someone called in a high, sweet feminine voice, "Swithin, my dear!"

He tipped his hat, waved at the caller, blew her a kiss, gave them another smile and hurried down the gangplank as quickly as he could. Soon, all too soon, he was lost amongst the crowds.

Mark said unnecessarily," Come Lucy, we must hurry."

Lucy was sorrowfully pleased—or was she pleasantly sorrowful? The way of it didn't matter. She had seen him again and had spoken with him, however briefly and obviously he had been hurt by her deliberate avoidance of himself. If he had been hurt, that meant he cared enough to be hurt. The implications of that were scarcely comforting, but they were something to remember—even if that memory proved regretful. And despite the fact that he had only heard it once and then ten whole days previously, he had not forgotten her name.

"*Balderdash*!"

The Old Lord was back from his sightseeing tour. "It's not," she mouthed defiantly.

"Who could forget your name once having met you?"

Lucy blushed and softly apologized for having misunderstood him. She was also glad he had joined them. His presence brought her out of her futile daydreams. It was time to get on with the business of the day, the night, Boston and a dwelling place. Though that was the last thing that had occurred to her, it was the first they must seek. The moon was increasing, and they could hardly put Mark in the cellar of some hotel! It would be equally difficult to leave the coffins in their room since most hotel maids came in without knocking.

Much as she missed him, Lucy was doubly glad her grandfather had not joined what she and Mark were, for sentimental reasons, formally calling the Household. He had been so adamant concerning her disposal of those coins he had given her on the night of his death.

On arriving in Liverpool, she had taken them to a numismatist, who gazed at them in wonder and then offered her a very small price for them. Even without the Old Lord nattering in her ear, she would have refused him. She had gone to several shops where she had received much the same treatment with each dealer trembling with rage as she refused and left. She had been about to give up when she had spied a little hole in the wall with a dirty glass window on which was inscribed in curly gold letters, *Isaacson, Coins*. She had hesitated at the entrance and then something, she was not sure what, had urged her inside. The dealer, a small, bent man with shaggy hair and equally shaggy eyebrows had peered up at her suspiciously, as if he were expecting to be gulled. However, when she produced her bag and showed him the coins, he had emitted a long quavering breath and stared at them in wonder, handling them with a tenderness and a respect that had made her want to cry.

"A bit o' history, my dear," he had murmured. "Drake was alive when this was coined . . . and maybe this was paid to a lad named Will, who'd once held horses outside the theaters, but of course it wouldn't have been a tip, it would've been payment for his scribbling. And this . . . look how its singed. Maybe it survived the Great Fire . . ." He had gone on giving her bits and pieces of England's past while she hoped against hope he would offer her the fair price none of the others had so much as mentioned. He had given her more than she expected. He had emptied an old battered box he had taken from beneath a plank in the floor, shoveling the money into her hands, muttering, ''Just to have them, my dear; just to touch them.''

Somehow she was quite sure her grandfather would not have protested that exchange, just as she was equally sure none of those gold pieces would ever be sold on the market. They would be kept in another secret place. Meanwhile she had the price of a house. It only remained to find it.

The moon was beginning to bulge dangerously, and Mark was so edgy that he could not accompany Lucy on a search which was becoming very discouraging. The sum she received from the dealer had seemed princely, but while she could have purchased a house, none that Mr. Soames, an enterprising young real estate agent, showed her were adequate. Either they were too new or too old, and all were far too small; she was close to despair.

Meeting her in the lobby of her hotel on the third day since they disembarked, the agent said hesitantly, ''There is a house that does fit your specifications, but . . . there is a drawback.''

''Drawback?'' Lucy repeated, finding that for no particular reason she felt excited rather than dispirited. ''What manner of drawback?''

''It's quite old,'' he said deprecatingly. ''It does have a lot of room, but there is it's location. It's very near the cemetery.''

She wanted to clap her hands. She wanted to waltz around the lobby. It was with considerable difficulty she retained a grave demeanor. ''My situation is quite desperate. My cousin's not well. Hotel food does not seem to agree with him, so if you would be so good as to show me the house, possibly I can bear with its situation.''

He looked crestfallen. ''It would hardly seem to me that a lady like yourself would be happy in such surroundings. Though it is large, it has been vacant for quite some time. There are rats. You'd need a cat or two.''

''That would present no difficulties.'' Lucy's excitement was increasing. She wanted to be polite but she did wish this young man were not so reluctant to show her the only house that might have real possibilities. "Might we go, please?" she prompted.

He nodded, still not stirring. "It was originally built as a manse, but the church to which it was attached burnt down a decade ago under very suspicious circumstances."

"Really?" Lucy managed not to appear pleased. Was he suggesting that it was haunted? She hoped so. The Old Lord was lonely and disappointed that none of his immediate family had joined him. He did converse with Molly, but he often had complained that not only was her Irish dialect a barrier but that intellectually she left much to be desired. Furthermore, his encounter with Erlina Bell had given him a definite prejudice regarding witches. Trying not to sound too hopeful, Lucy asked, "Is the house reputed to be haunted?"

He stared down at the carpet, saying equivocally, "There are a great many superstitious people in the city, especially since the influx of Irish in the last twenty-odd years. Not that they aren't a most delightful group of people," he added hastily. "There are a number living a short distance away from that house."

It sounded so absolutely ideal that Lucy could contain her impatience no longer. "Oh, do let's see it," she urged.

"Very well," he responded. Evidently, he felt it incumbent to add, "It was a very nice house when it was first built."

"When was it built?"

"At least a half century ago."

"That's not very old, not by our standards."

"Well, perhaps it will appeal to you," he said doubtfully, his admiring gaze on her face.

The house not only appealed to Lucy, it delighted her! He had not mentioned the trees, the elderly oaks, the tall elms and the red beeches. They stood close to its walls, their spreading branches with their summer coating of leaves obscuring some of the side windows. The building itself was four square, and there was a tangled growth of vines clinging to its brick facade. A massive front door was framed by two pillars, and there was a matching side door. The fact that the pillars were wooden and splintered and that the shutters that framed the eight windows facing front were askew meant nothing to Lucy. They could easily be mended and righted. Her main interest lay in the interior—with emphasis upon the cellar Mark would soon require.

She did like the way the rooms were situated. Rather than interlocking as they had in the castle and many older houses at home, with one room leading into the next, these had adjoining doors but also opened on a wide hall. On the lower floor there was a drawing room, a dining room, a library and a parlor. A kitchen and laundry room were in the rear. A wooden staircase in the hall led to four bedrooms on the second floor and to three smaller chambers and an attic under the mansard roof.

Happily, the rooms were commodious. True, it would take a lot of work to get the place in order. It was badly in need of repair. Plaster was peeling from the walls, and some of the bricks in the six fireplaces were dislodged. There was also a smell of mold, and though there was a large bathroom upstairs, evidently added by later tenants, its plumbing needed to be replaced. However, that could easily be done and would be—if only the cellar proved adequate!

Since the gas lighting in the nether regions of the house was very uncertain, Mr. Soames had recourse to a candle to light Lucy down the rickety stairs. He made excuses all the way, but on reaching the bottom she was delighted to find two more rooms, each with stout doors and small narrow windows. Evidently no one had ventured into them for a good many years. In the uncertain light from the candle, she could see cobwebs hanging from the ceiling. Generations of spiders had spun their webs across the windows and a dead bat lay on the floor. There were also rat droppings and a definite odor of mice and mold, but none of these obscured the fact that it was all quite, quite perfect.

Clasping her hands, Lucy raised speaking blue eyes to Mr. Soames' unhappy face. "It's lovely. It might have been made for him!" she exclaimed and immediately blushed, feeling rather than seeing his astonishment. "My cousin enjoys carpentry," she improvised hastily. "He'll find these rooms a real challenge." She added, "I must tell you that I love the house!"

"You do!" he exclaimed, adding dubiously, "Do you

think your cousin will agree?''

"Oh, I am sure he will. It's just right for the . . .'' She paused, feeling another blush heating her cheeks. She had been about to say "the household" but that would have sounded a bit ridiculous considering that she was supposedly talking only about herself and Mark. "Two of us," she finished.

"Well," the agent said, as they ascended the stairs, "I expect we can talk terms."

"Please." Lucy smiled, and her smile broadened as they returned to the drawing room. Until this moment, she had not noticed that its side windows faced the graveyard, just across a narrow street and behind a wrought iron fence. In her immediate vision were tombstones, variously surmounted by angels with widespread wings, by baskets of stone flowers and by admirably carved wreathes topped by mourning doves. She could also see a spread of clipped green lawns between them and graveled paths flanked by ornate iron benches with floral carved backs and legs in the shape of twining leaves.

"I wonder," she said. "Do they have crypts in that cemetery?"

"They do," he said, "but they're not selling so well. Most folks prefer a single gravestone."

"Oh, lovely!" Lucy cried, excited by this double-barreled response. Meeting his curious stare, she knew she was blushing again. Since there was no way she could explain her enthusiasm, she said merely, "I am completely satisfied with the house, sir. Do let's talk terms. The sooner my cousin and I can take possession of these premises, the better it will be." Scanning his face, she realized that in his estimation, this latter statement needed even more explanation. That didn't trouble her. Nothing could trouble her now that the Household had found a home which, she was sure, must be the refuge they all desired.

She wondered if the Old Lord agreed but received no corroboration. Evidently, he must still be mourning their expulsion from the Hold. As for herself, she felt singularly light-hearted. She was sure that by now the curse had been lifted. After all, its terms had been met—and fully. They had been expelled from the castle and even had seen it destroyed exactly as Erlina Bell's cottage had fallen. They had taken to the road and to the sea as well. Surely the witch must be satisfied!

On hearing her hypothesis, Mark disagreed. "If the curse were lifted, I'd be cured," he said morosely.

"Maybe you will be."

"Not with the way I feel."

"Oh, my dear, if there were only some way I could help you," Lucy cried.

"You've helped me more than anyone in my entire life—your sweetness, your kindness to me, to all of us. Oh, Lucy," his voice broke, "I do love you so much!"

Tears filled her eyes. "I love you, Mark, but . . ."

"I know, my dear," he said with a gentle resignation that wrung her heart. "I wish I could love you in that same calm way, my dearest. Oh God, I am accursed."

"So are we all, Mark," she reminded him with a slight sigh, realizing in that moment that of course Erlina Bell's vengeful spirit was not yet appeased. More had been destroyed than her cottage. There had been that mysterious elixir, the properties of which remained unknown.

"You aren't cursed, Lucy," Mark said positively. "Your sorrows are behind you."

Also behind her was Swithin Blake, who still walked through her dreams, but Lucy chose not to mention him to Mark. It would only increase the pain. Instead she said, "I can hardly wait until you see the house. I know you'll find it to your liking."

They all found it to their liking. They were particularly pleased because it appeared older than its years. Juliet and Colin immediately appropriated the rooms overlooking the graveyard. Their coffins would be placed in them, but only temporarily because they agreed with Lucy that a crypt would be infinitely more satisfactory. As Juliet remarked to Lucy, "There must be some of our own kind around, and besides we'll need to know more about Boston."

"Of course," Lucy agreed, glad that Juliet had not amplified her comment.

Mark and Lucy would have the other two bedrooms. However, on the night they moved in, the cellar received all their attention. Equipped with hammers, brooms, mops and buckets of plaster, Lucy, Mark, Colin and Juliet swept, scrubbed, mended and pounded. The Old Lord watched, while higher up Molly and the cat tried to accustom themselves to a house without ramparts and with numerous chimneys rising in inconvenient places on the roof. Their combined wailing sounded more fretful than ominous.

Three

As they worked in the cellar, Lucy, remembering Mr. Soames' vague references to suspicious fires and superstitious people, had hoped that for her great-grandfather's sake some manner of specter might emerge to mitigate his loneliness. However, by the time the first rays of sun were coloring the eastern horizon, she decided that the manse's quesionable reputation was based on appearance alone. Old, vacant, vine-shrouded, tree-shadowed dwellings always looked as if they were inhabited by disembodied spirits. This house was, as she regretfully observed to Mark, singularly free of phantoms.

His smile was wry. "It's well that it's also some distance away from traveled paths, else I'd be lending plenty of corroboration to the gossip. As it is, my love, we'll need to depend on you for that."

She laughed. If the truth were to be told, she was not really amused. Mark had belatedly reminded her of the reason for their presence in Boston. They were there because Juliet had overheard Bob Smith discussing spiritualistic phenomena with his fiancée, and she, Lucy Veringer, was going to add to the household resources by becoming a medium! But how?

There was a possibility that Bob had attended some of the

mediumistic circles in the city. Unfortunately she could not apply to him for information. That meant that she and Mark, when he recuperated, would need to attend some spiritual-istic meetings so she would be able to inquire into the practices of the mediums. And where might these be found? She doubted that they advertised in the newspapers. Once they had furnished the house, she would have to make discreet inquiries. No, she reasoned regretfully, she would have to delve into the subject before the house was completely finished. Their money was dwindling, and more would go in furnishing eight large rooms and the kitchen. She would do nothing to the top floor; they could not hire servants. She and Mark would divide the household duties and, as they had that night, Juliet and Colin would help out when they could. That was a real sacrifice on their part, Lucy thought grate-fully. Generally, they did not like to remain in the vicinity of their home. Not only did their continued presence give rise to some awkward questions regarding their habit of turning night into day, but they dearly loved to travel and, in Colin's case, paint. In addition to his portraits, he had done some admirable landscapes. Three of these—*Moonlight on the Thames, Night Scene in the Ruins of Athens* and *Midnight in the Colosseum*—were hanging in the Royal Academy.

She hoped he would be similarly successful here. Judging from what she had seen of the city, night would be kinder to Boston than daylight. Lucy released a small sigh. She was feeling homesick and she must not give into that. She must not let her thoughts be diverted from her duties. She went on up the stairs to the trunk in which she had packed Mark's collar and chains. As she went, she wished that the full moon would arrive later, but despite what she had heard about American enterprise, she doubted that even the Yankees had any control over the movements of heavenly bodies.

During Mark's confinement in the cellar Lucy did not leave the house. His howling and growling were louder and much more violent than usual. These were accompanied by rattling of his chains and by loud thumps as he threw himself against the doors in a frenzied attempt to escape. Fortunately they had reinforced the doors, and of course the windows were far too small to allow either egress or access. It was bad during the day—and it was terrible at night.

In the back parlor, sitting on three rickety chairs found in the attic, Colin, Juliet and Lucy regarded each other unhappily.

"It's probably the new location," Colin remarked after one particularly long and fearsome howl.

"Doesn't he know we've emigrated?" Lucy asked.

"*He* knows, but the beast in him does not," Juliet sighed. "It must be quite disoriented."

"Poor, poor Mark." Lucy wrung her hands.

"Poor on many counts," Juliet agreed soberly, her eyes on Lucy's face.

"I wish I could love him in the way he wants," Lucy whispered.

"You mustn't even consider it!" Colin warned.

"One werewolf's enough for Boston," Juliet agreed.

"Have you found any . . . friends?" Lucy asked delicately.

Juliet and Colin looked at each other and laughed soundlessly. "More than you'd believe," Colin commented.

"Some you wouldn't believe."

"I am never surprised by the number of politicians that swell our ranks," Colin observed.

The air became noticeably colder, and the windows rattled.

"Good evening, Father." Juliet rose and curtseyed.

"Good evening, sir," Colin echoed. He added interestedly, "Were you able to find out anything?"

Lucy raised her head and looked about her hopefully. The Old Lord had been scouting seances for her.

"*Amateurs, scalawags, magicians, scoundrels. Only one with any pretension to psychic power.*"

"One's all that's needed!" Lucy exclaimed excitedly.

"Do you have her name?" Juliet cried.

"Who is she?" Colin asked.

"*Her name is Sophronia Sloane.*"

They had found the name amusing, but when Lucy, armed with the Old Lord's succinct description of the lady's direction—street, house and number—found herself outside the cottage in question, she felt unaccountably nervous. She should have been reassured by the very ordinariness of the place, she told herself. Mrs. Sloane's one-story cottage reminded her of the tenant's dwellings near the Hold. It stood on a small plot of ground, slightly removed from a row of similar houses, distinguished from each other mainly by color and by elaborate jigsaw trimmings on the porches. Sophronia Sloane's house was constructed of grey clapboard. It had small, shutter-framed windows and a shingled roof. A neat lawn was divided by the flagstone path that led to a pair of steps going up to a porch just large enough to allow for a small hammock and a white wicker chair. An oak tree grew hard by one window, while masses of white and lavender sweetpeas and two pink hydrangea bushes grew on either side of the steps. In front of the house gold letters on a black signboard announced that Mrs. Sloane gave "readings" by appointment only. On Tuesdays, she conducted a "circle," for which one also needed an appointment.

Hesitating at the far end of the path, Lucy looked dubiously at the square, brown, uncompromising bulwark of the front door. She wondered if her nervousness could be ascribed to the fact that she had seldom gone anywhere alone. At home Mark had nearly always accompanied her to the village, but though he was recovered, the members of the Household decided he must remain behind. The Old Lord insisted that Mrs. Sloane was a real sensitive with a canny spirit guide named Wind-Flower of Nipmuck extraction. One or the other might ferret out Mark's problem—more likely it would be Wind-Flower, whom the Old Lord had described as being uncommonly prescient.

Summoning her courage, Lucy walked up the path and, reaching the door, lifted a knocker in the shape of a ship and let it fall against the plate. She waited a short while hoping that Mrs. Sloane would be absent, but as she was about to turn away, the door opened on silent hinges and a tall, gaunt woman with iron grey hair twisted back in a tight knot stood in the aperture. Meeting wide grey-blue eyes that seemed to peer beyond bone and flesh, into the mind itself, Lucy felt even more intimidated.

"Yes?" the woman said in a deep mellow voice.

"Please, I . . . I would like to come to the . . . circle," Lucy said, falteringly. "My brother . . ." She bowed her head as much to escape that penetrating stare as to simulate grief.

"You may come," Mrs. Sloane said, "if you are sincerely interested."

"Oh, I am." Lucy clasped her hands and raised her eyes, immediately wishing that she hadn't, for the stare was even harder.

"You are very sensitive yourself," observed Mrs. Sloane. "Have you been unable to contact him?"

Lucy dropped her gaze again. "I do not know how. That's why I have come to you," she whispered.

There was a pause. Then Mrs. Sloane said, "Very well, we'll make the effort. The price of admission to the circle is two dollars, payable upon arrival."

"Thank you," Lucy said softly. As she turned away from the house, she was both relieved and disappointed. She had expected—she was not sure what—but absolutely nothing had happened. That was unusual. Generally, when she became aware of something indefinable, it was subsequently defined. Mrs. Sloane had been strange looking, and her glance was certainly compelling. Yet her vision was not as broad as Lucy had expected. She *had* believed in the brother invented on the spur of the moment. In discussing the project, no one in the Household had suggested she lie. No one knowing her would ever suggest such a thing, since she did it very badly.

The more Lucy thought about it, the greater grew her confusion. The Old Lord had said Mrs. Sloane was very sensitive. If she were very sensitive, why hadn't she guessed that she, Lucy, was telling a falsehood? Probably she needed the two dollars. That suggested that the medium business wasn't as lucrative as Bob Smith had insisted. And if it wasn't lucrative, what would they do? Lucy sighed and then looked over her shoulder. In that moment, she had become aware that someone was following her—but she was mistaken. No one was behind her.

That the sensation persisted depressed her, suggesting that something was happening to her own powers of perception. Possibly it was the Boston air. She wondered if air changed from continent to continent. Perhaps Mr. Blake could have told her, having been in both.

Lucy grimaced. She had promised herself faithfully to blot him from her mind. Unfortunately, he would not blot. He returned to he throughts at odd times, times when he had no right to be there, such as now. She wondered where he lived. Boston was such a big city, not by European standards, of course, but large enough so that two people who had met on the relatively small area of a steamship could easily not ever meet each other again. It had been depressingly simple to avoid him on shipboard—how much easier in this bleak sprawl of a town, where she seemed to have lost her vaunted sensitivity. Tears blurred her vision. She wiped them away with a sweep of her hand and hurried in the direction of the graveyard, not a very comfortable landmark to be sure, but one which would always point the way. A long sigh escaped her. Much as she adored her family, she wished that three of its most important members were not ostensibly deceased.

Lucy let herself into the house. As she shut the front door, she had a vague impression that something had entered the house in her wake. That was really very odd!

"What is that creature doing here? And what does she mean by 'how?'"

Lucy, peeling off her gloves, looked up startled. "What's the matter, Great-grandfather?" she inquired.

"Whatever induced you to bring that . . . that savage into this house?" he blustered.

Hard on his question, Lucy's small knitted purse, which she had just deposited on the hall table, suddenly went flying through the air and fell to the floor just inside of the living room. It was followed by the hall table which rose about three feet in the air before falling on its side.

There was a clatter on the stairs as Mark hurried down. "What's all the racket?" he asked testily.

"I . . . I don't know." Lucy hurried into the living room to retrieve her purse. Before she could pick it up, the new and heavy oak table near the window began to rock back and forth, slowly at first, but gathering momentum. Books, a small vase and a lace doily slipped to the floor.

"It's an earthquake!" Mark exclaimed, as a new gas fixture began to sway.

"The floor's not moving," Lucy said doubtfully.

"Earthquake be damned. It's that overgrown papoose! Back to own wigman, Wind-Flower!"

"Wind . . . Flower?" Lucy questioned in amazement.

"Wind-Flower!" corroborated the Old Lord. *"Why did you bring her here?"*

"I didn't," Lucy said thankfully. "She must have followed me. I knew I felt something."

"An arrow in your back?" Mark laughed.

"Keep her away from me! I am not an exhibit in some bloody museum!"

"I have heard of poltergeists," Lucy said tentatively, "but grandfather seems to believe . . ."

"Polgergeists be damned. It's that blasted squaw who's making all the commotion here."

As if to corroborate his words, a book sailed across the room and crashed against the opposite wall. It was followed by a pitcher which shattered into bits.

"Good Lord!" Mark exclaimed. "What are we to do?"

"Send her away!"

"Be kind to her, Great-grandfather," Lucy pleaded.

"I like heap brave man, Wind-Flower wants."

"You said you liked her, Great-grandfather." Lucy pointed out.

"In her place, which is not here. Go away, Wind-Flower."

"I go, you come, I show you many things."

"What am I to do with the woman?"

"As she asks." Lucy felt a smile twitching her lips and quickly quelled it. The situation was not really amusing. "You might profit from the experience, Great-grandfather."

"You wise. I like you better than Mrs. Sloane. She ugly. You pretty. He handsome . . . like man-wolf, too," commented Wind-Flower.

"Listen to that!"

Lucy could hear yet not hear Wind-Flower's voice. As with the Old Lord, her words were an impression rather than a sound. Cast into the darkness behind her eyes was a face, dusky and framed in long black braids. The eyes, tilted at the corners, were dark brown and deeply sad. Their sadness reached Lucy. The woman, she understood, was weighted with loneliness. She had followed because of her loneliness, because she had recognized the Old Lord as another like herself, caught there in the middle of emptiness.

"Don't be angry with her." Lucy wafted the words at him. "Wind-Flower is desperately lonely."

"Yes, lonely . . . many times search for Red Eagle . . . not find. Gone long time . . . all gone long, long time."

"Catlin!" the Old Lord suddenly cried. *"I cannot find her."* The anger had gone from his voice, and Lucy felt that he suddenly sympathized with Wind-Flower.

A wave of sorrow swept over her. They were, all of them, lonely and forsaken, they more than herself. Juliet and Colin were more than herself, too. She was alive, breathing and here for a purpose. A medium could help to alleviate the loneliness of others. She had not thought of that before. In fact, she realized, she had been well on the way to believing she was as cursed as the rest of the Household, doomed to be forever alone and unhappy. That was not true. She had a mission. Her unique talents could be put to good use, bringing comfort and love to other sorrowing souls. She must learn how to be a medium.

"Go back, Wind-Flower," she silently beamed the words. "I must learn how it is done—to be a medium, I mean. Mrs. Sloane could instruct me, but only with your assistance."

"You no learn. You be you. I show."

There was a sudden pressure in the middle of Lucy's forehead. Accompanying it was a dull ache, and then she experienced a sudden lightness and a letting go.

"Lucy . . . Lucy . . ."

She heard Mark call out but could not see him or answer, even though she knew there was panic in his voice. Her next feeling was that her head had increased in size and that something was beating inside of it, not beating but throbbing, a throbbing like drums. *She* was a drum, and something or someone was pounding on the thin wall that protected her brain. Then there was darkness, a spreading darkness like dark waters lapping at her feet, rising to engulf her. Fear coursed through her and was blotted out. Everything was blotted out.

She woke to a long tearing scream. Her throat ached with it, and her tongue was moving. She heard words in her voice, but she did not remember speaking; she remembered nothing. Then, it was no longer her voice.

"Aeeeee! The cat! I will not stay. The cat is heap bad spirit! Spirit cat! I go."

"An' good riddance to you, ye wicked scamp!"

With Molly's howl fading from her ears, Lucy awakened fully to find Mark kneeling beside her, cradling her in his arms. "What happened?" she whispered.

Surprisingly, Mark was shaking with laughter which he was trying vainly to quell. "Wind-Flower blew away. Evidently she does not like cats in general and Grimalkin in particular. If I could see him, I'd pet him." His laughter ceased abruptly. "And you, my dearest, are you all right?"

"I expect so," she said vaguely. "My throat aches as if . . ."

"You'd screamed." Mark finished. "You did, and it wasn't your voice." The golden eyes were full of concern. "I cannot say that I like this, my Lucy, this invasion."

"Was I invaded?" she demanded wide-eyed.

"You don't remember anything?"

"Only darkness and . . . and sleep. But she did speak *through* me?"

"She did," Mark corroborated.

"I wish I'd been there."

"But you weren't. Where were you?"

"Nowhere." She shivered.

"I won't let you do this, Lucy."

"But I must." She regarded him earnestly. "I feel it, Mark. I feel it is almost a vocation."

"A vocation!" he exploded. "To make yourself some sort of . . ."

"Medium," she finished. "I can help people that way—lonely people, who are not as we . . ."

"Not cursed, you mean?" he inquired bitterly.

"There are other ways of being cursed," she said feelingly. "Not being able to reach the ones you love." Her huge blue eyes glowed softly. "I want to help them, Mark."

"Oh, Lucy, Lucy . . ." He rocked her in his arms. "None of us deserve you."

"Dearest Mark." She smiled at him. "But," she said more energetically now, "I will still need to attend a seance."

"*No, I think I may be of use to you there,*" the old Lord said positively and purposefully. "*I will be your guide and for purposes of identification, you may call me 'Beowulf.'*"

"Beowulf!" Lucy exclaimed.

"Beowulf?" Mark echoed.

"BEOWULF IN BOSTON," Juliet read and tossed down the paper. "And where is the 'sensational Saxon' now?" She inquired with a touch of sarcasm.

"On a scouting trip, no doubt." Colin said, looking at Lucy, who lay prone on the new sofa they had bought with the proceeds from four months of meetings. "You are looking unhappy, my dear."

"I think she's tired," Juliet observed. "And no wonder, with the parade that has been marching through here of late, not to mention all the letters she feels she must answer."

"I wish," Lucy said wearily, "that you would not speak as if I were not among you. I am here and awake."

"Poor love." Juliet's lips brushed Lucy's forehead. "I keep forgetting how frustrating it must be for you to be Boston's most famous medium and never to have met—even Napoleon. But it's just as well. He never should have been elevated from Corporal to Emperor, do you not agree, Colin?"

"My agreement or the lack of it will not change the circumstances." Her brother laughed.

"He is such a cantankerous little man," Juliet said, also laughing. "Isn't it amazing how many of the world's great leaders are so tiny? Alexander the Great, Attila—small and ill-tempered to boot."

"He keeps bringing them," Lucy whispered regretfully. "I know he enjoys their company, but the truly bereaved . . . Great-grandfather grows so testy when I so much as mention their needs."

"It's to be expected." Juliet shrugged. "Naturally father's excited by these associations." Impulsively, she turned to Colin. "Will you ever forget the time when we met Lucretia Borgia coming from an appointment in the Pitti Palace with the blood still pouring from her lips? Or when the Empress Catherine of Russia . . ."

"I am sure that poor Lucy does not want to share such recollections," Colin said. "And father's promised that tonight he'll not play to the galleries." He gave Lucy a commiserating look. "You'll have your say, my love—and no learned professors to goad you nor psychologists to test you."

"Is that true?" Lucy sat up.

"Mark insisted," Colin affirmed. "That is what I meant by a 'scouting trip.' He has scanned the letters of those who have applied for tonight's session."

"Oh," Lucy said, clasping her hands, "I am so pleased. The letters from those who have lost a loved one truly pain me."

"You take them too much to heart," Mark said from the doorway. He moved into the room, his eyes on Lucy. "You're looking very wan, my love. It's too much of a strain on you; your energy's being drained away."

"Oh no," she contradicted, "I really do not feel that. It is only that I want to help. I cannot believe it helps anyone to discuss gravity with Mr. Newton or battle stategies with William the Conqueror, especially when some poor woman longs to have a comforting word from a husband or a son who has passed over." She looked hopefully at Mark. "Will my powers really be put to that use tonight?"

"They will, my dear." Concern was still large in his eyes. "But I hope that the time will come when you'll have ceased to be a nine-day wonder."

"One-hundred-and-twenty day wonder," Juliet corrected lightly, casting a pleased eye around a room that was much better furnished than when they had moved in.

Watching her, Lucy could guess what she was thinking. While the small area of the back parlor could not compare to the mighty rooms of the Hold, it was certainly more homelike and redolent of the luxury in which Juliet had grown up. Due to the connections of the Old Lord, and to the business acumen of Mark, the attention that "Beowulf" had attracted had brought them money, practically from the moment they began the sittings. They were able to buy new furniture and, to Juliet's delight, new garments. She glanced at Colin's latest portrait of his sister.

She was wearing a blue moiré gown of expanding flounces edged with black velvet ribbons and extended by a wide crinoline. Her golden hair was drawn back into a snood with a few small curls escaping to flutter by her ears. As usual, she looked incredibly young and beautiful. Yet, the infectious gaiety of that pictured countenance depressed Lucy. In spite of the drawbacks to her situation, Juliet seemed not to have a care in the world and, as usual, Colin reflected her mood.

The talk of both was spiced with reports of the prestigious individuals they had encountered at various gala soirées, many of which they attended without benefit of invitation. Yet such was their charm and address that no one ever questioned their right to be among those present. Unwillingly, Lucy's thoughts sped to an article in the *Daily Evening Transcript* concerning a recent and unexplained outbreak of anemia among young men and women in the better areas of the city.

No one had succumbed to the malady, but its prevalence was puzzling the physicians, especially since each of the victims had complained that their weakness had been preceded by peculiar nightmares. Many theories had been advanced, but no one had deduced the cause. And no one ever would, Lucy knew. The learned doctors, the scientists, pyschologists, lawyers and judges who frequented her seances might believe in communication with the dead but never, by any stretch of their combined imaginations, would they believe that the source of this recent epidemic could be traced to this house or, more specifically, to the elaborate crypt Colin and Juliet had purchased a scant fortnight after their arrival.

Her thoughts skittered away from them. Lately, she had been asked to increase her sittings from two to three a week, mainly to accomodate the learned men who were coming from all over the eastern seaboard to attend them. Only Mark seemed to understand that she was tired, becoming more so after each succeeding session. Even though she depended on the combined energy of the sitters she was, as Mark theorized, being drained. She wished she could find a way to stop but that would mean resisting the rambunctious entity of her great-grandfather. She doubted she could, and besides, he was enjoying himself so thoroughly.

" *'Tis a marvelous feeling, Lucy,*" he had said on more than one occasion, "*to feel the blood rushing through your veins and to breathe the good air again.*"

That he was making use of her blood and her nostrils had never occurred to him. She would not remind him, nor would she complain about his exuberance to the rest of the Household. They were all so pleased at her success and its profits.

Last week they had actually been able to purchase the
charming little pianoforte that Juliet played so beautifully. It
also seemed to her that during the last three full moons,
Mark's howls had been infinitely less frequent and his periods
of recuperation shorter. Was the curse winding down? Mark
enjoyed his walks around the city and more than once had
expressed admiration for the American female. He had not
mentioned anyone specifically nor would he, she was sure of
that. She stifled a sigh. It was really no good to think of the
curse's cessation until they—Mark, Colin and Juliet—were
able to . . .

" 'Tis time, my dear.''

Lucy rose hastily. For once, she had not noticed the arrival
of her great-grandfather. She prayed he had not been a party
to her thoughts, but divining the fact that he was in good
humor, she guessed that he had not.

She went down the hall and into the living room,
furnished now with a center table flanked by ten straight-
backed chairs and the cushioned Queen Anne chair reserved
for her. It was a pity, she thought, that the table could
accomodate only ten people; for the sake of those who hoped
for words from the beyond, she wished it could be twice as
many. As she approached her chair, she heard gasps of
surprise and knew that each of those present was having
second thoughts about her vaunted abilities. There was a
paucity of light in the chamber, but most of it came from the
dim gaslit globe directly over her chair. It cast a pale green
light upon her face and diminutive body and, as had
happened before, those present probably looked upon her as
little more than a child.

She stood at the table, wishing she could make use of the
candelabrum placed in its center. She gladly would have
conducted her sittings by sunlight. She enjoyed awakening to
brightness and, at first, she had used several branches of
candles. However, the protests of those who believed,
erroneously, that spirits would only emerge in darkness,
caused her to abandon the practice and adhere to custom. It
was, she guessed, a custom promulgated by those spurious
mediums whose manifestations owed more to stage-magic
than to the spirit entities they professed to summon and
which were composed of cheesecloth rather than ectoplasm.

As she sank down in her chair, Lucy thought she heard a startled gasp. She looked around the table but could not distinguish the features of anyone present. She could tell from their shapes that there were more women than men—seven to three, in fact. That, she reasoned thankfully, would make matters much easier. Men were ever more skeptical than women, and the negative energy produced by a circle of psychologists, lawyers and judges made her very weary indeed.

"Miss Veringer?"

Lucy stiffened. Someone present knew her by the name she no longer used, having, for convention's sake, called herself Driscoll and setting about the fiction that Mark was her brother. She gazed around the table vainly trying to pierce the gloom, but to her regret the Old Lord, vigilant as ever, descended upon her. She felt the familiar pounding in her forehead and then nothing more.

At length, the entity known as "Beowulf" departed, and Lucy, opening her eyes, gazed tiredly around a table where everybody was excitedly talking or, as was the case with several women, weeping. She smiled, realizing that the Old Lord had made good his promise and brought back a group of what he would call "innocuous phantoms." She slumped gratefully among the cushions in her chair. Soon they would go and she could sleep.

"Oh, Swithin, he *was* your father. You can no longer doubt it!"

Lucy tensed, wondering which of the ladies had spoken.

"Wasn't it a miracle? Surely you must agree now?"

"It was remarkable, Mother," came the answer couched in terms she remembered so very well, even though she had met the speaker only twice. She felt rather than saw his gaze upon her as he continued. "I believe I have met the medium."

"Met her? But you never told me . . ." his mother began.

It was not Lucy's custom to speak to any of the people that came to her sittings. As the Old Lord had warned, *"Address a word to any one of them and the whole lot of them will be upon you like a swarm of locusts!"* However, upon this occasion she said, almost without conscious volition, "Yes, we have met, Mr. Blake. It is so very nice to see you again." She got to her feet.

"Miss Veringer!" Amidst a growing babble of exclamations and questions, Swithin Blake arose and strode to her side, grasping her hands warmly. "I knew I could not be mistaken," he said raising his voice above the clamor. "But why are you here?"

"I . . ." Lucy began and then, much to her consternation and subsequent regret, fainted dead away.

A month after her third and all-important meeting with Swithin Blake, Lucy, curled on the sofa in the library, watched him striding up and down with an ecstasy mitigated by pain. Since the moment when she had fainted at his feet, she had seen him two and three times a week during the first fortnight. In these last two weeks, he had been there nearly every day. Seven days, three hours and an untold number of minutes ago he had told her he loved her, and since then he had proposed at least 20 times, refusing to be discouraged by her gentle procrastinations. He had just proposed to her again, interspersing his pleas with concerned comments on her state of health.

She knew she looked peaked and could not tell him that much of her weakness was due to lack of sleep, as she tried to find a solution to what seemed an insolvable problem—her duty to the Household. If only she could have told him the truth—but that was impossible. Given his unexpressed but obvious doubts concerning the validity of her occult powers, he would scarcely give credence to anything she told him about her great grandfather, her great-aunt and uncle and her cousin Mark, whom he now believed to be her brother.

"But it is ridiculous. You tell me you are merely resting. How many times in this last month have you been 'resting' when I have come to see you? It would not surprise me to learn that you've contracted the anemia so prevalent in the city."

"Oh, I could not have that!" Lucy cried, with a haste she immediately regretted.

Swithin came to stand by her sofa. "Why could you not?" he demanded angrily. "These damned sittings are a drain on your energy, and you know it!"

Lucy's gaze shifted from his accusing stare to the folds of her new dimity gown with its pattern of blue and pink roses.

She replied diffidently, "I do not have anemia. The doctor will attest to that."

"Ah, so you have been to see a doctor," he said accusingly. "And what did he say was the matter with you?"

"Nothing." She raised her eyes that she hoped were candid. She did hate lying to Swithin, but there was no help for it.

"Nothing?" he echoed dubiously. "It is my belief that you did not go and are merely trying to fob me off, but you will not succeed. You are not strong enough to continue with these sessions. A fortnight ago you sustained another fainting spell. That is two in as many weeks."

"I did not faint last night," she reminded him.

"You were noticeably paler. Oh, Lucy," he said, sitting on the edge of the sofa, "if I did not love you so much, if I'd not loved you from the first moment I saw you, I would not insist that you abandon this pursuit."

"I cannot," she said in a low, unhappy voice.

"Why not?" He smote his hands together. "Oh God, I hate the way they are using you. I even hate your loyalty, noble as it is."

"They are not using me, Swithin," Lucy said gently. "I wish your mind were not sealed shut. In spite of all you've seen this past month, you are determined to believe that Mark is hidden in some closet or that I am a ventriloquist rather than a medium."

He looked at her in surprise. "I have never said . . . ."

"You've no need to say anything." She smiled at him. "I know you."

"I love you. I want you to marry me and come away from here, from this house that is redolent of death!"

"Swithin!"

"Is it not?" he demanded. "You are like some latter day Charon, ferrying souls back across the Styx and living on the edge of a cemetery. I do not give credence to the arguments that you can afford nothing better. I can take care of you, your brother and those mysterious cousins I so seldom meet."

"We belong here!" Lucy exclaimed. "All of us must stay together."

"Why?"

"I can tell you nothing more than I have told you," she

said miserably. "I cannot leave, and I shall not leave. I beg you'll not ask it of me!"

He stared at her for a long moment and then said incredulously, "Does your celebrity mean so much to you?"

"My celebrity?" She stared at him, wide-eyed with shock and hurt. "It means nothing to me!"

"Does it not?" he countered. "Does it not when each day you are receiving letters from men prominent in their fields, from judges, from physicians, from philosophers . . ."

"No, no, no!" she exclaimed.

"Then why?"

The moment had come. Experiencing the ecstasy of love for the first time in her life, Lucy had half-persuaded herself that Swithin would not need to know the truth, but there was no escaping her dark heritage. The time of the full moon was almost upon them. As she had done the previous month, she planned to make some glib excuse about Mark and the others. As well as she knew herself, she knew that having once received that knowledge, he would not reveal it. He would only go away and never see her again. A small sob escaped her.

"Lucy, Lucy, Lucy." He put his arms around her and held her against him. "What is troubling you?"

Before he could answer, a dish full of fruit which had been on the table, suddenly sailed across the room and dropped its contents over the couch, a rain of apples, pears and grapes.

"Good God, what's that?" Swithin stared about the room. In that same instant, a chair began to bounce up and down, and the table rocked from side to side. The overhead light swayed and another chair slid over to them. Swithin leaped to his feet. "We've got to get out of here. It's an earthquake!"

"No," Lucy said despairingly, "it's not. It's my great-grandfather, and he's telling me there's something you must know. He wants me to tell you now. Please listen."

"Lucy, my dear, you are not making sense. In an earthquake . . ."

"It is not an earthquake!" she repeated. "You see . . . everything is quiet now."

"But . . ."

"Please," she repeated. "Sit down and listen."

He stared at her confusedly. "Very well." He resumed his seat. "But I do not see what your great-grandfather . . . ah, well, continue, my dear."

He listened quietly while Lucy talked. His silence disturbed her. There seemed something ominous about it. She could not be quite sure of that, however, and she did not look at him. Consequently she was deprived of the play of emotion she might have seen on his features and, in speaking, she was also deliberately closing her mind to any vibrations she might have picked up.

As she talked, she strove to be emotionally detached from the agonies that had afflicted the Household in the years following the eviction of Erlina Bell. Even though the seeds of evil had been planted long before, it was impossible not to blame the greater part of their misfortunes on her. However Lucy could not remain totally detached, not when she spoke of Juliet's tragic encounter with Simeon Weir and the equally tragic death of her brother Colin. Yet, meeting them now, she was sure that Swithin would be hard put to imagine a time when Juliet had not been bright, gay and a little brittle. Her vulnerability was gone and Colin's as well. Lucy had an interior shiver, thinking that if such a horrid fate were to befall her, she would do as Colin had done and leave instructions as to the disposal of her body. Tony should have respected his brother's wishes in regards to both of them. Yet selfishly enough, she was glad he had not. Mentally, she fled away from these thoughts. She had to finish her narrative, her Arabian Night's fantasy that must spell the death of all her hopes concerning the only man she could ever love.

Valiently she continued and was surprised to find that as she finally concluded her history that the sun was definitely lower. In another hour or so, Juliet and Colin would emerge from their crypt. She looked at Swithin and found him grim. She had anticipated that, but she had not expected to hear him say, "Was it necessary to tell me all this?"

"I thought it was," she conceded, still too emotionally drained to fathom the workings of his mind.

"I could have accepted a simpler refusal," he returned witheringly.

"A simpler . . . ?" She stared at him in consternation.

"A yes or a no, would have sufficed—but this fairy

tale . . . ! What manner of fool do you think me? You may deceive yourself into believing you live in a world of ghosts and demons, and you may deceive half the population of Boston. However I, I hope, am a rational man. I haven't believed in Red Riding Hood and the Wolf since I was five!'' He rose and moved toward the entrance hall. "I will," he said heavily, "bid you good afternoon, Miss Veringer." He went swiftly out of the room, and seconds later the front door closed softly behind him.

Lucy slipped from the sofa and ran after him. She did not get very far, for she stumbled and fell. She did not try to rise but lay there, weeping as bitterly as she ever had in the whole of her life.

"Child, darling."

She felt the Old Lord close beside her. "Oh, Great-grandfather, he'd not believe me? Why?"

"He prides himself on being a rational man, child. As I, myself, once did, laughing at gods and demons alike and breaking the eternal laws. I only hope that . . .''

She was frightened at the sudden termination of his sentence. "What do you only hope?" she whispered.

"Nothing, child. You are weeping. Do not weep."

Lucy's curls were stirred by a gentle breeze that was no breeze but the five fingers of her great-grandfather, trying vainly to soothe her. "I love him. I did not want to tell him, but I could not leave you all, and he had to know the reason why. Why would he imagine I was refusing him?"

"Because he did not understand. He is sorely confused, as I once was. God grant he does not learn as I learned, but he will not. The curse does not lie on his head."

His words were meant to be comforting, but they were not. They filled her with fear. It seemed to her that the Old Lord was implying that Swithin was in some manner of danger. "I am worried about him. Is he safe?"

"Of course he is safe, my dear. I beg you will not fret nor turn your thoughts upon him too much. It will not do, you know."

"I do know. I am sorry that I told him so much, but I thought you wanted me to do so . . . and I knew I could trust him." She was suddenly aware that she was speaking to emptiness. The Old Lord had gone.

Lucy rose and fled to her room, flinging herself on the bed, but she no longer wept. It occurred to her that she was frightened for Swithin, but why? She did not know. And thinking of him, she grew angry, too. He should have believed her! Fear quickly replaced the anger again, and this fear was all the more fearful because it was dense, amorphous and unreasonable. Swithin would go home to his family and his comfortable house. He would forget about her and marry a young woman of good family and . . . Lucy could think no more, would think no more. She lay watching the clouds floating through the sky, clouds streaked with the rays of the descending sun, and wondered how many more sunsets she would see through that window in a room that was suddenly very lonely.

Four

Swithin Blake's anger had evaporated. Sitting in his late father's library, he stared gloomily into the darkening garden. He had been there a long time, pondering on the fantasies Lucy had spun for him, more than mere fantasies—a phantasmagorical! Yet she had seemed so earnest, so honest, as if every word that fell from her lips was no more than the truth—but how could it be true? He had always been a realist. How could he credit her tale? How could she expect that he would? A mocking laugh rose in his throat and turned into a sob. He had not lied when he told her he loved her from the first moment he had seen her. A vision of her dainty form and delicate beauty came to him. She was so lovely, and to see her in the darkness with all those strange voices issuing from those shapely lips had seemed arrant trickery to him, this despite the evidence of his senses.

During the time he had been participating in the circle, it had seemed as if his father really had spoken to himself and his mother. She believed it implicitly, but subsequently he had been extremely doubtful. He had been willing to accept Lucy's chicanery, telling himself that she was the tool of her brother or rather cousin Mark, which was the way they had first been introduced, he recalled now. And whether cousin or brother, Mark was a werewolf?

"No!" he exclaimed explosively. "No!"

How could she have expected him to believe that, to believe everything she told him? There had been such hurt in her eyes when he challenged her preposterous tale. Had it been assumed? No, it was real. He had to think!

Rising, he thrust his hands into his pockets and paced back and forth across the room, trying to understand why she had found it necessary to tell him anything so outrageous. His thoughts were momentarily deflected by the feel of something soft and squishy in his pocket. He found that it was a rather elderly grape and remembered what he had totally forgotten—the disturbance in Lucy's living room, the rain of fruit!

What had caused him to put that out of his mind?

Had he excised it unconsciously because it eluded explanation?

He stared at the grape and remembered the moving chairs.

Purposefully he strode from the library and went into the kitchen where Mrs. Anawalt, the cook, was preparing dinner. As he expected, the housekeeper was there, too, as was one of the housemaids. Tentatively he asked if there had been an earthquake that day. They looked at him with amazement.

"Oh, no sir," they chorused.

Thanking them, he came out and followed where his feet led him which was out of the doors and in the direction of Lucy's house. The sun was nearly down, and as he reached the street that lay along the graveyard, he remembered something to which he had paid little heed. She had mentioned that her aunt and uncle dwelt in one of the crypts. He remembered the pair and had thought it one of the anomalies of a big family that Lucy should possess an uncle who was her age and an aunt who seemed much younger. The iron gates of the cemetery were still open. On an impulse, he strode inside. Certainly, it would lend credence to her story if he were to see them in the act of emerging from their tombs.

Though he was not familiar with this particular cemetery, he rather thought that the larger monuments lay toward the back of the graveyard. He was nearing the path he thought might lead in the direction when he heard a step behind him.

"Why, Swifty, what are you doing here?"

He turned quickly and much to his surprise saw Bertie Lowndes, whom he had known at Harvard. He had lost sight of him in the last few years. "Hello, Bertie," he said cordially. "I haven't had anyone call me that in years." He stretched out his hand.

Bertie shook it. "I suppose not. Once you leave school all the old nicknames go by the boards. What, may I ask, are you doing here after dark? It is not a particularly pleasant place for a stroll."

Swithin glanced up and saw that it was growing very dark. "Oh, I know someone who lives near here. I thought I would take a short cut."

"I see."

"Come to think of it, what are you doing here? I'd heard . . ." Swithin paused, unable at the moment to remember just what he had heard about Bertie Lowndes. They had never been very close at the university. Bertie had been too inclined to burn his candle at both ends and had belonged to a rather fast set.

"What had you heard?" Bertie asked in an abrupt and even belligerent turn of voice, almost, Swithin thought, as if he were looking for an argument.

"Nothing, old man," he said quickly. "How have you been faring since leaving Harvard?"

"Well enough. I do not complain. It would be no use." Bertie shrugged.

"That sounds as if you might have experienced some disappointments," Swithin said sympathetically. "I hope they were not too severe."

"Not really. Where are you walking? I might as well go along with you."

Swithin experienced some little annoyance. It would be no use to go the crypts. Bertie had detained him too long; Juliet and Colin would be gone by now. He blushed, hoping that his old classmate wasn't a mindreader, but that, too, was in the realm of of the impossible. He said, "I'm bound for a house that is . . ." He glanced around and was even more annoyed. He was no longer sure where he was. In searching for the right path, he had stepped away from the fence, and now in the increasing darkness, he had lost his bearings. He said, "I don't actually know where I am. I know I want to go to the gates."

"I know the way," Bertie responded. "I will be glad to show you."

"That would be a real service," Swithin said gratefully.

"We will go in this direction." Bertie turned up a graveled path.

Following him, Swithin was vaguely troubled. Someone had told him something about Bertie, but for the life of him, he could not remember what it was. He had never really been a close friend to Bertie Lowndes. He had taken his legal studies at Harvard very seriously. Bertie, he recalled, had never been serious about anything except enjoying himself and in rather strange ways, now that he thought of it. He had formed some kind of a society, and there'd been a scandal of sorts. Again he could not remember quite what. Esoteric studies had come into it. Yes! Bertie had been playing around with the occult. And hadn't one of his cronies been hurt during a weird ceremony? He had not heard much about it, mainly because the whole matter had been suppressed by the college authorities. The young men involved had been expelled, Bertie among them. Excitedly, he brushed that recollection aside. He could not believe his luck! Bertie *had* been interested in the occult—that was definite—and he might be able to sound him out about Lucy's strange story.

He looked toward his guide, who was several feet ahead of him, standing near a little stone mausoleum. Swithin stifled a sigh, remembering his mission, but it was much darker now. He joined Bertie, saying, "I have a rather foolish question to ask you."

"Foolish, Swifty? In what way?"

"I have been hearing some rather fantastic tales of late. It seems that there are people who really think that . . ." He paused, embarrassed, wondering if it would not be better to dismiss the subject. Undoubtedly Bertie would consider him quite mad, for certainly he could no longer believe in the devils and demons he and his followers unsuccessfully had tried to rise. This, he remembered now, was what the furor had been all about.

"Think what, old man?" Bertie prompted.

"Well, that . . . ghosts and vampires really exist."

"Vampires, too? That's most unfortunate."

"Unfortunate?" Swithin flushed. "Well, I expect it is—to be so superstitious in this day and age."

"Exactly. I would prefer that everyone be as enlightened as . . . well, you, for instance. I am quite sure that *you* don't believe in that sort of thing, old man."

Swithin was even more embarrassed. "You're no longer interested in the occult, I see."

"I shouldn't say that." Bertie laughed. "But my interest has taken a different turn."

"That means that you are no longer so deeply involved?"

"Well, yes and no," Bertie said musingly. "Why are you so interested in ghosts and vampires? We were never very closely allied at Harvard, but I do seem to recall that you were more inclined toward scientific rather than psychic research."

"That's true," Swithin agreed uncomfortably.

"As I said before, I wish, old man, that everyone were like you."

"You have changed."

"Oh, yes, I have changed. Indeed, I have changed." Bertie laughed.

"Well, I suppose that's all to the good. Disregard my question, please." Swithin looked around him at a vista of old trees. Near them were moon-illumined gravestones, and a short distance away he saw another mausoleum. It seemed to him that they had penetrated deeper into the cemetery. It was very quiet here, preternaturally quiet. He did not even hear the usual chorus of crickets and frogs, which was odd. Generally they were everywhere. He wondered if Bertie were as knowledgeable about the lay of the cemetery as he had professed. "Where are we?" he inquired.

"To quote the late Mr. Poe, we have arrived upon the 'nightly shore.'" Bertie laughed.

Swithin also laughed. "That's not quite an answer."

"But it's all you need to know, old man." Bertie stepped close to him, and Swithin, seeing his face in the light from a three-quarter moon, was taken aback. Bertie did not look at all well. There were deep circles under his eyes, and surely he was much thinner than when he had attended Harvard. In fact he looked as if he were suffering from consumption . . . consumption! Swithin suddenly recalled what he had heard about Bertie.

"Good God!" he exclaimed and saw Bertie take a quick step back. "Do you know what I thought? It shows you that you can never credit rumor!"

"What manner of rumor would that be, old man?"

"I heard that you had contracted some manner of pernicious anemia and . . . and . . ."

"And died from it?" Bertie inquired.

"Yes." Swithin nodded. "That's what I heard."

"It was true, old man." Bertie smiled widely. "You were asking me about vampires, I think?"

Swithin, staring at Bertie's gleaming fangs, was filled with a horror that lived up to all the descriptions he had ever heard of it, turning him icy cold. Coupled with that was a terror which invaded every pore of his body. He wanted to turn and run, but he could not move. He was, as it were, rooted to the spot. In that moment, Bertie's hand fastened on his arm. His grip was strong and hurtful. Swithin tried to pull away but the hand that held him could have been fashioned from iron.

"You . . ." he mouthed. "You are . . ."

"Quite, old man. I do not know why you were wandering through this graveyard, but for me, your presence is most fortuitous. The search for sustenance is often wearying and can take the better part of a night. Of course, I would prefer a female." To Swithin's increased horror, Bertie licked his lips with the tip of a pale tongue. "But on the other hand," he continued blithely, "the idea of having you among our ranks is quite to my taste. You were always so tediously industrious at the university. Several of my professors pointed you out as the ideal student, calm, rational and brilliant. I hardly think that any of these qualities will sustain you at this moment which, I fear, will be your last. But I expect you will employ them to even better . . ."

"Bertie, darling, good evening! And Swithin! I wasn't aware that you knew each other." Juliet, in a white gown worn over one of her largest crinolines, stepped up to them. She was followed by Colin who was in evening dress.

"Bertie," he exclaimed. "Swithin, good to see you again. My father told me I might find you here."

Swithin found his voice. "Good evening," he managed to say.

Despite the friendliness of their greetings, Bertie Lowndes did not appear to welcome the sight of either. Still grasping Swithin's arm so tightly that the circulation felt as if it were shut off, he said coldly, "What are you doing here?"

"Darling, Bertie, is that the way to speak to us? Why are you being such an old grouch?" Juliet laid her hand lightly on Swithin's other arm.

"Go away!" Bertie said shrilly. "You have no right here. This man is mine!"

"Unless I am deeply mistaken about his proclivities, I hardly think Swithin will agree with you," Juliet quipped.

"You have no right to interfere," Bertie retorted menacingly.

Colin stepped closer. "This man is practically a member of our family, Bertie."

"Curse your damned family!" Bertie finally loosened his hold on Swithin's arm.

"You are too late, my dear, by some seventy-five years. That has already been accomplished, and now you really must go. It's damp out here, and I am sure Swithin's not feeling at all well." Juliet smiled sweetly.

"There are rules," Bertie said chokingly.

"Darling, don't be tiresome. We are two to your one. Get along with you, there's a good boy," Juliet spoke dismissively.

"If you taste one drop of his blood . . ."

"We won't," Colin assured him. "He is very nearly our nephew. As my sister has mentioned, it is time you were off."

Bertie glared at them, and then to Swithin's increased horror he seemed to dwindle and collapse. In less than a minute, a large grey bat flew off, awkwardly grazing a tree as he went and uttering a disgusted squeak as he vanished amidst its leaves.

"He's really very clumsy," Juliet observed.

"He doesn't have the hang of it," Colin agreed. "You really need a breeze. If he weren't such an unpleasant creature, I would give him a few pointers, but I really do dislike him. We're here through no fault of our own—at least that's true of you, my dearest Juliet—but it was his evil ways that did for him. Now, Swithin, we will escort you to the gates, and if you wish to see Lucy . . .'' He broke off in consternation as Swithin suddenly fell at his feet. ''Well,'' he said, looking at Juliet, who had dropped to her knees beside Swithin, ''I hope it wasn't his heart.''

''He has only fainted,'' she said. ''He has been through quite an ordeal. Shall we take him to Lucy or bring him back to his house?''

''I think Lucy must care for him,'' Colin said judiciously. ''Besides I hardly think he's ready to answer any of the inevitable questions that his mother might put to him at this time.''

''Oh, of course, I was forgetting about her. 'Tis so long since we have had a mother, I had not remembered how they do carry on.''

Summoned from her bedchamber by Juliet, Lucy stared down at Swithin, who lay unconscious on the sofa in the back parlor. He was very pale and slightly blue about the lips. Listening, as Juliet recounted the circumstances in which they had found him in the graveyard, she fixed horrified eyes upon them.

''He didn't . . .''

''No,'' Colin said quickly. ''Thanks to father's warning, we arrived there before Bertie could harm him.''

''But it was fortunate we arrived when we did,'' Juliet stated.

''Oh, yes.'' Lucy knelt beside him. ''I wonder what he was doing in the graveyard?'' She looked questioningly at Colin.

''Being a damned fool for not believing you, my own darling.''

Lucy shifted her gaze quickly and found that Swithin's eyes were open and that, wonder of wonders, he was smiling at her as tenderly as he had before she had told him about the Household. ''And you . . . do believe me . . . now?''

''Implicitly,'' he affirmed with a slight smile. He glanced toward Juliet. ''I am most grateful to you and your brother.''

''Please,'' she said blithely, ''it was the least we could do. You do not feel any ill effects from your encounter, I hope?''

''You will,'' Colin warned as Swithin shook his head. ''Your arm will hurt. You'd best soak it in warm water.''

''With a poppyhead,'' Lucy added. ''That will take the

swelling down.''

"There is some soreness and stiffness in the limb," Swithin discovered. "His grasp was very strong, but I should think the effects of it would have gone away by now."

"It will take time," Juliet said. "We have uncommon strength, all of us."

"Oh, I'm am so sorry you had so frightening an experience!" Lucy cried.

"I am not," he said gently. "For now I know and should have known from the first that you were telling the truth. Still, I must explain that this encounter did not prove the turning point in my belief. I was almost convinced of the truth before I went to the graveyard, but as it is with lawyers, we do look for proof positive. I had hoped to see your aunt and uncle emerging from their tomb. Can you forgive me for doubting you, my own darling?"

"Can you ask?" she breathed.

"Oh, Lucy." He reached out his good arm and drew her closer to him.

"We must go," Colin said.

"Yes, we must." Juliet nodded and smiled knowingly at her brother, realizing that neither Lucy nor Swithin was attending. "I pray he makes her happy," she continued as they came outside.

"I do not think they would need your prayers even if you were in a position to offer them."

"No, you're right," she agreed. "Lucy, alone among us, has finally escaped the curse." She looked up at him, adding anxiously, "I hope you agree."

"I think I do," he said. "There's a fine breeze tonight."

"So there is," she responded delightedly. "Shall we?"

A short time later two grey bats lowered themselves upon the wind and glided happily off into the darkness.

She had been so long a pale cypher and semi-invalid, shut into her suite of rooms and moving from bed to sofa and back, endlessly bemoaning his father's death, that when his mother railed against his marriage, Swithin was as astonished as he was angry.

He had come to her sitting room bathed in the glow of happiness that followed his proposal and Lucy's tremulous but delighted acceptance. He had not expected that, upon bringing her this news, his mother would stare at him in horror. He had not expected that she would wring her hands and muss, if not actually tear, her sparse grey locks.

"You can't," she wailed. "I will not have that wretched girl in this house!"

"As it happens, Mother, she will not come." He said between stiff lips.

"Will not come?" she repeated. "What can you mean?"

"I have agreed to remain with her—in her house," he said, relieving himself of the bit of information which, until this moment, he had feared to divulge. Fortunately his mother's incomprehensible attitude made it wonderfully easy.

"You have agreed to . . . to remain in that hovel?" shrilled Mrs. Blake. "What madness is this?"

Since madness would seem like the most logical explanation were he to give his mother even an inkling of the truth, Swithin said uncomfortably, "She feels that the location is more conducive to her work."

"To her work!" repeated his mother in ascending accents. "You mean that she would continue to . . . to . . . ."

"For a little while longer," he clarified. "You see, in three months time she will be the . . . uh, hostess for a contingent of scientists, lawyers, a newspaper editor, in other words, the most learned men in Boston, Marblehead and Salem. A professor from Harvard will be among those present. Lucy's reputation as a medium is widespread, Mother." His explanation sounded plausible because it was the truth. After that, he would have to concoct another excuse as to why he could not bring his bride and her "brother" into his large comfortable mansion. For a moment, he wished he could override Lucy's well-founded objections. Unfortunately that would not serve. Neither his mother nor the servants would understand Mark's monthly indisposition. He quelled a reminiscent shudder as he remembered the howls that issued from the cellar just last week. His own cellar was cavernous and echoing, and Mark would sound even more frightening in there.

"I feel that you are not telling me the entire truth," his mother observed with a rare perspicacity.

Swithin winced. He really hated lying to her, but nothing must interfere with his forthcoming nuptials. "I have told you the truth, Mother. Am I in the habit of prevaricating?"

"I have never believed you to be," she sniffed. Her sniff became a sniffle, as she continued. "I never thought you would marry behind my back! And to a . . . a medium!"

"I am not marrying behind your back," he said with diminishing patience. "I am in hopes that you will grace our wedding with your presence."

"I will not!" she declared in agonized accents. "I will not speak to that wretched girl. Oh God, with all your chances and . . . and Eliza!"

He raised his eyes to the heavens which ostensibly lay beyond the molded ceiling. Eliza Bishop had long been his mother's choice for him. Not only did the girl come from an old Bostonian family which traced its roots back to the founding fathers but she was the daughter of Mrs. Blake's oldest and dearest friend. Both women had done their best to promote a match between them. He and Eliza, also the best of friends, had often laughed about these abortive efforts, while they went their separate ways. Eliza was always falling in and out of love. His lip curled as he contrasted her with Lucy, whom he loved with all his heart and soul. Lucy was so brave, so staunch, so faithful! There would come a time when he would take her away from that miserable house beside the cemetery, but he would not think of that yet.

He said, "I am sorry you feel that way, Mother, but I will marry her."

"I curse the day that we went there," she cried.

"Do not be medieval, Mother," he said, unconsciously echoing his great-grandfather-in-law to be.

Mrs. Blake cried vociferously and continuously, but her protests were ineffective.

Molly and her cat also wailed, but since they had been engaging in this same chorus ever since they had arrived in Boston, no one paid much attention.

The wedding was private, attended only by Mark, reluctantly recruited to give the bride away, and Eliza Bishop who surprisingly enough had offered to be Lucy's maid-of-honor.

The ceremony took place in the First Congregational Church, and Lucy, looking exquisitely lovely in a white silk gown and a flowing tulle veil, both furnished by Juliet from sources she would not divulge, exchanged vows with Swithin, handsome and exultant in his dark suit and frilled shirt. Nothing untoward occurred to mar the day. If Mrs. Blake wept in her room and Mark felt as if his heart had been wrenched from his body, the bride and bridegroom were blithely oblivious to those woes as they climbed into the carriage that would bear them to Marblehead where they would have an ecstatic forthnight alone.

"Please, my love, be understanding," Lucy begged. "You promised, remember?" She raised herself on her elbow and smiled at him tenderly as she encountered her husbands' concerned gaze. "It will take nothing from me. I will be asleep, remember. Besides, it is late to cancel the seance. They will be here tomorrow." As he started to speak, she added defensively, "I *have* cut down on my other sittings these last three months."

"I have a feeling . . ." Swithin began. He was lying next to her in her large bed, and under the covers he ran a gentle hand over her belly, still flat but due to rise over the child she must have conceived as early as their wedding night.

Though they had been married three whole months, it seemed to Lucy that every time they returned to bed, the ecstasy of their first night together was repeated. She had never known what happiness could be until they had been joined, body and soul, together. And though she would never admit it to him, she, too, looked forward to the end of her seances. To remain a bridge between the living and the dead when life had become so wholly absorbing, so rich and wonderful, seemed wrong. She had discussed the matter with her relations, and the Old Lord agreed that in her delicate condition the seances might well be a strain.

"Only one last seance, Lucy, and you'll have made your mark. No more need you do. You'll have won recognition from the most important men in their respective fields." That had been Eliza Bishop's opinion. Eliza had become a real friend since her participation in Swithin's marriage. Passion was blotting out Lucy's thoughts, but just before her total surrender to it, she wished that Eliza might share her happiness and was a little sad about that, knowing that Eliza had loved Swithin all of her life.

"My dearest, my love, my sweetest Lucy . . ." Swithin murmured between kisses.

She answered his needs with her own and forgot the world.

On the day of the long-awaited seance, called by a facetious editor from the *Boston Globe* the "eccentric circle," Lucy waited in the back parlor until the group assembled. She was excited, and yet she could not help feeling a trifle intimidated by the credentials of the intellectuals who had come to test her veracity. No less a personage than the famous Dr. Samuel Gillette, professor of psychology at Harvard, would head the contingent and moderate the discussion which would follow. Others included Herman J. Riner, editor of the Edgecombe Press, a company which had published many esoteric classics; James T. Mitchell, a prominent Boston physician, equally well-known as an indefatigable psychic investigator; Origen Hoyt, an equally prominent psychologist; Ward Beauchamp, a controversial young Unitarian Minister; Stephen Hawley, a reporter from *The Evening Transcript*; Arthur Seymour, a principal of Patrick Henry High School and also known for his investigations of the famous medium Renate Caldino; and Thornton Brace, an astronomer of international repute. Two women would also be present: Mrs. Launcelot Osbourne, whose husband was a judge known for his scepticism, and Dolly Tate, who wrote for *Peterson's Magazine*. Eliza had also asked to attend, and Swithin, rather than Mark, would introduce Lucy and oversee the proceedings.

Lucy felt badly about Mark's refusal to attend. She had hoped that in three months he might have accustomed himself to the change in her circumstances, but though outwardly compliant, she knew he was still suffering. He had become quiet and withdrawn, and though he was pleasant enough to Swithin, she could feel his animosity. It was a pity she could not bring him together with Eliza, but her conscience forbade that—and fortunately they were not interested in each other.

She turned her mind back to the seance, wishing that it

were over. Despite her faith in the Old Lord's abilities to produce phenomena of no mean order, she could not help but be concerned over what she feared might be the influx of negative energy that always invaded a circle when there were doubters present. That would affect her directly, and she did not want to feel as tired as she often did after such a meeting, not now when she was expecting a baby. Happiness washed over her at the idea, and her qualms were soon forgotten. Even if she were weary after the sitting, she would have plenty of time to recuperate. She would not have to preside over another one for months. She could rest, relax and knit little garments for their son.

"Lucy," Swithin said.

She looked up at his anxious eyes. "Is it time?" She smiled reassuringly at him.

"They're all awaiting you in the front parlor," he said tensely.

"You mustn't worry about me, my dearest." She moved to him and reached up her hand to caress his cheek. "I'm used to this sort of thing—and you too should be, by now. It's the last I shall be holding for a long time."

"I do thank God for that," he said feelingly.

"But not where Great-grandfather or Mark can hear you," she cautioned. "Or Colin or Juliet."

"I know. Such names cannot be uttered in the presence of the damned without inflicting severe physical pain upon them."

"Oh, you are so understanding, love." She rose on tiptoe to graze his chin with her lips and was caught in his ardent embrace.

"Lucy," he murmured passionately, "you are my life."

"And you are mine, my beloved."

Reluctantly they drew apart, and Lucy, leaning on her husband's arm, came to take her seat at the table in the curtained and shadowy front parlor.

She was surprised by the varied ages of the group, which she had expected to be mainly in the fifties. Instead, those present ranged in age from Eliza's 25 to a possible 70 which might approximate the years of Samuel Gillette. He was a crusty-looking man with jutting eyebrows over pale blue eyes set in a hawklike countenance. His expression was fierce and intolerant, reminding her of a predator on the prowl for prey—herself, she decided as she met his suspicious and challenging glare. Riner, a thin, dark intense individual, also seemed to impale her with his own piercing stare. He, she decided, was in his mid-thirties, while James Mitchell and Origen Hoyt were both in their forties, calm and grave of demeanor. She judged them to be very conservative in dress and thought, waiting to be shown the validity of her mediumship, neither believing nor disbelieving. Ward Beauchamp, in dark clothes and a reversed white collar, did not remind her of the conventional minister. He was short, fair and with a pixyish face. His eyes, a bright hazel, were agleam with humor as if he found the sitting a huge joke. Stephen Hawley, the reporter, was young and not yet out of his twenties. He, too, was small but fiery-eyed and obviously a skeptic. She could actually feel his belligerence. Arthur Seymour, on the other hand, was fair, handsome, gentle and hopeful. She liked him immediately. She did not like Thornton Brace, the scientist, a tall, spare, dignified man of 50 with a shock of iron grey hair and narrow, intolerant grey eyes. She thought he looked at her resentfully, as if she were a specimen on a laboratory slide. Between Hawley, Brace, Gillette, Riner and possibly Beauchamp, there would be a great deal of negative energy, she feared.

Eliza appeared to be a trifle apprehensive. Lucy smiled at her. She was a beautiful woman with lustrous bronze hair and huge green eyes which radiated innocence and sweetness. It was a wonder that Swithin had not been attracted to her. Probably they had known each other too well—at least on his side. Mrs. Tate was a pretty little woman with dark hair and sparkling hazel eyes. Mrs. Osbourne was tall, imposing and in her late fifties. She was very much the grande dame, radiating dignity and self-importance as becomes one who headed committees to reform and rehabilitate fallen women and to abolish the consumption of alcohol and the use of tobacco. She was a charter member of the League of Decency and the most conservatively dressed among the ladies, wearing a neat grey silk gown over a small crinoline. Dolly Tate's crinoline was huge, her gown much frilled and beribboned as was that of Eliza. Lucy had the feeling that Mrs. Osbourne disapproved of them, but not, she decided, as much as she disapproved of herself. She was receiving withering stares from Mrs. Osbourne's cold grey eyes. Obviously the lady was of much the same opinion as Gillette and the other skeptics. It would be a pleasure to close her eyes and shut them out, of her field of vision. She was frankly glad that the Old Lord would soon be taking over for her.

After acknowledging the last of the introductions, Lucy leaned back in her chair and in that moment experienced a strong feeling of apprehension. She felt a pressing need to warn . . . whom? Much to her surprise, she also felt herself growing sleepy. That did not usually happen so quickly, and at this moment she did not want it to happen at all. Her alarm was increasing, and instinctively she knew it was important to remain awake. She tried to wing such a message to the Old Lord, but inxorably her eyelids were growing heavy. She could not hold them up. It was with an unanticipated, unusual fear that she felt the drumming in the middle of her forehead. She waged a losing battle against unconsciousness and finally with a little frightened moan, she went into darkness and oblivion.

Swithin had read the panic in Lucy's eyes. He stepped forward, wanting to awaken her, but in that same moment, laughter trilled forth from her throat, light, mocking and at the same time menacing.

He listened incredulously. In the last months he had been present at many seances. They rarely began so quickly, and the entities that came were generally solemn to the point of being pedantic, those who were not numbered among the so-called "dear departed," he amended mentally. These latter were often distressingly lachrymose, but those brought from distant planes by the Old Lord—and who were expected to be present today—talked of the new order and world harmony. In the case of Napoleon, a frequent visitant, he berated Tallyrand and Wellington, or in one poignant memory, he had shivered through the charred buildings and icy streets of Moscow. Julius Caesar in difficult Latin jeered at the blue-painted Briton, and a shade, identifying herself as Queen Elizabeth, bemoaned the bed manners of Sir Francis Bacon, thus adding an interesting sidelight to British history. None, however, had laughed so airily; it was a strangely beguiling sound, that continuing laughter.

"Who is present?" Gillette demanded, as leader of the group.

Silence answered him. The laughter ceased abruptly.

"Miss Veringer must have been laughing at us," Mrs. Osbourne stated icily, staring at the somnolent Lucy as if she had been one of her erring prostitutes, Swithin thought indignantly.

"I repeat," Gillette said loudly, "Who is present?"

"You are assuming a great deal if you imagine anyone is present," Thornton Brace said caustically.

"Please," Swithin protested gently, "we did not want any negative vibrations."

"I'm surprised at you, Mr. Blake," Stephen Hawley snapped. "I had the impression that you were a reputable lawyer but . . ."

"Hush," Gillette commanded. "We are not here to argue but to conduct a scientific investigation into the nature of the phenomena produced by this medium."

"Who is known to be remarkable," Seymour agreed.

"Indeed, she is," Eliza said staunchly.

Swithin listened with a mixture of gratitude and concern. The reference to his profession had shaken him. He had not really given much thought to the impression he must be making by acting as coordinator. Undoubtedly he would be mentioned in the newspaper but, he reasoned defensively, he was in good company. The people assembled here were prominent and respected and were lending themselves to this inquiry, except that they and Hawley, as well, were observers rather than a participant. He could imagine himself pilloried in one of the reporter's waspish articles, but he stifled a sigh, knowing it was too late to repine. It would not be the first time he had been involved in controversy, and undoubtedly it would not be the last, not with a famed medium for a wife.

"Who is present?" Gillette bent his fierce gaze on Lucy's unconscious form.

A bell rang, a little tinkle such as Swithin had heard when the host was lifted in the Catholic church he visited in Rome. But something told him that this particular sound had nothing to do with churches. It was playing a merry tune. What did that signify? Mediums sometimes produced musical notes from horns and tamborines, but Lucy had never introduced them into her sittings. In fact he had heard her dub them "irresponsible fakery."

Another bell rang, drowning out the tune. Its tone was deep and booming, followed by another and another until the room reverberated to the sound of bells. Startled, even frightened, Swithin pressed his hands against his ears, but even as he did so, the clamor ceased. There was a dead silence, broken only by the gasps of those at the table.

"Trickery!" Hawley said predictably but in a shaken voice.

"Indeed, I . . . m-must agree," Mrs. Osbourne said, sounding similarly discomforted.

"The spirits are out to confound us," Dolly Tate commented lightly.

Swithin was about to launch another protest when the voice in Lucy laughed again. "My name is Bell!" it announced.

Suddenly the table moved, up and down, up and down. The chandelier swayed, and the curtains at the windows fluttered as if in a high wind. An ornament of some kind crashed to the floor.

"A poltergeist," Arthur Seymour exclaimed.

"An evil spirit," Ward Beauchamp commented. "Interesting but spurious."

"Quite!" snapped Thornton Brace.

"Richard, poor, poor Richard," mocked the voice.

"Poor Richard? Has Benjamin Franklin invaded these hallowed precincts?" Dolly Tate inquired.

"Hush!" exclaimed Riner.

"*I command you to go away, woman*," boomed a deep hollow voice.

"Command away, Richard, but you are no longer a proud landowner with minions to serve you, to use their mallets and their sledgehammers to knock a poor woman's house to the ground and spill the elixir that she bartered her soul to concoct," railed the voice. "Did you imagine, Richard, that you could escape my vengeance by fleeing across the seas? Did you and yours hope to settle for a dynasty of Boston Veringers or Blakes, as the case might be? Not yet, my poor love. As 'twas for me, the byways of the world still beckon, and none shall give you nor those who bear even a drop of your blood in their veins a haven here. Yes, even the babe that grows in this womb will share my suffering!''

''*You're dead and can do nothing*!'' cried the hollow voice in tones that resounded through the room but seemed to come from nowhere.

''You're dead, dead, dead, Richard, and can do less!''

A man rose from the table and stalked toward the curtained windows. It was Thornton Brace.

''Sit down, sir,'' Swithin ordered. ''You are breaking the contact.''

''Contact, indeed. Arrant fakery!'' Brace retorted contemptuously.

''Sit down, man,'' rasped Samuel Gillette.

''Let him sit or stand,'' laughed the voice that issued from Lucy's throat. ''Erlina Bell does not need him. Erlina Bell does not need you, Richard, to bring her here. She had been waiting and watching, biding her time until it should be ripe, which now it is. Her hatred's not so easily appeased. You have been brought low, Richard, you and the rest of your wretched tribe, but I am not satisfied.''

''Who the hell is Erlina Bell?'' muttered Stephen Hawley.

Erlina Bell. Swithin had heard the name, but he could not place it.

''It does not matter who she is,'' Arthur Seymour said eagerly. ''She is an entity and possibly evil.''

''Possibly evil, possibly evil?'' chanted the voice. ''Entirely evil, entirely evil, Mr. Seymour, and you know about evil, do you not?''

Swithin saw him blanch. ''I . . . I do not understand you,'' Seymour said nervously.

''You understand, Mr. Principal,'' tittered the voice. ''Who last came to be caned in your office? Was it Howard or Johnny?''

''What are you saying, you lying witch?'' he demanded furiously.

''Hush!'' Gillette ordered.

Who was Erlina Bell? Swithin racked his brains and still came up with no answers. He was feeling very odd and more than a little dizzy. There was, he suddenly noticed, a strange smell in the room—of incense. Again he was reminded of a Roman church and wondered whether or not he was imagining it. No one had burned incense in this room during a seance, not since he had attended them, but the odor in his nostrils was heady, even beguiling, like some strange exotic perfume.

A dancer in a Parisian cafe on the Left Bank had been steeped in such a scent. He flushed at the memory of her golden body, naked in his arms. Why was he remembering that wild night, he, a staid married man of three months standing? Something deep within him chuckled and gave him the lie. His senses were stirred, and there were other odd images in his mind—he and that golden dancer, writhing together in her incense-filled room. In his ears was sound, music, another merry tune.

"Come and dance with me, dance with me, dance with me. All of you come and dance with Erlina Bell," trilled the voice. Lucy rose from table and whirled across the room.

Swithin leaped to his feet, full of trepidation, but Lucy came to a stop near the windows and stood beckoning with both little hands, a beguiling smile on her lips, provocative and wicked. He started toward her only to have his attention deflected by a movement at the table. Turning, he saw Mrs. Osbourne rise and step forward. She, too, was smiling. He wanted to order her to sit down, but he could not seem to frame the words. He could only stare as very deliberately she began to whirl around the room, and as she whirled, she tittered madly.

Stopping suddenly, she plucked furiously at her garments, jerking at hooks, ripping and tearing them when they would not yield. In an amazingly short time, her gown lay on the floor and she stood in camisole and crinoline over several petticoats, which she stripped off in rapid succession, still tittering. Her knickers and camisole followed. In a few more moments, she was naked as the proverbial jaybird and still tittering madly.

Swithin rose to stop her, but as he went toward her, he found he did not want to stop her, even though naked she was a pitiable sight with her withered breasts hanging down like the teats of a worn-out sow. She seemed completely unaware of the image she presented as licking her lips, she cried, "Come and dance with me, all of you! Come, come, come and dance with Satan upon this lovely heath!" Raising her thin legs she leaped and cavorted about the room, interspersing her movements with incredibly obscene gestures, her grey hair loosed from its pins and falling in thin locks over her bony shoulders.

Incredibly, Samuel Gillette brushed past Swithin, and he, too, was naked, his body even uglier than that of Mrs. Osbourne, being thin, bony and pallid with huge freckles on his back. Swithin's ears were attuned a great pushing away of chairs and looking back at the table, he saw that all the men were on their feet, their hands busy with buttons and braces as they endeavored to disrobe as fast as possible.

Music. He had heard the music before and now he heard it again, only louder. Coupled with it was low laughter, and what manner of tune could it be? It seemed to be produced by drums and violins. The drums were louder than the violins, a rhythmic beat that made him eager to move in time to it. His body was invaded by the rhythm, and he forgot his confusion and surprise, everything save the need to join in the dance. He was warm and growing warmer; his cravat was too tight, choking him. He ripped it off. His clothes seemed to be weighing his body down. He did not need them. If he were to dance, he must be free of all these restraints. He shrugged off his jacket and fumbled at the fastenings of his trousers, laughing as they slid to the floor. He stepped out of them, unlaced his boots and finally was naked, too.

He looked around him and saw that the group was forming a circle. Something inside of him told him he must stop them, but he did not want to stop them, could not stop them because there was a whisper in his ear, commanding him to obey the prompting of his senses. Someone tugged at his hand, and turning he found Eliza, beautiful in her nakedness, her bronze hair falling to her waist and a look in her green eyes he had never seen before.

"Come and dance, Swithin," she crooned. "Come and dance, my dearest love."

But he was not her love. His eyes fell on her breasts, and though he knew he was not her love, he wanted to . . . He was whirled around and around, and he found that Stephen Hawley was on his other side. He was growing dizzy as he continued to whirl and stamp and hop to the pounding of the drums and the shriek of the violins. It seemed to him that he had danced this way before, only it had been in the fields before a small stone house. He had danced and danced, and then, seizing the woman who danced beside him, he had thrown her to the earth and copulated with her, as had all of them, finding partners and raising the energy they needed to summon winds and sink ships, to raise demons and thwart the godly—to serve Satan!

The imagery fled, and he saw that the circle had broken up and some of the group were embracing. There was Arthur Seymour, his hair wet with sweat and plastered against his head. His calm dignity was gone. He was chanting loudly, each word from his lips an obscenity. Catching Swithin's eyes upon him, he smiled provocatively and moved nearer but was pulled away by Herman Riner, who kissed him full on his smiling lips. A second later Swithin saw them, still locked in an embrace, sink to the floor. He laughed and moved away from them. His loins throbbed. He wanted his dancer, his golden dancer. Her memory was large in his mind, but Eliza was beside him again, clutching him, her hands slippery with sweat, fastening about his thighs, sliding knowingly around them to caress him. They fell to the floor, and she was golden. He lay atop her, breathing heavily, thrusting himself against her, while she pressed open-mouthed kisses upon his chest. But this was madness! Lucy, Lucy! He pulled away from Eliza. Her frustrated screams followed him, as he stumbled blindly forward and fell. He rose, only to be pulled down by Mrs. Osbourne, who in turn was clutched by Samuel Gillette. She howled with frustration as Swithin wrenched himself away from them and saw that Eliza now lay with Stephen Hawley, who was eagerly finishing the invasion he had begun.

He heard a scream and recognized Lucy's voice. Staring in that direction, he saw only a mass of writhing bodies. No, there she was, fighting James Mitchell who was endeavoring to mount her.

He flung himself on the man and pulled him away, kicking him savagely in the ribs. Then Lucy was against him, naked, a wanton smile on her lips, caressing him, and in that voice that was not her voice whispering words that both thrilled and titilated him, while he knew somewhere in his befogged mind that it could not be Lucy who was inciting him to caress her in ways that would have been totally foreign to her. The wild music was loud in his ears but no louder than the beating of his heart as he possessed her. Finally, when he raised his eyes from his wife's beautiful little body, he saw Dolly Tate, fleeing from Origen Hoyt but laughing as he caught her, only to be pulled away from him by Ward Beauchamp, who pinioned her against the wall. At his command, she knelt, open-mouthed to service him. Origen Hoyt threw himself against the minister, who thrust a fist in his eye. Yelling, he stumbled back, while Beauchamp, pulling Dolly Tate down, began to caress her. She laughed loudly as Hoyt stumbled toward Lucy. Swithin knocked him down, only to be attacked by Thornton Brace, who also clawed at Lucy. Mrs. Osbourne suddenly joined them, clutching Brace, who thrust her back with a sharp elbow to her stomach. With a howl, she fell writhing to the floor. Hoyt, recovering, once more grabbed at Lucy. Brace stumbled toward Dolly Tate and tried to kick Beauchamp away, but the agile young minister grabbed at his feet and sent him crashing down, where Mrs. Osbourne, shrieking obscenities, clawed at Brace's bare chest. In Swithin's arms, Lucy laughed low and in her throat as James Mitchell tried to pull her away from her husband. Swithin, thrusting at him, was caught and pinioned by Hoyt. He tried to get away, but Hoyt proved to be stronger than he looked. Meanwhile Brace, freed from Mrs. Osbourne, joined Mitchell in capturing a giggling Lucy. Swithin writhed in his captor's grasp trying to reach her.

"Stop, stop, in the name of God, stop!" Mark stood in the doorway, screaming the forbidden name and wincing with the pain of it. Yet he cried out the command a second time, and Swithin became aware of a diminishing of the music.

"Begone, damned spirits, begone," Mark intoned. "In the name of God!" He coughed and blood gushed forth from his bleeding mouth.

Hoyt's arms fell away from Swithin. The music, the laughter, the shrieks of the women stopped.

There was dead silence in the room.

Swithin, shaking, looked around and blinked, not sure that he was seeing aright. Blinking did not help. The room was a shambles. The table was overturned. Amazingly, all the chairs were piled one on top of the other, and as he looked at them, they all came crashing down. The floor was covered with garments tossed helter-skelter, wherever their maddened wearers had tossed them. His gaze did not linger long on the floor, as he looked at the once dignified men and women who had entered this chamber a short time ago. They were a pitiable sight, their eyes wide in shame and horror, their bodies stripped naked, wet with sweat and, in some cases, bruised and bleeding.

Glancing at Eliza, Swithin shuddered as he saw blood running down the insides of her legs. As she met his gaze, she quivered all over, and sinking down, she put her hands around her knees, hugging them against her. Beside her, Stephen Hawley also sank down, his face white, his eyes filled with shame. Arthur Seymour, rolling off of Herman Riner, was also weeping. Looking down, Swithin gasped as he saw Lucy lying naked on the floor. He reached for his jacket to cover her and stopped, remembering that he, too, was naked. Confusion filled him. What had happened? How had it happened? He wished devoutly that he could not remember the madness that had invaded them all—but he could, in every last detail!

Suddenly the room was full of cries, screams and bellows, as those present pawed madly through the piles of discarded clothing, searching for their own garments, ignoring crinolines and pantaloons, climbing into such garments as must cover them easily and hastily. Swithin, kneeling beside Lucy, found her confused and terrified.

"What happened?" she moaned, as he helped her to dress.

"I am not sure, my love."

He was to repeat that statement many times during the next half-hour as he tried to give a lucid answer to those who accused, babbled and screamed impotent threats at them.

Finally Mark took over, and in a rough, snarling tone that Swithin had never heard for him, he said, "We are sorry for what has happened here, but given your august reputations, we fell that it is best you keep this matter to yourselves."

"You ought to be . . . to be . . ." Words failed Mrs. Osbourne, who was bent over double, clutching her gown about her as if she still felt herself to be the naked cynosure of all eyes.

Other malefic mutterings accompanied her unspoken threat, some erupting into accusations against Lucy, who stood trembling in her husband's arm.

"If you do not want any of this to leak out, I suggest you hold your tongue, the lot of you," Mark advised sharply. "We have no control over those we summon at a seance. I imagine this is not the first time such a thing has taken place, nor will it be the last. As experimenters and reseaches into the occult, you know that you are dealing with unknown and inexplicable forces."

"With demons," Dolly Tate mumbled, weeping.

"That is not unlikely," Mark responded. "And I wish to tell you that the medium is no more responsible for them than you or I. It is dangerous to tamper with the unknown, but all of you are aware of that, too."

"He's right," croaked old Gillette. "Let this occurence remain a secret, a . . . gentleman's agreement among us."

After an amazingly brief period of bickering the group, including Stephen Hawley, declared itself in sympathy with Gillette. No one spoke as they gathered their things together and hurried out, going off in as many different directions as there were people.

A moment after the room was cleared, Lucy, who had been very quiet, whispered, "Swithin, I do feel so very strange." Suddenly, she was a dead weight in his arms. Paling, he carried her up to bed. A shuddering breath escaped him as he saw how white and drained she looked, as if the blood had gone from her body. He did not need Mark to tell him that she had been felled by a great infusion of negative energy, but unfortunately it was nothing he could explain to the hastily summoned physician. There was a moment when he feared she would lose her baby, but against all odds she did not. However the physician left strict orders that she must remain in bed during the next six months.

"Else I'll not be responsible for either her safety or that of your child," he finished with a stern look at Swithin, as if he held him personally responsible for what had happened to his wife.

"I understand, sir," Swithin said in a low voice. But as he sat at Lucy's bedside, he did not understand at all what had happened or why. It was his wife who eventually enlightened him later that same evening.

"It's the curse, my love," she said weakly. " 'Twas Erlina Bell, remember?"

He did remember and wondered why he had not remembered at a time when it would have done some good, when he might have awakened Lucy and halted the seance. Was that the curse as well? He did not want to think of the seance or of his own actions and those of that exalted group of scholars and community leaders. Unfortunately it was not that easy to banish the episode from his mind. It had left him full of fears, not only for his wife but for all those who had participated. In common with himself, he was regretfully sure that they remembered what had happened in all its obscene and revolting detail. That in itself was a curse, and was it mere madness to fear that the curse had affected them all? It was equally mad, he realized, to believe in its existence.

Yet he did believe, and he scanned the papers every day during the week following the seance, fearing that Stephen Hawley might have yielded to the promptings of his pen. No word appeared, but he did learn that Arthur Seymour had inexplicably resigned from his post at Patrick Henry High School and at last report was bound for Paris. Herman Riner, that well-known psychologist, had closed his office and was also going aboard—destination unknown. Mrs. Launcelot Osbourne had withdrawn from all her committees, and rumor had it that she had been taken to a sanitarium, suffering from a mild nervous breakdown. Dolly Tate, amazingly enough, was marrying Ward Beauchamp, and they were going to Tahiti as missionaries. Samuel Gillette astonished his colleagues at Harvard by his abrupt retirement, and James Mitchell had announced that he was leaving his lucrative Boston practice for the poorly paid position of doctor in a Pennsylvania mining town. His pronouncement that he owed it to his soul made no sense to anyone save, perhaps, those who had attended the seance. Thornton Brace had also quit Boston for parts unknown. Eliza Bishop, Swithin heard from his mother, was engaged to Stephen Hawley; they would be married immediately.

He heard the news with regret. He could not imagine stately Eliza being wed to the diminutive reporter. However, upon a vision rising in his mind's eye, he guessed that they could not conclude their nuptials soon enough!

In the next few weeks Swithin realized that if none of the participants had discussed their experiences at what could be termed a history-making seance, there were rumors. These, he guessed, were generated by the servants of those who had attended. Crowds of the curious began to congregate around the house and some people had the temerity to pound on the door and demand to see the medium.

At last, Swithin could bring his bride home. His mother, shut in her rooms, did not protest. She, at least, had not heard the rumors and could not help being excited at the prospect of a grandchild. Mark stayed in the house near the cemetery, tended by Colin and Juliet when the madness was upon him. The Old Lord remained with them. Swithin could not bemoan the loss of his in-laws. In fact, if Lucy had been feeling better, his cup would have been full and running over. As it was, his joy was present but circumscribed. However, he was sure that when the child was born, all would be well.

As Lucy's time drew near, it was obvious to Colin and Juliet that she was losing strength, even though she was cheerful, happy and full of plans for the time when she would finally be allowed to leave her bed. She blamed her weakness on the pending birth of her child. Fortunately Molly did not disturb her with her wailing. She and Grimalkin much preferred the reassuring vista of the graveyard and stubbornly remained upon the roof of the adjacent house. It was there that Juliet sought them one night, a few days before Lucy's child was due. She had detected a different note in the banshee's howl. Flying up as a bat, she startled both Molly and the cat with her hasty transformation.

"Ach, Miss Juliet, 'tis a sad thing to see you," mourned the banshee.

"Never mind that." Juliet propped herself against one of the chimneys stacks. "I'm used to it," she said, shrugging. "I heard a new note in your caterwauling that sounds even more onimous than usual. What more can happen to us?"

"Ach, 'tis the poor little one." She unleashed a lugubrious sigh.

"Which?" Juliet asked but knew the answer. "Lucy?"

"Aye, little Lucy."

Colin, gliding to the roof, changed and asked gruffly, "When?"

" 'Twill be three days after her child is born."

"Ohhhh," Juliet moaned. "Why?"

"Because she be frail as a mayfly. 'Twas that Erlina Bell done for her apurpose. 'Twasn't to be expected she'd escape the curse. Now be off wi' ye. I must get on wi' me song." The banshee resumed her howling.

They moved away. "Oh, Colin," Juliet mourned. "We cannot let her go, nor our Lucy."

"We cannot help her," he said quickly.

"We can." Juliet put her little hand upon his arm. "You know we can," she said tensely.

"We'll . . . talk about it." There was reluctance but possible acquiesence as well as he changed quickly and flew from the roof, followed by Juliet. An even more ominous wail broke from the banshee coupled with a piercing screech from Grimalkin, which neither sister nor brother heard—nor would they have heeded the warning if they had.

Lucy awakened, feeling marvelously fit. She also felt considerably lighter. Much as she had longed for the birth of her child, her daughter Olivia, she had been tremendously heavy and weary at the last.

In spite of all her resting, it had not been an easy birth. She could still hear the doctor's gentle urging, "Push, push, push . . ." She had obeyed to the best of her ability, but it had been so hard that she felt as if she had been torn in half. Later, seeing the darling little red-faced baby with the dark swirl of hair which was the very same shade as Swithin's, she knew it had been worth every tedious second of the last six months, only she did wish that Swithin had looked happier.

He should have been happy, being the father of such a darling, but perhaps he had wanted a son. She had taxed him with that only to have him weep and say that he wanted exactly what she had given him—a daughter. He had agreed with a sob that he, too, liked the name Olivia, which she had culled from a favorite Shakespearean play. "Look you, sir, such a one as I, is it not well done . . ." she had quoted softly from *Twelfth Night*, Olivia's speech, only to have Swithin burst into even louder sobs. She had never seen him weep and it frightened her, especially as she felt so strange and weak.

"Am I going to die?" she remembered asking him, only to have him turn away, his shoulders shaking, corroborating her fears.

"You're not going to die, darling." Eliza had been there, too, looking pale. She was into her sixth month of pregnancy and married to Stephen Hawley, a poor exchange for Swithin, Lucy thought. It did seem as if she would die; she had been feeling so weak, especially at night. She had dreamed a great deal about Juliet and Colin, wondering why they had not come to see her. Last night she had dreamed that Colin had kissed and kissed her, but she would never confide that dream to Swithin. He would think she cherished some sort of secret passion for her uncle. Actually, much as she loved Juliet and Colin, she had always been a little revolted by their condition, especially since neither seemed in the least disturbed by what they had to do. She knew they had been once, but now they actually seemed to revel in it. They didn't even miss the sunlight!

"The moon is so beautifully bright," Juliet had confided once.

Lucy glanced toward her window but saw only darkness. It must be the dark of the moon, yet she could have sworn it was full when she drifted off to sleep last night. That was why Mark hadn't been to see her. Poor Mark! The last time he visited her he had looked so pale and miserable, all his bright coloring dimmed and his eyes like two burnt holes in a blanket, worrying over her, she guessed. But no one had to worry any more. She was better, much better. She could hardly wait until morning came and she could see Swithin. He wasn't sleeping with her now. They had been apart for six months, but now he would be able to come back to her bed and make love to her. She thrilled to the thought, and then she tensed, hearing a sound, a cry, a baby—her baby? No, it was an animal, a rabbit, she didn't know how she knew that, but she did. It had been caught by an owl, poor thing. The owl would devour it, drinking the blood.

A thirst grew in her, and she needed water or tea to quell it. Her throat was dry, so very dry. Had not Swithin left the pitcher near the bed?

She put out her hand and felt softness above her. The quilt? She tried to push it away and felt hardness now. She cried out in fear and then the hardness was gone.

"She's awake," someone said.

It was still dark, but looking up Lucy had no trouble seeing Juliet and Colin. "I need water!" she groaned.

"Water, so soon?" Juliet said inexplicably.

"Soon?" Lucy did not understand.

"Are you thirsty, love?" Colin asked ruefully.

"I am," she responded crossly. "Is there not a pitcher? I do not expect I should get out of bed, but I do feel much stronger."

"Do you, dearest?" Juliet asked.

"Yes, but I am so thirsty," Lucy complained wondering why they were not giving her the water she craved so desperately.

"It did not happen to me . . . so soon," Juliet muttered.

"Nor me, but circumstances alter cases," Colin responded.

With rising indignation, Lucy said, "Please, I beg you'll not stand there talking when I am so thirsty. I need a drink!" She knew she was acting badly, but she could not help it, listening to them nattering away when she was so much in need of water.

"We know, child," Juliet said. "Come." She pulled Lucy to her feet.

Lucy felt most peculiar, as if she had passed through something yielding that should not have been yielding. She had glimpsed the solidness of a door and a second later had been outside of it—without its opening! That had to be a dream! But she was outside. Grass was tickling her bare feet, and there were trees around her. Looking up, she was nearly blinded by the mere sliver of a new moon.

"How did I get outside?" She stared about her and saw great carved monuments white in the moonlight. "Why am I *here*?" she whispered on a rising note of panic.

"Lucy . . ." Colin began.

"Dearest," Juliet chimed in.

Lucy swallowed, trying vainly to vanquish that terrible thirst. Looking at her companions, she suddenly knew why she was there and knew what they had done. A terrible despair engulfed her.

"Why?" she cried accusingly. "Why, why, why did you do it?"

"My love." Juliet put her arm around Lucy's shaking shoulders and looked into her tearless eyes. "We could not bear to let you go."

"So you . . . so both of you . . ." She could not finish the sentence but knew the reason for her weakness of the last nights and knew that they knew she knew.

"Swithin!" she wailed. "My child . . . my child . . ." But in her new agony, she could not think of them any longer because she was so thirsty.

Later, when the radiance of the moon had dimmed and when Lucy had sadly and regretfully drunk the warm blood of a rabbit, hating the way it made her feel, full of life and well, she stared at her relations—resenting them, even hating them!

They understood.

"Dearest," Juliet said, "I know we shouldn't have done it."

"I shouldn't have let you talk me into it." Colin regarded Juliet ruefully.

"No, no, no, you shouldn't have done it!" Lucy agreed despairingly.

"But think," Juliet urged. "You'll be able to visit Swithin and Livia."

"Livia? Her name's Olivia."

"They will call your daughter Livia, my dear."

"Ohhhh," Lucy wailed blinking against the tears that did not, would never come. "No, I'll not see them, not like this. Oh, I am accursed." The truth of her cry came home to her. "The curse?" she whispered.

"Yes, yes, it must have been," Juliet cried, almost in relief.

"It must have been," he agreed.

"Will it fall upon my child?" Lucy demanded.

"Perhaps not," Colin said soothingly. "She's not a Veringer."

"The blood of the Old Lord runs in her veins," Lucy moaned. "Poor child, poor child, and poor Swithin, my love."

"You may see him, dearest," Juliet said.

"No, I will go away. You must take me far, far away. I may go, may I not?"

"All that's needed is a stone and Mark to help us when we need his help," Colin said.

"Mark! Does he know?" Lucy asked.

"Mark is here," he said, coming to stand beside Colin. There was a compassionate and sorrowing look in his golden eyes. "Lucy, my dear, none of this was my doing, but I am glad to see you and I am here to help you. I knew, knowing you, that you'd not want to stay."

"*And I knew, too, my poor child.*"

Lucy looked around and saw Richard Veringer as he had been in life, clad in dark knee breeches and a black satin coat, lace sparkling with diamonds at his throat, his hair lavishly powdered and clubbed at the back with a dark grosgrain ribbon. He did not look old. He seemed in the prime of life, but his eyes were aged and agonized.

"Great-grandfather," Lucy moaned. "Why did you let them do this to me?"

"*I was not consulted, dear child,*" he said ponderously.

"Oh, Mark." Lucy raised her eyes to his face. "Could you not out of your love for me pound a stake through my heart when morning comes?"

"Lucy, no." There was terror in his voice. "You'd not want that!"

"*No, child, you would not,*" The Old Lord whispered.

"You could not," Juliet said, exchanging an agonized look with Colin.

Staring at them, Lucy found to her own confusion and utter shame that, on thinking of it, she did not want it either. "I must go away then," she said.

"*We will all go away, my child. The world is wide,*" the Old Lord said.

"And we must never come back," Lucy told him solemnly.

"We never will." Juliet and Colin spoke almost in unison and with equal solemnity.

"You know I am with you, Lucy," Mark said.

Lucy found that she could smile. "My child will be safe," she murmured. With a little moan of fear, she stared at the Old Lord. "Erlina Bell must be satisfied by now."

"*I am sure she is*," he agreed gruffly.

"The sky is paling," Mark reminded them.

"Come, love." Juliet put an arm around Lucy's shoulders and led her back to her tomb.

Part Four

One

Livia Blake lifted a closely written page and waved it at the girl who stood before her desk. "Look at the number of misspellings in this story!" She shook her head, saying even more caustically than usual, "Had I not spoken with Mrs. Howard we would have come out with errors that would have made it totally useless as a news item. If the preparations for your forthcoming nuptials are going to interfere with your efficiency . . ."

"I am sorry," Miss Emily Harte began, "but . . ."

"You're being sorry is no excuse."

"But . . ."

"Do you wish to continue working at the *Marblehead Mercury* or would you prefer to resign?" Livia's eyes, a clear gold, seemed to flash fire.

"I want to continue," Emily said. "I do enjoy writing for . . ."

"Enjoy?" echoed Livia. "*Enjoy* suggests that you would be as happy cycling or dancing or swimming or camping. Writing for the *Mercury* is a vocation and an occupation. Have you any notion how very few women are engaged in the business of turning out a newspaper?" Without waiting for the response that was obviously trembling on Emily's lips, she continued sharply. "Very few is the answer. Women are not expected to be editors or reporters. They are expected to marry, as you will soon do, breed brats and turn their under-developed intelligences to cookery. You came to me because you said you wished to write. I have given you that opportunity, and the minute a gentleman looks sideways at you, you are ready to swoon into his arms and forget everything you told me when you applied . . . when you begged for this position."

There was a knock on the door. "Well?" Livia called impatiently.

The door was opened by Marian Sedley, the clerical typist who also served as receptionist for the *Marblehead Mercury*. She was a small, slender woman who was, at this moment, looking harried and extremely confused. "Miss Blake . . ." she said tentatively.

"Well," Livia snapped, "what is it, Marian?"

Miss Sedley pushed a straying brown curl out of her eyes, leaving a smear of black on her forehead. "There . . . there's a gentleman here."

"Indeed? And is he so frightening?"

"Frightening?"

"Judging from your expression, this gentleman wants to eat you for dinner and toss your bones over his shoulder when he is done."

"Oh, Miss Blake," Marian said, giggling nervously, "it's not that. It's that he wishes to place an advertisement."

"An advertisement?" Livia's eyes widened.

"Gracious!" Emily interjected. "A gentleman?"

"And very well-spoken, too." Miss Sedley turned a little pink.

Spotting this telltale hue, Livia said coldly, "Does the gentleman have horns and a tail or possibly purple feathers sprouting from his head?"

Emily giggled nervously, and Marian blushed an even deeper pink. "He is most personable," she murmured.

"I am glad of that," Livia said sarcastically. "I should be intimidated myself, if I thought our offices had been invaded by some monster rather than one who has merely come to place an advertisement. We have had advertisements before, not many, I'll grant you . . .''

"And never from a man," Emily broke in.

Livia opened her mouth for another withering retort and thought better of it. It was unwise to keep one of her few advertisers waiting. "Since you feel incapable of dealing with this crisis, Marian, I suggest you show the gentleman in here."

"I did not say I was incapable," Marian began, with a rare display of spirit, "but I just thought you'd like to know."

Some of Livia's hauteur vanished. "And so I would, Marian dear, though I could wish it were not such a nine-day wonder. Show him in, please, and Emily, you may go."

"Am I fired?" Emily asked timidly.

"No, not fired, just be more careful in the future. You do have the makings of a good reporter, should you care to continue in that position once you are wed."

"Oh, I will!" Emily promised. "Thank you, Miss Blake." she hurried out.

Livia Blake expelled a breath bordering on a snort. Since her recent engagement, all of Emily's vaunted arguments on the independence of women had gone by the boards. Let a man put his foot into the small offices adjoining her house and the two members comprising the staff of the *Marblehead Mercury* fluttered like hens before a rooster!

Of course Marian and Emily were both young or, at least, younger than herself, and Marian entertained the hopes that in Emily's case had been fulfilled when the minister's son proposed to her, turning her attention from her Social Notes column to fittings, bridesmaid selection, invitations and a honeymoon in Saratoga, New York.

Marian, who took the few ads that came into the *Mercury* and helped with the layout, was not bespoken but, at 22, she still had hopes. Livia, who had turned down more proposals than she could count in the nine years following her eighteenth birthday, had almost abandoned the hope that she would ever meet a man who pleased her to the point that she would be willing to place herself in the matrimonial harness. Invariably the young men who were attracted to her either turned a deaf ear to her outspoken views on the place of women in society or, if their hearts were set as much on her inheritance as on her considerable beauty, they listened attentively and then by some remark revealed their intrinsic insincerity.

"Fortune hunters," she muttered to herself and frowned, remembering that one Orville Cox was expected for dinner that night. He was the son of one of her father's Harvard classmates. He lived in Lynn, but when he had come to see Swithin Blake on business, she had met and liked him. He had looked upon her with the usual awestruck admiration, seemingly not caring that at five-feet-nine, she was a good two inches taller than himself. He was charming and had taken her driving after church on two successive Sundays. He had also been her escort at a local dance, and they had gone cycling together several times. These activities had led her father to cherish hopes he had not scrupled to hide from her.

"It would please me greatly if you and young Cox . . ." He had begun several sentences only to be discouraged from continuing in that vein.

"I like Mr. Cox, Papa, but I feel I must know him better," had been her response. It was no use telling him that though she liked Mr. Cox more than some of her previous suitors, she found his attitude regarding the *Mercury* very distasteful. It was plain to her that he thought it merely a plaything to occupy her before she married and turned her mind to the serious business of raising a family.

The *Mercury* was well-written, well-printed, and even if it was not a money-making endeavor, it was read. In fact, in the three years since she, with her father's backing, had launched it, the *Mercury* had picked up a circulation of something over a thousand. Its Social Notes were very popular, prized, it was true, mainly by matrons who were pleased to see the names of themselves and their guests in black and white. Still she also had been congratulated on her editorials and denigrated as well, when she plunged into the deep waters already stirred by Susan B. Anthony and Elizabeth Cady Stanton.

"Mr. Grenfall," Marian announced, cutting short Livia's ruminations.

"Please come in," she said, not glancing directly at her visitor and only getting an impression of considerable height and dark wavy hair. She indicated a chair facing her desk. "Will you sit down, please?"

"Thank you, Miss Blake," her visitor said in a melifluous voice.

Really looking at him for the first time, his appearance came as a shock, and if she were the type to flutter, it was very possible that he might have had such an effect on her. He was well and conservatively dressed in dark garments. To her relief, he had eschewed such facial adornments as side whiskers, a beard or moustache thus allowing her to see that his features were regular and his chin cleft. In addition to his height, which she placed at some three inches over six feet, he was well-built. His shoulders were wide, his waist slender and most of his inches appeared to be in his long legs. His eyes, she noted, were so brown as to seem black, and his glance was almost mesmerising, a notion she quickly rejected. She was further annoyed by a reaction that could almost be translated as attraction. His main attraction, she reminded herself crossly, was his willingness to advertise in her newspaper. However she could not help but be pleased that he regarded her without the initial surprise evinced by the bookkeeper, the printer and the several other men who had found that the O. Blake written in gold letters on her office door stood for Olivia rather than Osbert or Oscar. She would have used L for Livia but her father would not hear of it, even though he had always called her by that diminutive. "It was your mother's wish that you be christened Olivia," he had once explained.

She thrust these digressions to the back of her mind and said briskly, "My assistant informs me that you wish to run an advertisement in our paper."

"I do, Miss Blake," he looked at her earnestly. "I understand the *Mercury* appears twice a month?"

"Yes. We publish every other Tuesday from September through June."

"This is Wednesday. Judging from the copy I read, next Tuesday will be a publication date?"

"Yes." She was agreeably surprised that he had actually read the paper. She could not help inquiring, "What decided you to advertise with us, sir?"

"I based my opinion on the editorial content. Whoever wrote the article on street traffic has some excellent ideas about its regulation. I also enjoyed the piece on Mrs. Stanton.

I heard her lecture in Minneapolis, and I agree with the writer.''

Livia buttoned down a smile. It would not do to appear too gratified by one of the first favorable comments she had received on her editorials from a man other than her father. ''I am glad that you agree with our writers, sir.''

''I do. I have always been of the opinion that women must play a greater role in the affairs of the nation. I also like the other articles, and if I am allowed to choose a position for my advertisement, I would like to place it near the Social Notes which, I understand, are also widely read.''

Livia repressed another smile, appreciating his tact in inserting the word 'also' and thus suggesting that the editorials were as popular as the notes which of course they were not, as he must know.

''I could arrange that, sir,'' she agreed. ''Of course it would depend upon the content of your copy.''

''That is certainly understandable. I hope that you will agree with me that my choice is logical. You see, Miss Blake, I am a teacher of elocution, and since I am in Marblehead for an indefinite period, I should like the public at large to know that I give private lessons.''

''I see. I presume you come to the house?''

''Of course, Miss Blake. I could hardly receive my pupils in my lodgings.''

''Naturally not,'' Livia agreed quickly. She had heard a touch of hauteur in his tone and respected him for it. Her question had been foolish, she realized with some annoyance. Obviously he could not expect his pupils, female or male, to come to his lodgings, and if she had been thinking clearly, she never would have suggested such a thing.

''I will be glad to run your advertisement in the suggested space. Our rates are fifty cents a column inch.''

''I would like the first advertisement to be four inches long and two columns wide. Let's see. You publish Tuesday, which is May 4th, yes?''

''That is correct,'' Livia said, surprised and pleased by the amount of space he wanted. Four inches would be two dollars plus the extra width would bring it to six dollars. And he had specified that it would be for the first advertisement, suggesting that he would run the ad again.

"May 18th is the day you'll publish again, and accordingly I would like the advertisement to run again. Is it possible to reserve the same space?"

"I believe it's available, sir," she replied, making a determined effort not to sound either excited or pleased. Her attitude must be casual as if, she received such placements every day.

"Good. We are agreed, then. I will pay in advance, and I will give you the copy which I trust you to print in letters that catch the eye."

"Most assuredly, we will do that, sir."

"Now I understand that your Social Notes are widely read."

"They are—in town," Livia felt it incumbent to stress.

"The Marblehead public is the one I wish to reach. I would appreciate it if one of your reporters might cover the meeting of our literary society. It will be convening this Friday at eight in the evening."

"Your literary society, sir? Which one might that be?"

"It is called The Seventh Circle, and until a month ago we were located in Salem. Unfortunately our building burned down, and we were unable to find a satisfactory replacement. We were extremely concerned, as you might guess. Then one of our members mentioned that she knew of a place in Marblehead which we might lease at a price commensurate with our combined purse. We wrote to the owners and were able to secure the Pendergrass mansion. I suppose that you, as a native of this delightful town, are familiar with it?"

Livia had barely managed to stifle an exclamation of dismay. In a carefully neutral tone she replied, "Yes, I certainly am familiar with it. I had heard that it was going to be torn down."

"No, we saved it—at least until our lease runs out. A charming location, do you not agree?"

"It overlooks the sea," Livia said carefully, "but it is some distance from the center of town. Most of our literary groups are located there."

"So I understand. That is why I would be most grateful if one of your staff might attend our first meeting in our new home. We would appreciate a note."

"You might give me the information, sir. There is no

actual reason for any of us to go there."

"Oh, but there is, if you will permit me to differ with you, Miss Blake," he said earnestly. "You see several of our members are putting on a small entertainment, an adaptation of an Edgar Allan Poe story, *The Fall of the House of Usher*. It is an excellent dramatization, and I feel they should have some encouragement and recognition for a thoroughly professional effort."

"It does sound interesting," Livia mused. "Unfortunately, our one reporter, Miss Harte, is soon to be married and is in the midst of rehearsals for her wedding. Marian . . . that is, Miss Sedley does not write."

"Which leaves you," he said hopefully. "I cannot believe that a young woman who edits a bimonthly newspaper does not do some of the writing herself."

"I do," she admitted diffidently. Meeting his dark and eager gaze, she found it very difficult to explain that she was expected to cover the Thoreau Society meeting on Friday night. She also remembered that Marian had suggested more than once that she would like to be a contributor. Marian could not write very well, but she could and did gather facts. These could easily be rewritten and her new advertiser placated. It was good business, too. Not only did they rarely get advertisements, they had never had anyone suggest that such an insert, however small, must run twice. She said, "I expect I could come on Friday night. Of course, I could not stay long."

"We would only want you to see our playlet, and I, myself, would take you there and bring you back."

"That would be very helpful, sir," Livia said gratefully, for concurrent with her acquiescence had been her concern about transportation. Jack, their elderly coachman, did not like to drive at night, and she preferred not to press the matter. Furthermore, the old man would expect her to bring one of her friends with her, being quite unable to distinguish between assignment and a social visit. He would certainly not approve of her going as far afield as the Pendergrass mansion, especially in view of its unfortunate reputation. He would grumble all the way there and all the way back.

"We can count on your presence then, Miss Blake?" Mr. Grenfall asked eagerly.

"Yes, I will be there."

"I am delighted. We do want to attract new members, you know."

"I can understand that. However, I must warn you that you have a great deal of competition. There's Thoreau Society, a Johnson Circle and a Chronicle Group, the last being devoted to collecting items about Marblehead's Revolutionary past."

"I can imagine that the particular society must be flourishing in this year of 1881."

"It is, sir. We will commemorate the British surrender with a parade later in the summer."

"I hope I will be present to see it. Now, as to my advertisement . . ."

"Oh, yes, the copy." Livia felt her cheeks grow warm. She had almost forgotten his main purpose in coming to see her, and that was unusual. It was also confusing and annoying as well. Her manner was deliberately distant, even brusque when she finally showed him out of her office.

Though the rest of Wednesday was hectic and though Livia was certainly weary by the time she closed the door of what had once been her father's law offices until his retirement two years back, she was more restless than was her wont. She found herself thinking about Mr. Grenfall. She actually looked forward to covering the meeting on Friday, even though she wondered who had been unkind enough to suggest that he and his Seventh Circle take over the Pendergrass mansion, a place that had the reputation of being haunted, which of course was ridiculous.

However some very unsavory events had taken place there. It had been built by Nathaniel Pendergrass, a self-made millionaire, grown rich on munitions during the Civil War. Some 11 years ago, he had inexplicably killed his wife, his daughter, his son-in-law and himself. The rumors surrounding the murders and suicide had been ugly, suggesting that the old man had reason to suspect his wife and son-in-law were attracted to each other. It was also said that he, himself, had a most unfatherly feeling for his daughter.

Livia's lip curled. Even if the rumors had some basis in fact, she loathed the idea of the gossip. She had suffered enough from that herself. She had never forgotten the time when at the behest of Eliza Hawley, who was like an aunt to her, she had been bidden to stay with her and her large family in Boston.

Her father had been reluctant to let her go. Passing the library where they were arguing, Livia had found the door ajar. She remained to listen and had heard her father saying something about Lucy, the mother she had never known.

Aunt Eliza had replied soothingly, "That's an old story now, Swithin, and Livia doesn't resemble dearest Lucy in the slightest. I never saw two human beings less alike. Gracious, she's nearly as tall as you. She's dark and her eyes . . . Lucy's eyes were deeply blue and she had blonde hair and she was such a tiny little thing. Besides, you've been away from Boston long enough for people's memories to dim. After all, no one, outside the immediate group, actually knows anything. It's all conjecture and rumor."

"But . . ."

"Furthermore, I am of the opinion that you should have told Livia about Lucy."

"I have told her all she needs to know," he had responded firmly.

Though she had been intensely curious, Livia had managed to keep from questioning her father, mainly because mentions of her late mother depressed him and she hated to see him so unhappy.

Consequently she had gone to Boston to stay in her aunt Eliza's noisy household, where her nine children were always at loggerheads and where their parents also spent a great deal of their time arguing.

She smiled and then frowned at an old, odd recollection. Orin Hawley, Aunt Eliza's oldest son, who was only three months younger than Livia, had heard his parents quarreling and told her about it. "Papa didn't like your mother, but Mama does. She defended her when Papa said she was a fake who probably used some form of hypnosis on everyone who was there that afternoon when everything happened."

"What happened?" Livia had demanded.

"I don't know, but Mama got awfully cross and said that your mother was an angel in heaven, and then she said something about considering everything that took place, she wished she had been hypnotized and what's more she wished she might have remained in a trance all these years rather than experience the sort of life she was leading now! And then Papa hit her and she hit him back and they had a big fight. And then Papa had a black eye and Mama had a swollen cheek and then they both cried and kissed each other a lot and Mama became fat.''

"She became fat?'' Livia had been unable to understand that aspect of the matter.

"She always becomes fat after a big quarrel. I mean not right away but a few months later—and that time Eva was born. The next time they fought Jimmy was born.''

Livia always remembered that conversation with Orin because in those days she believed that Eliza's children had been produced because she and her husband quarreled so much. Orin believed it, too.

Livia chuckled. Orin knew differently now that he had wife and two children of his own. She also knew why his parents had quarreled over her mother. She had been a famous medium and Aunt Eliza believed in her so-called powers while Uncle Stephen did not.

She had become aware of Lucy Blake's reputation during that visit to Boston in her eighteenth year. They had gone to the theater and someone had said quite loudly. "That girl with Eliza Hawley, she's Lucy Blake's daughter.''

"The medium, you mean?'' had been the equally loud and surprised response.

"Exactly.''

"Well, I never. She doesn't look anything like her. Are you sure?''

"As I'm standing here. They live in Marblehead now, she and her father.''

Aunt Eliza had been very aware of this far-from-quiet exchange. Afterwards, she had told a curious Livia a little about Lucy's remarkable seances.

Livia bit her lip. Despite the great furor over Spiritualism in Boston with such well-known men as the psychologist William James in the forefront of the investigation, Livia was secretly and deeply embarrassed over her mother's connection with the movement. In her opinion, it was composed of wishful thinkers on the one hand, magicians and confidence men on the other. The fact that her father so rarely mentioned his brief marriage was evidence to Livia that he shared her opinion.

She often wondered why he had never married again or, as far as she could tell, ever become interested in another woman. Not that she minded that. She adored her father and would have hated a stepmother coming to possibly destroy their relationship as had happened when Thomas Saunders, her best friend's father, had married again. Livia frowned. Her father was ill and spent a great deal of time in his room these days, explaining that Dr. Parsons thought he needed rest, something corroborated by the physician.

She sometimes wondered if the doctor were telling her the whole truth about his state of health. She did not want to dwell on that. It was better to think of something more pleasant such as Mr. Septimus Grenfall, newly arrived in Marblehead, who was going to advertise in the *Mercury* and who had asked her to cover his meeting on Friday, two days away, rather two nights, when she wished . . .

She brought herself up short, amazed at the direction in which her thoughts were speeding. She had met the man for the first time that afternoon. They had spent less than half an hour together, and she was building upon this brief episode like . . . like Marian Sedley. Marian was inclined to picture every young man with whom she came in contact, standing up before the minister, exchanging binding vows with her.

Mr. Grenfall had been attractive and was older than she. Livia judged him to be about 29 or possibly 30. Mr. Cox was six months younger than she—not that that would have made any difference had she been attracted to him, which she was not. Maggie Iler, another good friend, had married a man three years her junior—but why was the thought of marriage flitting through her mind? Livia's cheeks burned as she hurried up the stairs to dress for dinner.

Shortly before she was to meet Mr. Grenfall, Swithin Blake asked Livia what she was covering that night.

"A literary society, a new one called The Seventh Circle," she replied.

"The Seventh Circle?" he asked. "That's a rather odd name for such an endeavor. A circle, did you say?" He frowned and ran a nervous hand through his white hair.

She nodded. "I do not know what it signifies."

"And you're going alone with the young man?"

"Yes, neither Emily nor Marian could come. Emily's in a dither over her wedding."

"Shouldn't you have another friend with you?"

"Oh, Papa, you are sounding just like Jack. This is an assignment, and Mr. Grenfall is most eager to be mentioned in our Social Notes—and, as I told you, he is an advertiser. I do not think he'll attempt to drive me to some lonely spot and have his way with me."

"You are a very beautiful young woman," he said dubiously.

"I am complimented, Papa, but Mr. Grenfall is more eager for pupils than conquests, I am sure."

He fastened an anxious look on her face. "Mr. Cox was most attracted to you, Livia. He was truly disappointed that you could not return his affection."

"I know that you're disappointed, too, Papa, but I believe you should accustom yourself to the possibility that your daughter may be an old maid or, in words I prefer, a single woman."

His frown spread from his faded blue eyes to his heavily lined forehead. "I do not like to contemplate such a possibility, my dear. Before I go, I hope to see you happily married. Aside from the loneliness you are bound to experience as you grow older, you would be missing out on one of the most gratifying, most beautiful relationships life has to offer."

"Oh, Papa." Livia hugged him. "I am so sorry that mother did not live longer."

It was a moment before he replied. "I wish you might have known Lucy. She was one of the sweetest women alive, self-sacrificing, noble . . ." He paused. "I have been thinking about her a great deal of late. I wish she'd been here to watch over you."

"You've been here, Papa." Livia blinked away tears she did not want him to see. "That is quite enough for me."

"You've been a great joy to me, my Livia, but I won't

always be here. We must be realistic. I do not imagine my heart will last much longer. And I have not been . . .''

"Oh, please," she protested, putting her hand over his mouth. "Let's not talk about these things."

"Dearest, we must call a spade a spade. Before I go, I should like to feel that you are creditably established. Young Cox . . .''

"Will have to be creditably established with some other girl, Papa."

"You've had so many offers, my dear."

"I know. Would you want me to marry just to be married, Papa?"

"No, of course not, but . . .''

Reading concern in his eyes, she felt it necessary to reassure him. "If the right man were to come into my life, I would most certainly accept his offer, but I would need to respect as well as love him."

"You told me that you respected young Cox."

"But I did not love him," she said patiently.

"If you knew him better, allowed yourself to know him better . . .''

"If I knew him forever, it would make no difference in my feelings about him. You yourself have always stressed the fact that one must be honest with oneself."

"And now I am hoist on my own petard," he said with a whimsical smile. He added, "Please come home early. I still do not like the idea of you going off with someone you do not know."

"Papa, I am sure your fears will be laid to rest when you meet him. He is well-spoken and," her eyes lighted, "don't forget he has advertised with us. I am in hopes that these inserts will encourage other gentlemen to place ads. If we had enough advertising, the paper could become self-supporting. What do you say to that?"

"I say don't count your chickens."

"Just like a canny New Englander," she teased, hugging him again.

Twenty minutes later, seated in Mr. Grenfall's trap, Livia was pleased. She had been pretty sure that her father's objections would be put aside once he met Mr. Grenfall. He had seemed to like him on sight. He had also been intrigued by his name. "Septimus?" he had inquired. "Are you a seventh child, then?"

"The seventh son of a seventh son," Mr. Grenfall had replied.

"Ah, your family runs to boys, then?"

"It does, sir. Girls, too. I have six brothers and four sisters."

"That must have made for a lively home atmosphere."

"Indeed it did, sir."

"I was an only child and my wife, too, but I must not detain you."

"I hope we'll soon meet again, sir."

"You must come to dinner one night."

Thinking of that conversation, Livia was surprised. Generally her father was much more reserved, but it was easy to see that he had formed an instant liking to Mr. Grenfall. She was glad of that, for now he would not worry any more. Though he had long been accustomed to her habit of striding around town without even a girl friend to accompany her, the distance between their house and the Pendergrass mansion was considerable.

"Miss Blake," Mr. Grenfall said, breaking the small silence that had fallen between them, "I am really delighted that you will be with us this evening."

"I have been looking forward to it," she said, adding quickly, "I am always interested in new literary societies."

"But we are not new—except to Marblehead."

"I understand, but it is new to me. What is the significance of its name, The Seventh Circle?"

"Circle is another name for our group and seven refers to our original membership. Of course we have expanded, but the name stuck."

"That's understandable. How many are in your group now?"

"Twelve. We are about to initiate a thirteenth. I hope you aren't superstitious."

"Heavens, no," Livia assured him. "I pride myself on being a realist."

"You should be proud of that."

Livia was surprised to find that the Pendergrass mansion looked almost as dark and deserted from the outside as it had in the intervening years since the deaths of its last occupants. It was a large square house with a mansard roof set with dormer windows. There was a pillared veranda on one side and a small porch to the other. As he drove up under a porte-cochere, a young man came out to hold the horse. Helping Livia out of the trap, Mr. Grenfall escorted her up three steps onto the veranda.

Halting near the wide front door, he pushed it open, disclosing a hall lighted by a dim gas globe swinging from a chain. An odd smell filled her nostrils as she entered. "You burn incense at your meetings?" she inquired in some surprise.

"Not at our meetings" he stressed. "This house had a very moldy smell when we took it over. We've succeeded in getting rid of most of it, but there is a residue and to combat it we use incense. It is a pervasive odor, I grant you, but the mold is worse."

"I am sure it must be," she agreed, thinking that the house could have done with a little more heat. There was a definite chill in the air. In fact it seemed colder inside than out. She could not restrain a slight shiver.

"Are you cold, Miss Blake?" he asked solicitously.

"A bit," she admitted, "though I do not know why I should be. I'm dressed quite warmly." She indicated her brown silk gown with its quantities of ruffles and its modified bustle.

"Quite warmly and most becomingly," he said. "Though I have never admired the bustle, it looks very well on those who are tall enough to carry it. On some young ladies, it appears to be carrying them."

His observation surprised her. The men she knew did not usually comment so frankly on fashions. They limited their remarks to compliments, and while in a sense he had complimented her, he also had been making fun of a style that she herself despised. She was not sure that this was proper, but to her surprise she found herself saying, "I'm inclined to agree with you."

"I'm glad you do. If I had my way, we should follow the lead of the ancient Greeks with their loose and comfortable tunics which did not impede, overburden or constrict."

She was definitely shocked by this statement but she merely said, "I am sure they were proper in their time and place. Greece is known to be a warm country."

"Very warm," he agreed. "Come, Miss Blake." Turning left in the hall, Mr. Grenfall led her down a passageway into a large room, not much brighter than the hall, the light issuing from several lamps set on tables and a piano. There were a number of young women sitting on couches and chairs as well as several young men. She had the impression that there were more than twelve people present, but on counting them she found that there were seven women and five men. The women, she noted with some surprise, greeted Mr. Grenfall with warm embraces. She was taken aback by these actions. At the meetings she had attended, members merely shook hands. She wished that Mr. Grenfall had not been so hasty in his introductions. She was having difficulty affixing the name to the individual, which embarrassed her, for not only would she have to converse with them but she needed them for her article. She would, she decided resignedly, have to ask for them again.

"Would you care to sit here?" Mr. Grenfall indicated a large comfortable armchair. "We will serve tea, and then Vivienne, Charles and Herbert will enact our little drama."

"I am looking forward to that," Livia said politely as she took the proffered chair. Scanning the people around her, she wished that the room was not so dark. She wondered which of the young women was Vivienne. None of them looked right for the role of Usher's desiccated sister. They were all attractive and some were beautiful. They dressed well though one or two were wearing very low cut gowns, hardly suitable for the occasion—or for any occasion. Livia had never approved of such displays. As Miss Falkner, one of her governesses, had said, "Provocative costumes are designed to appeal to man's lower nature. The intelligent woman uses her mind rather than her body to attract gentlemen."

At 17 Livia had taken this bit of wisdom to heart, and ten years of being a member of Marblehead society had done nothing to change her mind.

"Would you have tea, Miss Blake?"

Livia turned to find one of the pretty young women proferring a silver tray on which was a cup and saucer of fine bone china, a silver creamer and sugar bowl. "Thank you," she said.

"This is a special brew," the girl said. "You would be advised to try it without cream and sugar."

"As it happens, I do not use either," Livia said, as she took the cup. She refrained from adding that she was not very fond of tea, especially the kind served on such occasions. Generally it was a cheap brand rather than the China tea she occasionally drank. However, upon sipping this brew, she found it had a strange but definitely pleasant flavor. She drank every drop and did not protest when another woman stepped to her side to fill it again. She drank that, too, looking around the room as she did. Her eyes were becoming accustomed to the dim light. The floor, she observed, was bare of carpets, and there were a great many pictures on the walls. While some were landscapes and others portraits, she noticed two which struck her as being very old.

One was a painting of a large star, covered with scrawls, as if someone armed with a red paintbrush had deliberately defaced it. Another depicted a cross, but rather than being right side up, it was turned around—or perhaps the picture had been turned around? She glanced away and started as on a table she saw a polished human skull with a candle burning inside. She wondered if it were a prop for the playlet she was soon to witness. Another table caught her eye. There were two swords lying on it. Beside them were a number of dishes and a large bowl. Would they also be serving food? She hoped not. She did not feel hungry. She yawned and put her head back against the soft cushions of her chair. She was feeling rather sleepy which was not unusual; she had put in a hectic day at the paper. She had rested before dressing, but that was hardly enough to make up for the aggravations of the day—some copy coming in late and Emily wanting to leave early and Marian crying that she had only two hands. Livia closed her eyes, wishing devoutly that the playlet would get underway.

*   *   *   .

Towards morning, Livia, waking out of a deep sleep, sat bolt upright in bed, running her hands over her cotton nightgown just to make sure that she was wearing it. Once she was positive it was in place—buttoned up to her neck, sleeves fastened at the wrist, the rest of it tangled about her hips but there, where it should be—she pressed her hands against her burning face and unwillingly thought of the horrid dream that had seemed so realistic and which she could remember down to every last detail.

She had had some strange dreams in her life. In them she had visited places she had never seen. A moldering old castle with a drawbridge and moat figured in some of them. In another recurring dream she saw an angry dark little woman who jeered at her. As a child, the sight of her had sent her screaming out of her sleep. On those occasions her father had come in to comfort her. She was glad she had not screamed tonight since she would not have wanted him with her. She might have blurted out what she had experienced. It was all so very real. Why should she have dreamed of Mr. Grenfall and all the nice young people she had met there at the Pendergrass mansion? Supposing that dream had happened when she was still there, sleeping in her chair and not waking until Mr. Grenfall tapped her gently on the shoulder and asked if he could take her home.

She had been so embarrassed and confounded to learn that she had slept through the entire playlet and through the subsequent discussion. Though she was not a woman who cried easily, she had been quite unable to keep from weeping. She had been terribly ashamed over her most unprofessional lapse, and Mr. Grenfall had been so kind, so understanding. Everyone there had sympathized with her and talked about the exigencies attendant on editing a newspaper. Mr. Grenfall had said they could restage the piece the following Friday and asked tentatively if she might come again. She promised she would. Mr. Grenfall had been so understanding on the way home. Mr. Grenfall! She shuddered. He had figured prominently in her dreadful, shocking, indecent dream!

Lying back against her rumpled sheets, she closed her eyes and tried to sleep but could not do so. She could only think about that dream, which was unfolding before her inner vision like the panorama picture of the Civil War she had seen at a county fair two summers ago.

In her dream it seemed to her she had heard humming sounds, as if the group around her were humming an odd sort of a melody, one she had never heard. That surprised her because she had expected the play must be starting immediately. Then two of the women came to stand by her chair. One of them was the blonde girl who had served her tea, and the other a beautiful girl of 19 or 20, a redhead with long green eyes. She had a lovely figure, but Livia could not approve her deeply plunged gown.

"Come, my dear," the blonde girl urged. "We must go now."

Livia had felt disinclined to stir. "Where are we going? Isn't the play about to begin?"

Instead of answering, the blonde girl had said something that startled her. "Has she taken all her tea, Vivienne?"

The girl named Vivienne stared into her cup. "Every drop, Charlotte. And it was her second cup."

That conversation had not made any sense at all, but of course dreams seldom made sense and this one, despite its startling continuity, made even less sense than most.

The two girls had urged her to rise, and once she was on her feet, her head had seemed heavy with the room whirling around her. "I am so dizzy," she had complained.

"You will feel better soon, my dear," Vivienne assured her.

They all led her out of the room and into a smaller chamber just across the hall, a cloakroom with many hooks along the wall. On each hook hung a long black cloak.

She found that several other women had followed them into the cloakroom. They were busily removing their shoes and stockings. Charlotte and Vivienne were also taking off their shoes.

"You must remove your shoes and stockings, my dear Livia," Vivienne had instructed.

"Very well." Livia had not even protested, she recalled. Nor had she been surprised when she found the other women removing their gowns.

"You must undress, Livia."

Under the covers, Livia clutched her nightgown. Had she obeyed? She had! Obediently, she had stripped off all her clothes, not as quickly as the others had, but without any protest. She had received in their place a long black cloak. All the women were wearing those cloaks.

Then they filed out of the cloakroom and into the large chamber where she found that all the men were in red cloaks, including Mr. Grenfall. A man had been seated at the pianoforte. She remembered hoping that he would play because she loved music. She did not remember being in the least surprised or self-conscious at what was happening even though under her cloak she was as bare as the day she was born.

Her face burned. That had been bad enough, but there was worse to come!

She had looked toward Mr. Grenfall and saw that he was speaking to one of the men. She had wanted to speak to him, but she had not wanted to interrupt them.

"Very polite," Livia muttered and cringed as she recalled moving near to him, noting as she did that there was a fire blazing on the hearth. It took the chill off the room and even made her too warm. She had wanted to discard the cloak. Had she really wanted that? She could not imagine that even in a dream she would have contemplated anything so immodest, but she had, she had, in that terrible, confusing vision.

"Livia, my dear." Mr. Grenfall had stepped to her side.

Had he addressed her in that familiar way? Yes—and she had not even been surprised. She had smiled up at him, saying brazenly, "I was hoping you'd see me."

"How might I not see you, my sweet?"

"There are so many women about," she had pouted. Pouted? She never pouted.

In her dream, his obvious interest had actually thrilled her, and she had said, "Why do we need to wear these heavy cloaks. I am so warm."

Livia turned over in bed, pressing herself against her pillows and pulling the covers over her head, but one could not hide from a dream.

He had said, "It's cold in the cloakroom and the hall. You will not need to wear it here." He had gently untied the strings of her cape and slipped it from her shoulders. Subsequently he had removed his own cloak, and turning back to her, he had stared at her, his eyes roving over her body. "You are very beautiful," he had commented.

"Ohhhhhh," she moaned, squeezing her eyelids together, but not managing to shut out the vision of his body, which was also completely naked.

And what had she said? What had she done? Had she screamed and run? No. She had said, "Do you think I'm beautiful?"

And he had said, "Incredibly beautiful from head to toe."

And she had said, "Is there any reason why we should be naked?"

"Oh, yes, because of the energy."

"The energy?" In spite of her condition, she had been only mildly curious, standing there, naked beside a naked man and saying, "I don't understand about the energy."

"You will," he had replied, and reaching out, he had cupped her breasts in his hands, repeating, "Beautiful, beautiful. I had never expected that your body would be as beautiful as your face."

And what had she said? "I find you very handsome."

Livia burned with embarrassment as she remembered how she had gazed on his body. She had not been shocked but only interested to discover an essential difference between them. And that difference? In all the statues she had seen at the museum, it had been disguised by a fig leaf. In her dream she had seen that portion of his body without the fig leaf, a tubular shape half-masked by hair which was slightly darker than that which grew on his head and was very curly, almost kinky. She had also noticed a strange little birthmark that was shaped like a hoofprint and located just above the curly hair. She had wanted to ask him about that, but he had moved away and she had heard music coming from the pianoforte.

It was a catchy tune, and its rhythms invaded her. She began to move in time to them. Then Vivienne and Charlotte came to stand on either side of her. The whole group seized hands and formed a circle, beginning to move in time to the music. One woman however stood apart from them. She was older, perhaps 35. She stood at the table holding up the swords Livia had seen when she first entered the room. The older woman drank from a silver goblet. There was chanting, and though Livia did not know the words, she found she could follow it, which was always the way it was in dreams. There was more to the dream but she could not remember it, did not want to remember it, and she lay in her bed, feeling fearful and wondering if she were not going mad.

She shuddered, running her hands through her hair again. Something odd was certainly happening to her. She had never fallen asleep on an assignment. If Emily or Marian ever found out, she shuddered to think what they would say to her, she who was always upbraiding them for their lack of efficiency. As for her dream—her disgusting, dreadful, immodest vision—she could never tell anyone about that. And how was she ever to face Mr. Grenfall again? She had to face him! She had to repeat the assignment on the following Friday. She had promised. She could send Emily, but she really couldn't. Emily did not have the capacity to gather news at this time, and besides, she had promised to see that playlet. Six days intervened between now and next Friday. She was a mature woman, and by then she would have regained her equilibrium.

"You're very quiet this evening, Miss Blake." Mr. Grenfall slowed his horse to a walk. He looked down at her with one of his charming smiles. "It was very kind of you to agree to come again."

"I could hardly not come, Mr. Grenfall, after falling asleep at your meeting. I am really chagrined over that. I assure you it will not happen tonight."

"If it does, I'll not blame you. I know how very hard you work."

"You are most kind and understanding, sir. However this week was not as difficult as last. Once we meet our Tuesday deadline, we can relax a bit."

"I see. I'm glad. I think you'll enjoy yourself."

"I am sure I will."

Though she had been dreading this evening, dreading to

see him again, Livia did not experience the embarrassment she had expected upon greeting him. In fact, before the reality of his presence, the dream faded away, and any qualms she had entertained were based on her foolishness in allowing what was no more than a nightmare to distract her as much as it had. Certainly she could not dread Mr. Grenfall. She truthfully could no longer deny that she was attracted to him, and she felt unhappy about that. There were so many lovely young women in the group. She could not imagine that he would single her out. He had given her a most admiring glance tonight. Probably he approved her new gown, bought, if truth must be told, because of what he had said about the ancient Greek costumes. It resembled a Grecian tunic and its yellow hue was flattering to her dark complexion, also bringing out the lights in her eyes. She had often wondered how she happened to have what Orin Hawley had called "yellow eyes." She much preferred the adjective "golden" used by her father. He did not have much of an explanation for her unique coloring, save to say that she took after one of her mother's relatives. Livia had learned long ago that he did not like to discuss his wife's family.

"Here we are, Miss Blake." Mr. Grenfall brought his horse to a stop at the porte-cochere of the old house.

"Oh, so soon," she said. "I was not sleeping," she added quickly. "I was thinking."

"May I offer a penny for them?"

"What?"

"Your thoughts."

"They weren't very interesting, I fear."

"Anything that you would think must be interesting, I am sure." The groom had come forward to hold his horse, and climbing nimbly out of the trap, Mr. Grenfall came around to lift her down.

He was very strong, and for a moment she felt quite hepless in his grasp, a most unusual sensation. Even more unusual was the fact that she enjoyed it. And that, Mr. Grenfall, is one thought I would never share with you, she silently assured him.

A short time later Livia, setting down her third cup of aromatic tea, actually scanned the bottom of the cup in search of another sip. She wondered whether it was China or Indian but that did not matter. She would have to ask Vivienne or Charlotte where she might buy it. Looking around, she saw Vivienne coming toward her. She was wearing a blue gown that night, not as complimentary to her vivid coloring as the green she had worn at the previous meeting. It, too, was plunging, showing a great deal of her bosom. Her arms were bare, and Livia envied her. She felt uncommonly warm in her tunic.

"Good evening, my dear," Vivienne said cordially. "Are you ready to join in the dancing?"

"Quite ready," Livia assented eagerly.

"Come, then." Vivienne beckoned, and Livia hurried after her into the cloakroom, stripping off her garments gladly. She felt so much freer without them. The cloak was not heavy, but she would be pleased when she could discard it. She slipped it off and threw it over a chair a second after returning to the meeting room. It was easier going through the motions of the dancing, and this time there was a different chant—a name was spoken, one she knew. It was that of Judge Elias P. Martin, a wealthy man and head of several philanthropic organizations. He was also running for congress on a reform ticket.

"Elias, Elias, Elias P. Martin," Livia chanted with the rest of them and knew that she hated him, had always hated him and wanted him dead.

"Die, die, die, Elias," she chanted. And there were other words she did not recognize but knew they would spell the end of this holier-than-thou-do-gooder, who had sworn to abolish corruption in Boston's police force, something none of them wanted, least of all herself.

"Die, die, die Elias!" she screamed, leaping and whirling until her body was slippery with sweat and she was weak with the effort. Finally the older woman appeared and lifted her swords. The air was heavy with incense and with it was mingled another odor which, Charlotte explained, was burning salt.

They drank from various vessels. Livia remembered that from the previous week, and she also recalled the names of her companions: Charles, Mabel, Robert, Joyce, George,

Myrna, Christopher, Anna, Eliza, Vivenne and Charlotte—and, of course, their leader, their High Priest, Septimus, Septimus, Septimus, so beautiful in his nakedness. With the exception of Eliza, the older woman, they were all such attractive people. She wondered why she had never met any of them in Marblehead, but of course they hailed from Salem.

She remembered something Septimus had told her. He had mentioned that a thirteenth member of the group was going to be initiated. Later, when she lay beside Vivienne catching her breath from the rigorous dancing, she mentioned that initiation, wondering when it would take place and whom they had chosen.

"You will be our thirteenth member, my dear," Vivienne said.

Livia regarded her in startled surprise. "I thought I was only here to observe."

"Oh, no, we need you. You will observe and then you will be initiated."

"I am really to be a member!" Livia exclaimed.

"Our thirteenth member, yes. We have tested you and found that you will be a most welcome addition to our group," Charles, a handsome young man who lay beside her, corrobrated.

"Oh, I am delighted!" she exclaimed happily.

"So are we all." Charles ran his finger down her back.

Livia giggled. "That tickles."

"Sorry," he apologized. "I wish someone would scratch my back."

"Turn over and I will," Livia said readily. He had a beautiful back, she thought, as she began to run her nails across it very lightly. His skin was smooth and there was no hair on it. Some of the men were very hairy, front and back. She had noticed that when they danced. However Septimus was also free of hair save between his legs. "There," she said lifting her hands from Charles' back. "Is that enough?"

"Fine." He turned over and smiled at her lazily. "What may I do for you?"

"You can rub my feet," she said.

"At your service, madame." He winked at her, and

placing her feet across his legs, he began to rub them gently.

"Oh, that is so relaxing," she said gratefully. She glanced around the room and spotted Septimus talking with Charlotte. Much to her delight, he caught her eye and smiled at her warmly. Senses deep within her stirred. Her body throbbed, and she wished it was he who was lying beside her.

Another man joined the little group just as Charles stopped rubbing Livia's feet. The new arrival's name was Christopher, and he was almost as dark as Septimus. In addition to the dark curling hair on his head, his chest and belly and the heavy growth on his arms and legs, there was even some on his feet. He was still breathing hard, she noticed.

"The dancing is very tiring, do you not agree?" Livia said to him.

"Yes." His dark eyes roved over her body. "But it does raise the energy."

"They talk so much about energy," Livia commented, "but I don't understand why it is needed."

"You will." He edged closer to her. "You have exquisite breasts, my dear," he observed.

"That's what Septimus said, but I don't see anything unusual about them."

"They're so firm and round. Eve's apples, my dear. I should like a taste of them." He leaned forward.

"Christopher, darling," Vivienne drawled.

To Livia's surprise, he rose immediately and strode away. "Why did he leave so suddenly?" she asked.

"Christopher's a relatively new member. Sometimes he forgets why he is here."

"Oh, I see." Livia did not understand Vivienne's explanation and that troubled her. She had always prided herself on her acumen, however it would not do to question Vivenne further. A trained reporter could not sound as if she were unsure of herself.

Charlotte said, "We must go and get cleansed."

"Cleansed?" Livia inquired.

"Yes, dear, as we did last week."

"Oh, yes, now I remember." Livia followed them into the chamber that contained the sunken tub, not unlike those that were known to be in Roman villas. This one was square and fashioned from white marble. The water was very blue and filled with rose petals. Stepping down the three steps that led into the tub, Livia was immersed up to her shoulders. As it had been last week, the water was warm. She could swim, and she paddled back and forth until Vienne slipped into the pool and soaped her all over. Beckoning Livia to come out, Charlotte turned a fine spray of water on her, washing off the suds. Afterwards she spread a towel on the floor and, as she had the previous week, Livia lay down on it. Charlotte used another towel to dry her hair while Vienne began to massage her, and Livia, feeling pleasantly drowsy, soon dropped off to sleep.

"Miss Blake, wake up. You're home."

Livia awoke with a start and found she had been resting her head on Mr. Grenfall's shoulder. She tensed and regarded him in horror. "I . . . I didn't fall asleep again!" she cried.

"I am afraid you did," he said gently.

"What is happening to me?" she demanded fearfully.

His dark eyes, illuminated by the carriage lantern, burned into her eyes. "There's nothing the matter save that you work very hard and it's May."

"What does May have to do with it?" Amazingly, she was feeling a little better about this second lapse, as if he had somehow removed her troubles from her mind, an odd supposition certainly.

"May is before June, and in June you will be closing your office for a well-earned rest. You're not made of iron, Miss Blake, you know. You are only flesh and blood."

His mention of flesh and blood brought a flush to her cheek, but she did not know why. His reasoning seemed extremely logical though. "I expect I have been working too hard this year. We're short-staffed. Emily's away so much of the time."

"Perhaps you should hire another reporter to shoulder some of your load."

"I could not do that though Emily would take it very much to heart. And, as you have pointed out, we are very nearly through the season."

"You are a very nice person, Miss Blake."

"Thank you, sir," she replied, feeling hurt and disappointed. She had been experiencing a closeness with him that his last observation had obviated. "I had best go in," she added.

"I will see you to your door," he said. "Might we hope that you will come again next Friday? I am really determined that you see our play, whether or not you report on it."

She expelled a short, embarrassed breath. "I'll come and see it, and I will report on it. And if I fall asleep this time, you must stick pins into me."

"I would never want to hurt you in any way," he said with a seriousness that surprised her. Helping her down from the trap, he accompanied her to the porch. Standing in front of the door, he said softly, "I'll come for you next Friday, Miss Blake." Taking her hand in his warm grasp, he brought it to his lips.

This unexpected gesture startled her, and the feel of his lips against her hand sent an odd shiver through her body. She suddenly was amazed and startled by the specificness of what she wanted from him. "Next Friday," she said shakily, embarrassed because she sounded like a schoolgirl.

"Goodbye, then." He released her hand and went swiftly down the steps and climbed into the trap.

Livia stood at the door, watching until he drove away. Waiting until the last sounds of its wheels coupled with those of the horse's hooves were out of her ears, she went inside and up the stairs to bed.

Towards morning, Livia wakened with fragments of another strange, embarrassing dream floating through her mind. It was not quite as vivid as it had been the previous week, but there were enough images to shock and terrify her. She could not understand why she should be visited by this nightmare. It had left her feeling all churned up inside. She did not want to think about the dream. Her thoughts turned to Mr. Grenfall, who had been so impersonal the previous night.

"And why not?" she muttered. "I hardly know him."

Sitting up in bed and clutching her knees, she stared into

the darkness wondering why the truth should be so unsettling. She had met him only four times—twice at the paper, twice at the meeting—and still she felt she knew him so much better than that. She didn't. He had every right to be impersonal and even annoyed. She had slept through two meetings she, a trained reporter who had managed to stay awake through one of President Garfield's campaign speeches. Yet she could not keep her eyes open in that house! Possibly it was the incense that made her so sleepy. She wished she might ask Mr. Grenfall to refrain from burning it next Friday, but she could not presume on so brief an acquaintance. Still, he did want her to view his playlet, and the poor actors must be quite frustrated by now.

She turned over on her stomach and tried to go back to sleep and fragments floating through her head, she had an image of him naked!

Finally, defensively, she slept only to have another nightmare, not as horridly embarrassing as her other two, but she had not liked it either. In it a horrid old woman screamed and screamed. She had a cat with her that screeched like the toms that stalked the fence tops on hot summer nights. Her ears rang with the sound as if she had actually heard rather than dreamt it.

She glanced out of her window. The sky was paling. She winced. She did not feel at all rested and it was almost daylight. She closed her eyes again, and this time her sleep was mercifully untroubled.

On her way back from her third and equally disastrous visit to The Seventh Circle, Livia blinked against tears. She hated the sobs that were welling up in her throat. She had always been so strong-minded and capable, but this Friday's meeting seemed to be the culmination of all the confusion she had experienced this past week.

She had fallen asleep again!

And the people in the group were so understanding and so forgiving that it hurt her. She liked them all so much, what she had seen of them, but she could not return a fourth time. The situation was totally out of hand, not only her curious habit of falling asleep almost the moment she set foot in that house but the distracting dreams that were beginning to haunt her every night of the week. Not only did she dream, but during her working hours she entertained memories of those dreams that shocked and horrified her. These frayed her temper, and she took it out on the girls. On Wednesday, Marian had threatened to quit, and Emily, castigated for an abominable piece of writing, *had* quit. She had returned, but both girls were eyeing her askance. She had the feeling that they held whispered conferences in the other room. She had come out of her office twice to find them very close together and looking extremely self-conscious as they moved away from each other.

Then there was the matter of Elias P. Martin, the famous philanthropist, who had been running for congress until a heart attack had sent him to the hospital. According to Emily, who had hastened to the hospital to see if she could get some information on his condition for an item in the *Marblehead Mercury*, he was near death.

On receiving this news, Livia had had difficulty concealing a smile of pure pleasure. There even had been an incredible moment when she had been actually glad the man was dying. Why? He was the soul of integrity, at least according to her father, who was seldom wrong about politicians. His opponent in the race was totally corrupt, and yet she had felt not only pleased at the idea of Martin's possible passing, she had muttered under her breath, "Die, Elias, die!" Then, immediately afterwards, she had turned cold with terror, remembering that in her dreams, she had singularly wished him ill, she and all the other people at Mr. Grenfall's literary society. And no one could understand why he had had a heart attack. He had been in singularly good health, his doctor had declared to the assembled reporters.

It was such a strange coincidence—her dream and his attack!

Her father, who seemed to be growing weaker by the day to the point where he rarely left his bedroom, had noticed her distraction. "Dearest," he had said only last night, "you seem very preoccupied of late."

"Not really, Papa," she had assured him hastily. "It's just that so much of the work at the paper is falling on my shoulders. I will be glad when we shut down."

"Yes, you do need a rest, and perhaps you should not rise so early. You do need more sleep."

Sleep!

Livia was beginning to dread the thought of sleeping. She wished she could tell her father exactly what was troubling her, but of course that was out of the question. She could never let anyone know about the dreams, or rather visions—vile visions that tormented her and at the same time were beginning to fill her mind with impure thoughts and desires to match them!

It was terrible to remember those dreams so clearly and how Mr. Grenfall had appeared to her, his beautiful body naked. She shuddered. They were nearing her house and her horrid thoughts had distracted her attention from the man himself. And this was to be the last time they would see each other. The idea filled her with a new agony, one that was physical as well as mental. She wished . . . but she could not consciously entertain the wish that had just flashed into her mind, bringing with it embarrassing bodily reactions.

If only she could get away. Unfortunately her father's worsening health precluded that. She dared not leave him, but at any rate she soon might be taken away to a madhouse!

Mr. Grenfall had halted the trap, and now she would have to bid him a long goodbye. As he helped her down, a gust of wind caught her hat and she clutched the brim. It was a stormy night with a hint of rain in the air, more than a hint, she realized, as a drop splattered against her cheek.

"Come." Mr. Grenfall hurried her up on the porch. "Will we see you next Friday?"

"No!" she cried. "I . . . I cannot come. I do not see why you would want me to catch up on my sleep as I have been doing," she said, managing a light laugh.

"Sleeping or waking, I want you there," he said insistently.

"Come, Mr. Grenfall, that does not make sense," she reproved, glad that she could sound so calm. What she had told him was no more than the truth. Why would he want her there? She had yet to see his playlet, and she had not give his society so much as a mention in the paper.

"Perhaps next week you'll not feel like sleeping."

"I never feel like sleeping but I do. I do not understand myself." Inadvertently she added, "I do not understand anything of what is happening to me. My dreams . . ." She paused, staring at him in consternation, wondering what had made her blurt out her fears.

"Your dreams," he asked. "What sort of dreams?"

"They . . . they're rather disturbing," she said, striving to remain calm.

"Would it help you to tell me what they are about?"

She blanched, wondering what he would say if she were to reveal their content. She said hesitantly, "There's this old woman with tangled white hair. She screams very loudly. She has a cat that seems to be on fire and it also screams."

"For a very good reason if he is on fire," he commented with a half-smile which vanished quickly. "The old woman sounds as if she might be a witch. Perhaps there's the ghost of a witch in your house. Several were hanged for witchcraft in Marblehead, you know."

"Mr. Grenfall, I hope that an intelligent man like yourself does not believe in witches," Livia said tartly.

"But I do," he replied, "having met you, my dear Livia."

She regarded him with an astonishment mingled with shock. "You are becoming extremely familiar on very short acquaintance, sir."

"I do apologize," he said hastily. "Please forgive me, Miss Blake."

"Very well," she replied, well-aware that she should never have countenanced his surprising employment of her Christian name, but on this, their last meeting, she did not want to order him to leave, as she should have done. She did not want to leave it all. Tears she could not blink away filled her eyes. Fortunately, the porch light was too dim for him to see them.

"Miss Blake," he said solicitously, "I feel that you are deeply troubled over something. Can you not tell me what is worrying you?"

His perspicacity startled her. "It is nothing," she said with a brusqueness she had not intended. "I . . . my dreams . . ." She clicked her teeth together in a palpable effort to keep any further confidences from escaping. What was the matter with her?

"More dreams," he said. "I know a little something about dreams. Maybe I could help you."

"I doubt that anyone could help me," she said, immediately regretting this second confidence.

"I could help," he insisted, "and . . ." He paused as a wind-borne gust of rain splattered them.

"Oh!" Livia exclaimed. "You'd best come inside." She opened the door and motioned him to follow her into the hall. "Do be quiet," she whispered. "My father sleeps downstairs in the room across from the library."

"I will be very quiet," he murmured.

"We can sit here," she said, pointing to a settee. Her nervousness increased. She should not have brought him inside. What could he tell her about her dreams? What could she tell him? She ought to ask him to go, but the rain was becoming heavier. He would be drenched. Probably it was a cloudburst and would be over shortly. Then, she could ask him to . . . She stiffened. There were footsteps coming across the floor.

"Livia, dear," her father called from somewhere down the passageway.

She cast a nervous glance at Mr. Grenfall. "Best go up to the first landing," she instructed. "Yes, Papa," she added in a louder tone of voice. Her tension increased as she watched Mr. Grenfall start up the stairs, but he moved very quietly.

"Did you just get in, dear?" Swithin, clad in a long brocade dressing robe, came into the hall. "You are rather late, are you not?"

"The weather . . ." she explained.

"Yes, it's bad, isn't it? I am glad you're home, my love."

"So am I, Papa, but why are you out of bed?"

"I've had trouble sleeping. I've been in the library reading."

"The library's damp."

"I have a fire going. Should you like to join me?"

"I am very tired, Papa. I must go to bed, and so should you."

"I will presently." He kissed her. "Good night, my dear."

"Good night, Papa. Please don't stay up too long."

"You mustn't worry about me so much, my dear." He moved back toward the passageway.

Livia stood on the stairs waiting until she heard the library door open and close. She joined Mr. Grenfall on the first landing and started as she heard a violent clap of thunder. "Oh, dear, it is coming down," she whispered. "We'd best talk in my room. Papa would hear us if we remained in the hall." Immediately after this statement, she wondered if she *had* gone mad, inviting a veritable stranger into her bedroom. Yet it would give her a little more time with Mr. Grenfall before they parted for good. "Follow me," she muttered.

"Very well. I have something I must tell you, too." he whispered.

Her shutters were banging back and forth as she ushered Mr. Grenfall into her bedroom. As always, she had left the oil lamp on the nightstand burning. Its soft glow afforded a dim view of her fourposter canopied bed with its red and white cretonne hangings matching the curtains at the window, her dresser, the highboy and the two cosy armchairs facing each other on either side of the fireplace. The light was further reflected in the mirrors over the mantel and the dressing table. Also reflected in the mirror was the door to her bathroom, an innovation added by her father several years ago. It had delighted Anna, her maid, she remembered inconsequentially, and she was glad that her views on the working woman had caused her to insist that Anna go home after she helped her dress. Neither their cook nor maid lived in their house.

She looked about her nervously, wondering why a room that she had always believed to be quite large had seemingly shrunk to half its size. She preferred not to dwell on this anomaly.

Trying to subdue a combination of nervousness and regret for having invited him into her bedroom, Livia indicated one of the armchairs and said with a creditable insouciance, "Will you sit here, sir? I must secure the shutters." She hurried across the room to the east window and, pulling the shuters closed, wished she could remain there, speaking to him over her shoulder. Then telling herself sharply that her mental processes were beginning to resemble those of a girl of eighteen rather than a woman well into her twenty-eighth year and a newspaper editor to boot, she came back to the fireplace. Seeing that he was still standing, she slipped into one of the armchairs. "Please sit down, sir," she invited.

He cleared his throat. "I prefer to stand," he said heavily.

Though the light in the room was too dim to illuminate his features, Livia felt that he was disturbed. In fact, she had the strange impression that their moods had been exchanged and that it was he who needed soothing rather than herself, which had to be ridiculous and only emphasized the disordered state of her mind. She had seldom met anyone more self-possessed than Mr. Grenfall.

"As you choose," she said.

After an awkward little silence, he said, "You have been worried about your dreams?"

She nodded. "I have sometimes felt as if I might be going mad!" she exclaimed, again regretting another foolish outburst.

"No," he said positively yet gently. "You're in no danger of that."

Though he could have no comprehension of what she meant, she felt oddly reassured. "I . . . I suppose I am being silly."

"No," he said. He added, "Miss Blake, have you any knowledge of an . . . Erlina Bell?"

"Erlina Bell?" she repeated, wondering at his question. "I've never heard the name."

"That's just as well. Still, she knows you and . . ." He paused, drawing a long breath and releasing it in a sigh. "But first things first. I can see you are deeply troubled and confused, but I can see more than that, Miss Blake."

"More . . ." she repeated. "I do not understand."

He sighed again. "I hold myself responsible for the anguish you have suffered—are suffering. I never imagined that I could feel this way or that I could so bitterly regret all that has happened in the last three weeks. Before I tell you anything more, let me assure you that I am truly ashamed of myself."

Listening to this amazing declaration, her own confusion increased. "All that has happened in . . . in the last three weeks? I am not sure I understand you, Mr. Grenfall."

"You have been frightened and bewildered by your dreams. I . . ."

"Please," she interrupted. "I should not have mentioned them to you. You are a stranger . . ."

"We are not strangers." He stepped closer to her. "I know what has been tormenting you."

"You couldn't! You couldn't begin to understand the pain, the degradation, the . . ."

"Degradation? No, that's not true. You've not been degraded. You've been embarrassed, but only in retrospect. I am deeply sorry over that. I did not anticipate your dreams. There was a great deal I did not anticipate."

She regarded him incredulously. "You speak about anticipating my dreams. How might you have anticipated them?"

"Because I am to blame for all that has disturbed you. Erlina Bell led us to you. It is only in the last week that I have begun to understand her real motivation. Her vengeance has long tentacles."

She had wondered about her own reason, but now she feared for his. He seemed to be speaking in mad riddles. "I do not understand you. Who is this Erlina Bell?"

"The spirit of a witch, whose thirst for revenge has yet to be slaked. She first came to us during our Candlemas celebration."

"Candlemas?" she questioned.

"For Christians it is a church feast but its rites are older than your church and we name it as one of our four great Sabbats."

"What is a Sabbat?" she asked, trying vainly to understand what he was telling her and at the same time becoming more and more perplexed by his evident depression and regret.

"A Sabbat is a meeting of the witches. The four great Sabbats take place in summer, winter, spring and fall. During the rest of the year our covens, which number thirteen, meet on Friday or Saturday evenings for rituals and—relaxation. These weekly meetings are called Sabbats. There is a monthly gathering known as an Esbat.''

"Witches . . .'' She faltered. "There are no such things.''

He looked away from her, saying gratingly, "I find myself actually wishing that were true. Yet more than that I wish your father had not raised you in such ignorance. I cannot blame him from wanting to protect you from the horrors of your heritage, but it would have been easier for you if you'd known, easier and safer so you might have protected yourself.''

"I do not understand you.''

"Your mother . . .'' he began.

"I know that my mother was a well-known medium. My father did not tell me but someone else did.''

"Do you know anything else?'' he demanded.

"I don't understand you,'' she repeated and then recollected something he had said a moment ago. "Thirteen! Vivienne said I was your thirteenth member. You meet on Friday nights. I have read about witchcraft, the Salem trials, the beliefs . . . You're not telling me that you . . . that I . . . ?''

He actually looked relieved. "Yes. For the last three weeks, my dear one, you have been present and participating in our weekly Sabbats. We are witches, my love. I am what is called a High Priest, and Eliza is the High Priestess.'' As she started to speak, he raised his hand. "Best let me continue,'' he urged. "On the night of Candlemas we conjured up certain spirits. Erlina Bell was one of them. She told us of a young woman now twenty-seven years old, her climacteric year, which means a year of destiny. She told us that we could tap a source of power as yet undreamed of and there for the taking—if we brought this woman into our coven. She gave us your name. We were dwelling in Salem, and she told us to move here. It took us several weeks to effect that move, and through my own arts, I was able to learn a great deal about you, including where I would find you. I met you, and the instant we locked glances I knew that the power was there. We knew, too, that the negative energies in the Pendergrass mansion would help us draw it forth. Murder, you see, leaves behind a psychic residue—and there were three murders and a suicide. You felt the chill in the air immediately. You are very, very sensitive—hence your dreams and hence your power.''

''Power? I do not understand,'' she cried.

''You may remember Elias . . .''

''Elias P. Martin,'' she whispered. ''Die, Elias . . .'' She stared at him in horror. ''I remember . . . oh, I remember now. You are saying that I *helped* . . . no, I cannot believe it.''

''You helped,'' he said. ''That was part of the binding.''

''The binding?''

''In another week I could not have freed you. In another week, at the monthly Esbat, you would have been our creature, but that will not happen. I love you too much to destroy the intrinsic you, as the others have been destroyed and set upon the lefthand path from which there is no turning back, no will to turn back. I have told myself that you were not conscious of what was happening, but as I have said, you are sensitive—more so than any of us realized.''

''What do you think I know?'' she questioned. She was confused by his mention of poor Elias P. Martin, confused and terrified. Memories were flowing into her mind again. ''What do you think I know?'' she repeated, fearing the answer, fearing and yet pitying him for his obvious anguish. ''Tell me.''

He said very deliberately, ''I think you know that you have lain naked in my arms. I think you know that you have danced naked in our rituals. I think you know that you and those of my coven joined in raising the negative energy that felled Elias P. Martin. You do not know that we are paid to achieve these effects, paid to kill or drive mad. That is how we exist and grow rich. And when we find anyone with power such as you possess . . .''

''I have killed a man!'' she suddenly wailed. ''Oh, my God, I have killed and . . . and I have really been with you, and . . .'' She thrust her hands against her chest, as if to shield her body from his eyes. ''How has this been possible? I do not understand.'' Tears began to pour down her cheeks.

''Martin's not dead. And we would have been responsible for his demise—not you. It was not your design nor desire. It is your heritage, my poor girl. You are a child of the Veringers—I have divined that through my own arts—and over the heads of your family hangs the curse of Erlina Bell. It sent your mother and her family halfway across the world, wanderers all, the living and the dead. You, too, are doomed to become a wanderer. I might have saved you from this present evil, but Erlina Bell's not finished with the Veringers or those who love them as I have come to love you.''

''You love me,'' she whispered.

''I think I might have loved you from the first moment I saw you, but I did not recognize the emotion. I have never loved before. I was not meant to love. I am the seventh son of a seventh son, born to a family steeped in witchcraft and Satanism. I have served these dark powers all my life, but tonight I renounce them.''

''The dark powers . . . Satan?'' She backed away from him. ''You are telling me that I . . . Oh, God, am I doomed to the fire everlasting?''

''There is no such fire, my love. It is only a metaphor, a description of what has been called the 'dark night of the human soul.' But you will not experience that. You are neither doomed nor damned.'' He reached out to her.

''Keep away from me!'' She shuddered. ''I begin to believe you. And you . . . you brought me to them. The strangeness was real. I loved you and . . .''

''Did you? And now, no more? I swear to you, Livia, that part of my life is at an end.'' Moving to her, he put his arms around her.

She thrust him away. ''Please go.''

''No, I cannot go. You need my protection. Believe me, my own love, my dearest.'' He fell to his knees. ''I kneel before you. I beg you to forgive me.''

She did not want to look at him, but she did and could not doubt him, could not doubt the anguish in his beautiful, dark eyes, shamed eyes that were full of tears. He was not a man who cried easily, she knew that about him. Somehow she knew a great deal about him, without knowing why or how.

''Oh, Mr. Grenfall . . .'' She knelt beside him, touching his wet cheeks with a gentle finger. ''You must not weep.'' She stifled a sob and found that she, too, was near tears again. ''Oh,'' she cried out, caught in a vortex of emotion, ''I do love you.''

"My dearest." He embraced her, kissing her hair, her cheek, her mouth.

Her body throbbed with a need she barely understood. She opened her mouth to his kisses and moments later felt him fumbling with the hooks at the back of her bodice. She brought her lips close to his ear. "Let me," she whispered. "I think I am beginning to remember a few magic tricks."

Laughing softly, she slipped from his arms and stripped off her garments as quickly as Vivienne and Charlotte had done that first night in the cloakroom. And all the while, she was aware that a great weight had been lifted from her mind and heart. She was not going mad. She might have been shamefully misled. She might have ventured close to the edge of a yawning abyss, but what she had experienced had been real, not imaginary.

She let her garments fall to the floor. Turning, she saw him with the dim light on his magnificently muscled body. He looked even more like the wonderful Greek statues she had seen in the museum, but they were only cold marble. His arms were warm as he lifted her against his chest and carried her to the bed.

Later, rejoicing in a pleasure that had blotted out the brief, sharp pain that had accompanied surrender, Livia freed herself from her lover's arms and whispered, "I hope all that has passed between us is not another dream."

He did not answer her, but very soon she found herself in ecstatic agreement with one of her governess's contentions that actions speak louder than words.

Two

Jamie Wilson was annoyed. His small brown eyes were filled with anger and his lower lip was thrust out. It was an expression that spoiled his still-boyish good looks and added at least five years in lines around his mouth and across his forehead. At this particular moment, he looked all of the 39 years to which he never admitted. His ire was occasioned by disappointment. He had expected to meet Lucy Veringer by the gates of the cemetery, and she had not arrived.

Probably, at the last moment, she had been unable to get leave from the old crone to whom she acted as companion and whom she had described as a regular horror. No, he amended mentally, she had not actually told him that her employer was a horror; she had mentioned that she was difficult. The old bat did not go to bed until the wee hours and kept poor little Lucy at her side reading to her out of dull books, fetching and carrying, even though she had been hired as companion, not maid. Poor little thing! She was so pretty. She ought to be warming someone's bed rather than straining her eyes over the religious tracts her elderly employer preferred.

He had hoped that Lucy might give the woman those pills he had slipped to her last night. That would have sent her off at a good hour, and then he could have come to the house. He would have had ample time to make love to Lucy, and later, when she was asleep, he would have taken such jewels and silver as he could find and gone his merry way. As it was, he would probably have to wait until tomorrow night. Lucy was timid about administering those drugs, but she was becoming more and more passionate. He smiled. He could always get 'em going. He had a way with him. Every girl he had ever met had told him that. It was not entirely his looks. He had a gift of gab and a way of making the girl he was presently seeing think that she was the ony one in his universe, even when he wasn't really attracted to her, which he practically never was. Lucy was something different—a real treat! He would be sorry when he left her, but that was the breaks. Once he got into the house, that would be the end of the romance and onto the next.

He chuckled. He often wondered what happened in the morning when the mistress or master discovered that their jewelry and silver plate had taken wing. He had learned that one girl he'd cozened had been sent to prison for a good long time. Another had killed herself, fool that she was. She had fallen for all his fine talk and actually believed he meant it when he whispered that they would marry. She had cried and cried when he had his way with her. She'd been a virgin, he recalled. He would not be surprised to learn that Miss Lucy was also a virgin, such a pretty creature. He could easily lose his head over this morsel. He had met her, of all places, right here in this graveyard. She had gone to put flowers on her late mother's grave. She had been so frightened when she saw him looming out of the darkness. Though hardly more than medium height, he must have looked very big to that tiny little creature.

He had come into the graveyard because he had seen a policeman he thought he knew. Having no desire to renew that acquaintance, he had dashed in here. Fortunately, he had caught his breath by the time Miss Lucy Veringer came down the path. He had walked her to the gates, and they had fallen into conversation. She had been very shy at first but had gradually warmed to him. They always did. They had parted with her promise to meet him last night, and she had been Johnny-on-the-spot!

"Good evening, Jamie."

He turned. There she was, such a pretty little thing, with her fair hair piled up on her head under a wisp of a bonnet. She was wearing a long dark cape, but he could see the gleam of satin beneath it.She had come to meet him wearing her best bib and tucker. He had made a real hit with her, there was no doubt about that.

"Hello there, Miss Lucy Veringer." He smiled widely and bent to kiss her. She had allowed him to kiss her last night, and she had kissed him back, very shyly the first time. He had kissed her again, and then she had given him a tiny little nip. It had set him on fire! He gestured at a stone bench. "Come and sit down, lovey."

"Very well." She took a seat and did not protest when he sat very close to her.

"I suppose you didn't put the powders in the old lady's tea, did you?"

"I did, Jamie. It's all arranged," she told him breathlessly.

"Lucy!" He bent to kiss her on the lips.

When he finally released her, she said nervously, "Oh, Jamie dear, you don't think they'll hurt her, do you?"

"Not a smidgin," he replied with a low laugh. "They'll just let her sleep a little harder and longer than usual, and meanwhile you'n me'll have ourselves a better time on a softer spot than this here stone bench."

"I shouldn't let you come to the house, Jamie," she said anxiously, "but . . ."

"But you can't resist me?" he inquired audaciously.

"That's true, Jamie."

"Can we go now?"

"Not yet. She doesn't have her tea immediately. Usually she takes it after she says her prayers."

"Christ, I can hardly wait. Mind if I have another sample, lovey?"

"A what, Jamie?"

"I want to kiss you again, baby mine."

"Please do." She was in his arms, and damned if she wasn't going for his neck. He winced. Her nip was a little harder than last night, but he didn't mind, not if she let him return the compliment.

"Let's have a taste of . . ." he began and paused. She was still at his neck, and he was beginning to feel sort of weak. "Hey, honey, go easier," he muttered. She did not appear to hear him. He tried to push her away, but he couldn't budge her. Fear shot through him. He was feeling weaker, sort of all gone inside. "Hey!" He made another effort to break free but he couldn't, and then he found he didn't want to get away. Whatever she was doing was sort of pleasant. He was getting sleepy. He didn't really want to sleep out here. He wanted to cuddle in her little bed and . . . he stopped thinking.

Lucy raised her head, and bringing a dainty scrap of cambric to her lips, she wiped them and rose. She had never drunk so deeply of that life-sustaining fluid, but it was necessary. She needed as much strength as she could get. She glided across the grass to the tomb she would not be using again. Mark was waiting for her. She paused and let her fangs retract; it always distressed him to see them. Then, stepping to his side, she said softly, "Have Juliet and Colin returned yet?"

"Not yet. Do not look so unhappy, my love."

She had not realized that her distress was mirrored on her features, but Mark always knew her state of mind. "I do dislike it. I stopped just short of killing him. I've never done that before." She put her little hand on his arm, adding anxiously, "I do wish they'd hurry."

"And so we have, dearest." Juliet came to her side with Colin only a few paces behind her. "Oh, you do look blooming, darling." She smiled at Lucy. "You must promise to do this more often."

"Don't," Mark chided. "You know how Lucy feels about draining them."

"But he's such a nasty little man," Juliet said.

"It's the principle of the thing," Lucy said unhappily.

"One of these days, you . . . ah, well, what's the use? I shouldn't be lecturing you tonight, should I?"

"No." Colin gave her a long-suffering look. "We have a train to catch. Have you bestowed our bags and boxes aboard, Mark?"

"Need you ask?" his grandnephew demanded indignantly. "When have I ever failed you?"

"Never, old fellow. Don't be so touchy," Colin begged. "I have enough temperament about me already." He had a pointed stare for his female companions.

"I'll let that pass," Juliet said, sticking her tongue out at Colin. "You're an absolute wonder, darling Mark," she continued. "Thank Beelzebub that the full moon doesn't fall on Friday."

Lucy said, "Let's just hope that we are there on time."

"You are not to fret." Juliet moved to Lucy. "Swithin's ill, but Molly has said . . ."

"I know what she has told you," Lucy returned impatiently, "but aside from my darling's illness, I cannot help but feel there are other problems Molly's not mentioned. I fear for my daughter, too."

"I beg you'll not borrow trouble," Juliet cried. "We have enough as it is." She paused, staring at Lucy's stricken face. "Oh, my dear, forgive me. You'll think I have no heart. Come, we'll hurry. See you at the station, Mark."

He nodded, watching the three bats winging their way through the trees. A moment later, striding out of the cemetery, he stopped to alert a policeman to the presence of the unconscious man he had seen lying under a park bench not far from the gates.

Her father had taken a sudden and unexpected turn for the worse. Livia had scarcely left his side during the week following her coming together with Septimus. The time had passed slowly, and in addition to her distress over her father, Livia was struggling with the promptings of a body awakened to an excitement that could be assuaged only in her lover's arms. That comfort was denied her. Leaving her bed just after midnight on Friday, Septimus had spoken strangely about purification and protection. He had not been very explicit, but he had promised to return on the afternoon of the following Friday—to be with her throughout the night.

"You will need me, my love," he had said. "Above all, you will need my protection."

"Protection?" she had asked, aware then that he was deeply concerned, even frightened and, in her new knowledge of him, she realized his fears were for her rather than for himself. "What sort of protection?" she had demanded.

"I must fashion shields," he had said obscurely. "You'll know what I mean when I return. It's best not to be too specific now."

Those elliptical comments had been all she had to comfort her during days that seemed 48 hours long. She had not even the solace of work. She had dismissed the girls and closed the *Mercury* early. She spent most of her time in her father's room, occasionally relieved by Mrs. Nelson, the housekeeper, and as Friday drew near, she was morbidly certain she would never see Septimus again.

Late on Friday afternoon, Livia, sitting with Swithin, who was awake and restless, was informed by a disapproving Mrs. Nelson that there was a Mr. Grenfall on the front porch demanding to see her, even after being informed that she was tending her sick father.

"Stay with Papa, Mrs. Nelson," Livia ordered, ignoring the woman's affronted expression. "I'll be back in a few moments."

Hurrying down the stairs, she opened the front door and then stood still, staring at him in dismay. He looked much thinner than he had a week earlier; he was pale as if he might not have been eating enough. "What's the matter?" she asked anxiously.

"Nothing, my love." He moved into the hall swiftly.

She read concern in his eyes, but intermixed with that was a look that sent shivers of delight coursing through her. "Papa is ill," she said. "I must stay with him until he falls asleep. Do you mind waiting in the library?"

"No, but I hope he falls asleep sooner rather than later. Can you not have the housekeeper stay with him?"

"No." Livia's lip trembled. "He wants me by his side and . . . he's very ill, Septimus."

"I thought he might be," he said enigmatically. He put out his arms and let them fall to his sides. "I mustn't touch you," he said ruefully.

She gave him an anxious look. "There's something wrong, isn't there?"

"It is Friday," he reminded her, "and you must be protected. Come to the library the minute he falls asleep."

"I will," she promised, concerned by his concern, frightened by his fears, knowing instinctively that he was rarely fearful. She led him to the library. There was a paraffin lamp on the desk and another on the table, and since it was dark in the room, she lit both of these.

"Do not let the housekeeper come in here," he warned.

"She won't. She'll be outside of Papa's room once he falls asleep."

"Good."

As luck would have it, her father was unusually restless that afternoon. It became increasingly evident to Livia that, in addition to his physical discomfort, he was mentally uneasy. More than once, he sighed deeply, saying, "My dearest, I do not know. I just do not know how it came about."

"What, Papa?" she asked finally.

"Perhaps it will not be as bad as I imagine," was his only response.

It was not until after seven that he slept. Livia went to fetch Mrs. Nelson, and having left her in the small sitting room adjoining the master bedroom, she went down to the library. Entering, she stopped short on the threshold. The carpet had been rolled back and in the center of the room was an immense circle etched in chalk and having within it a large five-pointed star. Strange symbols were etched upon each point of the star, and a chair had been placed in its center. Her first thought was what would the housekeeper think. She also had an impulse to laugh but that was checked immediately when she met his concerned and somber gaze. She started toward him.

"No," he said quickly. "Step into the circle and sit on the chair."

"I do not understand. Why?"

"For reasons of safety."

"What is the significance of this star?"

"It's not a star. It's a pentagram. It will afford us some

means of protection. I wish you might have come sooner, but perhaps it was ordained that you could not."

"Ordained?"

"It will be a contest," he explained. "The golden bowl is broken. The seals have been stripped from the door."

"I wish you'd stop talking in riddles," she complained.

"Metaphors rather than riddles." He suddenly smiled, but it was a strained smile. "The tomes I have been consulting are full of them, and I'm afraid they've coated my tongue. Please, my dear, sit in that chair. Now!"

Livia moved toward the circle, but as she reached the edge, she found herself oddly reluctant to obey him. Speaking with a forced lightness, she said, "Septimus, dear, what is all this hocus-pocus? I really need an explanation."

"They are getting to you. I beg you'll not heed them. Go into the circle, at once!"

"Who are they? I don't understand you."

"You have only to understand that you must get into the circle and remain there until I tell you that you may leave."

She did not like his abrupt manner, and she resented the fact that he was issuing commands. "My dear, I've left Mrs. Nelson with Papa. I will have to relieve her eventually."

"Go into the circle," he ordered. "Do not make me carry you to that chair. That is what they want. Please, Livia."

Something inside of her was telling her she must not obey him, but she could not resist the appeal in his eyes. She stepped over the chalk-drawn rim and another step brought her to the chair. As she sat down, she felt a lessening of her inner tension. Still, she was curious as to how this diagram could protect her. He had never given her a full explanation of what he meant by protection and purification. "Well, I'm here," she said, "but I am not sure why."

"Because we are dealing with forces inimical to us both, and my powers are no longer at their height. But with you in the center and I at the rim . . ." He gave her a regretful look. "I wish I did not love you so much, my darling."

"Why do you wish that?" she asked, happiness flooding through her.

"Because," he said somberly, "it has filled me with fears that are new to me. If I am to protect you, I mustn't be afraid.''

"Of what?'' she probed.

"Of what can happen.''

"The others!'' she exclaimed. "You think they'll come.''

"Yes, they will come.''

"The doors are locked.''

"Locks will present no problems for them. They will be here at eight. The clock's already struck the half-hour. That's why I wanted you to come sooner.''

"I told you why I could not. Oh, Septimus, I am so worried about my father. I . . . I think he might be dying—and soon.''

"You must not think about that now. It will weaken you. You need all your strength for what lies ahead.''

She rose and moved toward him. "But . . .''

"Stay in the chair!'' he commanded. "Go back to it at once.''

Startled, she obeyed without question.

"Livia, you must stay where you are,'' he said sternly. "Know that in the last week I have fasted and prepared myself for this night. I have power and I have increased it, it is not as strong as it might be. I am depending on our combined energies to stand against them, and though you have always been strong, some of your energy has been drained from you, too.''

"How?''

"Because we have been together.''

She smiled mistily at him. "I've not lost anything through that, my darling. I have gained in strength. Before last Friday I was only half-alive.''

"Oh, my love,'' he said yearningly. "I wish I could hold you in my arms, but as I told you earlier, I dare not touch you or I will be weaker yet. If I'd only known how much I would love you, but what could a child, dedicated to Satan before his first breath, know of love? How could I recognize it until . . .'' He groaned.

"I am glad you didn't recognize it,'' she said softly. "If you had, you might have become afraid of it—of me. Perhaps you'd not have come to me. Whatever happens, I shall never cease to be thankful that you did.''

"Livia,'' he moaned, "I want to make love to you. My

body craves you, my soul adores you, and that is the way it
has been this whole agonizing week. And that worries me. I
have to be strong. Listen to me, my dearest. Those who are
my followers, I have trained them well in evil. They will send
you dreams, but they'll not seem like dreams. They'll entice
and beguile and summon. They will send you pain; it will be
an illusion but will not seem like an illusion. That is why you
must not step beyond the circle, and it is why you will want to
flee from it, but you must not, no matter what happens
or . . ." He broke off as the windows rattled. "It is
beginning. Stay in your chair. Do not leave it."

"That's only the wind," she said soothingly, surprised that
his strange exhortations were not frightening her.

"It's not the wind." He stepped into the circle, standing
at the perimeter, his body tense.

Livia rose from the chair. "Septimus, dear."

"Sit down!" he commanded.

She hesitated. She wanted to be with him, but finally she
obeyed. As she did, she felt a pressure around her as if the air
had suddenly grown heavy, had developed substance.

"Livia . . ." Septimus's voice sounded fainter, as if rather
than in the circle and only a few feet away from her, he was a
room away. "There is still power to be used, your power,
weakened but present because of your heritage. You must
not let them take you. They'll try, even though without me
to lead them, they are also weakened. I am on your side.
Remember."

"I . . ." She paused as she heard the doorbell ring, heard
the sound almost gratefully because of the strangeness of
what he was telling her, because he seemed to think that a
circle drawn in chalk on the floor could afford protection—from what?"

"Do not doubt me," he warned.

She flushed. It was almost as if he had read her mind, but
no one could do that. "Darling," she said, "someone is at
the door. I'll have to let them in. Mrs. Nelson's with Papa.
He's no longer sleeping downstairs, but you know that. We
took him to his own room when he became ill. It is more
comfortable." She rose.

"Haven't you been listening to me? Sit down," he cried.

"But . . ." she began.

"Sit down!" he ordered.

"Ohhhh . . ."

Livia stepped forward. "That's Marian. She sounds as if she's in pain. What's she doing here?"

"It's not Marian. Sit down please. They know about the circle. They want you out of it. On your life, remain where you are."

She sat down but looked at him unhappily. "It sounded like Marian."

"Oh, Miss Blake, help me!"

Livia clutched the sides of her chair, staring at Septimus. It was no good telling him that was Marian calling to her, his glance anticipating her assurances.

"Stay where you are!" he commanded.

"Livia, why have you left me alone? I need water, child," her father called from just beyond the door.

Terror filled her. He had come downstairs in his condition! There was no mistaking his gentle, feeble tones. He had woken up, and Mrs. Nelson must have been out of the room.

Livia did not look in Septimus' direction. She rose and started toward the door, but as she stepped over the rim of the circle she was thrust back. She fell hurtfully. She was on her feet in an instant, her ankle aching, but she was also remembering that never, even in extremis, would her father have been able to rise from his bed and come down the stairs. He was too ill. She limped back to her chair and looked toward Septimus, glad he had not scolded her.

He was not there. She stared around the room and did not see him anywhere. Angered at her disobedience, he had left her alone.

"Septimus," she called frantically.

"Septimus!"

"Septimus!"

"Septimus!"

"Septimus!"

"Septimus!"

Shocked and terrified, Livia heard the name shot back at her like echoes in a cavern, booming at her from all sides of the room, but he was not there.

A wind was rising outside, and it seemed to her that his

name was on the wind, only it was Septimus's voices he heard
in its wail. "Stayyyyyy . . . stayyyyyyy . . ." it urged.

"Where are you?" she cried.

"You!"

"You!"

"You!"

"You!"

"You!"

Echoing words, one after the other, drummed into her
ears.

There was a smell in the room, noxious, horrible, rotten
and putrefying.

Livia coughed and flung a hand over her nose, but the
smell remained because it was coming from her flesh. She
stared at her hand and wailed in horror. The skin was
wrinkled, splotched with huge brown spots. She screamed
and her voice was old and cracked, a thin wail from a
withered throat. The wind blew around her, icy cold, pushing
her toward the rim of . . . what? She could not remember;
the wind was no longer cold but was dry and hot. She must
open a window else she would suffocate.

"Livia, Livia, Livia, do not step beyond the rim."

The voice was only a thread of sound, and she did not
know what it meant. What was a rim? She looked about her
but could see nothing because she had no eyes. Her eye
sockets were on fire with agony, blood pouring down her
cheeks and dripping from the tangled veins which had once
nested her eyes. Screams tore from her throat, screams of pain
and fury. "Eyes, eyes, eyes, give me back my eyes," she
howled and beat blindly on whatever substance lay beneath
her. She crawled forward, because something was urging her
forward.

"Dreams, Livia, dreams, dreams . . . do not leave the
circle!"

She must leave, even if she had to crawl. She must crawl
like a worm, for her arms and legs were gone, too. She was
nothing but a rotting trunk. She writhed and pulled herself
along the floor like a giant worm. Where was Septimus, and
why was she lying on the floor?

She looked up and could see the hooded figures standing

around her beyond the rim, trying to draw her forward. They were reaching for her.

She rolled back, trying to rise and go somewhere . . . where? The chair . . . but she could not rise. She was in terrible pain. Her head felt as if it had swelled to twice its size. Her temples throbbed, each throb a separate beat of agony. Sharp pins were pricking her arms and legs. Her breast burned. Knives seemed to be slashing at her belly. Terrible pressure was being applied to her ankles and feet, as if they had been squeezed into iron boots.

She drew herself into a ball, trying to stifle her cries but to no avail. Great groans were being wrenched from her as she felt the pain inside and out. Her heart seemed to have been pulled from its moorings, throbbing out its message of torment to every lacerated portion of her anatomy. And through it all, she knew that it could be stopped, that all pain would cease immediately. The hooded figures at the rim of the circle were chanting, and in their chant she heard the words that told her that once beyond the rim of the circle, she would be free of the agony. It was the circle itself that was filling her with such excruciating, atrocious pain. Mindlessly, she edged forward, forward, dragging her useless limbs toward that barrier of monolithic figures. Once she was among them, she would be free from this intolerable suffering. Closer, closer, closer, she came to their bare feet.

"Livia, no, no, no, it is an illusion. I suffer as you suffer, but it is an illusion."

She was past believing that warning. An illusion could not cause such frightful torture. She must walk but could not walk! She could not rise; her limbs were knotted. She must crawl. They were stepping back, preparing to let her through. There was a crash as if something had slammed against the glass, and at the same time she heard another sound, as if a door had banged back against the wall.

The pain was suddenly, miraculously gone. Livia staggered to her feet. Looking down, she saw to her horror that she had been very close to the rim of the circle. As she moved back hastily, an arm went around her waist. She tried to pull away, until on looking up she saw that Septimus was holding her. A cry escaped her. He was so pale and hollow-eyed as if he had suffered a grave illness.

"Ahhhh!" A long scream deflected her attention from him. Looking around her, she saw *them*, clad in the hooded capes she remembered from the dreams that had not been dreams. They had come. Of course, they had come! They had been standing at the rim of the circle chanting, but they were not chanting now. They were screaming, all of them, running hither and thither around the room, bumping into each other and cowering in fear as if trying to get away from something. Several of them were looking upwards, their hoods fallen back. She recognized Charlotte and Vivienne, and there was Christopher, dodging from—bats! Three huge bats were wheeling and darting about the room, descending to attack with powerful claws, to beat with mighty wings. She moved closer to Septimus, clinging to him fearfully. She had never seen bats attack anyone. They were such shy creatures, flying out at eventide to become lost in the trees, but these were not shy. And there was someone else. He had just walked in through the garden entrance, a tall man with golden hair and strange slanted eyes. He was smiling, but it was not a nice smile. He was angry, furious. He had left the garden door open, and now he was picking up one struggling cowled figure after another and throwing them out into the garden as if they had been made of rags rather than flesh and blood. Oddly, Livia did not feel afraid of him. Instinctively, she knew he would not hurt her. He had caught Vivienne in his arms now, and it seemed as if he would throw her out too, but no, he had changed his mind. Clutching her against him, he ran out into the darkness. Vivienne's loud scream beat against Livia's ears and was abruptly replaced by her wild laughter.

Her strange hysterics was drowned by screams from those members of the Circle who still remained inside. Septimus's arm suddenly grew rigid. He was staring straight ahead. Livia, following that mesmerizing gaze, saw to her amazement that an attractive and well-dressed young couple had arrived. One was a very pretty girl with blonde hair piled in a high pompadour. She wore a loose silk coat over an evening dress that seemed far too sophisticated for one of her years. She could not be more than 18, and Livia judged her to be even younger. The man with her seemed about 22. He, too, was in evening clothes, and though his coloring was dark, his features proved that he was either a brother or a cousin of his companion. Who were they? She did not think they were members of The Seventh Circle. No, she was sure they were not, for the four or five people remaining in the room were giving them a wide berth. In fact they, whom she now recognized as Christopher, Joyce, Charlotte, Charles and Mabel, were shrinking back, their faces drained of color and their hands raised as if they were warding off more bats.

The bats, she realized with no little relief, were gone. Even though they had certainly created a welcome diversion, she could not like the ugly creatures. And where had they come from? The more she thought about it, the stranger their fortuitous arrival seemed—almost as if they had been sent! She paused in her thinking. On the face of it, the idea of bats being sent was ridiculous. It suggested that someone had been able to tame and guide them: She had never heard of anyone taming bats. It would have to be done at night because they all slept during the day but at night were hungry and hunting.

"Livia, are you feeling better, my love?"

"Better, yes." She looked up at Septimus, and meeting his concerned gaze, her memories of the past few hours descended like a dark cloud. Hours? Had it been only hours? She glanced at the clock. It was a little after 11:00. She had been in the library for three hours; it had seemed more like three centuries. Yet the fear and the agony were fast fading from her mind. In their place were only questions, and these were being deflected by her curiosity concerning the brief bat invasion. "I am so confused," she murmured. "These people . . . where did they come from? And why are the others so frightened?"

They were more than frightened, she realized. They were hysterical, practically gibbering with fear as they bolted for the garden door, their screams reaching her from the garden and then fading into the night.

"To answer your question," Septimus said gently, "I believe they were afraid of what my psychic antennae tell me are your distant relations."

"My relations?" Livia looked at the young couple and received cordial nods from them both as they came over to her.

"My dear child," the girl said. "You are Livia, are you not? But I could not be mistaken, even if I had not known you were present. You have Mark's eyes, and you bear a certain resemblance to my elder sister Kathleen. Also you have my father's height. Don't you agree, Colin?"

"Yes, my dear Juliet." He looked about him. "Where has Lucy gone?"

"I didn't see her go." Juliet frowned. "But Swithin is ill."

"Yes, she must have gone to him, poor love."

"Who are you?" Livia demanded. "How can we be related and . . . did you say . . . Lucy?"

"You'd best sit down, my dear." The girl looked at her compassionately. "We have a great deal to tell you."

"My father . . ." she began concernedly.

"Your father, my child, is in very good hands," Colin assured her.

"Yes," Septimus agreed, "I am sure that is true." Leading Livia to the couch, he sat down and drew her against him. Feeling his arms around her, she could no longer protest. Gratefully, she rested her head against his shoulder while Colin and Juliet, pulling up two other chairs, prepared to discuss family relationships.

Swithin Blake awakened from a disturbing dream in which he had been back in his family mausoleum in Boston, mourning the death of the only woman he had ever loved. But when he opened his eyes and looked toward the chair near his bed, he found to his extreme relief that it had been a nightmare. He smiled at Lucy. "I fear I ate too much at supper."

Her beautiful eyes lingered on his face. "I didn't notice that, my love. You are not generally a heavy eater."

"There must be some reason why I had such a terrible dream," he said shuddering.

"A terrible dream?" she repeated. "What did you dream, my dearest love?" Her hand, cool against his forehead, gently swept his hair back.

"I . . ." He paused and chuckled. "Do you know? I can't seem to remember. It wasn't very pleasant. I am sure of that."

"I'm glad you don't remember it." She looked at him

lovingly.

"Why are you sitting so far away, my darling?" he inquired. "Come to bed."

"Very well." She dropped the cloak she was wearing and revealed a lacy shift beneath. Slipping under the covers, she snuggled against him.

"Oh, Lucy, Lucy," he said tremulously. "It's been such a long, long time."

"A long time? Since we finished supper and came upstairs?"

"It has seemed so to me. I wonder why."

"You've had a little illness. I expect that's why you're a bit confused."

"Have I been ill?"

She stroked his hair. "Don't you remember?"

"Yes, I think I do, but I'm better now. How could I not be with you beside me, my only love. Do you know that you are all the world to me, Lucy?"

She did not answer. She kissed him gently on his forehead and fluttered her long eyelashes against his cheeks before pressing her lips against his mouth.

"You are here," he murmured joyfully. "Have you come to stay?"

"When have I ever left you, Swithin?"

"I thought you . . . had."

"We agreed that it was a dream."

"A dream, yes. And may I have no more like those, ever in my life."

"I promise you, you will not." She kissed his ear.

"I shall hold you to it, my heart." He sighed, and his voice grew weaker. "I am tired. I don't want to be tired with you beside me, my Lucy. I've missed you so dreadfully all these long years."

"But I've been here with you. My, my, you've had some odd fancies tonight." She put her arms around him protectively.

"I expect I have. Kiss me again, Lucy."

She held him very tenderly and pressed another kiss on his lips. She heard his deep, rattling sigh, then felt him relax and lie very still, as once her grandfather had. She remained beside him a few minutes longer, and though he was past hearing her, she said softly, "Goodbye, my life, my love." Slipping from the bed, she draped her cloak about her and went softly down the stairs and out into the rose garden.

As she had expected, the sun was a faint red glow along the horizon and the nightbirds were flying to their nests or to their caves, while in other nests a sleepy twitter reached her ears, a twitter and a stirring. She bent to smell the dew-touched roses, and with her two fingers she nipped one off and kissed it. It was growing brighter in the east. She had always loved the sun. She was allowed one glimpse of its brightness, and in that moment she murmured, "Swithin."

The sun was beginning its progress across the heavens when Mark, carrying a weary but still excited Vivienne in his arms, was arrested by something he saw on the grassy path that stretched between the rose bushes. He hurried the woman into the library and with unceremonious haste placed her on the couch, saying commandingly, "You'll wait until I return."

She laughed up at him. "Yes, Master of all Masters," she teased. Having made his wants known, he strode from the room and back into the gardens.

Mark bent over what he had seen on the path. Tears formed in his golden eyes and slid down his cheeks. Amidst the keening of the banshee and her cat perched on the roof, he thought he heard his great-grandfather's sorrowful lament as well. Kneeling, he bowed his head. Later, he began to dig a grave for Lucy among the roses.

Part Five

One

The woman was tall and striking. She held herself like a queen, and though obviously past middle age, her face had an enduring beauty. If her skin were lined and her mouth pale, her eyes, golden rather than the unimaginative "hazel" used to decribe them on licenses and passports, were bright, young and, at this particular moment, fierce.

She stood beside a huge pile of luggage and boxes like St. Michael at the gates of Paradise. There was a flaming sword in her fiery glance. She seemed to be daring anyone to challenge her right to be on the platform. She appeared totally oblivious to the fact that she was inconveniencing the people that surged about her, awkwardly avoiding her crush of paraphernalia, as they met relatives or rushed to the trains that thundered into and out of New York's Grand Central Station in this autumn of 1921.

Livia Grenfall was even angrier than she looked. Curse or no curse, she had been hoping that after New York she and her family could purchase the little Connecticut farm that their fabulously successful run at the Palace had enabled them to afford. She had the very place marked out in her mind. It would be in the vicinity of New Haven. It would be large enough to accomodate Septimus, herself, their children Richard and Kathie, and their adopted son Mark III, as well as Juliet and Colin, whenever they showed a disposition to alight in one place. And of course her great-great-great-grandfather could settle in, too, even though he would probably cavil at anything smaller than his ancestral castle. She was sure of that just as she was equally sure that it was Erlina's Bell's curse that had doomed him as well as themselves to the series of fleabag hotels they had occupied in practically every city from here to Nome, Alaska.

Looking at the train wheels, she could hear them chugging in her head, and just by way of diversion she mentally examined the cities they had covered, starting when Septimus laid down one magician's cap and took up another. He had really surprised her when he informed her that he was a master of illusion and legerdemain, practices that supported him when he wasn't heading covens. This secondary activity was far more lucrative than the elocution lessons he had given during his brief stay in Marblehead. It had been necessary because after her father died, there had been barely enough money to bury him. Mismanagement, speculation and irresponsible spending had devoured his fortune. The house had been mortgaged, and the furniture had brought a mere pittance.

"Well, my dearest love," he had said after the depressing revelations of the will, "we shall call ourselves The Great Grenfalls." A mild suggestion that the *Marblehead Mercury* could be put on a paying basis had been gently but firmly ridiculed, and the advantages of herself in spangles and tights left no room for argument. A smile curled at the corners of her lips. She had not been of a mind to argue. If Septimus had insisted she be fired from a cannon, she would have agreed. Even now, she was still apprenticed to his sorcery.

Boston to New York was her first experience in a train, also her first efforts at finding explanations for the pair of coffins that were an intregal part of the theatrical props they transported from town to town. That first journey had brought her into such towns as Oshkosh, Kansas City, Toledo, Youngstown, Macon and Mobile. It had been grueling. The well-bred and once well-to-do young lady from Marblehead found that her training as a newspaperwoman was of scant assistance when it came to coping with the exigencies of the road.

It had taken her months to accustom herself to upper berths and unheated cars, to sitting or even standing up all night when trains were crowded. She had loathed the cheap hotels or boarding houses where, like as not, they would be turned away by signs advising that the hostelry in question did not accept dogs or actors. Nor had she been very helpful when assisting Septimus with his illusions. He had been wonderfully patient with her and with her newly acquired relations, even though among the living there had been Mark Driscoll and his bride, Vivienne Mantell.

Septimus had never liked Vivienne, and he liked her less when she joined them on the road. She hated traveling, but notwithstanding the vast difference in their ages, she appeared to adore Mark. She had once shocked Livia by confiding that his lycanthropy added a special ingredient to their lovemaking. However her passion for him had not kept her from being flagrantly unfaithful to her lover. She left him for months at a time, coming back when she chose. He finally married her when she became pregnant with what she insisted was his baby.

Livia grimaced at the memory of Vivienne; screaming her lungs out giving birth to Mark III in an East Saginaw boarding house in the year 1895. Compared to the agonies she had endured giving birth to Richard, the following year, and Kathie, two years after that, Vivienne's travail had been remarkably easy. Unfortunately, it had taken place during a full moon when Mark was locked in the specially designed steel trunk Septimus had made for him. It had also been during a full moon that Vivienne had decamped, leaving them with her seven month old infant and the responsibility of informing her husband she had gone with a team of acrobats headed for Peoria. Probably it would not have added to Vivienne's vaunted self-esteem had she witnessed Mark's heartfelt relief. According to Juliet, Mark had only one love in his life, and that had been her mother, Lucy.

Livia shuddered. It was unworthy of her, she knew, but she was still pleased that she had not been introduced to her vampiric mother. It had taken a great deal of mental adjustment to accept Juliet, Colin and Mark, not to mention the Old Lord, whom she could actually see if she put her mind to it, just as she could hear Molly, the banshee, and her ill-natured cat. Of course it was touching to think of her mother's true death in the rose garden at sunrise. It had been a terrible shock to Juliet and Colin. When they were able to talk about it, they had told Livia that Lucy had always loathed her condition. They speculated that finding Swithin dead on the terrible night of the witches had been the final blow. Lucy had looked forward to meeting her daughter, they assured Livia, but she had never ceased to long for her husband in the years they were separated.

Livia understood that. Though she adored her own children, her passion for Septimus exceeded anything she felt for either of them. It was the ruling factor in her life. In common with the foolish and lustful Mary of Scotland, she would have followed him around the world in her nightie. In a sense, that was what she would be doing once they boarded the train that would take them on their longest journey ever—across the country to a place called Hollywood. It was a town which, according to Mrs. Soames, the wife of a juggler who had shared their stint at the Palace, had nothing to do with either holly or woods.

"It's hot as hell, dearie. Don't never snow out there 'cept up in the mountains. And it's half bean fields and beaches. Most folk go out there to die. An' you can't tell me that movin' pitchers is here to stay. Mark my words, you'n yourn'll be back on the road quick as this." She had snapped her fingers.

Livia secretly agreed with her, however the children were excited. Richard had been signed to play Cagliostro and Kathie would play the magician's wife in a monumental epic called *The Queen's Necklace*. Septimus had been hired as advisor for the magic part of the production. Only she and Mark III had no connection with the movie, and for her part she was absolutely delighted.

"Livia, love."

She glanced up quickly at the shout that echoed across the station. Septimus, accompanied by Kathie, Richard and Mark III, was hurrying toward her. As they approached, she was conscious of a slight pang. Mark looked so very much like his father, who had died two years ago. For once Vivienne hadn't lied. Livia remembered how the older Mark had prayed that his son would not inherit his tendencies and had wept when he found the baby had the telltale hair on his palms. Septimus, too, had been close to weeping but for another reason. Full moon days would be doubly difficult. However, he had set about constructing a small steel trunk with the requisite shackles and airholes. Fortunately, for the first six years of the child's life, they had not needed to use it except when traveling. On moon days, he resembled an adorable little wolf cub. He had been very good with the children, and they had been able to sneak him in and out of the hotels with a minimum of trouble. It was only in his seventh year that he began to exhibit tendencies that required more stringent measures. All the rest of the month he had been of inestimable help in transporting luggage and caring for the two younger children. He still was. For his sake, as much as for their own, she was glad they had been able to schedule their trip so that Mark would not have to join Juliet and Colin in the baggage car.

Her family joined her, and the men, annoying several willing redcaps by possessing themselves of the luggage, started toward the train. Walking with Livia, Septimus gave her a fond smile as he said for perhaps the five thousandth time, "Well, my dearest love, the Great Grenfalls are on their way." He added with an impudence she could not quite appreciate, "When we get to the club car, we must all drink a toast to Erlina Bell."

Seated in the sunken living room of his immense Spanish mansion perched on a cliff overlooking Hollywood Boulevard, Morris Goldbaum, head of Goldbaum-Magnum International Films, Inc., pressed his lips against his ivory and gold telephone saying loudly and indignantly to his secretary Ruth Fiske, "You do not mean to tell me they are complaining about the best accomodations this side of the Los Angeles river? Of all the unmitigated gall! If I ever saw a boarding house breed, they are it. What happens, I ask you, to performers once they get off the train in this city? The hot air gets to their head. It is hot air you are giving me, also. What,

I would like to know, is the matter with the Egyptian Palace hotel? No expense has been spared. They have the Nefertiti suite. Have they seen the Babylonian Pleasure Gardens? And the Javanese Pavilion?''

Repressing a small shudder as she mentally envisioned the sights in question, Miss Fiske wondered if the producer had concluded his diatribe. Receiving an angry demand for an answer, she said, ''They have told me they must have a house.''

''Ah, a house is what they want, eh? That is all? Gold-plated, perhaps, mit a swimming pool; ja?''

''Actually not, Mr. Goldbaum,'' she said soothingly.

''You surprise me. Maybe they are wanting me to build them something?''

''Actually, they specified an old house.''

''An old house?'' he howled. ''In California is nothing old. Did you tell them that?''

The secretary ran a nervous hand through her dark auburn hair, wondering if she dared mention a very sore subject to her employer. Usually, Mr. Goldbaum, kindest of men despite his choleric outbursts, was agreeable to her suggestions. However, he hated being reminded of the mansion he had purchased in Boyle Heights, near the Hollywood Bowl and not far from Rudolph Valentino's famed Falcon's Lair. Similarly huge but of an earlier vintage, having been built at the turn of the century, it rose on a high hill with such Victorian excesses as gables, hanging balconies, turrets and Venetian arched dormer windows.

Ruth knew it bore a definite resemblance to some of the elderly mansions that a poverty-stricken young tailor named Goldbaum had admired in his native Weisbaden, Germany. He had purchased it on the proceeds of *Scented Kisses*, his first major success. His second, *Passion's Pawn*, provided a paint job and repairs, while *Heart's Aflame* enabled him to purchase the furnishings. He had been planning to move into his prize, unoriginally christened ''The Castle,'' when Letitia Lawrence, sophisticated femme fatale of the London and New York stage, agreed to star in *Pearl of the Prairie*, a saga of the cow country. Since the actress was known to be flighty and temperamental, Mr. Goldbaum slipped on his kid gloves. Included in the preferential treatment accorded his star was an agreement to honor her request for the sort of privacy enjoyed by that "Swede barber's assistant" by which she meant Greta Garbo. Accordingly the producer moved her into The Castle for the duration of her stay.

Unfortunately, Miss Lawrence developed a passionate crush on Hank Wilmot, her leading man, whose embraces under the stars painted on the canvas backdrop of a tumbleweed-and-sand-strewn set had been extremely realistic. Upon learning that his private life was complicated by a wife he loved devotedly, Miss Lawrence pettishly hanged herself on the $5000 blown-glass Venetian chandelier in the main hallway of The Castle. Her anguished suicide note addressed "To Hank" was found on her pillow. She had also sent carbon copies of this missive to the editors of the *Hollywood Citizen-News*, the *Los Angeles Times*, the *Herald-Express* and *Movie-Star Parade Magazine* in the fond hope of ruining Mr. Wilmot's career.

Unfortunately the fact that so famous a beauty had died for love of him increased Mr. Wilmot's box-office appeal to the point that from playing rugged cowboy heroes, he was currently being cast as sensuous matinee idols. At present Henry (no longer Hank) Wilmot was finishing a picture entitled *Burning Love*, in which he was portraying just the sort of dashing seducer Miss Lawrence hoped he was. Ironically enough, he was in the throes of a divorce that would leave him free to wed Paula Sinclaire, his leading lady.

Possibly out of frustration and anger or because she had had enough time to regret her impulsive action, the defunct star remained in residence at The Castle, producing a series of uncomfortable psychic manifestations. These had routed its owner and several other tenants. The mansion had remained unoccupied for the past two years while Mr. Goldbaum deliberated as to whether or not he would put it on the market. As he had remarked sadly to Miss Fiske, "It's like selling my heart's desire."

Consequently, the secretary's suggestion was tentative. Holding the receiver a protective three inches from her ear, she asked, "What about The Castle?"

The anticipated explosion failed to take place. "Ach, why not?" Mr. Goldbaum demanded in a definitely mollified tone of voice. "They stay a short time only and with coffins they travel. They should feel at home, ja?'' He added cravenly. ''You show them through the house, Miss Fiske. I send my limousine? Have you met them yet?''

''No, sir, we've only spoken by telephone.''

''Put yourself at their service, please. And you will bring them to Culver City tomorrow, ja? And Miss Fiske, how are they liking it here?''

It was a loaded question and required a tactful answer. ''I haven't had an opportunity to inquire,'' was the one she chose.

''Inquire, please,'' he ordered. ''You know always I am interested in what strangers to our beautiful city will say.''

''Yes, sir.''

''Goodbye, Miss Fiske. When through with them, you may take the rest of the afternoon off.''

''Thank you, sir.'' Miss Fiske thoughtfully replaced the receiver and gazed on the grey file cabinets across the room. She hoped that the producer would not pursue the matter of the Grenfalls' reaction to the ''beautiful city.''

As an emigrant from Germany via the Lower Eastside of New York City, he was at once extremely proud and billigerently defensive of the region known as Southern California. In common with many recent settlers, he eagerly solicited what he firmly expected must be similar opinions, collaring incoming actors, directors and scenic designers, inviting them to tell him how they liked the area.

He beamed when they praised its climate, its floral and arboreal beauties, its wonderful ocean and long white beaches, its towering snow-topped mountains and its vast stretches of desert. He glowered if they also decried its indifferent transportation and large assortment of peculiar inhabitants. A slur against Los Angeles or Hollywood was akin to mud being tracked on a temple floor. Miss Fiske, who was very fond of her employer, frowned. Being a native Californian, she was used to the epithets hurled by disgruntled Easterners. Less defensive than Mr. Goldbaum, she took them in her stride, attributing them to jealousy. However, she *had* felt her hackles rise when Mr. Grenfall, after various amused jibes at the so-called pleasures of the Egyptian Palace Hotel, had asked mildly if the prevailing architectural influences all ran to spotted dogs, derby hats and Dutch windmills.

Evidently Mr. Grenfall had seen very little and assumed a great deal. It had been partially with the intention of finding his family their requested house and partially by way of figuratively rapping him on the knuckles that Miss Fiske had suggested The Castle. While the mansion would definitely provide the quiet, seclusion and space he had mentioned, its design, or rather the lack of it, must put the proverbial mote in his artistic eye. Hopefully its ghostly phenomena would also afflict him.

Her green eyes agleam with gentle malice, Miss Fiske separated her receiver from its hook, and dialing the number of the Egyptian Palace, she asked for the Grenfall suite.

By the time Mr. Goldbaum's long black Mercedes limousine had negotiated the high hill crowned by The Castle, Ruth Fiske, seated beside Bob, her employer's chauffeur, was having second and third thoughts. Taking her eyes from the tree-shadowed edifice looming over the steep, winding driveway, she cast a furtive glance at the rear-view mirror and looked down quickly. Her conscience assailed her anew as she saw the bright anticipatory smiles on the faces of the five people occupying the rear of the car.

She swallowed the lump in her throat. If, rather than talking to Mr. Richard Grenfall on the telephone, she had met him in person, she would have never mentioned the house. She could only hope that once he and his family came inside and felt the dank chill that no amount of central heating could counteract, their enthusiasm would be similarly chilled. There was also the outside chance that the late Miss Lawrence would help matters by causing the chandelier to swing slowly back and forth. That action, without benefit of breeze, had driven at least four prospective tenants away. For her own piece of mind, Miss Fiske forebore to dwell on what had happened to the nervous systems of those who had briefly taken up residence in the place. And, of course, the building was overpoweringly ugly.

On this particular afternoon, its overdecorated porch, its circular weather vane topped tower, its third floor balcony set under a gable and fronted by a free-form wooden cutout, its second floor balcony half-hidden by the misplaced pediment that ornamented the arched opening on the porch, and all of its other Victorian excesses, not excluding stained-glass windows, caused it to look as intimidating outside as it was to be inside. The interior view was something she had not yet seen, having entered Mr. Goldbaum's employ only eight months previously. However, she was reasonably sure that no one with any pretensions to good taste would want to live there—certainly, no young man as elegantly turned out, as handsome of feature and person as Mr. Richard Grenfall, who had just this minute leaped out of the car to open the door for her.

Reading admiration in his dark eyes, Miss Fiske said in a small deprecating voice, "I'd forgotten that this house was so far off the beaten track. With the appalling lack of proper public transportation in the city, I fear the location would be too inconvenient for you—all of you. Culver City is way on the other side of town."

"Oh, you need not worry about that, my dear," Mrs. Grenfall said, strolling over to them. She had much the look of Richard around the eyes and in the shape of the face, Miss Fiske decided.

The secretary's glance fell on Kathie Grenfall, dark like her brother and her parents, but with her mother's golden eyes. She was so beautiful that Miss Fiske had been delighted to discover that her relationship to Richard was one of sister rather than cousin. Mark Driscoll was a cousin. He, too, was very attractive with his red-gold hair and his slanted eyes which were similar in color to those of Kathie and her mother, but he was more hirsute than Richard. His chin was faintly green, and she guessed he must have to shave twice a day. Hair grew thickly on his wrists and the backs of his hands. There were even hairs on his palms; she had felt them when they shook hands. Thinking about them now, some faint disquieting memory stirred in her mind and was forgotten as the elderly Mr. Grenfall joined them. He was certainly a handsome man. With his dark hair only slightly sprinkled with silver, his narrow moustache and his short dark beard, he looked every inch the stage magician. His eyes were practically mesmerizing, and his body was slender, graceful and almost sinuous. He had a rather foreign air, but his accent was definitely Eastern seaboard as he said briskly, "Well, let's go inside. Do you have the keys, Miss Fiske?"

She would have given much to explain that she had forgotten them, but given Mr. Goldbaum's all-abiding faith in her efficiency, she dared not confess to so fearful a lapse. She reached into her small purse and reluctantly brought them out. "Come with me," she said resignedly and walked up the path leading to the front steps, praying that when they entered the hall, they would be met by that all-pervading chill and the swinging chandelier. As she fitted the key into the ornate lock beneath the heavy brass doorknob, she mentally challenged the phantom actress. "Do your worst, Miss Lawrence!"

The key turned with regrettable ease, and Miss Fiske, who had never encountered Miss Lawrence or the other psychic phenomena, hoped devoutly that she could maintain her equilibrium. Pushing open the door, she stepped inside, pausing just eyond the threshold. A small cry escaped her as she encountered a blast of air so icy that it seemed to have risen from the very bowels of a glacier.

There was a creaking rusty sound in her ears, and raising her eyes, Miss Fiske saw the chandelier moving back and forth quite as if someone were standing back of it, pushing it as they might a schoolyard swing!

A scream formed in her throat and was resolutely forced back and down. Half-fearfully, half-triumphantly, Miss Fiske turned to her five companions. With only the slightest tremor in her low, rather husky voice, she said, "You see, it's quite unacceptable, isn't it? There's such a draft, and I don't know what's making that chandelier swing back and forth. The chains are rusty. It could fall at any moment. We'll have to find something else for you. You must agree."

She received no response. They weren't looking at her. their eyes were fixed on a point far above her, and gazing in that same direction, Miss Fiske could not stifle the scream that tore from her throat. From a noose at the end of a rope that encircled the base of the chandelier just above an ornamental glass drop dangled a shadowy figure, repulsively blue and bloated with its tongue lolling from the side of its distorted mouth.

Confronted with Miss Lawrence's enthusiastic response to her prayers, the secretary felt herself growing dizzy and faint. "P-Please," she begged. "D-Do let's go. I . . . I . . . I'm sorry to have brought you here."

"Please don't be sorry, Miss Fiske," Richard Grenfall said with a charming smile. "You couldn't have done better. This is quite perfect."

"Darling," his mother warned, "don't make any snap judgments." As the trembling, shuddering secretary gazed gratefully at this infinitely sensible woman, the lady continued. "We can't be sure of anything until we've seen the cellar."

At that moment, there was a terrible gurgling scream from overhead. The doorknob flew out of Miss Fiske's hand and the door slammed loudly, evidently driven in that direction by a numbing blast of wind that seemed to be coming from the inside of the house. As the secretary, well over the edge of terror, fell fainting to the floor, she heard or thought she heard Mrs. Grenfall say concernedly, "Grandfather, dearest, what on earth is the matter?"

As Richard lifted Miss Fiske to a nearby hall settee, Kathie, who communicated with her ancestor better than the rest of the Household, heard his views on the cheap, theatrical upstart who was currently endeavoring to establish territorial rights in a house that didn't even belong to her!

"In my day, she'd have been a bloody orange seller. They'd never have allowed her to set foot on the stage!"

"Grandfather!" Kathie reproved.

"Please don't stop to palaver with him," Livia said tartly. "We have to see to this poor girl." Turning to Richard who was kneeling beside the fallen secretary, she added, "How is she?"

"She's still unconscious," he said worriedly. "I'd best take her out to the car."

"Can't someone stop her doing that with the chandelier?" Septimus demanded.

Looking upwards again, they saw that the chandelier was swinging back and forth and around and around, imitating the action of a pendulum. The chain was creaking fearfully. Evidently, the actress wanted to intimidate the intruders headed by the Old Lord and was choosing this way to make her displeasure felt.

"Look out!" Mark exclaimed. "I think it's about to fall!"

Thanks to his warning, they were all able to jump back as

the chains of the heavy fixture, already overstrained by her suicide and further weakened by her habit of activating it so often, crashed to the floor, leaving only the smaller end of the chain dangling from the high ceiling.

"Oh, dear, what a mess," Livia commented. "We'll clean it up later on, but that will certainly cut her claws. Now, may we please go down and see the cellar?"

"They have the house taken?" the producer yelled into the phone the next morning. "What, what? Speak up, Miss Fiske. I can hardly hear you."

Miss Fiske, still recuperating from her first brush with the spiritualistic world, managed to raise her shaking voice. "They like the cellar," she stated, hoping he would not ask for a further explanation.

"The cellar yet?" he questioned, defeating her hopes.

"It seems that it's large enough for their purposes."

"What purposes? Wild parties, no doubt?"

It was on the tip of her tongue to contradict him. None of the family, especially not Mr. Richard Grenfall, looked as if they favored that popular recreation, but since she could not comprehend their enthusiasm for the cellar, she found it easier to let the matter stand. "Possibly," she replied cravenly. "They said they'd be obliged if you'd replace the chandelier with a fixture that did not swing."

"The chandelier?"

Miss Fiske hastily removed the phone from her right ear and rubbed that assaulted appendage. "Didn't I tell you that the chandelier fell?"

"Gott in Himmel!" screamed Morris Goldbaum. "Have you any idea of the cost? Imported it was from Venice, blown especially for me, and they are not two minutes in the house and broken it is?"

"*They* didn't break it, Mr. Goldbaum. It fell of its own accord, I expect." She paused, not wishing to rub salt in his many wounds by mentioning Miss Lawrence's contribution to the breakage.

"It has never fallen before," growled Mr. Goldbaum. "Ach, what I must put up with actors. Very well, do as they ask. Only spare the expenses, please."

Extracting the kernel from the nut of that conversation,

Miss Fiske leaned her chin on her hands and her elbows on her desk. She heaved a long sigh. "Actors," he had said. That was the trouble. In her eight months with Mr. Goldbaum, she had seen them come and go. Some remained longer than others. Generally they came for one picture and went back to stages located either in New York or London. Mr. Richard Grenfall was here for one picture. Undoubtedly he would leave immediately he was finished filming it—and that should not matter to her. No sensible secretary or young woman from California ever made the mistake of falling in love with an actor. Everyone remotely connected with the burgeoning film industry knew that actors were heartless, faithless, often mindless and always supremely egocentric. They lapped up praise and adored anyone who adored them—but briefly. This applied to all of them, but if they were as handsome as say John Gilbert or Ramon Navarro or Richard Grenfall, who to her mind was better looking than both of the aforementioned and definitely in a class with John Barrymore, they were impossible! Their only love could be found in their makeup mirror. Their other love would be their leading lady, in this case the exquisite Katherine Grenfall—but she was his sister! Miss Fiske hated the feeling of hope that flickered in her mind despite her large portion of common sense.

"Desist, my girl," she muttered. She called the studio electrician and exlained about the chandelier.

She hated herself still more when she dialed the number of the mansion, hoping against hope that *he* would answer the telephone. Her loathing for herself increased several notches when, as she heard his voice on the other end, her heart leaped and her breath grew short. It was very difficult for her to say calmly, "About that chandelier, Mr. Grenfall . . ." She was close to swooning when, at the end of their conversation, he said wistfully, "I hope that you are not doing anything tonight, Miss Fiske."

Her answer, the stock one she gave all actors, should have been, "Unfortunately I am. I'm very busy." Despite her well-developed instincts for self-preservation, she said, "No, I'm not busy. Why?"

"I . . . would like to see more of the city. I was in hopes that you might show it to me, you being familiar with it. And possibly we might have dinner?''

He actually sounded shy! Shy? An actor? Incredible! Striving to keep her tone level, she said, ''I would be glad to show you the city, Mr. Grenfall, and I'd love to have dinner with you.''

''Oh, that's fine, Miss Fiske. Oh, I hope you'll not think me remiss for not asking how you feel.''

''I feel fine, Mr. Grenfall, just fine!'' she exclaimed and immediately blushed. She never should have sounded so enthuiastic.

''I'm so glad. Shall we make it at six . . . and please give me your address, Miss Fiske.''

''And how is Miss Fiske?'' inquired Livia, who had come down the stairs in time to hear the end of her son's conversation. ''Has she recovered from her experience?''

Richard's smile faded. His expression was rather gloomy as he nodded. ''She seems to have suffered no ill effects.''

Livia moved to him and put a hand on his shoulder. ''What's the matter, dear?''

''I like her,'' he said defensively.

''That's hardly surprising,'' she replied tolerantly. ''She's a most attractive young woman.''

''Intelligent, too, in spite of . . . of . . . and you really can't blame her for that,'' he said obscurely.

''Of course you can't,'' Livia said kindly. ''When I was her age, I am sure I would have fainted, too. I'm glad I'm inured now. That woman, did you hear her last night?''

''I think Kathie must say something to the Old Lord,'' Richard said. ''Of course, I heard them. They were having a dreadful go, and once we start filming, we'll need our sleep. Damn, I wish I knew more about acting, Mother. Being a magician and pretending to be one must be very different.''

''I am sure it is, darling, but look on the bright side of it. You are getting paid well, and you won't have to speak.''

''I'll have to seem as if I am speaking,'' he pointed out. ''Even if the titles will do the rest, I don't want to end up with egg on my face.''

''You won't, darling,'' she assured him. ''And you will look very handsome as Cagliostro.''

''Juliet says she met him in Rome, and he was squat, flat-faced and thick-limbed.''

''Well, I don't expect they'll insist on realism,'' Livia told him comfortably. ''And thank you for the suggestion about Kathie. I will get her to speak to the Old Lord. That's a much better idea than what your father had in mind.''

''What was his solution?''

''He wanted to conduct an exorcism, and at the present time he needs as much energy as he can get. I'm sure his work at the studio will be wearing. They'll be at him with questions night and day. And there's no telling when the picture will be finished, and off we'll go on the road again.''

Richard's brow grew even darker and his gaze more somber. ''I took a walk through the gardens this morning. There's also an orchard.''

''I know. I saw it from our bedroom window. Orange trees.''

''And lemon, avocado, kumquats and olives—all growing alive out of doors!'' he said almost worshipfully.

She gave him a pitying look. ''Yes, dear, it's very nice but need I mention . . .''

''No!'' he replied explosively. ''You need never mention it at all. I have lived with the knowledge for twenty-seven years or very nearly. We dare not stay in any one place for more than a couple of weeks or something will happen and we'll have to go! Excuse me, Mother.'' He went swiftly out of the room.

Livia sent a commiserating look after her unhappy son. At least Richard, at twenty-six, was not in ignorance of what could happen because of deeds committed over a century before he saw the light of day. Richard and Kathie had grown up with the Old Lord, with Colin and Juliet, and with Mark's infirmity. Ignorance in this family was definitely not bliss!

She thought about Ruth Fiske, a very pretty girl, efficient, reliable and sensible except where it counted the most. Anyone the children loved would have to know, and though she had no intention of being an interfering mother, she doubted that Ruth and Richard would suit each other, judging from the way the girl had reacted to Letitia Lawrence—no pretty sight, of course. Maybe she was making too much of it. After all, they had just arrived and Richard had known other women, quite a few of them, in fact.

Generally he did not become interested after a single meeting, but he was of an age when he might want to settle down. It was a pity that they would have to leave Hollywood. Judging from the few words she had managed to exchange with them before they retired to the cellar, Juliet and Colin liked it, too. She stifled a sigh.

It had taken a combination of willpower and tact to keep from warning them to be careful. In the years that dear Mark had been alive, she had learned their story, something neither of them had ever divulged to her. They did not confide in her very much. Though they liked her, were even fond of her, she knew they could not help comparing her unfavorably to her mother, whom they had adored. She shivered, as she remembered what form that adoration had taken! And it was certainly indicative of their thought processes.

Mark's uncle Tony had told him of their transitions—Colin following his beloved sister into the dark realm of the Undead. In those days, they had been gentle and vulernable. However, unless she were deeply mistaken, a large part of their humanity had dissipated. That had been all too evident on the road. As they traveled from place to place, there had been numerous cases of amnesia reported in the local papers, and in Des Moines, after a rather long fast, Juliet had slain a postman and Colin had done the same to a lady of the evening. Fortunately neither victim had pursued them, but she did not like to dwell on what might be taking place in Des Moines. The Household would be billeted here far longer. She only hoped that Juliet and Colin's natural caution would reassert itself. She did not believe they would regain their humanity; for one thing, they weren't human.

"Livia's upset about us," Juliet remarked as Colin helped her out of her casket that evening.

"I know. She's not really very good about concealing her emotions, poor woman."

"You're much more tolerant of her than I am. There are times when I really don't like her, even though she is Lucy's daughter. I fear she takes after Swithin's side of the family."

"You don't really mean that," Colin reproved, as she tied his tie. "For one who knew nothing about the Household until her twenty-seventh year, she has done famously. Look how splendidly she has coped all these years what with Mark, the children and this constant traveling. Judging from what Septimus has told us, she has been afflicted by the curse even more than the rest of us.''

''Not more,'' Juliet contradicted.

''For a neophyte,'' he corrected hastily.

''You are making me ashamed of myself,'' she admitted. ''I expect I still can't help thinking that if she hadn't been born, Lucy might still be alive.''

''You're forgetting that devastating seance and Erlina Bell. And I hardly believe she'd have survived to the age of eighty-nine, curse or no curse. She was such a delicate little thing.''

''Wasn't she?'' Juliet agreed mournfully. ''The sweetest girl in the world. I do miss her, but I fear she doesn't miss us at all. I wonder where she is?''

''I don't know. It's not given for us to know, as I needn't tell you. But since we're evil, I suspect . . .''

''I don't feel evil,'' Juliet interrupted. ''Do you, Colin?'' She regarded him earnestly.

''I don't think we should have been so enthusiastic in Des Moines.''

''That was a mistake,'' she agreed, ''but we were both so famished and that postman was such a horrid little creature. If he hadn't made all those disgusting overtures to me when I happened to meet him at the pillar box, I don't think I would have been so angry.''

''Angry or hungry?''

She stuck her tongue out at him. ''I have already admitted that I was starving. And you needn't go all sanctimonious on me. Don't forget your whore.''

''I am doing my level best to forget her,'' he replied ruefully. ''I paid for my greed. Her blood was full of impurities.''

''Isn't it fortunate you're undead, else you might have caught something really nasty,'' she teased.

''There are compensations in everything, I suppose. Where are we going tonight?''

''Let's just explore,'' she said. ''And I should like to get some pretty clothes. This town's famous for its midnight suppers and after-hours parties. I really don't have a thing to wear. Isn't it lovely that they have ready-made clothes these days? We won't have to mesmerize dressmakers and haberdashers or raid anybody's closet. We can just slide into the stores and steal to our heart's content.''

"There are several reasons why I like this century,'' he mused. "I wonder what it would be like to be alive in it.''

"Oh, Colin,'' she mourned, "I beg you'll not talk that way. It always makes me feel so dreadfully guilty.''

"Love,'' he said, slipping an arm around her waist, "if it were not for you, I shouldn't have passed through some very fascinating times. You've nothing to reproach yourself about, nothing at all. Now let's go.'' Before she could comment, he changed into his bat shape, and with Juliet close behind him, he flew out the window, skimming gracefully past the eucalyptus trees.

Coming up out of the cellar where he had just finished attaching steel plates to the cell where Mark would stay in a couple of days, Septimus sank down in a comfortable but elaborately ugly, red plush chair, ornamented with gold tassels and finished off with gold clawed feet on large golden balls. All through the house the tendency was toward overstatement; an impoverished child's view of palatial surroundings had been his observation to Livia, when he had first seen this gaudy interior.

"This house also reminds me,'' he now commented to his wife, who was lying on a long, deep, down-cushioned sofa covered in golden damask, "of some Swabian brothel.''

"And what would you know about Swabian brothels, love?'' she inquired.

"I have a vivid imagination,'' he said, smiling. Rising from his chair, he moved to his wife, and lying down beside her, he caressed her in a way that still sent thrills coursing through her body. "Aside from the furniture,'' he said a few moments later, "the space in this mansion is wonderful. It has been a long time since we've been in such a situation.''

She had the tact not to remind him that they had never been in such luxurious premises; even her father's house could not compare to this semi-palace, though its excesses did assault her sense of taste. She said merely, "The location is lovely. Richard likes it, too.''

"And Mark."

"Juliet and Colin, too."

"I haven't spoken to Kathie," Septimus mused, "but I saw her walking through the gardens. She looked happier than I have ever seen her."

They turned and stared at each other. "Do you suppose?" They laughed wryly, having both spoken the same words at the same time.

Septimus pressed a long kiss on his wife's mouth. Moving back he said, "My darling, I've been talking to the Gower Booking Office. We've been discussing slots in Fresno, San Luis Obispo, Sacramento and San Francisco. There's definite interest, and the start of our new tour depends on when shooting's completed."

"I'm glad you saw them, darling," she said approvingly. "I'm glad California's such a large state. They say that the northern area is just as beautiful as the southern."

"I've heard that, too, and the theaters in San Francisco are almost as plush as those in New York. Belasco got his start on the Pacific Coast, if you remember."

"Yes, and beyond the Pacific Coast is Hawaii."

"And beyond Hawaii, Japan and the rest of the Orient."

"All Asia—Siam, Persia, India—" She broke off as a gust of wind blew through the room causing all the crystal drops on the beaded lampshades to clash together and sending several small objets d'art tumbling to the floor.

"Oh, dear, what can be troubling him?" Livia inquired.

Kathie hurried into the room. "What have you been saying to upset grandfather? What's all this about India?"

Looking into her daughter's distressed face, Livia said gently to her and to the vague shape she saw towering at her side, "Calm down, both of you. We were only talking."

"He doesn't want to leave, either," Kathie said as the shape seemed to dissolve.

It was the "either" that really wrung Livia's heart. It spoke volumes about her daughter's life since infancy. The house was so beautifully situated, so large and comfortable, and poor Kathie was so weary of traveling. She herself was also road-weary—so many, many miles covered and more stretching ahead of them. In another few months, she would celebrate her sixty-seventh birthday. Septimus was approaching his sixty-ninth. They shouldn't be expected to put on shows sometimes in two different towns in one week!

"Love," Septimus whispered, "let's go to bed."

"Very well," she agreed, excited by the touch of his caressing fingers and responding to the urgency of that request. Three decades dropped away as, bidding Kathie goodnight, Livia and her husband went up the long winding staircase.

Kathie watched them enviously. They were still so very much in love. It was hard to imagine what they could see in each other after 41 years of marriage! They were both so old. Of course neither looked old, but it was the years that counted.

Love to Kathie was an undiscovered country and likely to remain that way. Her parents, she thought, had been extremely fortunate. Given her father's former connections, he was really the ideal husband for a girl with a curse on her head. As for herself, she was just as fortunate that she had never been a party to that unfortunate emotion, especially when her choices would be so severely limited.

Though Kathie adored her father, she did not want to fall in love with a hereditary witch or a reformed Satanist. At 24, she knew precisely what she wanted and was sensible enough to realize that she probably wouldn't get it. Her preference was for Englishmen. She had met quite a few British actors on the road and they always appealed to her, though she had never let any of them know that. One of them she remembered in particular. He had called her "Miss Frosty." His name was Matthew Vernon. He wasn't a good actor, she recalled, but as he confessed one day, he didn't want to be an actor. He had been learning the stage for an entirely different reason. She had never discovered what that reason could be. They hd been conversing while she was in the wings waiting to go on and be sawed in half. Her call came, and when she returned, he had gone. She had not seen him again.

She wondered why she even remembered him, but she did, more than the others she had met in her ceaseless peregrinations back and forth across the United States. She had thought him interesting and she knew he liked her—but love her? That was another matter. That meant that he would have to accustom himself to Mark, the Old Lord, Colin, Juliet, and she knew that some people even might be daunted by her father. In addition to his conjuring, he could, if he put his mind to it, raise and lower windstorms.

Kathie went slowly up the stairs to her room. Later, lying in an immense canopied bed set on swans' wings, something that would have delighted her years ago, she listened to a chorus of crickets and frogs and wondered why she was crying. Tomorrow promised to be an exciting day. They would be going to Goldbaum-Magnum for the first time and would be meeting the producer and the director. They would also learn their rehearsal schedules and be given the scripts. She wondered how long they would rehearse and how long they would be working on the movie. She had heard that it had taken the famed D.W. Griffith six months to complete *Birth of a Nation*. Of course it was a very complicated movie. *The Queen's Necklace* was also complicated. They were going to reconstruct the whole city of Paris in 1785. Her father was advising them on the authenticity of the sets as well as upon Cagliostro's magic.

They little knew that he would be getting the information practically first hand from Juliet and Colin, who had been sojourning in Paris five years before the French Revolution and who, in addition to being presented to the unfortunate Marie Antoinette and King Louis XVI, had also had a nodding acquaintance with the Count and Countess Cagliostro.

"A freemason and supposedly an adept in magic," Colin had said. "He was a very generous man and certainly not a villain. His wife Lorenza was very beautiful. They say that half the court was in love with her and the other half her lovers, but judging from what I know about her, I feel that was an exaggeration. And my dear Kathie, you far surpass her in beauty!"

"Colin!"

That was something Kathie had never let herself dwell on, either. The very thought of it frightened her. Though he had never been anything except avuncular where she was concerned and though she knew that if he had any particular preference for her above Richard, it was because she resembled her grandmother on the Veringer side, she still could not help rejoicing in their relationship. She loved to look at him. He was so slim, so elegant—his face was almost beautiful. To her mind, he bore a resemblance to the pictures she had seen of Lord Byron. She had told him so once and received a rather cool response. Colin had known the poet and, as he had told her crisply, to know him was not to respect him! Still, she did detect the resemblance, and there had been moments when he had been about to leave for some gala evening that she almost forgot his unfortunate situation.

"Oh, dear," Kathie whispered and thought defensively of Matthew Vernon. He was similar in type to Colin, she realized, now that she allowed herself to consider them both, a pastime in which she rarely indulged. Surprise shot through her. Yes, they were similar in face and form, both darkly and aristocratically handsome. English with a touch of the Scot.

"The border breed, my dear," was how the Old Lord characterized Colin's looks. Was that why she had been attracted to Mr. Vernon? Startled she glanced upwards. Had she heard a distant wail? Was it Letitia Lawrence or Molly? They sounded very much alike. She hoped it might be the actress, but no, it was Molly. She also heard the cat—but why?

Kathie put her head under the pillow to close off that mournful sound. She wondered miserably what more could possibly happen to them. She refused to speculate and defensively went to sleep.

In his room, Mark, standing at the window, was beginning to feel logy and dispirited. Ignoring the palm trees and eucalyptuses under the rising moon, he glared at the chill satellite. Another two days and it would be full. As it reached that period, he felt estranged both from his family and the world. His arms and legs ached, and there was a throbbing all through his body in anticipation of the moment when he must change. He also knew that immediately upon closing his eyes this night, the dreams would come. He would see himself, sleek and furry, running swiftly over terrain he had never viewed in his waking hours. Huge trees would tower over him, their branches twisted and gnarled under their sparse coating of leaves. The ground beneath his paws was rock-strewn. There would be tall gallows bearing whitened skeletons, and the roads over which they loomed were crooked and unpaved.

As he loped along, his senses would be curiously sharpened so that he was aware of a number of scents, some delicious enough to make his mouth water and his stomach groan—rabbits in their holes, badgers in their burrows, squirrels curled in tree hollows, birds in their nests. Each had a different odor and would be delicious in its own way, but better things lay ahead. Out on an undulating stretch of moor would be sheep, which he saw not as white and woolly but lying stiff and stark on the ground, their throats torn out, their insides half-gutted, as he devoured great hunks of their flesh, their blood soaking his muzzle and himself howling with the pleasure of the kill!

It was a fantasy he never shared with anyone, not even Juliet and Colin, whom he knew could understand his craving and match it with their own. They would not really be in sympathy with him, he knew. No one could understand what it meant to be a werewolf. There were times when he felt dreadfully alone and envied Juliet and Colin because they had each other. He envied Robert even more. He could make love to a girl and often had. It was true that he never allowed himself to become serious, but at least he was not totally incapacitated for two to three days each month. He did not need to look at the moon and see it only as a threatening body that filled him with increasing dread because of the oblivion that overcame him, together with the ever-present fear that someone would let him out by accident some night and he would turn on those he loved, which he had been warned was the nature of the beast. Coupled with that fear was a new dream in which a small, dark woman came and jeered at him while he was chained in the cellar.

"The son of a witch and a werewolf ought to have more gumption," she had said.

In that dream, she loosed his chains and guided him through the cellar, up into the house and out into the moonlit night. He had been experiencing that dream ever since they started for California. It seemed very real. He groaned. Half of him hated the dream but the other half longed to feel the earth beneath his paws—and the witch knew it. She laughed at him for that hidden longing, that unfulfilled desire. That woman had a name, one he knew and dared not mention to any of his kin.

She had told him that her name was Erlina Bell.

TWO

Goldbaum-Magnum occupied some four acres in a town called Culver City which lay several miles distant from The Castle. It was bounded by a thoroughfare called Venice Boulevard, and the best way to reach it was to drive down Sunset Boulevard to Sawtelle Boulevard which would bring them to the aforementioned Venice Boulevard.

Those were Miss Fiske's directions which they had given to the cab driver. However, the cabbie, an amiable, transplanted and homesick New Yorker, learning that his passengers had come from that city, talked warmly and wistfully of its wonders while taking a circuitous route that brought them to Malibu, a beach town several miles up the coast highway. From Malibu they drove to Venice Beach, and connecting at last with the proper boulevard, they rolled up in front of the studio gates some 40 minutes later than they should have.

Septimus, sitting with the nostalgic driver, did not comment but his glance at the meter and another glance in the rear-view mirror spoke volumes to his children. Subsequently he turned that glance on the driver, and as they emerged from the taxi, Kathie and Richard were not surprised to hear the cabbie say, "That'll be fifteen cents, sir." He magnamimously refused the nickle tip that Septimus attempted to press upon him.

"Papa," Kathie reproved as she watched the mesmerized driver speed off. "He should have had at least fifty cents."

"He planned on five dollars," Septimus said sententiously. "If there's anything I cannot abide, it's a cheat."

Richard did not join in their laughter. He was thinking about Ruth Fiske and was glad she was not present to see his father flexing his arcane muscles, even though he could only agree that it had been no more than the driver deserved. More specifically, he was thinking about the previous night when they had driven up Mulholland Drive and looked at the spread of twinkling lights that were Hollywood and Los Angeles. He had longed to embrace her. That was what was happening in most of the cars parked around them. Unfortunately there had been no opportunity. Those lovely lips, which seemed made for kissing, were in almost perpetual motion as she told him about Hollywood, about Mr. Goldbaum's relief that they liked the house, about the forthcoming picture which would be the most expensive ever produced by G&M. The evening was nothing like what he had expected.

"An easy conquest," jeered his other half.

That was what he had wanted the previous night. He could still smell Ruth's subtle perfume and envision her lovely profile as illuminated by the headlights from another car that had parked shortly after they rolled in.

In the bright light of morning, Richard was just as glad she had not proved "easy." He had met plenty of that sort on the road. Try as his mother did to protect him from what she dubbed "harmful experiences," he had been just 14 when he helped one Vera, the Snake Charmer, carry the box containing her pet python up to her room in the same boarding house where they were staying.

Vera had proved to be just as strong and determined as the python when her arms snaked around him. He had been very sorry when Vera, taking Charles, her python, had gone on the road the following week. Sally, a kootch dancer, had quickly taken her place, and after that there had been Tanya and Manya, a very pretty pair of Siamese twins. Later experiences were less exotic but equally rewarding. They were also too numerous to remember without the aid of the card file he did not possess. Yet oddly enough he had not even protested when the secretary, eluding his attempt at a good-night kiss, had thanked him for a lovely evening and, refusing to let him accompany her to her door, hurried into her house. He was still addressing her as "Miss Fiske."

Under these circumstances, it was all the more surprising to him that he kept muttering to himself, "Ruth and Richard. Richard and Ruth."

Usually he needed a great deal more encouragement than she had provided. She did have beautiful eyes, and her figure, as he had noted the previous day, was extremely good. He was glad she had not followed Juliet's example and shingled her hair. He would have liked to see her with her long, heavy auburn tresses falling over her shoulders and bosom; his fancies precluded teddies or other underclothing. In fact his fancies . . .

"Richard," Kathie said quite loudly.

Startled, he turned to find that the guard was opening the gates for them, Septimus having presented their passes. He flushed and followed them inside. The signs in the mammoth studio were varied and confusing enough to bring him out of his dangerous daydreams.

The guard that volunteered to show them the way to Mr. Goldbaum's office took them down a wide cement walkway amazingly bordered by the sort of neat white houses found in the residential section of many American towns. Clipped green lawns stretched in front of them, flowers growing in neat beds near the front porches.

"Do people live in the studio?" Kathie asked him.

"Some try," the guard said, "but they wouldn't much care for these here places. C'mon, little lady, and have yourself a look-see. C'mon, all of you."

Following him up the cement driveway by one of the houses, they were amazed to find that beyond those curtained windows were only unfinished boards to prop up the line of facades.

"They're sets!" Kathie exclaimed incredulously. "But they look so real!"

"Better have," said the guard. "Camera picks up every little thing. Goes for people, too. You oughter see what we have to do with some of the dollies that come waltzin' in here. Won't need to do much of a job on you, miss, that's a fact. But we'd better get goin'," he added hastily before she could thank him for the compliment.

Coming down the driveway they passed what appeared to be a bombed-out village, and coming around the bend they met a bevy of pretty girls in Japanese costumes complete with heavy black wigs and delicate painted parasols. Following them were a pair of nuns screaming with extremely unlady-like laughter and smoking cigarettes in long jade holders. An Arab shcik followed close behind them, walking with a girl in a riding habit.

As they passed, the guard jerked a thumb in their direction. "They ain't Rudy and Agnes, Valentino and Ayers to you. They're extras from *Arabian Knight*, spelled K-n-i-t-e. It's a spoof on *The Shiek* worked out by Mickey Moriarity, hell of a funny feller, beggin' your pardon, miss." His smile at Kathie was so close to a leer that she was extremely glad by the time they were ushered into Mr. Goldbaum's outer office.

The waiting room was furnished with one long leather-covered couch and several straight wooden chairs. Framed photographs of scenes from *Passion's Pawn, Pearl of the Prairie* and the recently completed *Lottie of Lonesome Gulch* decorated the walls. There were also several framed Awards for Artistry and a huge garish poster depicting a shrinking maiden in a tattered evening gown being menaced by a leering man in evening dress. Huge splashy yellow letters proclaimed this to be a scene from *Injured Innocence*.

The long sofa was placed under the poster, and at one end sat a small man in a loud checked suit, bright ascot scarf and rakishly tilted derby. As Kathie, her father and brother sat down, he cocked a bright interested eye at the trio, his gaze lingering so long on Kathie that she flushed and looked down to see if the seams in her hose were straight.

"I'll bet youse are waitin' to see Mr. Goldbaum, huh?" he asked, looking interrogatively at Septimus.

"We are," Septimus replied coolly.

"So'm I. Betcha you're here to discuss *The Queen's Necklace*, huh?" Before Septimus could reply, the man continued brashly, "I knew it. I read the papers. You, her'n him're from the East Coast. Had yerself a magic act. Betcha don't even have an agent, huh? That's bad. You oughter have an agent. You need to know more'n how to get a rabbit out've a hat. An agent's the man'll get youse a fair shake. That's the only way. An' you might not know it but I'm the best in the business. You can talk about Ted Small an' any other of them guys, but nobody knows more about flesh on the hoof than little old Sammy Shelton an' that's me." He reached into his breast pocket and brought out a card. "Anybody asks you who your personal representative is you tell'm Sammy Shelton. Otherwise you're goin' to get screwed for sure."

"Mr. Shelton, I don't remember giving you an appointment." Ruth Fiske, standing just beyond the door to the inner office, spoke in glacial accents.

Mr. Shelton assumed an expression that expertly mingled surprise and hurt. "Why, Miss Fiske, honey, I'm their personal representative."

Before Miss Fiske could protest, and before Septimus, who was clearly about to burst forth with a hot denial, could utter a word, Richard said gently, "I'm afraid that position is already filled, Mr. Shelton. I am acting as my family's artistic representative."

Shelton's mouth fell open but closed instantly only to open again with an astonished, "Ya can't be your own agent. It ain't done. We artist's reps'll have your hide. You won't work here in this town, mister, an' you can put that in your pipe'n smoke it. An' let me tell you . . ."

"That is enough, Mr. Shelton." Septimus turned his dark stare upon the agent. "You will leave, please."

Richard winced and exchanged a long-suffering look with Kathie as Mr. Shelton rose and without another word walked stiff-legged to the door. As it closed behind him, Miss Fiske turned an amazed glance on them. "My goodness," she breathed, "you must have hypnotized him. I've never seen that little vulture . . ." She blushed. "Excuse me. Won't you come in? Mr. Goldbaum will see you now."

Richard did not venture another look at his sister or his father. Otherwise he would not have been able to contain the wild laughter that threatened to escape from him. It was not happy laughter. The accuracy of Miss Fiske's observation had erected another wall between them. Though she had been joking, the three of them knew she had hit the nail squarely on its proverbial head. Mr. Shelton, finding himself outside on the sidewalk in front of the studio, would soon be as confused as a certain cab driver upon realizing that the receipt of their ride did not tally with the meter.

"Are you really repping for your family?" Miss Fiske demanded.

"Why yes." Richard still avoided looking at his family. "I am often employed in that capacity."

"Well, that's fine," she exclaimed enthusiastically. "That should make matters much easier, Mr. Grenfall. I wish all actors were equally qualified. You've no idea how they are victimized by those bloodsuckers. Mr. Shelton actually takes fees from aspiring youngsters whether he gets them work or not."

"So I've heard," Richard lied, thinking that her eyes were very beautiful, more beautiful even than they had seemed last night, two shining emeralds but more lovely than emeralds. He added strongly, "I can protect my family."

"Richard has a fine head for business," Septimus said.

"I'm delighted to hear it." She moved back. "Please come in. Mr. Vernon's been delayed but he should be joining us presently."

"Mr. Vernon?" Kathie questioned.

"Our director," the secretary amplified, as she led them into a palatial office that reflected the decorating scheme on view at The Castle.

Once more it was a matter of no one meeting anyone's eyes as the full glory of peacock blue walls painted with golden tigers with red stripes burst upon them. An immense desk lacquered in Chinese red and ornamented with gold at all four corners further stunned them and minimized the effect of two huge turquoise blue Fu dogs positioned at either side of a couch covered in red leather. In front of the couch was a low table inlaid with mother of pearl. A tiger and a leopard skin were spread on the oriental carpet, and close beside a wide peacock chair stood a small table balanced on elephant's tusks. An African shield hung on the wall behind the couch. The monarch of all he surveyed was seated in a gold and scarlet thronelike chair behind his desk. He had wide shoulders and a plump body, at least as far as they could see which was only to his waist. However he rose immediately proving himself to be about five feet six. His round face was lighted by large sparkling blue eyes, much enlarged by the thick rimless glasses balanced on his short nose. His mouth was small and full, his head bald, his expression benign. He was clad in a white linen suit that, along with a black string tie, called to mind mint juleps on a Southern veranda, but his speech was coated with a heavy German accent.

"Ach, you are here." He smiled expansively, the while his eyes narrowed. "And how the house are you liking?" He looked surprised but gratified by their assurances that they were delighted with it. "And disturbed you've not been?"

"It's very quiet and peaceful," Kathie said.

"It can be," he allowed. "I am glad you are finding it to your taste." He gave them another side glance. "And you find it quiet?"

"Very quiet." Septimus nodded.

"Gut, gut, please to sit down." He waved an arm at the various seating accomodations in the room. Turning his eyes on Miss Fiske, he suddenly barked, "Pictures! Their pictures I will need."

"I have made appointments with the photographer, sir," she said.

"Gut." He looked back at them. "You have the story of this picture read?"

"They have not yet received the synopsis, sir," Miss Fiske put in quickly. "If you will recall, it was finished only yesterday. I have copies here."

"Ach, then I must explain. "You," he pointed at Kathie, "are the wife of the magician Cagliostro, who is the villain. Ach, a Satanist he is and controls half of Paris. The ladies come to him for seances and for the black masses he conducts in the cellars of Versailles."

Septimus, with Cagliostros' benign freemasonry in mind, was about to contradict the producer, but Mr. Goldbaum's voice flowed on carrying the unspoken protest away on the current of his enthusiasm. "Cagliostro is old and ugly, ja? His wife is his victim, poor young girl, who of him is so afraid. He looks at her and she trembles. Brrrr. Also under his thumb

are the Queen and King of France. The beautiful Marie
Antoinette has a son who is sick, ja? Always he is bleeding,
bleeding, bleeding—prick his finger and he bleeds like a pig
who is stuck. The magician Cagliostro makes the hocus-pocus
and cures this bleeding son, and so Marie Antionette protects
him even though she knows he is no gut!'' Mr. Goldbaum
frowned and pounded the table. ''No gut, but she thinks he
is gut, and the King, he is a numbskull so he goes along with
it. Why worry? He on Zizi depends. Zizi is his name for his
Queen.'' Again Septimus would have spoken, mentioning
the recently murdered Nicholas II of Russia, his Empress and
Rasputin, but again he was defeated by the power and thrust
of Mr. Goldbaum's storytelling.

''Then comes this Grand Duke and he does not trust the
magician, especially since he has the eye on Madame
Cagliostro, the beautiful young girl. Also he is at court out of
favor and cannot go to the big parties they throw at Versailles.
So this diamond necklace he buys and wishes Calgiostro to
hand it over to the Queen because they are such good friends,
ja? Cagliostro has the influence and he don't have any. So
Cagliostro will do it for a big sum of money, but he is one
smart cookie and doesn't want to get involved so he sends his
beautiful wife to deliver the necklace and on the way she is
captured by Danton, who has found out about it.''

''Danton?'' Septimus managed to question.

''He is for the people of Paris. He is also a handsome young
man like Richard Barthelmess or Ramon Navarro or Rudy
Valentino and he falls in love with the beautiful young wife.
Ach, she is so beautiful!'' The producer gazed at Kathie for a
moment. ''He finds out that the necklace is for the Queen
and it has all these big diamonds so it is worth lots of money.
He decides to sell it so that the people of Paris can have
bread. He will put a fake one in its place.''

Richard's astonished gaze fell upon Miss Fiske's face but
found that the secretary's attention was riveted to the
notebook she held in her lap.

''Meanwhile,'' the producer continued, ''he and Madame
Cagliostro are in love at first sight. He detains her while they
are the necklace copying. Danton and Madame Cagliostro go
in for a little innocent smooching but nothing more because
immediately he sees her, he respects her. But Cagliostro looks

into his crystal ball and finds out what is happening. Ach, he is angry. He goes off in his coach and separates the young couple. In the Bastille he throws Danton. He gets back the necklace and puts it in his safe and gives the copy to the queen who thinks it is the real thing and is very grateful. Diamonds she likes a lot. Meanwhile, the beautiful Madame Cagliostro sneaks away from her husband and gets to the Bastille where she gives a rope ladder to Danton and he climbs out. He incites the people of Paris and there is a big revolution and the Bastille is knocked down. Ach, what a scene that will be! Cagliostro is guillotined and so is the Duke and the King and the Queen and Danton marries this beautiful girl.''

"Ah,'' Septimus was the first to break the slight silence that ensued upon the conclusion of Mr. Goldbaum's narrative. "An ingenious plot.''

"Yes, a few departures from history are made, but the audiences must have someone for whom they can root, ja? And so there is handsome young Danton and beautiful young Madame Cagliostro.''

"Who live happily ever after?'' Kathie murmured.

"As far as we know,'' shrugged Mr. Goldbaum. "As far as the audiences know. And do you not see the opportunities for spectacle? The court of Versailles? The fall of the Bastille? Cagliostro in the cellars with all those beautiful ladies? The black mass? Danton on his big white horse waylaying the coach of the beautiful young Madame Cagliostro? It will be bigger than *The Birth of a Nation*! Spectacular! Stupendous. It has everything, ja? Orgies, battle scenes, the guillotine, the mobs of Paris, a thousand extras will we use! And in the theater they will play on two pianos the Marseillaise!'' He rubbed his hands together, adding gleefully, "Even Griffith will not be able to top this, ja?''

"I shouldn't think he could,'' Septimus agreed.

More congratulatory comments were obviously being invited but the Grenfalls were fortunately spared from inventing them by the abrupt entrance of a tall dark young man who was breathless and disheveled. There was a trickle of blood running down his forehead from his hairline. "My apologies, sir,'' he addressed Mr. Goldbaum in a clipped British accent. "I am sorry I am late, but I was caught in the

French-Indian wars on the back lot and sustained a slight wound from the arrow."

"An arrow, Matt?" Ruth Fiske rose swiftly. "I do hope you weren't hurt badly?"

"Not at all. No more than a scratch, Ruthie." He smiled at her reassuringly.

"I have some first aid material in my desk," she said.

"What were you on the back lot doing?" Mr. Goldbaum demanded severely.

"I thought I'd take a shortcut, sir."

"Ach, haste makes waste."

"And lays waste," Vernon quipped.

Two members of the Grenfall family had listened to the brief exchange between Miss Fiske and Mr. Vernon with definitely heightened interest. Kathie, of course, had recognized the director immediately and with an odd little flutter of the heart had also noticed his astonishing resemblance to Colin or to Lord Byron as the case might be. She had also noted his familiarity with Miss Fiske as well as the latter's evident concern over the rather deep scratch he had sustained. It was borne in upon Kathie that Miss Fiske was really a very pretty girl, who undoubtedly saw a great deal of Mr. Vernon at the studio and possibly away from it. She discovered within herself an astonishing and embarrassing antipathy toward the secretary, whom, heretofore, she had liked.

Much the same feelings were passing through Richard, try as he did not to glower at Mr. Vernon whose exchange with Miss Fiske had not pleased him. The concern reflected on her face for what was, after all, no more than the merest pinprick had annoyed him. It had also added a new dimension to his thinking. The lovely Miss Fiske must meet many directors and actors every day which was a sobering and disquieting notion. He had never realized that her job was replete with such temptations.

Mr. Goldbaum said, "Now that you are here, Matthew, may I introduce Miss Katherine, Mr. Septimus and Mr. Richard Grenfall?"

Matthew Vernon, acknowledging the introductions, turned an appreciative eye on Kathie saying, "Miss Grenfall, I didn't recognize you with your clothes on!" He immediately flushed a deep red, adding hastily, "I mean . . ."

"He means," Kathie said with admirable if icy composure, "that we met while I was waiting in the wings to be sawed in half by Papa—in tights."

The laughter that followed fortunately cleared the air, and after the introductions the Grenfalls were given the script and Vernon's rehearsal schedule.

"I would like to do a reading of the first scene which will take place in the Paris apartment of the Cagliostros, so please study that portion of your script." Vernon told them in crisp businesslike tones.

"Will we be introduced to the rest of the cast?" Kathie asked.

"Not all of them, Miss Grenfall. Some are still working on other films. We hope to stage the final scenes first. These will need a great many people, and while they are still shooting the French-Indian wars, we will be able to use the extras for the toppling of the Bastille. Then there is the question of Mr. Conover Bliss, who will be performing the role of Danton. Mr. Bliss is due to star in *Sinister Sisters* at Grand Films so we will have to do your scenes with him first. Consequently I would like you to pay close attention to the Danton-Madame Cagliostro scenes and Mr. Grenfall," he turned his eyes on Septimus, "I would like to speak to you about Cagliostro. I understand you are an authority on the subject."

"I have been," Septimus mumured.

"Good." Mr. Vernon did not appear to notice the irony implicit in his tones. "Now perhaps you would like to see Paris?"

"Paris?" Richard questioned.

"The set," Mr. Goldbaum put in. "It is nearly completed."

"That would be lovely," Kathie said.

After the tour was completed, a taxi was called for the three Grenfalls. Bidding farewell to Mr. Goldbaum, Miss Fiske and Mr. Vernon,they clutched their scripts and solemnly walked out of Mr. Goldbaum's office, making their way back to the studio gates. It was not until they were in the taxi that Richard broke the silence by saying, "Paris . . . plaster of Paris!"

Their loud and sustained laughter startled the driver

enough for him to eschew the roundabout route he had been happily contemplating. He drove them straight to their destination and breathing a deep sigh of relief, sped away. After living in Hollywood for a number of years, he could recognize lunatics when he saw them.

Chief among the supper clubs that were springing up in the vicinity of Hollywood and further West was a little-known-to-the-general-public but extremely well-patronized nightery called simply "Kitty's." It had the reputation of being considerably more than a mere dine-and-dance spot. Kitty, its proprietress, was a rambunctious lady of fifty-odd with a whiskey voice and a face she cheerfully described as a "clock-stopper." In addition to providing the best food and booze in town, she took the name "club" seriously enough to provide several upstairs rooms which could be booked from one to eight hours a night. The cost was exorbitant but the facilities, running to ceiling mirrors and black satin sheets on extra-wide beds were, as many guests agreed, worth the price of admission.

It was an open secret that many film deals were consummated in Kitty's upstairs quarters. The boxoffice blockbuster, *Roman Nights*, brainchild of Frankie Farrell of Fairburn Films, Inc, occurred to that youthful genius after he saw Gloria Gower spread-eagled on Kitty's shiny black sheets. Those same sheets were the inspiration of Palette Productions' *The Downfall of Dee-Dee*, loosely based on Shakespeare's *Othello*. *King Leer*, another Palette production, also found its inspiration at Kitty's.

Consequently, everybody who was anybody in filmdom and lots who were merely hopefuls, considered an appearance at Kitty's a must. The trade up the stairs resulted in carpet and treads needing to be replaced at least once a fortnight. Its owner did not cavil at the cost of replacing expensive Oriental runners nor did she mind the wear and tear on sheets that sometimes did not last an hour. A well-stocked linen cupboard at the far end of the hall was often empty by sunrise, but Kitty could expect a percentage of what she called "ceiling contracts."

She received more than a mere percentage from her "cellar contracts." These involved servings of that popular white powder affectionately termed "coke" or pipes filled with opium or heroin injections. There was much more camaraderie in the two long cellar rooms. These were supervised by Kitty's silent partner and supplier Ah Hung Low, whose face, if not his activities, was famous. For one reason and another it was always on Ah Hung Low that producers and directors called when an extra Chinaman was needed to glower from the screen. Naturally, with so much going on at Kitty's, the aura of dope and hope was so vivid it was a wonder it did not shine like an extra electric light at the top of Kitty's small red sign. If it could not be seen, however, it could be felt.

In the past 135 years, Colin and Juliet had become peculiarly adept at recognizing the effluvium of evil. It was an unavoidable aspect of their condition. This nose for the noisome had resulted in some unique and enlightening experiences. Sometimes when they were in the mood for reminiscing Colin would recall the time they visited the cellars of Malmaison to watch a defrocked priest celebrate the Black Mass that was supposed to bring Napoleon back to his Josephine even on the eve of his wedding to Princess Marie-Louise of Austria. Though the ceremony was not immediately effective, they agreed that it filled the Emperor with a false sense of power, one that culminated in his ill-advised effort to conquer Russia.

In 1893, they had visited Paris in time to see the notorious Marquis de Guaita slay a rival by means of a Black Mass, and they had returned to that city for the famous "Paris Working" of Aleister Crowley in which he committed sodomy for Satan. Currently they were thinking of joining Crowley at his so-called Abbey of Thelema, actually a Sicilian farmhouse in the vicinity of Celafu. Though his sorcery was open to question, he was always amusing and both had reached the stage where they felt far more comfortable with the rogues and rascals of this world. As Juliet was wont to say, "Evil is always so marvelously entertaining."

Consequently, when they saw the spurious Spanish outlines of Kitty's Place rising on a cliff overlooking the sea, they were both enchanted by its promise. That they themselves exuded a similar promise was immediately apparent. There was a definite lull in the conversation as Colin, wearing the extremely well-fitting tuxedo acquired during a midnight stroll through one of the better men's shops in the area, escorted Juliet, a vision in silver lamé sparkling with jet and crystal beads on a low cut bodice and edging the hem of a skirt that showed a great deal more of her shapely legs than was strictly fashionable in this year of 1921. Her short hair was banded with a silver ribbon and her slender feet were encased in high-heeled silver pumps.

Juliet was scarcely aware of the effect she was creating. She was listening to the loud strains of the jazz band and wishing it was even louder. After rising from the dawn-to-dusk oblivion that was never disturbed by a single dream, she craved the gaiety and laughter that helped her forget that she had missed seeing some 53,730 suns, she who still remembered how much she had loved those beneficent rays. In fact, it was her memory of leaning out the window of her room at the Hold to see the eastern horizon turning red that brought her plight home to her even more than that which she must do to sustain herself. For reasons she could not quite fathom, she had been feeling a little melancholy this night, to the point that when Colin came to lift her from her coffin, he had said knowingly, "Cobwebs, love?"

"Cobwebs," she had acknowledged defensively. There was no use trying to keep anything from her brother.

But now, entering Kitty's Place, she could not retain her cobwebs, not with the orchestra playing a tune that made her long to dance.

The proprietress, a huge woman, looking even larger in a bright red dress sparkling with sequins and with diamond braclets traveling up to the elbows of both her brawny arms, came forward, a scowl on a wide face amply powdered and heavily rouged. Her eyes, small and gimlet sharp, accorded her would-be guests with a lowering suspicious stare. "Kinda young, ain't ya?" she snapped, her gaze wandering up and down Juliet's slender shining figure.

Juliet returned her stare calmly. "I am older than I appear," she purred.

"Would you care to see our birth certificates?" Colin extracted a hundred-dollar bill from his pocket, placing it on the hostess's plump palm. He was amused to see her beringed fingers close on it with the mechanical rapidity of a steel trap.

"Enjoy yourselves," she boomed. "Mack," she bawled to a slender man in black tie and tails, "show these here kids to a table, huh?"

"We've already dined," Colin said. "We'd like to dance and . . ."

"And booze, I suppose, or maybe . . . smoke?"

"Maybe."

"Anything you want, we got it. The three S's, that's us. Sin, sex and smoke." She gave them an impudent grin. "And don't worry none about raids. The cops are on the take."

"Does that orchestra ever play a tango?" Juliet asked.

"You a Rudy fan? I go for Latin lovers myself. Sure, I'll put a bug in Frank's ear. That's the gink that's leadin' the band."

"Thanks." Colin pressed another bill into her hand.

"Geez." She looked down, her eyes widening as she saw another hundred. "You got what it takes'n we'll take what you got." She clapped a hand to her mouth and looked actually discomfited. "Listen to me. I sound like I'm comin' unstrung." Her grin appeared again. "Maybe you'd like to go downstairs, huh? Lotsa partyin' goin' on down there'n upstairs, too. You let me know when you dogs get tired'n I'll find a nice comfy place for you to lie down." She fluttered one of her heavily beaded eyelashes and moved away.

"If you get to those black satin sheets before I do, let me know," Juliet whispered.

"I'm not that thirsty, yet," he muttered.

"You . . ." Juliet paused as the music suddenly changed from "Ain't She Sweet," to "Jealousy." "A tango," she announced.

Colin dutifully led her onto the floor, but before they had accomplished their first swoop, he felt a light tap on his shoulder and turned to find a tall, slender young man with slicked-back black hair and dark langorous eyes—at least they would have been langorous if he had not been staring so avidly at Juliet.

Colin, glancing at his sister, received the high sign he expected. He relinquished her into her new partner's arms and finding a nearby potted palm in the curve of the stairs, he stood beside it, half-concealed by its fronds, searching out the various women who were minus escorts. He recognized half a dozen famous faces but regarded them without interest. He was not there to court publicity. A dance with any one of them would be accompanied by photographs, the results of which he did not like to contemplate. He glanced at several unknowns. They didn't interest him either, mainly because they looked the worse for the quantities of booze they must have imbibed. He still remembered the time in New York when he had drained a tipsy socialite with disastrous results to his own constitution. He had managed to make it back to the cemetery, but Juliet still talked about how she got him into his coffin just in time.

One of the women had to be *the* woman. Though his need was, as yet, just a little tickle in his throat, it would grow. Before the night was out, his thirst must be slaked. However he had time. He frowned as a cry of protest touched by fright reached him.

"But Mr. Galgani, I didn't come here for *that*. You said I'd meet a lot of people—producers."

"Aw c'mon, Morna, you're so big on begin' a vamp, whyn't you try'n vamp me?"

"I don't want to go upstairs. I've heard about . . . about what's up there. Ow, you're hurting my wrist!"

"Lissen, you little twit, I spent a hell of a lotta dough on bringin' you to this here clip joint an' . . ."

"You said . . ."

"I said we'd have ourselves a damned good time'n we will. All you gotta do is be Theda and bare it." His loud laughter made Colin wince. "Get it," he chortled. "Theda Bara?"

"I get it and I don't want it," she retorted bravely. "Now take your big paws off of me and . . . ahhhh." She screamed as Colin heard the sound of a slap.

Fury raced through him. Making his way around the curving newel post, he looked upwards and saw a squat, chunky man in ill-fitting evening clothes half-dragging a slender young woman in black chiffon up the stairs. Swiftly he mounted them, arriving at the top a split second behind the couple. Moving down the corridor, he managed to get ahead of them and turning swiftly said softly, "I don't think this lady wishes to go with you, sir."

"Yeah," he received a lowering glare, "an' I don't think

it's any of your damned business what she wants."

"Oh, please." The girl stared at Colin out of dark eyes heavily rimmed with mascara. Her dark hair framed a thin pretty face in heavy bangs. Spit curls seemed pasted to both cheeks. Her mouth was unfortunately a trifle wider than the bee-stung pout she had painted on it. She wore quantities of cheap but flashy jewelry in the form of beads and chains around her slender neck, bangles on her wrists and a snakeskin belt complete with serpentine head hugging her slender waist. Moved as he was by her plight, Colin, recognizing the popular "vamp" look, had difficulty swallowing a grin as he wondered what several vampiric ladies of his acquaintance would say were they confronted with the girl and her costume. He wished he might tell her that with the possible exception of his sister Juliet they dressed very quietly.

His stream of thought was interrupted as a heavy hand landed on his shoulder. "Like are you goin' to stop botherin' us, sonny boy? Or do I have to give it to you with the knuckles?"

"I shouldn't suggest that you do," Colin said pleasantly, his hand closing on Mr. Galgani's thick wrist.

"Aowwww," the bully screamed. "Leggo, yer breakin' my wrist!"

Colin did not even glance at him. Relaxing his hold, he offered his arm to the girl. "Come, my dear, let's go downstairs."

Her huge dark eyes were wide and tears gleamed in them. A good portion of her mascara was running down her purposely whitened cheeks. "That was wonderful of you, but . . . look out!" she screamed as the big man slammed against them, grabbing for Colin's sholder. He turned, and in another instant Mr. Galgani was tumbling down the stairs. Reaching the bottom, he jumped up and dashed through a forest of tables, knocking down a few as he went and finally running out of the club.

Though her hand had tightened convulsively on his arm, Colin was inordinately pleased to find that the girl seemed totally in command of herself. She was actually smiling as they reached the bottom of the stairs.

They were confronted by an angry and blustering Kitty. "Look," she began, "I don't go for no rough stuff in this here joint. Tony Galgani is a good friend of mine."

"You ought to be more selective," Colin said softly. "But as it happens, this young lady and myself are just leaving." Moving past Kitty, he said solicitously, "Do you have a wrap, Miss . . ."

"Moran," she supplied. "Morna Moran, but look, you needn't bring me home. You were swell. You were really swell, but I don't want to make you go to any more trouble."

"It's no trouble," he assured her. "I wouldn't want you to go home alone."

"Well, I guess I won't say 'no,' then, Mr. . . . ."

"Colin Veringer," he supplied.

"Gee, that sounds English," she commented with a touch of hauteur.

"Don't you like the English?" he inquired.

"Well, I guess I do like some of them," she allowed. "My grandfather came over to the U.S.A. because of the potato famine, but I guess you didn't have anything to do with that."

"No," he said quickly. He himself had dark memories of that period—the Irish starving in their wasted fields. It had really reached him, and now he also remembered why. He said, "I'm half Irish, myself."

"Hey, how's about that!" She clapped her hands. "That's really peachy-keen. Did your folks come here because of the potato famine, too?"

"Other reasons. Let's go, shall we?"

"Sure thing. I really don't like this joint. Can you imagine that big galoot told me he had all sorts of connections in the movies? Didn't tell me he had another sort of connection in mind for me." She flushed. "I'm sure glad you showed up when you did."

"I'm glad I did, too."

"Hey, I really like you, Mr. Veringer."

"I like you, too, Miss Moran.

They were playing another tango as Colin and the girl skirted the dance floor. He came to a stop as he saw Juliet. She was still in the arms of the Valentinoesque young man and arched in so deep a bend that her head nearly touched her partner's pointed patent leather pumps, but in another second they were moving across the floor, their heads and shoulders immobile, their clasped hands thrust forward, their expressions seemingly frozen into passionate frowns, a pose that was quickly abandoned as Juliet sighted Colin. Still clutching her partner's hand, she hurried toward her brother, saying breathlessly, "Colin, I want you to meet Gareth Garnet, who is, as you can see, a marvelous dancer."

"It is you who are marvelous, my dear." Garnet visited a glowing look on Juliet but produced a jealous glare for Colin.

"You are both marvelous!" Morna exclaimed.

"I agree," Colin said enthusiastically. "Juliet, dear, this is Morna Moran."

"Delighted," Juliet responded, looking at her questioningly.

"I'm taking Miss Moran home," Colin amplified.

"Will you be coming back for me?" Juliet asked.

Gareth said hastily, "I'd like it if you'd let me see you home, Miss Veringer."

"Oh, you're related!" Moran blurted and blushed.

"Yes, we're brother and sister," Colin explained and was immediately surprised by his admission. Usually he and Juliet posed as husband and wife. He glanced at his sister, expecting to read surprise or possibly annoyance in her expressive eyes, but she wasn't even looking at him. Her gaze was fastened on her partner's face. "Come," Colin said to Morna. "Let's go."

It was in keeping with her fantastic costume, he thought amusedly, that Morna should claim a long black cloak from the hatcheck girl.

Coming out of the club, she suddenly left him to run toward the cliff's edge, staring down at the glistening white swirl of surf. "Smell that air!" she said ecstatically as a rising breeze whisked her hair back from her face and sent her cloak billowing out behind her.

Colin stared at her, feeling as if he were seeing her for the first time. Her profile was faintly Grecian and definitely beautiful. Desire rose in him. He wanted to embrace her but did not dare. Now that she was no longer frightened, there was a joyous innocence about her that he wanted to preserve a little longer. This would not be the last time he would see her, he knew that, and an embrace would certainly open the door to other desires. He said, "Why do you wear black? You ought to be in colors or, better yet, white.''

She whirled around to face him. ''Holy Gee, I'm supposed to be a vamp. You know . . . like Theda Bara? Haven't you ever seen her?''

''I don't think I have. Of course, I've heard of her.''

''I guess you don't see many movies, huh?''

''Not many, but you have?''

''I'll say.'' She grinned at him. ''I've even been in a couple, not so's you'd notice me.''

''I'd always notice you.'' He smiled down at her, finding that he really meant it.

''No, you wouldn't,'' she said positively. ''I was a Babylonian priestess in *Intolerance* four years ago. Not even my own mother, God rest her soul, could've picked me out.''

''Four years ago!'' he exclaimed. ''You must have been a mere child.''

''Oh, go on.'' She giggled. ''I was eighteen. I just turned twenty-two. I bet you aren't much older than that yourself.''

It always startled Colin when anyone tried to guess his age and arrived at what would have been the correct amount of years—they had that is, if met in 1788, the year of his transition. Usually it did not carry with it the regret he suddenly experienced at this moment. It was hard for him to say casually, ''That's about it.''

''I knew it,'' she said happily. ''I'm sort of psychic, I guess, at least where ages are concerned, and maybe a couple of other things, too. The Irish are fey. Anyhow, as I was telling you, you really need a big break if you're going to climb out of the extra ranks. I thought I'd done it when I was in *The Love Flower* for Mr. Griffith again, and I actually had a scene but it ended up on the cutting room floor. You can't get anywhere unless you doll up fancy and maybe somebody sees you and thinks you're the cat's whiskers. That's why I came here with Tony. He said he'd introduce me to a lot of people. He said I was star material. I guess I should've known he was the big kidder.''

There was so much wistfulness in her tone that Colin found himself saying, ''It might be that I have a few connections, too.'' At the same time, he resolved to get in touch with Richard or Septimus as soon as he could.

''You have connections?'' she questioned excitedly. ''You

look just like a movie star yourself."

He laughed and shook his head. "I don't photograph well."

"I can't believe that," she exclaimed, staring up at him. "Maybe you ought to look in your mirror more often."

He wondered what she would say if she knew he hadn't seen himself in a mirror for over a century. Thinking about that, he remembered that he was thirsty. He said quickly, "I'd better take you home. I'll see if I can get a cab."

A short time before dawn, Juliet skipped down to the cellar. She was humming to herself as she sped toward that part of the labyrinth reserved for herself and Colin. Upon entering the wide room, she found her brother wrapped in the Chinese robe he donned for his "rests."

"Oh, you're here. *Did* you?"

"No," he said shortly. "Did you?"

"I didn't either, but I am going to see him again."

"Same here," he returned. "I had a rabbit tonight. What about you?"

"A squirrel," she replied, and meeting her brother's surprised stare, she added flippantly, "I wasn't really thirsty."

"I wasn't either," he lied, as he lifted the lid of his coffin.

Juliet slipped out of her garments and hung them on a long steel costume rack provided by Septimus, who had filched it from the Empire Theater in Peoria. "He's a good dancer."

"I noticed."

"And what does she do, that strange looking girl?"

Since he was too tired to either argue with Juliet or defend Morna, he said merely, "She wants to be a vamp in the movies."

"Well, she's certainly come to the right place for instruction," Juliet drawled.

"Do you know? I'm not entirely sure of that—or maybe she has. It all depends on Richard." With that enigmatic remark, he slid into his coffin.

Juliet started to ask him what he meant but thought better of it. Colin was in one of his moods tonight, that was obvious. She, too, was in a mood, she who had gotten out of the habit of wishing for anything was thinking of Gareth Garnet, as she pulled down the lid of her coffin, and wishing that she were allowed the luxury of dreaming.

Ruth Fiske, seated on a canvas chair next to a similar chair which bore Matthew Vernon's name in white letters on a tan background, watched as Richard and Kathie Grenfall rehearsed a scene from the screen play of *Cagliostro and the Queen.* That was the new title and, she was sure, one that probably would be changed again very soon, given Mr. Goldbaum's mercurial decisions.

She was glad that the producer was busy in his office this afternoon rather than storming around the set. That would have been something he surely would be doing had he been privileged to view his new stars enacting the moment when Cagliostro persuades his timid wife to deliver the necklace to the queen.

Kathie, she noted with surprised approval, was even better than she had been the previous day. The girl was all shyness and distress as she mimed her fear of embarking upon *The Questionable Quest,* the title that would be flashed upon the screen between shots. Richard, on the other hand, stood stolidly, frowning only when sharply prompted by the increasingly, impatient director. Otherwise the expression came and went like the sun on a cloudy afternoon.

"Son," Septimus yelled from his vantage point behind Ruth's chair, "for God's sake try and act!"

Of course he was totally out of line, and Matthew Vernon would probably give him a good strong lecture or perhaps not, given his obvious penchant for Kathie Grenfall. Ruth firmed her lips. It was a pity that Richard had to act. He had better talents. He had come up with some very canny clauses to the contracts he prepared prior to embarking upon rehearsals. Though Mr. Goldbaum had howled "foul," he had signed. Later he had agreed with Ruth that Richard did have the makings of an excellent and, amazingly enough, fair agent—something the industry badly needed. But, as she had on the last two mornings, she wondered why their New York talent scout hadn't fastened on Septimus rather than his son for the role of the magician. The Cagliostro dreamed up by Joe, Dave and Aaron Goldbaum, the producer's nephews, had called for an older man. Almost immediately she recalled that Septimus had not been performing on the afternoon Richard and Kathie were spotted. Her thoughts were abruptly scattered as Matthew Vernon predictably called for a recess and came storming over to Septimus, his eyes alight with ire and his lower lip thrust out.

With a sinking heart, Ruth recognized the expression. The director had worn it on the day he had tossed Evangeline Goldbaum, her employer's beautiful but interfering bride off the set. Evangeline had gone into strong hysterics and ordered her husband to fire Matthew. With the business acumen and common sense that had built the Goldbaum-Magnum enterprise, the producer had immediately made arrangements to divorce the lady. It would be a pity if he fired Septimus, who did seem to know as much about the period as was necessary for a picture of such doubtful authenticity. She wished she might say something that would throw oil upon Matthew's boiling waters, but she knew from experience that it was no use.

"Mr. Grenfall," the director began, "will you please change places with your son? I have decided that as an actor, he might very well be the best agent in Hollywood. I will not have him mucking up this production any more than it has been mucked up already by possibly the worse script that was ever invented by man—or rather men. It would take a magician to save it, and I understand from your daughter that you are a superb magician!"

"Sir, are you saying that you believe my son to be a bad actor?" Septimus inquired sternly.

"Mr. Grenfall, I am telling you that he is a rotten actor," the director said clawing at his hair. "I can do nothing with him. Griffith could do nothing with him. By now Von Stroheim would have murdered him!" He clawed at his hair a second time. "If he stays, I will not be responsible for my actions!"

"Save your tresses, Mr. Vernon," Septimus said soothingly. "I will be glad to stand in for my son if, of course, he agrees." He glanced in the direction of Richard who was talking with Kathie. "If I may be allowed to broach the subject to him . . ."

"Please do," Matthew said tensely.

As Septimus strolled casually across the platform, Ruth also tensed. Until this moment she had not thought of the effect that Matthew Vernon's announcement must have on the man she was sure she loved, even given her innate prejudice against actors. They had been out together two more times, and each time she saw him, she found that parting from him was full of that "sweet sorrow" so admirably described by Shakespeare. However, actors, even those so monumentally inept as Richard, did have tender egos. She watched breathlessly as Septimus, facing his son, put a hand on his shoulder, speaking quietly and probably apologetically, she guessed, wishing that the back of Septimus's head were as eloquent as his dark eyes.

She shuddered as a great yell erupted from Richard. The sound, replete with that resonance learned in a lifetime spent facing audiences who were not shy about chanting, "Louder!", beat against Ruth's eardrums. It seemed full of grief. Tears pricked her eyes, and she sank lower in her chair.

"Ruth!" Richard was at her side in three bounds. "I don't have to do the damned thing!" he cried triumphantly. He stared down at her, his expression of joy slowly fading. "My dear, why are you crying?"

She stared up at him, her poise irretrievably shaken, "I . . . I thought it would hurt you to be told that you were no longer needed," she confessed.

"Hurt me? I'm ecstatic. I hate acting."

"Oh," she said joyfully, "I knew you couldn't be an actor."

"And that pleases you, doesn't it? Why?"

"Because I really don't respect actors and from the first I did respect you."

"Oh, Ruth . . ." He paused, feeling rather than seeing his father's eyes on him. More than his father's eyes, he could feel the whole Household staring at him. Though that was clearly his imagination, he groaned, and moving away from Ruth he turned toward Matthew Vernon saying jerkily, "I guess I'll go home if you don't need me any more." He could also feel Ruth's beautiful eyes, puzzled and perhaps even sorrowful. He wished that she were in his arms.

"That'll be okay, Mr. Grenfall. Sorry," Matthew said gruffly.

"I'll go, too." Kathie joined them.

"But I'm not through with you, Miss Grenfall," Matthew protested.

"I am through with you, Mr. Vernon. Don't you have any heart—firing my brother right in front of everybody?" Kathie caught Richard's arm. "Let's go," she muttered under her breath.

"You don't need to come," he muttered back.

"Yes, I do," she whispered. "Start walking, please." As they moved out of earshot, she continued, still speaking sotto voce, "I'm leaving for the same reason you are. I know how you feel about Ruth. I feel the same way about Matthew, but we'll be on the road again soon. I'm sure of it."

"Oh God, darling, so am I. And even if we could stay, they would never understand."

"No, they wouldn't," she agreed sadly. "Remember how Miss Fiske reacted that first day?"

"That's what I'm remembering," he groaned.

Septimus, facing an angry Matthew and a Ruth, who was looking at him with puzzlement written large upon her features, shrugged and said, "I'll have Kathie back tomorrow. They're very close, she and her brother, and obviously she misunderstands the situation."

"If you can't explain it to her, we won't have a picture," Matthew said.

"I'll explain it to her, never fear." Septimus followed his son and daughter.

"I need a drink." Matthew stared bitterly down at Ruth.

"So do I!" she exclaimed with equal bitterness.

"How's about getting soused?"

"You're on," she said clutching his proffered arm.

The sun had descended, and in the cellar the beast rattled its chains, snuffled and whined. It was dreaming again.

Slipping out of her coffin, Juliet said, "Poor Mark, he's bad tonight."

"Naturally," Colin said. "It's the first night of the full moon. It's a pity. He was really getting interested in the art of makeup, and they offered him a job at Magnum after he gave them those suggestions on the movie."

"A vampire movie." Juliet giggled. "Fancy them not

knowing us any better than that, making the men all bald and ugly with fangs jutting over their lips. Good gracious, they'd all starve to death!"

"That's the German influence. They're copycats here in Hollywood in case you didn't notice." Colin cocked his head. "Listen to Molly."

"Oh, she's really at it tonight, isn't she? I get so used to hearing her that I really don't hear her, if you know what I mean. And that actress, too. She's beginning to sound very hoarse."

"Trying to top our Molly and Grimalkin, too." Colin smiled but his eyes remained somber. "I have a feeling we'll soon be on the road again."

"Do you really think so?" Juliet inquired anxiously.

"Don't you feel it?" He gave her a penetrating look.

"I like it here," she said in a low troubled tone.

"As long as you can dance with Gareth Garnet, I expect."

"Have you seen much of that silly Morna?"

"She's not silly!" he exclaimed angrily.

"Nor is Gareth. He likes to talk as well as dance."

"That's reassuring," Colin commented acidly.

"Colin, I won't speak to you when you're in such a mood." She dressed hastily, slipping into a flattering pink sequined shift that stopped just below her knees.

Colin was clad in a Harris tweed suit. His coat hung open over a blue silk shirt, and he was wearing a loose kerchief instead of a tie. His brown and white Oxfords came from an expensive store in downtown Los Angeles.

Juliet said lightly, "My, don't we look deshabille. No dancing tonight?"

"My life's not bounded by the dance floor," he retorted, and then moving to her, put an arm around her. "Sorry, Juliet, pardon my bad mood."

"And mine, love," she apologized. "I almost wish we were on the road this very minute. It's getting so hard not to . . ."

"I know," he said hastily. "For me, also."

"I've never . . ." she began.

"Nor have I," he concurred. "I'm beginning to understand a lot of things."

"So am I." She looked sadly up at him. "But I do love you

so much, Colin.''

''I love you, too, my dearest.''

Their glances, unhappy and full of a new understanding, met; then both turned aside.

''My God, you look beautiful,'' Gareth Garnet said half an hour later as Juliet joined him on the corner of the block she had told him was her own. She was glad he believed the elaborate story she had concocted about a sick aunt who didn't want her going to dances.

''How are you, my dearest?'' she said warmly.

''Relieved because you're here. Usually I'm not a very fanciful guy, but every time we say good night, I get this crazy feeling we'll never see each other again.''

''And you're wrong every time.'' She laughed a trifle shakily and tucked her small hand into the crook of his arm.

He gave it a little squeeze. ''I want to keep on being wrong, too.''

''Where are we going?'' she asked.

''House of a friend of mine—big dance floor, big orchestra, lots of notables of the Hollywood variety.''

''That sounds like fun.''

''It wouldn't be, if you weren't with me, Juliet. God, I am crazy about you.''

''Crazy, period,'' she teased.

''Maybe,'' he said soberly. ''I think about you all the time. You're in my blood, baby.''

''Ugh, don't talk that way,'' she begged. ''It's so clinical. How did the shooting go today?''

''Great when I didn't have to kiss Barbara la Marr.''

She gave him a stricken look. ''Don't say that,'' she reproved.

''Why not? I mean it. I don't want to kiss anyone except you.''

''You should . . .'' she began.

''Hey.'' He stopped walking and stared down at her indignantly. ''Do you go around kissing other guys when I'm not with you?''

''No.''

''Then why shouldn't I feel the same? I'm not the Sheik of Araby, even if I do look like Rudy. And the next picture I make, I'm being me—and me's a one-woman man, so put that in your pipe and smoke it!''

"Got a pipe on you, love?" she murmured happily.

Her lips grazed his neck, and her little fangs shot out. The need was upon her, the need and the thirst. Rabbits and squirrels and birds were not enough. She wanted him and had been wanting him not only for sustenance but for love. Love! It seemed to her that the word had become solid. It clattered through her brain, rattling in her skull. He was trying to push her down on a sloping lawn. If they lay together, she would not be able to stop herself. She thrust him back. "Let's go to your party, dearest. I don't want grass stains on my dress until later."

Excitement electrified his tones. "Don't think I won't hold you to that," he said.

"I'll never forgive you if you don't." She forced herself to smile up at him and was glad for once that she was denied the solace of tears.

Morna, wearing a simple green sleeveless shift, was waiting for Colin. She watched from her window as he walked up the flagstone path to the small door of her one-story cottage. She had never been so glad that it was her cottage, inherited from her late father. It was not particularly well-furnished nor was it in a very good section of Hollywood, but at least she didn't have to share it with anybody. She made good money as a secretary in an insurance office so there was always food in the icebox and the electric bill was paid along with the water and the telephone.

Earlier she had observed Colin from her front window as he strolled along the sidewalk. The moon was bright and round tonight, and the sky was encrusted with stars. She ran a nervous hand through her hair and frowned. Turning swiftly, she hurried into the bedroom to glance in her mirror. Her eyes were wide and a little frightened. She did not want them to be frightened; rather she did not want him to see that they were frightened. She was not actually afraid. She loved him too much for that. She had only seen him three times, but it seemed to her that she had known him much longer than that. Her love for him was boundless and deep. She would do anything for him, anything he wanted. She tried to smile at the idea of such passion. Passion was only for the movies, where it was all silly and overstated. She was no longer interested in the movies and hated to remember the dumb getup she had worn the night they met. She must really have disgusted him!

When the doorbell rang, she dashed into the living room and flung open the front door. "Hi," she panted.

"Hello, Morna," he said gravely, as she held the screen aside for him. "You seem out of breath."

"I was combing my hair, like Rapunzel in the fairy tale, only I bet she was a blonde."

"I like brunettes better," he said softly.

"I'm flattered." She forced a smile. "Come in, Colin. Make yourself at home." She pointed to the couch.

"Thank you." He kissed her on the cheek and sat down on the couch.

It was time for her to offer him some wine but she didn't. He had refused it the last time he had come, which was last night. It was also the first time she had let him into her house, the first time he had made love to her. It had been an experience she wanted to repeat and repeat, but first she wanted him to feel at ease. He hadn't been quite at ease the previous night. She sat down beside him, touching him all the way from his shoulders to his legs.

"I've missed you," she said.

"And I've missed you," he told her.

She put her hand against his cheek, feeling the coolness. She said hesitantly, "I watched you come up the street."

"Did you?" He leaned toward her, pressing his lips against the hollow at the base of her throat.

She waited, unafraid, but he lifted his head.

"Colin, my dearest darling, I watched you . . . and you cast no shadow."

He tensed all over and drew away from her.

"No!" She flung her arms around him. "I know, I know, and I want you to love me in any way you can. I want to give you anything you need, no matter what it is!"

Anguish twisted his features. "Morna, you . . . you can't know." He strove to recapture his equilibrium. "There isn't anything to know. I really don't understand what you think you mean."

"Don't shut me out, Colin," she cried. "I've known ever since the second time we were together. I can tell. I read up on a lot of stuff when I decided to be a vamp. I'm sort of thorough when I get to researching anything. I look for derivations—and I'm psychic. Besides there are a lot of giveaways, like you never wanting to meet me for lunch and always having had your dinner and never drinking anything either, only pretending and emptying the glass when you thought I wasn't looking. And I saw you didn't cast any shadow that second night, too. I guess that wouldn't occur to anyone who didn't know, but I want you to know that I'm not afraid of you, Colin. I love you too much."

"You . . . you're talking nonsense."

"I'm not, my darling," she said gently, positively. "I love you. I want to be with you and share everything. I wouldn't be saying any of this if I didn't know you cared for me, too."

"I do." Something inside of him was hurting, and memories buried over a century before were flowing back into his mind. There once had been girls, young and lovely though never lovelier than Morna, who had opened their hearts to him in the days before he had been lost in the woods, the dark woods through which he had been traveling ever since.

"Love me, please. Come with me." She took him by the hand and urged him from the couch. She led him into her bedroom and moved away from him, but only for the moment it took her to slip out of her green sheath. Then she put her arms around him again.

He tried to resist and could not. Warmed by her passion, he lay with her, caressing her. Her body was beautifully white, and through her delicate veins flowed that life-giving fluid which she was so generously offering him. His lips fastened on her neck, on the great veins that he could nip open so gently, so painlessly that she would not even feel it, but instead he moved back, kissing her rosy nipples and caressing her gently. Then he arose.

"Please stay," she begged.

"I love you," he said.

"Then . . ." She stretched out her arms. "Be with me."

"I love you too much, child—and you are a child. I wish I'd met you in another summer, Morna." He dressed hastily and embracing her once more, he left her, walking out of her house and down the street under the huge round moon that denied him a shadow.

The house of Oliver Arno, the head of Arno Films, clung to a cliff high in the Hollywood Hills. Constructed along Spanish lines with white stucco walls and a red-tiled roof, its greatest asset was its vast patio which, according to some facetious spirits in the movie colony, was large enough to harbor and sustain the hordes of poor relations who hung around the producer.

On this night none of the aforementioned were in evidence, but dancing to the strains of a top jazz band were a great number of filmdom greats. If Mary Pickford had not deigned to put in an appearance, there was Charlie Chaplin dancing with a delicious teenager. Lillian Gish, wraithlike in chiffon, leaned on the arm of tall D.W. Griffith, and John Barrymore winked at Dolores Costello. Richard Barthelmess, his usually slick black hair mussed as he kidded around with Mae Marsh, also had an eye for Juliet. Douglas Fairbanks, swashbuckling even offscreen, was toasting Marguerite de la Motte, who had been his leading lady in his great success *The Mark of Zorro*. There was the usual complement of directors, rival producers and such agents who had managed to storm the barricades.

Juliet had just finished a tango with Gareth. She stood close to him, clutching his arm and wishing devoutly that Oliver Arno, who was coming toward them, pushing several of his guests aside in the process, would not reach his obvious destination. Of course, she dared not waft such signals toward their host because he was also producing Gareth's next picture called, appropriately enough, *Tango of Death*.

"Why haven't I seen you before?" Arno's stare took in all of Juliet. His small beady brown eyes, set on either side of a red bulbous nose, gleamed lasciviously. He was holding a glass of whiskey, and it was obvious that he was more than a little drunk.

"Gareth," he said lurching to the young man's side and clutching his arm, "Whyn't you ever bring the little lady around to the studio?"

"I've asked her, Oliver, but she won't come."

"Well, maybe she'll come for me." Arno grinned. "You two really look great together. You'd have the gals swooning in the aisles, and she'd have the guys tryin' to crawl into the screen. I've got Helena Browning ticketed for *Tango*, and Dane Fuller's been bustin' his balls tryin' to get me to pull a switcheroo and drop you out on your ear, Garnet. Only he's got two left feet when it comes to dancin' an' he ain't no Valentino. Don't want no college boy for this pix . . . don't want this Browning dame if I can have you, Miss . . ." He leered at Juliet. "Don't think I caught your name, honey."

"Veringer," Juliet said.

"Veringer, huh? That's a bit long for screen credits, but we can change all that. Tell you what I'm going to do, Miss Veringer, honey. I'm goin' to schedule a screen test for you tomorrow mornin'. Be there at makeup come five o'clock on the nose. Will you do that?"

"You bet she will!" Gareth said excitedly. "She's a natural for the screen."

"You don't need to tell me that, Gary. I saw her from across the room. It's like she's got a light shinin' inside of her. And she'll photograph like a million bucks. She's got the right features." He moved around Juliet. "Yeah, from all angles she's perfect. You let me run some film on you, honey, an' then you come to my office and we'll talk contracts."

It had been difficult for Juliet to keep herself from telling Mr. Arno that his manners were atrocious. He had been talking as if she were not there. She could have been a slave girl she had once seen in a Moroccan market half a century ago. It was a marvel he hadn't wanted to examine her teeth. It gave her considerable pleasure to say, "I can't do that, Mr. Arno."

"Of course you can, darling," Gareth said. "I'll do the test with you."

She shook her head. "I'm really not interested."

"You're never tellin' me you're turnin' down a chance to star in an Arno film," bellowed the producer.

"I must," she said unhappily.

"But Juliet," Gareth began, "we could be together, dance . . ."

"Please don't press me," she interrupted, hating the hurt

she read in his eyes, hating the way it was making her feel. "I must go now," she added. Turning toward Arno, she said, "Thank you for a very pleasant evening."

He glared at her. "I think you're nuts." Turning on his heel, he walked away.

Gareth stepped forward, his fists knotted.

"No, my love," Juliet said, placing her hand on his arm and holding him there. "It's your career."

"He has no right . . ."

"Shhhhh," she begged. She made herself smile. "I guess nobody's ever turned him down. It's a new experience for him, so you have to make allowances."

"Why did you turn him down?"

"I don't want it, darling."

"We could have been together."

"We *are* together. Please take me to my corner, dearest. My aunt . . ."

"If you'd only agree to the test, you wouldn't have to cater to that old witch," he said hotly.

"Shhhh." She ran her hand down the side of his face.

Catching her by the wrist, he pressed a kiss into her palm. "I love you."

"I love you, too, Gareth."

"Will you go with me to Kitty's tomorrow night as planned? I hate the place, but they do have a great orchestra. And I want to see you in that costume you mentioned."

"I'll be there." She managed a smile, difficult in view of all she was feeling.

It was early when Juliet came back to the cellar, but she was tired and dispirited as she had never been before in all her lengthy existence. It seemed to her that she was looking down a tunnel of times to come, and now she remembered a tale her nurse had once told her about the goddess Aurora.

The deity of the dawn had loved a mortal, Tithonus, a Prince of Troy. Aurora begged Jupiter to grant her lover eternal life, but she forgot to ask that he remain forever young. And he had grown old, old, old—as Gareth would, as most of her victims had because she could seldom bring herself to kill them and condemn them to this weary immorality. Yet there never had been one whom she loved as she did

Gareth. She had never loved anyone except Colin, whom she still loved but in a different way—as a sister, she realized with a feeling of shock. She realized something else, too. She had never experienced such anguish in all the years of what, for want of a better term, she called "life."

Colin returned shortly after she arrived. Looking at his face and his tortured eyes, vulnerable as she had never seen them, she said, "There's a costume ball at Kitty's Place tomorrow night. We're supposed to wear costumes from our favorite period in history. Shall we go?"

"Of course," he said brightly.

His assumption of gaiety was so unconvincing that she almost wept, but at the same time she was glad of it. "Colin . . ."

"Yes, my love."

"I'm tired."

"So am I."

"Really?"

"You hardly need ask."

"I know."

They gave each other detailed descriptions of their evenings.

"Isn't it odd," Juliet murmured when Colin had finally finished speaking, "that we should feel the same way at the same time."

"Haven't we always?"

"Out here, it is such a beautiful place."

"There are always serpents in paradise," he said ruefully.

"I didn't think I would call mine—love."

"Nor I."

Juliet cocked her head. "Listen to Molly."

"She knows," he said.

"I hope she doesn't say anything to father."

"She's never been one to keep her own counsel, but it can't matter."

"It's growing early," she reminded him, as she moved toward her coffin."

"Yes." He hastily undressed. "Until tomorrow night."

"Until tomorrow night."

They smiled at each other lovingly.

Three

Toward morning on the second night of the full moon, Livia awakened with a start. Edging away from Septimus, she looked through the windows, thinking that Molly and Letitia Lawrence must be on that segment of roof right overhead. She wondered why they were howling so loudly. They were a weird trio, Molly with her shrieks, Letitia with her choking gurgles, and Gremalkin joining in with his usual squall. That she usually did not hear them so clearly worried her. Generally they were like rain on a tin roof, something that reached you but didn't make any real impression. Tonight they were making an impression. She envied Septimus his ability to sleep through their caterwauling. Even though he possessed the psychic sensitivity to hear them, he could always blot them out, something she could never do. It was impossible to guess what had started them off, but it was all of a piece. Kathie and Richard were also disturbed, coming back from the studio both miserable, both sure that something was about to happen to send them forth upon the road again.

Until this moment she had been reasonably sure that the trouble was borrowed, born out of all their previous experience. If Richard had been relieved of his acting chores, Septimus had agreed to take his place. Kathie was doing very well, and that timorous but nice Miss Fiske had praised Richard's cleverness with contracts. It had seemed to Livia that for the first time in their gypsylike existence, they stood a chance of settling down. She had almost been afraid to think about it, but staying did seem feasible with three members of the Household gainfully employed here in Hollywood. She had said as much to her children, but now she was uncomfortably aware that the rooftop residents were definitely opposed to this opinion.

What could happen?

Mark?

Septimus had been nervous about the reinforced cellar walls being as strong as they should be. He had spoken about putting Mark in his special trunk, but by the time he had arrived at that opinion, it was too late for such precautions. Mark had already been given the freedom of the room. He had been restless today. Passing the door leading to the cellar, Livia had heard the rattling of his chains, suggesting that he was pacing back and forth. Yet, it did seem a shame to keep him in that trunk. He always complained of severe muscle cramps when released.

Juliet and Colin?

She had seen very little of them of late. They seemed to be very happy, but they always were. She dismissed them and concentrated on Kathie and Richard again. Until today, Kathie had been in very good spirits. She had spoken a great deal about Matthew Vernon, whom she had met briefly on the road. That was a pleasant coincidence—or perhaps it wasn't. Matthew might actually have been instrumental in getting her this job. Probably he was in love with her—so many young men had been. And Kathie? It suddenly struck Livia that her daughter might very well be in love with the director. She was sure that Richard yearned for Ruth Fiske. Her eyes widened. That could be why both were so melancholy! They were in love, and of course unhappy. The Household weighed heavily upon their shoulders. Livia frowned. The Household *was* a problem. Not everybody was fortunate enough to marry a witch or a sorcerer. Probably Molly and Letitia were equally cognizant of that. Maybe

Richard and Kathie were unaware that their fears of being up-rooted again were actually based on the fact that neither was willing to tell the object of their desire the truth. Maybe they really wanted to leave. Her thinking was becoming con-voluted, and she hoped she was wrong. She did not want to leave. She loved everything about this area, which among its many virtues was the lack of a main street. She had walked up and down so many dusty, depressing main streets. Livia yawned and gratefully resigned herself to sleep. Her last waking thought was that everything would be all right. She could not remember when she had last believed that.

She had waited until the coffin lids were closed. She had waited until Livia, waking nervously from sleep, had slipped back into oblivion again. Then she oozed into the room where the beast lay drowsing and hovered over him with her headful of dreams, willing him to receive what she was sending.

He lay there, his long grey shape stretched upon the floor, his horrible half-human head resting on his front paws, paws with sharp curved talons that could tear the living flesh from the bones, fangs that could bite and destroy and infect—and which in the course of his life had accomplished none of these three acts! Instead he had been impotent, surrendering him-self to chains, lulled by his intrinsic kindness. Kindness! How she loathed the word!

For a century it had mitigated the force of her vengeance. The Veringers and those of their blood had suffered and would still suffer, but not as she, living and dead, had intended they should suffer. Their plight had not driven them apart but had brought them ever closer together. Consequently her anguish remained unappeased, her hatred unsatisfied.

Oh, how she abominated them for thwarting her plans, thrusting her forth upon the roads when she had been so very near to discovering the power that would have rendered her beautiful and immortal! The elixir had been strained of nearly all its impurities. The ceremonies and the sacrifices had raised the demon who had told her of the final ingredient needed to achieve the proper consistency. Another night, only one more night, and she would have had the world at her feet! Then, he had come, Richard Veringer, accompanied by the louts that knocked down the house, hammers and mallets crushing the old stone, destroying the beakers, letting the precious fluid sink into the earth. She had been forced out upon the road, a ragged vagabond again, with nothing but the virulence of her curse to comfort her—and now it was weakening, due to her own foolishness and her belief that there was never a place that would receive them. How could she have known about Hollywood? If she were not careful, they would soon be free of her malevolence.

Mark was her one hope. Let him out, let him run over the ground, let him destroy, and in destroying cut the thread that might have become a lifeline. She could not sever the chains nor batter down the steel, but he was strong and unaware of his strength. He must be made aware of it, of the thrill of earth beneath his unfettered feet, of the smell of blood. None of them had ever preyed on their own, but let him dream of tearing their flesh, as he had last night and the other night she had invaded his dreams. On the second and brightest night of the full moon, let him be guided by her hatred!

She stood before him, knowing that he saw her with the eyes of his mind, knowing that he heard her with the ears of his mind. And when she asked him her name, she heard it come hissing out of his slavering jaws.

Erlina Bell.

She laughed silently and poured the dreams into his moon-maddened brain. Under their onslaught, he twitched and snarled and howled, while outside the knowing bats darted into the holes under the roof, the snakes slithered into the shrubbery, the horned owls sought their hollows, and the smaller insects died, their tiny bodies plummeting into the rose bushes. And she, with her load of dreams, rose from the monster and slunk into the house.

Kathie awoke from a strange dream in which her brother had predominated. In it she felt that he was in deep trouble, and she had wanted to comfort him and be with him as she had when they were children, when they had slept in the same bed, entwined together in scruffy boarding houses where the sheets were mended and old and sometimes even unwashed. The mattresses had been hard or lumpy or both, the blankets thin. They had clung to each other for warmth. They had been very small then. Later Richard slept with Septimus and she with her mother or, when they could afford it and the act was prospering, they had the luxury of their own bedrooms. Now, quite suddenly, she longed to be with Richard and feel his arms around her, shielding her from her fears of strange houses with strange sounds in them and lately the continuous wailing of the banshee.

She heard them both now—Molly and Letitia. She craved the comfort Richard could give her. She did love him so much. It occurred to her that she really resented Ruth Fiske, who wasn't nearly good enough for him, but then again nobody was. Richard was so handsome, so kind and gentle. Her resentment against Matthew Vernon overflowed, firing poor Richard! How could she act with anyone else? She was used to her dear brother, needed him with her, wanted him. She flushed. She wanted him in ways that had never crossed her mind before, ways that were making her heart beat faster and her throat pound. Impelled by desires that both terrified and excited her, she slipped out of bed and started down the hall to his room.

Richard stirred in his sleep and woke up, thinking of Kathie. He had been dreaming about her, her beautiful face, her slender virginal body. She had seemed incredibly desirable. To think about her was to forget that he had ever been attracted to Ruth Fiske. He felt the depression that had sent him to bed early that night magically lifting. If they were on the road again, he would have Kathie to himself. He thought of Matthew Vernon, hating him because Kathie had a notion she loved him. He wanted her and needed her; it did not matter that they were brother and sister!

There as a little tap at his door.

"Yes," he called. "Who is it?"

"Kathie . . . may I come in?"

"Kathie, yes!"

She stood in the doorway, wondering suddenly what had prompted her to come to him. She was really so tired. It must be very late or extremely early; she wasn't sure which. She said crossly, "I'm so sleepy."

"Do you want to . . . crawl in with me?"

"No, what an idea! I think I must have been walking in my sleep or something. I'm sorry I woke you up."

"That's all right."

"I did have a funny dream, but I can't remember it now."

"So did I," he said, feeling much the same way she obviously did. "This house is conducive to dreams."

"I agree. We'll have to move once we get enough money salted away."

"Right." he said enthusiastically. "I'd like to be in Hollywood proper, maybe near Gower."

"I'd rather be farther out by the beach." She yawned. "But I don't really see us leaving town, do you?"

"No, I like the idea of being an agent, or rather an 'artist's representative.' Honesty doesn't seem to be the best policy among most of them out here. I'd like to change all that."

"I'm sure you will," she assured him. She yawned a second time. "I think I'd better go back to bed. Good night, darling. Sorry I disturbed you."

"That's okay, babe. Anytime."

After his sister left, Richard was annoyed, wondering what had brought her out of bed at this hour. A dream? He, too, had dreamed, something about her, but he couldn't remember what it was. He lay down and was asleep at the same time he put his head on the pillow.

Erlina Bell seethed in the hallway and fled back to her one hope in the cellar. She had been more successful with Colin and Juliet, but unfortunately they were no longer of any use to her.

Kathie awoke to the sound of her alarm clock which she had set the previous evening for seven. She must have automatically reset it for five last night and was glad she had. She felt much better today, better about the part and better about Richard, who would certainly be a more successful agent than actor. To be absolutely honest, he had given her nothing in the way of a response. She might have been acting opposite a wooden pole. The difference between them was that she enjoyed acting and he did not. She much preferred it to being sawed in half, being made to disappear, and generally assisting her father and brother with the illusions, which included feeding the rabbits and tending the baby chicks and the goldfish. Furthermore, all that had been required of her on stage was her capacity to look well in a series of low-cut skintight blouses or close-fitting leotards. Of course there had been her smile and sustaining that *had* required considerable acting ability. She had smiled while the saw seemed to grind across her middle, and she had smiled while disappearing and reappearing. She had smiled when Richard's daggers skimmed over her head, her shoulders, her arms, her hips, her legs and ankles. She had smiled even when one of them had gashed her side and another had clipped her on the ankle—on two separate occasions three years apart. Richard was usually very accurate.

As Lorenza de Cagliostro, she did not have to smile quite so often, and she could speak with Matthew Vernon, who did seem to like her. She really felt much, much better about everything. And she would go to the studio after all with her father. They had to be there at seven, so she had better get up.

Coming down the stairs a half hour later, Kathie looked up at the new chandelier which Mr. Goldbaum had insisted on installing. She half-expected to see Letitia Lawrence dangling from it looking horridly blue as she did at unexpected moments. Fortunately these were few and farther between, since the actress seemed to have found a kindred soul in Molly. She suddenly remembered her conversation with Richard in the night. Why had she gone to his room? She hadn't done that since they were children and living in all those miserable old boarding houses. That life was at an end; she was sure of it. Their combined salaries could get them a comfortable house. Maybe they even could afford separate houses, and the Old Lord hopefully might prefer to stay with her parents.

Thinking of him, Kathie became aware of the fact that he was not far away from her. She quickly banished the thought of living in a house free of his presence. She did not want to hurt his feelings. She cast a side glance at the chandelier—no, Letitia Lawrence was not there. That was odd. Often she followed him, but if they moved, she would not be with him. She could have this house to herself again.

"Good morning, grandfather," she whispered.

She received no response and had an impression that he was deeply troubled. She did not want to know what it was, not on this fine morning when her mood was so good.

She continued on down the stairs and had just reached the hall when the doorbell rang. She stopped short in surprise. It was early for visitors. Who could have come calling at such an hour? The postman? Probably. She opened the door and found a harried-looking Matthew Vernon outside. He was inside in a trice. Upon closer examination, she found he was not only harried but looked weary, distraught, rumpled and unshaven, as if he had been up most the night. If he had slept, he had done so in his clothes.

"You must . . ." he began and broke off in consternaton, staring over her shoulder. "My God, who's that? You have another actor in the family? But where does he get off raiding wardrobe?"

Kathie, already shaken by his presence and his appearance, was further shaken. "What are you talking about?" she demanded incredulously. "Have you gone mad?"

He regarded her as if *she* were the one who had gone mad. "All right, maybe he didn't raid it, but why the Eighteenth Century getup? We don't usually audition actors in costume, complete with powdered wig, though I must admit his fits better than most. Who is he?"

Kathie reached for something to steady her. It turned out to be Matthew's arm. "You *saw* him!" she gasped. "How is it possible? No one outside of the family has ever seen grandfather, and none of us have ever seen him that clearly!"

"Your grandfather, whom . . . none of you has ever seen . . . clearly?" He backed away from her. "You're not suggesting that he's a ghost!?"

"He is my great-great-great-grandfather," she whispered because her voice had suddenly failed her. "Richard Veringer, Earl of More."

"Earl of . . . of More!" Matthew repeated incredulously. "You are descended from the Earl of More?"

She did not appreciate the note of disbelief she heard in his voice. "As it happens, yes. Not all actors come from the slums of New York."

"But . . . but this is incredible," he shouted. "We're related!"

"We are?" she demanded. "How?"

"My dear, this might come as a shock to you, but my real name, my family name is Veringer. I am the present Earl of More!"

"The . . . present Earl of . . . of More," she repeated faintly.

"Yes!" he shouted. "But we can't call it consanguinity!"

"Consanguinity?" Septimus repeated from the hall doorway.

"Consanguinity!" Matthew actually shouted. "Kathie, my dearest, I have been up all night. I have been in agony. I don't care if you come back to work or not, or I do, of course, I do, but mainly I care for you. I have been in love with you ever since I saw you four years ago and you looked at me as if I were a stray cockroach!"

"I did not!" she cried. "You didn't remind me of . . . of a cockroach at all. In fact . . ."

"In fact, will you marry me?"

"Marry you?"

"Yes, will you?"

"Yes," she cried and then stared at him. "I mean . . ."

"You said yes. You must mean yes."

"But I hardly know you."

"We've known each other at least four years, and why do you think I asked old Goldbaum to hire you?"

"*You* asked him?"

"I did. I fell in love with you at first sight, Miss Frosty."

"Why didn't you wait for me?" she demanded unreasonably.

"Wait for you?"

"You weren't there when I came back from being sawed in half," she said, luxuriously allowing herself a touch of the old anger and pain, now that it could be so easily alleviated.

"I couldn't. I had to catch a train for the West Coast." The full import of her words dawned on him. "You missed me!"

"Terribly," she admitted. She sighed happily, even though half-stifled by his embrace.

Several delicious moments later, Kathie looked at him in sudden trepidation. "But . . ." she began tentatively, "there's a great deal more to this household than . . . grandfather. There's a . . ."

"Do you think anything matters when there's you?" he asked tenderly.

She was afraid that it did and knew she ought to mention the curse, but curses were such dark things and she felt so happy on this bright morning.

"Will you stay for breakfast?" Septimus had returned to the doorway.

Matthew looked at him out of glowing eyes. "Oh, yes sir, please. But we'd better hurry. It's almost time for rehearsal."

Dreams had failed her but Erlina Bell, perched on the spare tire of Matthew Vernon's elderly flivver, remained undaunted. Something else had occurred to her, and that, she thought gleefully, would get the whole passel of them on the road again—those who were in shape to travel!

Kathie sat in Matthew Vernon's tiny office on the lot at Goldbaum-Magnum, staring at the construction that was Paris in front and papier-mâché, timber, plaster and chicken-wire in back. Her exultation of the morning had passed and in its place was a pervasive melancholy. It seemed to her that the vast set could be a simile for her situation—happiness in the front and the curse behind. She had read that same fear in her mother's face when she and Matthew broke the news, with Matthew telling them all about his ancestor's long-ago razing of the Hold. He had described the handsome Manor House built in its place and now given over to the National Trust because of death duties. He had laughed at his empty title and talked about their future in Hollywood. But could they have a future here?

Kathie doubted it. Something would happen and they would be packing bags and trunks. There would be the endless treks from railroad station to theater and from theater to railroad station or pier. How could she bring such unhappiness to the man she loved? He was doubly vulnerable to the curse, married to her and related as well, even if that relationship were extremely distant.

She looked out of the window. Above the set rose the tall palm trees, like feather dusters perched on long thin handles, silhouetted against the darkening sky. She would have this

one night with him, she decided defiantly, and
tomorrow . . . She would not think of tomorrow yet. She
wished he would hurry. It had been a day of delays. The
master script had disappeared from Matthew's office and had
been found in Cagliostro's "bedroom." One of the men
working on the set had fallen from a tall ladder and an
ambulance had been called. The actress playing Marie
Antoinette called in sick. The rehearsal schedule had been
rearranged only to have the lady appear saying that she had
never called. She had wondered loudly and profanely who
had been playing practical jokes. They had not started
rehearsals until two in the afternoon, and at four-thirty Mr.
Goldbaum had called an unexpected script conference,
explaining in vehement terms that he was at odds with his
three nephews as to the authenticity of what they were
presenting. Matthew had tried to argue with him, saying that
he had pointed this out a long time ago and couldn't they
discuss it in the morning, but Mr. Goldbaum had been
adamant. Matthew had told her ruefully that it might take a
while and would she mind waiting. When she had agreed,
she had not expected that it would take over two hours. Yet,
in a sense, she was glad that it was going on so long. It had
given her time to think, but that time was past and she was
getting nervous. She was not sure why. She just wished he
would hurry.

The night watchman, starting on his rounds at seven,
limped across the "bombed-out French village" at
Goldbaum-Magnum. He had thought he heard a noise
behind one of the mock-ups of the huts, but he could see
nothing. He went on toward Paris, 1785; nearing it, he had a
sour grin for a vista he remembered reasonably well, even
though there were few links to join it to Paris, 1917, to which
he had come amidst fanfares and shouting. Some of the guys
were even singing the Marseillaise, and of course a lot of
sentimental dopes were humming "Over There." He had
hummed along, not that he had felt particularly sentimental.
Actually he had been scared at the thought of getting in the
thick of things. Reminiscently, he rubbed his arm—stiff it
was, just like his gimpy leg. Right leg. Left arm. It could have
been worse was what his mother had said. Sure, he could've

come home in a wooden box with the stars and stripes covering it. But here at Goldy-Mag, short for Goldbaum-Magnum, they hadn't been able to give him his old job of studio carpenter back. At first they had a hell of a time thinking of anything he could do. Then some bright joker came up with the idea about him being a watchman. That was a hell of a note, going to bed when everybody else was up basking in the sunshine. However, as his mom said, it was a hell of a lot better than selling pencils on some street corner in downtown L.A. or being stashed out in one of those rest homes they had in Mar Vista.

He saw a light in Matt Vernon's office. Must be working late as he sometimes did. Maybe he could drop in and pass the time of day with him—or night. Vernon was a nice guy for a limey. He limped over to the door and peered inside. His eyes narrowed. There was a girl sitting by old Matt's desk and him nowhere about. She was some looker. She must be the filly they'd brought in from New York. He'd heard she wouldn't break any mirrors. They were sure as hell right. She had it all over Mary Miles Minter and La Pickford to boot. He hoped the door wasn't locked. He would sure like to exchange a few words with this little flapper. He scratched on the door. She glanced up all smiles and then disappointment set in. Probably she was waiting for Matt. He wouldn't keep a girl like her waiting. He tried the door and found it was unlocked. Usually he wouldn't have come in, but hell, there she was, all alone and him with nobody to talk to. All he really wanted to do was pass the Goddamned time, and she was sure pretty, prettier than all those blasted Frog dames who never gave him the time of day. She wouldn't be able to turn him off so quick; there was only him and her for a bit. He opened the door and ambled in. Closing it behind him, he leaned against the door saying, "Hiya, honey."

The banshee was wailing, the cat was screeching, Miss Lawrence was gurgling.

Livia paced the floor in her bedroom, her hands to her ears. What was afflicting Molly? What did she foresee? If only she could reach her on her perch, but that was impossible. She wondered where the Old Lord could be? He would be able to interpret and confide—and why was Kathie so late? It was already 7:30! And where was Septimus? He had gone out to get the evening paper an hour earlier and wasn't back yet. She was nervous and unaccountably worried over him. And why hadn't Richard come home? She felt so dreadfully alone. She couldn't even hear Mark's howls from the cellar and the moon was rising. That ought to have comforted her, but it didn't. He always howled when the moon rose. Was she getting deaf? It wouldn't be surprising. She was at that age.

She hurried downstairs and stopped short in horror near the cellar door. It was hanging on one hinge. Something had battered it down from inside! How had that happened? Then she saw the crumpled newspaper on the floor.

"Septimus!" she shrieked, staring into the blackness behind the broken door.

A cold wind blew through the hall. The front door swung open and then banged shut.

Livia fainted.

It had been a desperate day, a last chance day. Her energy was leaving her quickly, and she didn't know why. Still the stage was set and ready for action. The beast was on the loose; guided by her, he loped through the dark streets toward their goal. He was her puppet. They were all her puppets; she had a handful of strings and all she had to do was jerk them. After that she would not care what happened to the poor few remnants who were left to plod their weary way toward oblivion. She would be vindicated at last.

Why hadn't Matthew returned?

The watchman was talking and talking. He stood between her and the door, a medium-sized but hulking figure of a man, most unprepossessing in appearance. He talked to her in a low voice, grinning at her with an appreciation she was beginning to loathe and even fear. He had been smoking the whole time, without asking so much as a by-your-leave! He had lit one cigarette from the next, and the air was heavy with the smell of cheap tobacco.

Kathie's nails were digging into her hands. She longed to tell him to go, but there was something in his eyes that gave her pause. Then she heard a sound outside—a footstep? With exaggerated relief, she said, "I think Matthew's coming."

"Yeah? I don't hear anything." He opened the door and glanced out. "Nope, baby, false alarm."

His use of the term 'baby,' both grated on her ears and frightened her. He had no right to talk to her like that, to compare her to all the other 'dames' who had sat in Matthew's office, making him sound like a combination of Casanova and Don Juan. The watchman must be a little crazy. He had been hurt in the war, he'd told her, playing on her sympathy in the beginning. Now he had taken a match from his pocket and struck it. He was holding the flame toward yet another cigarette. He paused.

"Hey, there *is* something out there. Sounds like a dog's sniffin' around. Who'd be walkin' his damned dog on a set? Dogs ain't allowed!" He pushed open the door, and Kathie came out after him, unwilling to stay inside and have him return to taunt her. As she closed the door firmly behind her, she heard a deep growl followed by a prolonged howl. She felt as if each separate pore in her skin had become an icy pricking needle! She recognized the howl, had heard it all the years of her life on nights when the moon was full. There was a loud yell from the night watchman. He tried to run and stumbled, falling on a heap of gunny sacks.

Looking around her, Kathie saw a huge greyish shape in the darkness. There was laughter, a woman's laughter, high and eerie, fading and swelling. It was all about her, that shrieking, terrible laughter. Then it changed in timbre and became low and gloating. It seemed to Kathie that her bones were turning cold inside her flesh. She shrank back against the door, one hand searching out the knob and finding that it would not turn. A wind was rising; it blew against her, tearing at her garments, almost as if it had developed fingers. Out of the corner of her eye, she saw the watchman, still screaming, run awkwardly away. Meanwhile there was smoke in her nostrils. A fire was rising from the pile of gunny sacks where he had cowered. The flames were leaping high, fanned by that infernal wind, and they seemed to be coming in her direction. She tried to run but she could not move.

Across the clearing came the beast. She could see him now in the lurid light of the flames—the fearsome head with the bestial features, retaining human characteristics but stretched and elongated, half-covered with bristling red hair and made even more horrible by the madness she read in its fiery, golden eyes. Mark's eyes! Its body was that of an animal, covered with grey-red hair. It was coming closer and closer to her. It rose on its hind legs, its muzzle wrinkled in a snarl and deep, low growls issuing from its throat. It arched its long back. It was about to leap at her.

"Mark, Mark, Mark, down boy!" she screamed senselessly, foolishly to the unhappy creature.

Incredibly, it stopped in mid-leap and, staring at her, uttered a long sorrowful howl and fled from her, its tail between its legs.

"Back, come backkkkkkk . . ." The scream resounded in her ears as the fire drew nearer, the smoke choking her. Suddenly another wind blew from behind. She felt battered between the two of them. And in that wind, which seemed to be fanning the flames away from her and driving them back, she heard a voice she seemed to know from half-forgotten dreams. "*Go back . . . go forth, woman. The price has been paid and our sanctuary found!*"

"Kathie! Kathie!" Matthew called frantically.

She wanted to go to him but the fingers of the opposing wind still pressed fiercely against her. Then, with a despairing shriek, the pressure was relaxed, and Kathie heard the Old Lord cry, "*Go, child, and let me guide you . . .*" At that same moment, she was blown into Matthew's arms.

Moments later, standing with him across the street, she watched the huge bonfire that had been the set of Paris, 1786, turn the sky a flaming orange. Looking at it, she wondered dolefully if Matthew would be able to fit into her father's magic act.

Four

Kitty's place was bright with lights. In the large parking lot Mercedes limousines rubbed fenders with svelte Pierce-Arrows and custom-made Packards, as well as a dozen other makes of auto not excluding the ubiquitous tin lizzie. All of these had disgorged brightly clad, incongruous occupants who seemingly hailed from Spanish haciendas, medieval monasteries, fairy tale palaces and every period in history from a fig-leafed Adam and Eve to Edward VII's court. Sheiks, gypsies, Robin Hoods, pirates, nuns, bears and gorillas, crowded into the establishment. In spite of the pick of studio wardrobes and elegant made-to-order costumes no one took the eye more than Juliet in a replica of the white gown she had worn for her birthday ball and Colin in a copy of the suit he donned that same night.

Juliet's golden curls, heavily powdered, looked like spun glass above her delicate, beautiful little face. The excitement in her eyes recalled those moments when life had seemed a glorious adventure to her. Her expression held no trace of the wry sophistication which had been so evident in the years that followed. She seemed incredibly young and glowing, a beacon light among the weary pleasure seekers that thronged about her on that glistening floor. In his powdered wig and white brocade suit with the diamond sprinkled lace at his throat and a court sword at his side, Colin resembled a prince from a fairy tale. They arrived late and did not stay long, just long enough for Juliet to dance with an eager and adoring Gareth, but for once they did not tango. Instead they whirled around the room to the strains of a Viennese waltz.

Gareth, in the white robes of an Arabian prince, stared at her incredulously. "You look, my love, as if you had just dropped from another world."

"Perhaps I have." She gave him a roguish smile.

"I'm ready to believe that. I think I always have."

"What can you mean by that?" She had meant to speak lightly but could not quite achieve the proper tone.

"I'm not sure," he mused. "I wish the music would go on forever."

"Nothing goes on forever."

"I . . ." He paused, frowning as a Pierrot in wine-splattered white satin and a Columbine in a wilted net tutu careened into them, nearly knocking them to the floor. "Damn you, Dane, why the hell don't you look where you're going!" Gareth exclaimed furiously.

"Sorry, Gary." The Pierrot turned a handsome, boyish and very famous face toward him. Juliet recognized him as Dane Fuller, a talented and popular actor with a flair for comedy on screen and a penchant for trouble off. He was with Helena Browning, his sometime leading lady and, some said, his partner in disaster. Though she had the serene beauty of a madonna, at least when her face was in repose which it practically never was, she was known for her comic and cruel impersonations. She was also known for drinking the night away and burning her candle at both ends.

Looking at her, as she blushingly and tipsily apologized for slamming against them, Juliet felt sorry for the girl. Though she was little more than 20, she already appeared weary and dissipated. Obviously that candle was melting fast.

Almost as if she had guessed Juliet's thoughts, Helena gave her a drunken salute. "You're not so perfect, either, Miss Prim," she said giggling.

"C'mon, Hel, let's raise some hell," burbled Dane Fuller. "Wanna go for a swim?"

"Sure, why not?" She laughed loudly and, tripping over his feet, sat down in the middle of the floor. "Look at me," she chortled. "I'm hitting bottom like they always said I would." She giggled wildly as her escort lifted her in his arms and bore her off.

"I'm sorry about that," Gareth said regretfully.

"Let's not think about them," Juliet pleaded.

"No, let's just dance. Juliet, my dearest, I do love you so much."

"I love you, too," she said, thinking now of Lucy. She was actually envious of her. Lucy had known love and birth before death, while she . . . but it was too late to dwell on that. She must be grateful to Lucy for having shown herself and Colin the way—and what would happen afterwards? Oblivion?

"Juliet!" Gareth raised his voice. "Where are you? I can't reach you."

"I couldn't be much closer." She tried to smile, but was not successful.

"There's a strangeness about you."

"So you've already suggested."

"More than ever. Juliet, my darling, please reconsider Arno's offer. You don't want me to be saddled with a leading lady like Helena Browning, do you?"

"No, I really don't," she said far more sincerely than she had intended.

"Please, darling, make that test."

She did not want to lie to him on this night of all nights, nor did she want to see the unhappiness in his eyes. Reluctantly she said, "Maybe I will."

"Will you?" he asked joyfully. "Promise."

"I will think about it, but I must leave now."

"Leave? You've only just arrived."

"We've been here quite a while. You just didn't see us."

"I couldn't have missed you," he burst out. "What sort of game are you playing with me?"

No game, Gareth." She stood on tiptoe to caress his cheek and kiss his lips, then breaking from him, she fled across the dance floor where Colin waited for her. She grasped his arm. "Let's go."

They threaded their way through the shrieking crowds, stepping over some drunken merrymakers who lay sprawled on the floor and avoiding others who were dancing on the tables and grabbing at them. The music was loud, the laughter, born of wine and booze, was even louder.

Colin said regretfully, "We shouldn't have come here."

"No, we should have come here," she contradicted. "This is the world we know," she whispered and tensed, feeling rather than seeing that Gareth was close behind them. "Hurry," she urged. "I dare not look at him again."

Colin moved swiftly then, as only he could move, as only they could move, skirting the crowds, reaching the entrance, losing themselves among the trees and finally, effortlessly, gliding down the cliffs to the white sands stretching below.

"Juliettttttt . . ." She heard her name called frantically.

"And not even a glass slipper for him to find," Colin said.

"Don't," she begged.

"I'm sorry, dearest."

They stood on the sand. A gentle breeze fanned their cheeks. Though it was still dark, there was a lightening along the horizon. Juliet, standing beside her brother, wondered how much of the dawn they would be allowed to see. She had always been afraid of the dawn before.

A shriek of laughter disturbed her mood, and she saw the Pierrot and Columbine run screaming across the sands but fortunately not in their direction. Soon all she could hear was their howls of laughter as they disappeared down an incline in the sand.

"The sea is beautiful tonight . . . and such a lovely moon," she said.

"One more moon day to go," Colin remarked.

"Poor Mark, I wish . . ."

"Don't think about him," he said.

"No." She held her brother's arm, watching the waves swelling, breaking and retreating from the shore.

Later, when the firemen who had tried in vain to put out the blaze that had consumed Paris, 1786, though not much else of the giant studio complex, they found the night watchman crawling around on all fours and yelling loudly. When he became somewhat calmer, he still couldn't describe the dog that had knocked him down and run away. At least they ascertained that it was a dog. The other attributes, the eyes, the ears and the fangs, were strictly from the realm of an imagination fed on bathtub gin.

Bathtub gin was the excuse the police formulated for the well-spoken, extremely surprised and strangely exultant young man they found wandering along the shoreline tracks just outside Culver City. Naked as the day he was born, he was staring up at the moon as if he couldn't believe what he was seeing. He was also rubbing his hands together and repeating, "No hair . . . no hair on my palms."

No one even attempted to translate that remark. Somebody loaned him a coat, and of course they took him to the Culver City police station. Since they didn't smell any liquor on his breath, they decided he was on dope, particularly when he said with something approaching ecstasy, "I can look at the moon and I don't feel a thing."

"Pain," supplied one of the jailors. "Don't you mean you're feelin' no pain, buddy?"

He received no answer. The young man just continued to stare out of the cell window at the huge round moon.

His eyes were eager and hopeful as he moved across the sands. He was wearing the black and silver suit that had once been his favorite and his powdered hair was pulled away from his face. He came to where they stood, just at the edge of the water. He said in a voice that was hollow yet resonant, "My dear, dear children."

Colin and Juliet regarded him incredulously and, at the same time, regretfully.

"Father . . ." Colin was the first to speak. "We didn't think you knew."

"I knew, and also knew that it was useless to argue with you, but now . . ."

"No, you mustn't argue," Juliet whispered. "Just stay with us until the sun rises. It can't be very long now."

"The stars are dimming and the moon is low," Colin agreed. "And we'll pretend it's a night when Father came in to see that we were both asleep."

"How did you know that?" the Old Lord inquired.

"Because we were never asleep." Juliet laughed tenderly.

"Oh, my dear, dear children." He stood between them. "I love you both so much. I fear I never expressed that love enough—not for you nor for your dear, dear mother, whom I have never ceased to miss or mourn. If I had known what I know now . . . but enough of recriminations. Heed me. All is not at an end for you. A new knowledge has come to me tonight, and I must share it with you.''

''Oh, Father, we know you love us and we love you,'' Colin said, ''but it has to be an end. It must be. We are weary of what we have become.''

''I understand that.'' The Old Lord stared about him. ''But you needn't be what you have been. It is all part of something that is passing.''

''What?'' Juliet asked.

''Look . . . there!'' Colin exclaimed.

Juliet had been staring at her father. She tensed. ''The sun?'' she whispered.

''No, there by the water's edge,'' the Old Lord said, adding obliquely, ''That is what was promised me.''

''What are you saying, sir?'' Colin stared at him confusedly.

''Oh . . .'' Juliet dared to raise her eyes. ''The poor Pierrot and the Columbine . . . lying so still. They must be drowned!''

''Come with me, my dears.'' The Old Lord strode down to the wet and shining strand. ''Follow me,'' he added impatiently.

''We must get help!'' Juliet cried.

''It is too late,'' Colin said. ''It's nearly dawn.''

''Come,'' the Old Lord repeated sternly, as he strode ahead. He was standing by the bodies when they joined him. ''Try them on. You'll find they fit.''

They stared at him incredulously.

''You'd not be telling us that we . . .'' Colin began.

''I am telling you what Molly told me. She saw it all. You know she was both witch and seeress in life. But you must want it, too. Heed me. At the moment the sun appears on the horizon, you will be without form or substance. Yet you will exist and may exist and live out these interrupted lives in your own way. If you choose, stand by that woman, Juliet, and you, Colin, stand by the man. You must hurry. Let your essence merge with them. There'll be a time of sleeping, of waking, of remembering and . . . of loving.''

They still stared at him questioningly.

"Hurry," he urged. "Take your positions. There's but one chance—at the first gleam of sunshine on the far horizon."

"But how . . . ?" Juliet whispered.

"You will know how," he urged.

Juliet and Colin stared at each other. "Do you think we might?" Juliet asked tentatively.

"We can try," he affirmed.

They moved quickly.

"Ah, the sun!" cried the Old Lord.

Livia sat beside the cellar door, staring stonily at the crumpled newspaper in her hand. She was trying to summon enough courage to go down and look, but as yet she could not bear to even contemplate what she was sure she would find. Septimus! If only he had continued to practice black magic, he might have subdued the beast, but he had renounced all that upon their marriage and his entrance into the terrible Household, where black magic should have been a requirement.

"Livia!"

She started and stared into the cellar, but the familiar call wasn't coming from there. And then Septimus came into the hall, looking grimy and smelling strongly of woodsmoke, but neither mauled nor bitten and most definitely alive. "I've got bad news," he said. "Paris is destroyed."

"Paris," she repeated blankly.

"I had one of my premonitions and I went to the studio and . . ." he broke off staring at the cellar door. "Where's Mark?"

"I don't know," she cried. "But you . . . you are safe." She ran to him and clutched his hand.

"Where is Mark?"

"I don't know. I came down and found the door that way. I haven't looked into the cellar, but it was broken from the inside—the door, I mean."

"That means he's out. Have you called the police?"

"I fainted and afterwards . . ."

"You fainted?" He looked at her concernedly. "How are you now?"

"I'm all right. I guess we had better call the police."

"God, yes, we can't have him wandering around the neighborhood."

"What can we say?" she cried.

"Say that our pet wolf . . ."

The telephone rang. "Oh, God," Livia wailed as Septimus grabbed the phone. "Don't talk long."

"Hello," he said edgily. "What . . . You! . . . You are? . . . You aren't? Yes, yes, of course, immediately. Right. Goodbye, see you soon."

"For goodness sake, why did you have to talk to him so long. We've got to find Mark."

Septimus stared at her blankly. "I can't believe it!"

"Believe what?"

"Mark!"

"Mark!" Livia grabbed his arm. "Someone called about Mark? But that's impossible, no one knows . . ."

"That *was* Mark. He's in jail," Septimus said jubilantly.

"In jail?

"In jail! I can't believe it."

"Septimus," Livia said between her teeth, "will you please explain yourself? How could he be in jail?"

"He says he's cured."

"Cured!"

"There's no hair on his palms, and he wants his pants, shirt, shorts socks and shoes."

"I don't understand!" Livia actually stamped her foot.

"I'm sorry, my love." Septimus opened wide his arms and catching her in them, hugged her warmly. "He's naked. They've got him booked for indecent exposure. In Culver City, of all places!"

"My God, what happened? How? Oh, it doesn't matter, does it?" She hurried toward the stairs and staring up saw Letitia Lawrence hanging on the chandelier and looking particularly blue. "Do go away," she said tartly and hurried on up to ransack Mark's wardrobe.

Much miffed, the specter sailed up to the roof to sit with Molly and Grimalkin. "I do not enjoy it here," she said, "I am not appreciated."

"It's off to Ireland, you should go," Molly said.

"Raggghoowlll," commented Grimalkin."

"Listen to the love," Molly said fondly. "He's wantin to

go, too. And it's my impression, we soon will.''

"I wish I might," Letitia Lawrence sighed.

"And why shouldn't ye?" Molly inquired. "There's always a cryin' need for banshees."

Miss Lawrence gave her a long look. "Now that," she mused, "is a thought." She added wistfully, "do you suppose I could be assigned to a castle?"

The nurses at the Santa Monica Hospital were in an uncharacteristic flutter. They had seen many celebrities in its corridors, but Helena Browning and Dane Fuller were something special. A whole country had taken the pair to their hearts. It would be terrible if they died, and they certainly had been close to death when they were brought in.

In a room with green pimpled plaster walls, Dr. William Jacobsen, Miss Bonnie Clarke, a nurse, and Mr. Luther Burns, the agent for both young performers, stared at the girl on the bed. She had been looking almost as white as the sheets, but now she was showing signs of returning consciousness.

"She's coming round," Dr. Jacobsen observed. "It's a miracle. There was so much water in her lungs. If it hadn't been for modern lifesaving methods, I don't think . . ."

"Don't say it," Mr. Burns groaned. "Don't even think it. This girl's a hot property."

"Caviar on your table, I know," commented the doctor sarcastically.

"Father . . ." the girl muttered.

"Hey, she's really out of it!" Mr. Burns exclaimed. "Her father hit the skids five years back. Drank almost as much as she does. What d'you want to bet the first thing she asks for is a whiskey and soda?"

"Colin . . ." the girl murmured.

"What'd she say?" Mr. Burns jumped up and bent over the bed.

"She said Colin," the nurse told him.

"What's a colin?" Mr. Burns demanded. "Gee, she's really pretty far gone. I wonder how he is. Guess I'd better . . ." He broke off startled as a door was thrust open and a tall, pale young man entered, followed by a frantic nurse.

"Gee whiz!" Bonnie Clark exclaimed.

"Mr. Fuller," shrilled the other nurse. "Mr. Fuller, you're in no condition to . . . I never would've told you her room number. The doctor'll have my . . ." She broke off, flushing, as she met Dr. Jacobsen's icy blue stare. "Geez, I couldn't keep him down," she bleated.

The man she had called Mr. Fuller moved weakly and shakily but managed to get to the girl's bed. Sitting down on the edge of it, he stared at her. "You?" he managed to say.

The girl opened huge brown eyes. "You?" she echoed.

"Yes."

The looks they exchanged were so full of love and happiness that Mr. Burns, meeting the reporters from the *Hollywood Citizen-News*, the *Herald-Express*, the *Los Angeles Times* and the *Los Angeles Examiner*, who were congregated in the hall outside, got all choked up as he told them about his two clients' miraculous escape from death. "I guess they'll get married after all," he concluded.

A world of newspapers headlined the story of the Fuller-Browning escape from drowning. In some of the local papers was another item. Two skeletons in eighteenth century costumes had been discovered on the beach. From the labels inside the garments, the police learned that they had been made by a famous costumer, who had reported them stolen several days ago. No one could explain the skeletons.

Morna Moran read the item and wondered.

Livia, Septimus, Kathie and Richard read the item and remembered Juliet and Colin leaving for the party the night when everything happened. They wept until the Old Lord, interrupting their dirge, said to Kathie that their tears were not needed. He would not expound any further on the subject.

It was just as well that he had given them that advice, for while they still wondered, their grief was partially assuaged and they could turn their minds to what Septimus and Livia believed to be their last interview with Mr. Goldbaum. He would want them to leave his house, of course. And where would they go? They would have to arrange a tour. Kathie would probably be joining them, and Matthew would be coming with her.

They were naturally nervous as they filed into the

producer's office. Only Richard was in a really good humor. He was remaining in Hollywood and thought Kathie also should stay. He was sure he could get her acting jobs. Mark was similarly confused. He could find work as a makeup artist, but he was also becoming interested in astronomy, now that he could look at the heavens to his heart's content. The only trouble about being an astronomer was the fact that he would have to go to college, and he had not even obtained his high school diploma. In fact, he had never even attended grammar school, something that would be difficult to explain considering the fact that he was both literate and intelligent.

It was Kathie who had suggested an alternate solution. "Have you ever considered astrology?"

He had not, but on reading several books about it, he found it fascinating. He also thought he had a real feeling for it. As he sat waiting for Mr. Goldbaum to summon them into his inner office, he wondered about the producer's signs. A few moments later, following his family into the great man's office, Mark needed only a glance to tell him that Mr. Goldbaum was a Capricorn with Pisces rising—a strong yet mystical individual with a Venus in Scorpio that gave him the touch of dishonesty he needed for the motion picture business. Mark decided that he liked Mr. Goldbaum, and to the surprise of the whole family, the producer seemed to be in an exceptionally good humor for one whose studio had been half-gutted by fire.

"Well," Mr. Goldbaum said, surveying the rather glum group facing him, "Paris has burned but Magnum will survive that. Also it will survive similar catastrophes and out of the cinders will rise a new picture. *The Devil, You say*! What do you think of that—a catchy title, ja?"

He looked around him, and from force of habit Ruth Fiske, seated next to Richard, said, "Yes, Mr. Goldbaum."

He beamed at her. "*The Devil, You Say*. That should bring audiences in, especially when we have a perfect devil and his daughter, who will be redeemed by the love of a good man. We have in mind Charles DeWitt if we can pry him away from Colossal Inc. It is he who will teach the devil's daughter how to love. That is the gist of the plot, and we'll film it on the lot. Already the scenic designer is sketches making. And I suppose you are wondering what we will use for actors.'' His benign gaze fell on Septimus. ''I hope you will not be taking this personally, Mr. Grenfall, but always the devil you are bringing to my mind. And Miss Kathie, no one is better able to play the daughter. Only in publicity we will not say she is your daughter, eh? Gut! And now as to salaries . . .''

''You can't talk to them about that, Mr. Goldbaum,'' Richard interrupted. ''I am their agent.''

Some of the producer's cordiality vanished. ''Ach, an agent you are becoming?''

''Have become, sir,'' Richard corrected.

''When do you start shooting?'' Mark suddenly surprised them all by demanding.

''Ach, another relative, and what do you contribute, young man?'' Mr. Goldbaum regarded him suspiciously.

''A horoscope.''

''An astrologer, you are? What sign am I?''

Ruth Fiske shot an anxious look in the direction of Richard. No one but she knew about Mr. Goldbaum's closely guarded interest in astrology. If Mark were to make an error it could prove disastrous. She held her breath as Mark answered with what she feared was not only confidence but overconfidence. ''Capricorn with Pisces rising, Venus in Scorpio, Moon in Cancer . . .''

''Say no more.'' The producer clapped his hands together. ''You are right. You must stay with me this afternoon. There is much that I would like to know.''

''I can't stay this afternoon, Mr. Goldbaum,'' Mark said with a firmness that shocked his family.

''When may I call you?'' The producer shot the question at him.

''I will call you, sir,'' Mark replied.

''Ach!'' The producer gared at him and then grinned. ''Mine own you are giving back to me, ja? You are a smart young man. Maybe I can find a place for you at Goldbaum-Magnum.''

There was a great deal more to discuss before the six of them left. They walked hastily out of the studio. It was not until they reached the limousine they had hired to take them there that they broke into a sustained yell and hugged each other all around.

"It seems too good to be true," Kathie finally said.

"It's not," Mark told her. "You'll be a star. It's in your stars." He hugged her.

"I'm going to be married to an actor," Livia marveled.

"And I'm going to be married to a wife." Septimus kissed her on the cheek.

"What does that mean?"

"You are going to sit on a fine cushion and sew a fine seam."

"I am going to cue you in your lines, write a column for the *Hollywood Citizen-News*, furnish a small house for us and have big family parties for the children and . . ."

"As you choose, my love." Septimus kissed her again. "I exist only to give you your heart's desire."

"You've given me that already," she said softly.

Two weeks after they had been brought into the Santa Monica Hospital, Juliet and Colin were pleased when Luther Burns hurried them out a side door and into the limousine sent by Oliver Arno, thus eluding the reporters.

Fortunately Dane Fuller and Helena Browning had been living together. Consequently Juliet and Colin did not have to go off to separate living quarters at this crucial time when they were getting acclimated to their new bodies. Neither of these had been in tiptop shape when they had been brought int the hospital. Late nights, coke and booze had made definite inroads on their constitutions, but Dr. Jacobsen had comforted them by saying that they were both young enough to overcome these ill effects. The producer had added his own comments on the subject, holding out the bribe of a higher salary if they stopped and the threat of firing if they did not. Naturally Mr. Burns had also had his tidbit to throw in.

The constant harping on that aspect of their presumed former lives had been amusing, confusing and annoying to a pair who had not ingested any foreign substance or even any solids for the last 133 and 135 years. Yet for the most part they had been patient, since actually it had been the least of their worries. During their fortnight in the hospital, they had had to relearn habits discarded over a century ago, and though they made remarkable progress, daylight still held terror for them and the night was almost equally frightening.

Everything was so dark, and the moon so dim and distant!

"It will take time," Colin had warned Juliet.

"Time," she had agreed.

They dismissed Mr. Burns once they arrived at the large English Tudor mansion on Los Feliz Drive, a few doors off Wilshire Boulevard. Mr. Burns had let Colin know that Dane Fuller had bought the house several years ago, while congratulating him on his purchase.

Coming inside, they found the rooms large and furnished tastefully, in keeping with the style of the house. They were delighted to find that there were two large bedrooms upstairs as well as two guest chambers, all with their own beautifully appointed bathrooms. One of the big bedrooms yielded the garments worn by Miss Browning, and in Dane's bedroom a mixture of casual and formal clothes was found, none of which appealed to Colin's more conservative tastes.

"We'll have to collect some of our own clothes from Goldbaum's," Juliet began and stopped, staring at him confusedly. "But I am . . . was . . . smaller than Miss Browning."

"And I," he said ruefully, "am just the type for Mr. Fuller's wardrobe."

"You can't call him Mr. Fuller," she chided.

"I was following your lead, sister dear."

"Oh dear, oh dear," Juliet sighed. "I fear this is only the beginning of the complications. We weren't allowed visitors in the hospital, but we're not in the hospital any more."

"An obvious fact and one that does not bear repeating."

"Don't be horrid. You're going to be just as mixed-up as I am. Whatever are we going to do? We aren't only inhabiting their bodies—we're inhabiting their lives!"

"But you almost drowned, my dear children, and so many allowances will be made for confusion and a possible loss of memory. Few questions will be asked. Your condition will be understood. I have tried to prepare the Household in some small way, but I think you might like to surprise it."

"Father!" they cried in unison and gazed about the large room not seeing him.

"You cannot expect to see me," he answered their unspoken thoughts, his voice no more than a windy whisper in their human eardrums.

"Oh, Father," Juliet said sadly and yearningly. "You'll not leave us?"

"Not yet, sir," Colin added.

"You will leave me," the Old Lord said gently. "Wait and see if you don't."

"Never," they chorused, drawing near to the place where they thought he might be and, because of their new vision, not knowing they were wrong and quite alone.

"But what happened to them?" Oliver Arno stamped up and down his office, glaring at a crestfallen Luther Burns. "You mean they won't get their memories back? But I've invested a hell of a lot . . ."

"Look, I'm telling you what they said. The girl's willing to take a crack at the part. She says she'll be glad to read with Gareth Garnet."

"And what did Dane say? I've got him slated for *College Capers on Parade*!"

"He's not ready."

"But it's been a whole damned month! Do you know what this delay is costing me?"

"Down to the last decimal point, Oliver," Mr. Burns said sympathetically. "But call it an act of God and get in touch with your insurance company. I mean these kids were almost mixing with the fishes. The nurse said it was a miracle they survived."

"What the hell use is a blasted miracle if I'm going to lose a million on this Browning bitch and another on Fuller? Better they should've stayed at the bottom of the Pacific and then I'd really have been able to collect."

Burns knotted his fist but smiled his agent's smile. "Well, you got the girl, maybe. Let's see how she does. That dip in the sea didn't hurt her looks any."

"That's one blessing. Try for another," growled the producer.

"Well, how do you like this? She don't have to talk so the folks out in front don't know she's got this damned monotone."

"Oh, all right," Arno growled. "But I'm not making any bets on this one."

* * *

"I'm nervous," Juliet said. "I wish you were going with me." She looked at Colin oddly, adding, "You really look like a movie star—all that swimming."

He stretched his tanned arms high and glanced out at the blue waters of one of the few private swimming pools in Los Angeles. "It's helped me get used to this body."

"I'm nearly used to mine, but I wish I were still a blonde."

"You can always become one."

"I'll leave that to you. How do you like your blue eyes and that bright golden hair?"

"I can see out of my eyes, and my hair keeps my head warm. You're going to be late, sister mine."

"What are you going to do?" Juliet asked. "Swim?"

"I haven't made up my mind," he said evasively.

"I don't believe you."

"That's your privilege." He grinned. "That sounds casual enough, doesn't it?"

"It also sounds rude," she accused. Moving forward, she flung her arms around him. "Have a wonderful time, whatever you decide to do," she said meaningfully.

"You can still read my mind," he discovered.

"And you mine."

"Yes."

"Will you wish me a . . . wonderful time, too?"

"I will, my dear. I will and do."

Luther Burns, looking harried, stood to the left of the set they were using for Helena's Browning's test shots. At the last moment the producer had decided that she must not only speak but do part of a tango with Garnet.

"I didn't tell her about this," the agent protested.

"I only got him to agree this morning," Arno said. "He's been in a hell of a funk lately. How's Dane?"

"Still down in the dumps," Burns said. "I think he got more water than she did."

"Water'd do it, I guess," Arno said sourly. "Been different if he'd drowned in gin."

"Here she is," Burns said. "You gotta admit she's a looker."

"Yeah." Arno gave her a lackluster stare. "We're not going to waste too much film on her. A couple of minutes ought to give me some answers."

The taxi driver drew to a stop and looked at his fare with wide eyes. "Here we are, Mr. Fuller." He grinned at the dollar bill Colin gave him. "I'm not never goin' to spend this. I'm goin' to frame it."

Colin gave him a nervous smile, nodded and started up the path to the little house. He was aware that he should have visited his family once he gained enough confidence to be out on his own, but he had not even thought of them until this minute. They fled his thoughts again as he reached the front door and started to press the buzzer. His hand dropped to his side. He was aware of a shyness he had not experienced in decades. He also remembered what he had forgotten in his eagerness to see her. She might not be home. He would soon find out. He put his finger on the buzzer and in his excitement kept it there.

"All right, all right." He heard her voice, and then she opened the door. She was looking belligerent. She was also pale and dragged out. She wore no makeup, her eyes were bloodshot, and she was much thinner than he remembered. The bright red kimono she wore accentuated her pallor, and her air of belligerence did not vanish immediately. "Will you take your finger off the bell? I'm here."

"Oh," he said, "I'm sorry."

"Goodness!" she suddenly exclaimed. "Don't I know you?" Before he could answer, she continued uncertainly. "You're Mr. Fuller. Dane Fuller, aren't you? Or maybe his stand-in?"

Colin had forgotten about what Juliet sometimes called their "borrowed plumage." In his eagerness to see her, to hold her in his arms, to love her, he had not taken into account what she would see once she opened her door to his famous face.

He said wryly, "I should be one or the other, Morna." The unaccustomed throb of his heart in his chest seemed to be activating pulses through his entire body.

Morna looked at him wide-eyed, and as he had hoped but dared not expect, her confusion dropped away from her like a discarded cloak. "Come in," she said softly, joyfully and with the strange awareness that had startled him weeks ago.

As he entered, she shut the door behind him. Turning to him, she said. "You will tell me the how of it later. Right now, I only want to feel your arms around me, Colin."

Much later, lying with her head in her bed, his lips upon the throbbing hollow at the base of her throat, he raised his head and stared lovingly down at her. "I had forgotten . . . but you have given it back to me, you alone, Morna."

"What had you forgotten?" she asked, running her hand down the length of his back, rejoicing in the warmth of his body.

"There's an ecstasy about being human."

"There is now," she agreed.

"Morna, I love you so much."

"I love you, Colin."

"You'd better learn to call me Dane."

"Colin," she whispered stubbornly and fell asleep in his embrace. He, lying awake a little longer, thought he must go soon. Then looking out of her window at the sun-drenched landscape, he realized he could stay. He reveled in that golden glory. It would be so wonderful to paint by sunlight. He looked down at the sleeping face of his love and knew exactly how he would position her for her portrait.

Burns and Arno were seated to the left of the cameraman, watching the woman they knew as Helena Browning as she danced with Gareth Garnet.

"She's damned good," Burns said with a sincerity that surprised him. "She never used to be that good. Her double had to do her dancing for her."

"Now he tells me," Arno commented, glancing at a young woman who was staring at Miss Browning in utter amazement. She had come rushing into the studio on the pretext that she was Burns' secretary and was bringing some important papers. She bore a slight resemblance to Helena Browning but, to the producer and the agent as well, she was no more than a smudged carbon. Arno's gaze shifted back to the dancing pair. He noted that Garnet appeared bemused and confused. He didn't blame him. He said, "Okay we can cut the test. I've seen enough to convince me. She's great."

Gareth Garnet was standing just beyond the door when Juliet emerged from Arno's office. "Hi," he said casually.

"Hi," she said lightly. "I really enjoyed that test. You gave me some swell support. Thanks."

"So did I," he said enthusiastically. "You're a remarkably good dancer. I'd never realized that before."

Juliet's heart skipped several beats, or at least it felt that way. Had Helena Browning danced with him? How well did they know each other? She searched for an explanation and produced one she hoped might suffice. "I've been practicing."

"It shows," he told her. "I understand from Arno that you're in."

"Yes, he wants me. I don't know about Dane though. Actually, I do. Dane doesn't really want to come back. He'd like to paint."

He said earnestly, "Are you still with him?"

"We live in the same house, if that's what you mean." Looking up into eyes which, she suddenly realized, were just a little darker than her own, she had to add, "But that's all over. I'm leaving as soon as I can get another place."

"You should," he said, frowning. "You need to get away from him, especially after what happened. You could've been killed."

"I wasn't though," she said softly.

"Would you have lunch with me?"

"I'd be delighted."

"How would you like to drive out to the beach . . ." He paused and stared at her apologetically. "I'm sorry. I guess you've had your fill of the ocean."

"I could never have my fill of the ocean. I love the sea, especially at the this time of day with the sun so bright on the waves. Let's go!"

"I'm parked just inside the main gates." He slipped an arm around her waist. "You're really a wonderful dancer," he said as they walked toward his car. "I've only known one other woman whose steps went so well with mine."

"And who was she?"

"Her name was Juliet," he said.

"Was?" she repeated. "Is she dead?"

There was a pain mirrored in his dark eyes, but as he looked down at her, it faded. "No, of course she's not dead. I only meant that I haven't seen her lately. That's Hollywood for you. People come and they go. It's too damned easy to lose touch. I'm glad the test pleased Arno. I'd hate to think of you leaving town so soon." He paused and then said, "But you must excuse me, Helena. I'm forgetting you're pretty well established."

Juliet said, "I keep forgetting that, too. But I am, aren't I?"

"Yes, thank God." His arm tightened around her waist. "I'll bet you're hungry or . . . maybe you'd like a drink."

"If it's water or tea or coffee. But I think I'd prefer something to eat."

"Come on, then." He bent to kiss her on the cheek. Straightening up, he added, "I know a great place. Right on the edge of the sea."

The following morning while letting herself into the house, Juliet was just about to close the front door when a cab drew up and her brother got out. She waved and went inside, waiting for him in the front hall. As he came in, she looked at him lovingly.

"I'm moving out," she told him ecstatically.

"Gareth?" he asked.

She nodded.

"May I bring Morna here?" he asked.

"Of course, but first . . . isn't it time . . ."

"Past time," he agreed.

They came into The Castle's front hall, and turning toward the living room, they saw Livia throwing dust covers over the furniture and Septimus closing the windows. A whistle from on high signaled Richard's presence in one or another of the bedrooms. They stood where they were until Livia turned and gazed at them blankly. Brushing a hand over a strand of hair that was hanging over face, she said crossly, "He hasn't sent anyone to view the house already, has he? I certainly should have had more warning."

Septimus's hand fell from the window he was closing. In two strides he had reached the hall, and to his wife's amazement he embraced the female half of the duo, a lovely young woman who returned his embrace with fervor. Then, he embraced the man.

"Ohhhh," Livia whispered, staring at Septimus. "To think that you knew before I did."

"That's what grandfather meant!" Kathie ran down the stairs followed by Richard.

"Hi." Mark came from the dining room. "Great to see you."

"Great to see you," Colin said warmly.

They were silent then, staring at each other lovingly and yet with a touch of regret.

"But of course," Livia said briskly, "we'll see each other from time to time. After all, none of us is going very far."

"No," Juliet said. "We couldn't tempt fate."

"Oh, I think we could," Mark contradicted, "but we wouldn't want to."

They all laughed and agreed.

"Where's grandfather?" Kathie asked. "He should be here to bid any of us goodbye."

"I don't think he is." Juliet looked uncertainly at Colin.

"I don't feel him at all," he said.

"Perhaps he's already gone somewhere," Mark mused.

"Where would he go?" Septimus asked reasonably.

"He's somewhere around," Livia said positively. "He'll join us at our hotel. Or maybe he's waiting until we find a house."

"That's probably it," Juliet said.

"I hope so," Kathie said. "But of course, he has to stay with one of us."

"Of course," Livia agreed. "He'll come when he's ready."

The Old Lord, who had been Richard Veringer, Sixth Earl of More, did not come back until the shades were drawn in the house and the rooms empty. The roof was empty, too. Its three inhabitants had flown off to the green hills of Ireland. He sat in the garden among the unfamiliar orange and avocado trees and listened to the wind rustling through the eucalyptuses. He thought of a time when a young man had waited outside the door of a theater, impatiently watching for it to open. He had bribed a coachman, he remembered . . . and there had been a midnight supper in his lodgings waiting . . . and that was how it had all started.

"Richard."

He tensed and looked up. She was dressed in a white satin gown with immense panniers. Her hair was powdered and piled up on her shapely little head. She was as slim as a fairy and incredibly beautiful. Her eyes were blue, as blue as the lakes of Kilarney and brimming over with love for him.

"Catlin," he said incredulously and joyfully. Rising, he held out his arms.